"It's coming fast, Coyote! Range five miles . . ."

"Mustang! When I give the word, break right. I'll go left."

". . . four miles . . ."

"Roger that, Coyote!"

". . . three miles . . ."

"Now! Break!"

Coyote pulled the stick hard to the left and forward, going into a dive to pick up extra, crucial speed. Stealing a look back over his shoulder, he could see the onrushing missile now, a pinpoint trailing an endless thread of white scrawling across the eastern sky. As Mustang slipped off to the right, the missile tracked left.

It was after him and Cat . . .

Titles by Keith Douglass

THE CARRIER SERIES:

CARRIER
VIPER STRIKE
ARMAGEDDON MODE
FLAME-OUT
MAELSTROM
COUNTDOWN
AFTERBURN

THE SEAL TEAM SEVEN SERIES:

SEAL TEAM SEVEN
SPECTER
NUCFLASH

Book Six
COUNTDOWN

Keith Douglass

J
JOVE BOOKS, NEW YORK

CARRIER 6: COUNTDOWN

A Jove Book / published by arrangement with
the author

PRINTING HISTORY
Jove edition / February 1994

All rights reserved.
Copyright © 1994 by Jove Publications, Inc.
This book may not be reproduced in whole or in part,
by mimeograph or any other means, without permission.
For information address: The Berkley Publishing Group,
200 Madison Avenue, New York, New York 10016.

ISBN: 0-515-11309-3

A JOVE BOOK®
Jove Books are published by The Berkley Publishing Group,
200 Madison Avenue, New York, New York 10016.
JOVE and the "J" design
are trademarks belonging to Jove Publications, Inc.

PRINTED IN THE UNITED STATES OF AMERICA

10 9 8 7 6 5 4 3

PROLOGUE
Friday, 20 February

Jackboots crunched through the shards of glass and splintered masonry littering a floor once richly carpeted, now charred by blast and fire. The tapestries that had covered one wall had all been torn down, as had the gilt-framed, life-sized portraits of Gorbachev, Yeltsin, and that bastard Leonov. Filing cabinets had been overturned, their contents scattered and burned. The smell of fire and high explosive still clung to the place. An ornate desk lay half buried beneath a fallen, inner wall, while windows smashed by the concussion of multiple RPG rounds gaped open to Moscow's leaden February sky, allowing a bitter swirl of snowflakes to dance across the debris.

Marshal Valentin Grigorevich Krasilnikov surveyed the wreckage of the office for a grim moment, then holstered the Makarov pistol he'd been gripping in one black-gloved hand. The traitor had fled, but damn it, how had he known? *How* had he known?

A soldier crowded past the half-opened, partly unhinged door to the shattered office. "Comrade Marshal!"

"Yes, Sergeant Borodin."

The soldier, an AKM assault rifle clutched at a rigid port arms, stiffened to attention. "We have searched the entire office wing, including the basement. He is not here."

"Has Doctorov arrived yet?"

"I do not know, Comrade Marshal."

"Find out. If he has not, notify me the moment he does. And

1

put your best men to searching and guarding the prisoners. It may be that some know of Leonov's whereabouts. It would be inconvenient if they died before telling us what we need to know. *Most* inconvenient. Do you understand?"

"Completely, Comrade Marshal."

"Good. I hold you responsible, *Lieutenant* Borodin."

The man clicked his heels and smartly slapped the bright orange butt of his AKM, sounding a crisp, military crack that echoed in the charred and smashed office. "Thank you, Comrade Marshal!"

He turned, and Krasilnikov was left alone once more in the ruin of what just five hours earlier had been the command center of a democratic Russia.

Demokratichyeskii Rossiya. Krasilnikov snorted at the absurdity of the thought. *Pah!*

The anarchy unleashed across the *Rodina* during the past decade was unmatched by that of any period of history since the Great Patriotic War, since even the epic sacrifices of 1917. First there'd been the so-called *glasnost* and *perestroika* of Gorbachev . . . followed by the abortive coup of '91, the accession of Yeltsin, and the wholesale dismemberment of the Soviet Union, she whom Krasilnikov had pledged to defend with his life. The Communist Party banned, the state-run economy plundered, the Warsaw Pact vanished with the winds of counterrevolution howling from Berlin to Vladivostok.

Krasilnikov and a dedicated handful of other senior officers had worked to set things straight, restore order where chaos reigned as a new and manic Czar. The puppet "democrat" who'd followed Yeltsin to power over the pathetic tatters of a great nation had been assassinated in Oslo—ostensibly by western anarchists, but in fact by agents of Aleksandr Doctorov's revitalized and rededicated security apparatus—and in the wake of that assassination, an alliance of KGB, military, and hard-liner party men had secured power once again in the capitals of the former Commonwealth of Independent States.

That had been only the beginning, of course, as the Soviet Union rose reborn from the ashes. The operation known as Rurik's Hammer, the lightning military conquest of all of Scandinavia, had been designed to solidify popular support for the resurrected Soviet government at home despite the rationing, the purges, and the KGB crackdowns; to cow a fragmented and weakened NATO already overextended in the war-ravaged Balkans; and to remind continental Europe of the might of Soviet arms.

But Rurik's Hammer had failed . . . and failed miserably. The vaunted Baltic and Red Banner Northern fleets had suffered ignominious defeat at the hands of a single American aircraft carrier battle group operating off the Norwegian coast, and U.S. Marines had stormed ashore at Narvik, trapping an entire Soviet army above Trondheim and forcing its surrender. The twin naval engagements at the Fröyen Banks and off the Lofoten Islands—the Battles of the Fjords, as they were coming to be called—were already being hailed as two of the classic encounters of military history. Even now, eight months later, the Red Banner Northern Fleet had not yet recovered but remained in port, impotent and all but useless.

The military fiasco in Norway had led to the collapse of the neo-Soviet dream, of course. Krasilnikov and his supporters had been forced to strike shameful deals with Ilya Anatolevich Leonov and his Popular Russian Democratic Party simply to maintain some voice in Russian government, and then been made to stand by helplessly and watch the inexorable disintegration of Mother Russia, the destruction of all that the glorious Revolution was and could be, begin all over again.

Enough was enough! Not even the legendary patience of the most stolid of Russian peasants could endure so much. The coalition of Soviet marshals and generals, KGB leaders, Communist Party hard-liners, and pro-Soviet nationalists had begun plotting the coup almost from the moment the shattered remnants of the Red Banner Fleet had limped into port at Murmansk. Their plans had culminated early this morning, as carefully screened, pro-Soviet army and KGB units stormed the Kremlin. Tanks now controlled every major intersection and boulevard in downtown Moscow, while crack Spetsnaz forces held all four of Moscow's international airports and the complex of military control and communications centers that ringed the city. This time, there would be no repeat of the pathetic half measures and hesitancy of the leaders of the coup attempt during the summer of 1991. There would be no civilian mobs rallying at the barricades this time, no army unit defections or CNN special reports "live from Moscow."

"Comrade Marshal Krasilnikov," a smooth, familiar voice said at his back. *"Dobre den."*

Krasilnikov whirled. Aleksandr Dmitrivich Doctorov stood in the doorway, hands buried in the pockets of his black trench-coat, a fur *schapska* perched on his balding head.

"Doctorov," Krasilnikov said, deliberately ignoring the other's greeting. "The bird has flown his cage."

"So I was informed on my way over here."

"It would seem we have had a major failure of intelligence."

The head of the *Komitet Gosudarstvennoy Bezopasnosti*— the infamous Committee for State Security—stiffened ever so slightly at that challenge. Did he hold a gun within his coat pocket? "There was no failure, Comrade Marshal. Leonov was *here*. If he escaped, he must have had advance warning. Perhaps from one of your officers."

Krasilnikov was careful to keep his own hand away from his holstered Makarov. "That is not possible."

Doctorov stared at Krasilnikov for a moment and then, surprisingly, he nodded. His hands came out of his pockets and he rubbed them together briskly, warming them against the bitter Moscow cold that had invaded the office of the erstwhile Russian president. "Actually, Comrade Marshal, I suspect that this time my opposite number with the *Upravleniye* is to blame."

"General Suvorov? Why should he—"

"An army helicopter was seen leaving the city twenty minutes before your men were to move in, Comrade Marshal. The tail number was that of an aircraft assigned to the GRU command staff."

Krasilnikov digested that. The Military Intelligence Direc-torate, the *Glavnoye Razvedyvatelnoye Upravleniye*, was larger and in some ways more powerful even than the more notorious KGB. Never had there been so much as a gram's worth of love lost between the two powerful intelligence agencies, and their rivalry had caused trouble for Soviet policy and image more than once in the past. But Krasilnikov had been certain that Suvorov was solidly in the coup's collective pocket.

"The helicopter's destination?"

"South. It may have gone to a military airfield outside Orel. An airfield still under PRDP control."

"This," Krasilnikov said softly, "changes everything."

Doctorov favored him with a death's-head smile. "It means, my dear Comrade Marshal Krasilnikov, that our beleaguered nation's troubles are but beginning. If Leonov is alive, the democrats in the army and the nationalists in the republics will rally to him. It means what we have feared all along."

"Da," Krasilnikov said, and his eyes were fixed on the swirl of snowflakes dancing through the shattered window of the office. "It means another civil war. A bloodbath."

"Come, Comrade. The capital, at least, is ours. As are the northern military sectors and the bulk of the Red Army. We must compose our message for the rest of the world."

"Yes. Before they descend on us like wolves."

Thunder keened from the gray skies as a trio of MiG-31s roared low over the city. Krasilnikov cast another quick glance about the ruined office, then hurried after Doctorov.

There was so very much yet to be done.

CHAPTER 1
Tuesday, 10 March

"Damn but the weather's dirty tonight." Captain Matthew "Tombstone" Magruder stood in *Jefferson*'s Primary Flight Control, "Pri-Fly" to the initiated, and worked at not sloshing hot coffee down the Air Boss's back. He could feel the pitch to the supercarrier's deck as she plowed through heavy seas invisible in the darkness 120 feet below. "For once I'm actually glad I'm not up there."

"What, am I hearin' this right, CAG?" Commander William Barnes grinned up at him from a coffee mug of his own. "AIR BOSS" was stenciled across the man's sweatshirt and the back of his chair, while his coffee mug proclaimed, "I'm the BOSS." He was the man responsible for controlling all air traffic in the carrier's immediate vicinity from this glassed-in eyrie, including all launch and recovery operations. "Man, this has got to be some kind of first. Usually all I hear is you bitchin' about what you wouldn't give to be able to log more hours."

"Hours, yes. But not in *that*. Case Three if ever I saw it." Case Three was a bad-weather carrier approach, with a ceiling of two hundred feet and visibility of a half mile or less. In blue-water operations like this, with no friendly airfields within range, those limits could quickly drop to zero-zero, no ceiling, no visibility.

"Hell, the Met boys say it's going to get even worse," the Boss said. He jerked a thumb toward Pri-Fly's aft windows.

"We're tryin' to get these people down before it turns to snow."

It was raining now, a cold, thin half-water/half-sleet that lashed across Pri-Fly's slanted windows. It was also pitch black save for the rain-smeared gleam of flight-deck acquisition lights and the glow from the big Fresnel lens apparatus aft and to port, where the Landing Signals Officer and his crew were already talking the next aviator down. The scene was repeated in black and white on the big PLAT monitor suspended from Pri-Fly's overhead. Glancing up at the screen, Tombstone could see several members of the deck crew, bulky in their cold weather gear, trotting out of the camera's range.

"Two-oh-seven," the LSO's voice crackled from an overhead speaker. "Call the ball."

There was a moment of static, then a new voice sounded from the speaker. "Clara." That one code word meant simply that the approaching aviator could not yet see the ball . . . or the storm-masked *Jefferson*.

In normal peacetime operations, the flight deck was shut down when Case Three conditions dropped below a half-mile visibility—fifteen seconds' flight time for an approaching aircraft.

"Home Plate, Two-oh-seven," the voice added a moment later. "Wait one. Okay, got you! Two-oh-seven, Tomcat ball. Three point three."

The terse information confirmed for the men adjusting the tension of the five parallel arrestor wires stretching across the after part of the flight deck that it was an F-14D Tomcat coming in for a trap, that the aircraft had 3,300 pounds of fuel left aboard, and that the pilot could now see the yellow beacon, the "meatball," of the carrier's landing approach guide indicator. Having made countless traps himself, including Case Three landings on nights as dark, wet, and raw as this one, Tombstone could see the approach setup clearly in his mind's eye. So long as the aviator kept the ball centered between the horizontal lines of green lights to either side, the aircraft was holding the proper angle of approach for a good trap.

The Tomcat was also being guided in by *Jefferson*'s Instrument Landing System, "riding the needles" in on the correct glide slope. By coupling the ILS with the Automatic Carrier Landing System, or ACLS, the approach could actually be turned over to a computer, which could land the aircraft with no human hand at the controls.

As Tombstone knew from long personal experience, Navy fliers had distinctly mixed feelings about the ACLS, and the hairier the approach, the less they liked it. Hell, *no* pilot liked to fly with someone else at the controls, and when that someone else was a goddamned computer . . .

Had 207 sounded just a little too tight? Hell, an approach on a night like this would unsettle anyone, and Lobo, Lieutenant Hanson, was still relatively new at this.

"Roger ball," the LSO's voice said, calm and reassuring. "You're looking good. Come left, just a hair . . . little more . . . that's good. Centerline good. Deck going down, power down . . ."

Tombstone was staring into the night astern of the carrier, but try as he might he still couldn't see any sign of the approaching Tomcat . . . and then the big aircraft *exploded* out of the gloom off *Jefferson's* stern, wings swept far forward and flaps down for maximum lift, acquisition lights at belly and tail and wingtips flashing frantically but damned near masked by the rain as the F-14 swept across the roundoff at the end of the flight deck, wheels kissing steel as the tailhook struck a skittering salvo of yellow sparks, then neatly snagged the three-wire and dragged the hurtling mass of machinery to an almost instant halt even as its two big F110-GE-400 engines howled to full throttle.

The moment the tailhook had successfully engaged the arrestor wire and it was clear the pilot wouldn't have to pull a "bolter" off the deck and come around for another try, the aircraft's engines spooled down again. The whole sequence, from Tombstone's first glimpse of the Tomcat materializing out of the dark to the moment it backed slightly on the carrier's roof, spitting out the wire, had taken only seconds, and he let out a small whoosh of pent-up air. Two-oh-seven was safely down, a perfect trap. Engines whining, the F-14 began nosing around to starboard, slowly following a yellow-jerseyed deck handler who backed away from the aircraft step by step, a pair of light wands waving up and down as he directed it toward an out-of-the-way spot on the flight line.

"Two-one-eight," the Air Boss was saying into the heavy microphone on the console in front of him. "Charlie now."

That was the command to the next aircraft circling west of the *Jefferson* to break from its holding pattern, or "Marshall Stack," and begin its approach to the carrier.

"Two-one-eight, copy," another voice said from the speaker, hard-edged and professional. "We're heading in."

"Ah, listen, Two-one-eight. Visibility on the deck's down to half a mile or less. Wind at one-nine knots from zero-four-zero, but we're getting occasional gusts at two-five."

"Wonderful, Home Plate. Just shit-fire wonderful. Sounds brisk and refreshing."

"Ah, Two-one-eight, we've got the beer chilled and waiting for you. Just bring back our airplane." Barnes released the switch on the mike and thumbed through a clipboard on his console. "Who's got the front seat on Two-one-eight tonight anyway?"

"Conway," Tombstone said. He didn't need to check the roster. "Call sign Brewer."

The Air Boss leaned back in his chair and glanced up briefly at him. "CAG, you look as shook as a rookie making his first trap. What the hell are you doing hanging around here bothering working men for anyway? Don't you have some papers to shuffle or something?"

Barnes said the words with a crooked grin that robbed them of their sting, but Tombstone felt the stab nonetheless. God, to be skipper of VF-95, Viper Squadron, again.

Those were Viper Tomcat-Ds recovering on the *Jefferson* under the Air Boss's watchful eye now. Tombstone was now the CO of CVW-20, commanding officer of *Jefferson*'s entire air wing of some ninety aircraft, but he still couldn't help holding a special place in his feelings for the Vipers of VF-95.

"Hey, c'mon, Bill," he said. "I just came here to do some slumming, you know that. If you prefer, you can let it out that I'm here to boost morale and encourage the troops."

"I think you're scared those nuggets of yours out there are going to get lost."

They laughed at that, but Tombstone was more than a little nervous and had to resist the impulse to pace the narrow stretch of Pri-Fly's free deck space. An aircraft carrier's roof, her flight deck, was already the deadliest workplace on Earth, and the harsh blend of darkness, wind, and sleet transformed it into a death trap. Back in the Vietnam War, medical researchers had wired naval aviators to record pulse and respiration and other telltale physical signs, then monitored them as they carried out their missions. Nothing, not the headlong rush of a catapult shot, not SAMs streaking toward their aircraft in the skies over Hanoi, not air-to-air combat, not even the jolting instant of stark terror during an ejection, could cause the same heart-pounding, sweaty-palmed terror every aviator felt making a final approach toward a carrier at night.

And wind and rain just made it worse, of course. Still, carrier operations went on, whatever the weather, whatever the time of day or night. Especially *now* . . . with this undeclared war with the Russians, or whatever the hell they were calling themselves these days. Tombstone glanced across the compartment to the Pri-Fly tally board, where an Assistant Air Boss was keeping tabs on *Jefferson*'s far-flung net of aircraft.

Storm or no storm, at this moment six S-3A Viking ASW aircraft were probing across an arc far in advance of the carrier battle group, searching for seaborne traces of Russian subma-rines that might be trying to use the rain and wind as cover for a stealthy approach and kill. Somewhere in the darkness a mile or so off to port, an SH-3 Sea King helicopter mounted lonely vigil, ready to attempt a rescue of an aviator who, God forbid, got into trouble during recovery and had to punch out in this soup. High up and to starboard was one of *Jefferson*'s four E-2C Hawkeyes, providing the entire, far-flung battle group with early-warning radar that could penetrate the sleet and dark across hundreds of miles and, at need, serve as airborne combat command centers. CAP, or Combat Air Patrol, was being provided by four F/A-18 Hornets of VFA-161, the Javelins. They'd screamed off *Jefferson*'s deck into the rain thirty minutes ago, taking up their patrol stations so that the Tomcats of Viper Squadron could return to the carrier.

As it was, except for the increased number of Viking sub-hunters aloft, it was a fairly light deployment. *Jefferson* and the entourage of warships comprising Carrier Battle Group 14 were currently cruising east-northeast through the Norwe-gian Sea two hundred miles south of Iceland. Carrier Battle Group 7, the U.S.S. *Eisenhower* and her consorts, was already somewhere well to the northeast, five hundred miles ahead, moving to cover the Barents Sea approaches out of Murmansk and the Kola Peninsula just in case the Red Banner Fleet

elected to sally forth for a rematch after its defeat at *Jefferson*'s
hands off Norway the previous year. CBG-3, meanwhile, with
the U.S.S. *Kennedy*, was in the North Sea off the Skagerrak,
overseeing the final collapse of neo-Soviet troops in Denmark,
Norway, and Sweden. *Kennedy* and the warships with her were
the cork in the Baltic's bottle, keeping any surviving Russian
ships at St. Petersburg safely docked and out of action.

No, *Jefferson* shouldn't have to worry about Russian attacks
tonight. But they *did* have to worry about the weather.
Tombstone felt the deck rise beneath his feet, felt the slightly
sickening twist of the carrier corkscrewing through the worsening waves.

"Two-one-eight," the LSO said over the speaker. "Call the
ball."

"Home Plate, Two-one-eight, Clara, repeat, Clara. I'd call
the damned ball if I could see it. It's getting damned thick up
here."

"Is Two-one-eight the last one up?" Tombstone asked.

"Yup." Suddenly, Barnes's voice was tight and sounded as
dry as Tombstone's. There was no light banter in the compartment now.

"Two-one-eight," the voice crackled over the speaker. "Tomcat ball. One point eight."

Eighteen hundred pounds of fuel left? They were damned
near running on fumes.

"Roger ball. Deck coming up, power on." Tombstone found
himself holding his breath . . .

. . . and then the Tomcat boomed out of the darkness, red
and green navigation lights winking, arrestor hook groping for
a wire, but high . . . *high* as the LSO's voice shouted, "Wave
off! Wave off!" and the meatball flared red. The Tomcat hit the
steel hard, sparks exploding into the night well beyond the
number-five wire, too far up the deck for the tailhook to snag
hold, but the aviator's hand had already rammed the throttles
full forward, sending twin spears of yellow flame thundering
against the night in a desperate bid to regain suddenly precious
airspeed.

"Bolter! Bolter! Bolter!" someone was yelling over the
intercom system, as Tomcat 218 screamed past *Jefferson*'s
island, rushing down the angled flight deck and back into the
night.

Stoney was still holding his breath as he watched the twin flares of light marking the engines, like glowing eyes, stagger beyond the deck, dipping toward an invisible sea, then come up, rising . . . rising . . . struggling aloft against wind and gravity and drag.

Then the Tomcat was gone, swallowed once again by the night.

"Okay, Brewer," Barnes was saying into his microphone. "Once again around. Just like a walk in the park."

"Ah, roger that, Home Plate," the voice replied. "Just remember that the parks are getting damned dangerous. 'Specially at night."

"So, Captain," Barnes said conversationally after a moment. "What're the chances that the Russkis are gonna fold?"

It was clearly a ploy to ease the atmosphere of growing tension that filled Pri-Fly like some noxious cloud. The Russian War had been the steady, number-one topic of conversation aboard every ship in CBG-14 ever since they'd left Norfolk the week before.

"Zero to none," Tombstone shot back. His heart was pounding hard enough that Barnes could surely hear it. "The Reds don't dare show the cracks in the foundation of their coup. It looks like Leonov is going to keep hammering away until something gives. The only out the neo-Soviets have is to turn this into a general war. A *world* war."

"My, CAG, but you're just full of cheerful thoughts tonight," Barnes said. "Think it'll go nuke?"

"It could. I don't think anyone wants it to, not even Krasilnikov. And yet . . ." He shrugged. "This is the first time we've had an honest-to-God civil war in a country where *both* sides have nuclear weapons. And, well, fratricidal wars are always the bloodiest, the most down-and-dirty vicious wars of all."

"Hey!" Barnes said. "Remember when we all thought the world would be a safer place with the Soviet Union gone?"

"What do you want," Stoney replied, grinning. "A return to the good old days of the Cold War?"

The neo-Soviet empire had appeared to collapse in the wake of the brief, hard-fought naval campaign off Norway nine months earlier. Tombstone could close his eyes and still remember the roar and thunder of battle, the pillars of smoke climbing heavenward marking the funeral pyres of ships, the hurtling aerial combat machines jousting in tournaments of death at Mach 2 and beyond. Tombstone himself had been in a Hornet flashing low across the deck of the Soviet supercarrier *Kreml* just as the Baltic Fleet's flagship had exploded in flames. His heart still raced each time he thought about it.

The *Thomas Jefferson* had been hurt badly off the Lofoten Islands in the final chapter of the Battles of the Fjords. She'd limped back under her own steam, first to Scapa Flow, then to Norfolk, but her flight deck had been so badly ripped up that nothing could land on it but helicopters. By the time the old girl had reached her home port, there'd been talk of scrapping her.

Events across the Atlantic had dictated otherwise. UN troops had briefly occupied Moscow and St. Petersburg, as Red Army units in Scandinavia began surrendering en masse. There'd been talk of a joint allied military government to oversee the recovery of Russian democracy. Ilya Anatolevich Leonov and his Popular Russian Democratic Party had made their appearance, rising from obscurity to control of the new Russian government almost overnight. The UN forces had withdrawn, and a breathless world had continued to watch the growth of the world's newest and most astonishing democracy, live from Moscow on CNN.

Which was why the news of the military coup in mid-February had been so devastating. Overnight, it seemed, the old Iron Curtain had slammed down yet again. The only news emerging from the crippled Russian giant consisted of dark, nightmare tales of purges and people's courts, of mobilizations, KGB arrests, and assassinations, of a hard-liner Red Army marshal named Valentin Grigorevich Krasilnikov who, to judge by the stories spread by the trickle of refugees out of Russia, held close spiritual kinship with the restive shade of Stalin.

The war begun by the Soviets in Scandinavia, it was clear now, was resuming. News that Leonov and some of his supporters had fled Moscow and found refuge in the southern Urals was the first word of civil war. As former S.S.R.s chose sides, as Krasilnikov's Red Army and Leonov's Blue Army clashed in a bloody meeting engagement at the Voronezh River, it became clear that events in the former Soviet Union might well be capable of holding the entire world hostage.

Both Reds and Blues possessed nuclear weapons. How long would it be before one side or the other used them?

The repairs to the *Thomas Jefferson* had received top priority in a nation already struggling to improve its military posture. In record time, *Jeff*'s flight deck had been restored, and her normal complement of ninety-plus aircraft in ten squadrons had been returned to her.

Now, the *Jefferson* was returning to the same waters where she'd been savaged nine months earlier. She was the same ship, but many of her people were new . . . and that included the majority of the air wing's aviators. Casualties among *Jefferson*'s fliers during the Battle of the Fjords had been atrocious, and the Navy Department had been pulling out all the stops to get qualified personnel in to replace those losses.

"Two-one-eight, you're lookin' just fine," the LSO's voice said. "Call the ball."

Static crackled over the speaker, and Tombstone pictured Conway in the Tomcat's cockpit, straining for a glimpse of *Jefferson*'s meatball through that ink-black soup.

"Two-one-eight, call the ball. Acknowledge."

"Okay, gentlemen, got it," Conway's voice replied. "Two-one-eight, Tomcat ball. One . . . ah, make it zero point niner."

There wouldn't be fuel enough for another touch-and-go.

"Two-one-eight, roger ball. You're right on the money. Deck coming up. Power on."

Tombstone leaned forward, knuckles white against the handle of his forgotten cup of coffee.

"Power *on*, Two-one-eight! Up! Up!"

God, Conway was low, hurtling toward *Jefferson*'s ramp at 140 knots. . . .

The Tomcat materialized out of the night like a gray ghost, nose high, landing gear and arrestor hook seeming to reach ahead of the plummeting aircraft in a desperate search for the deck. The F-14 cleared the flight deck's roundoff by a handful of feet, slamming the steel just beyond with a jolt that wrenched its nose down sharply. Throttle up . . . but then the tailhook engaged the number-two wire and yanked the aircraft to a halt. The engine throttled down.

"Thank you, God," Tombstone said. "Thank you, *dear* God."

A pair of powerful 7x50 binoculars swung by their strap

from a hook beside the Air Boss's station. Tombstone picked them up and raised them to his eyes. Tomcat 218 was now approaching the spot left for it, guided by the yellow shirt and his glowing wands. The rain appeared to have lessened in the past few minutes, but it was rapidly being replaced by the first swirling flakes of snow. The Tomcat's wheels left tracks in a thin slush already gathering on the black-painted steel of the flight deck.

Two-one-eight's deck crew crowded around, ramming chocks home beneath the wheels and beginning the complex tie-down process to secure the aircraft against blasts of wind, natural or manmade, across the flight deck. The crew chief turned a key and unfolded a ladder from the fuselage. The canopy popped open, then raised itself back.

Tombstone focused the binoculars on Lieutenant Commander Conway and the aircraft's Radar Intercept Officer, Lieutenant Damiano. Still seated in their aircraft, bathed in the harsh glare from a light on the carrier's island above their heads, they seemed unshaken, running through their shutdown procedures with the professionals' routine and unflappable calm.

Not for the first time, Tombstone marveled at the changes that were overtaking *Jefferson*'s air wing . . . that were sweeping throughout the entire American military. He'd thought that the high casualties off Norway, the graphic horrors of modern naval warfare, would have had the exact opposite effect on recruitment and training policies and American popular opinion than that he'd been witness to these past few months. Sometimes it was still a bit hard to believe.

Through the binoculars, he watched Conway and Damiano remove their helmets and hand them to their crew chief, then begin unfastening the harnesses. Tricia Conway's blond hair was cut short to accommodate her helmet; Rose's hair was jet black and a bit longer. Their flight suits could not completely disguise the decidedly female curves of their figures. Lieutenant Chris Hanson, having just clambered out of her Tomcat parked a few yards away, reached the foot of the ladder and was shouting something at Conway, giving her a happy thumbs-up.

This, Tombstone decided, was definitely a whole new Navy from the one he'd joined over a decade before. Twenty-eight new flight officers, pilots and RIOs, had reported aboard the *Jefferson* at Norfolk two weeks ago. Of those twenty-eight, twelve were women.

The great, long-awaited social experiment, American women in combat, was beginning aboard the U.S.S. *Thomas Jefferson*.

CHAPTER 2
Tuesday, 10 March

Navy fliers never referred to themselves as *pilots*. The Air Force had pilots, men who landed on fifteen-hundred-foot runways, *stationary* runways, men who didn't have to contend with pitching decks or equipment failure in the recovery gear. The Navy had aviators, and naval aviators wore that word as a badge of supreme accomplishment, pride, and honor.

Could a woman be an aviator? That was the question. Tombstone Magruder still wasn't entirely sure of his own feelings regarding women aboard combat ships or flying combat missions. To be honest, he had no doubts whatsoever about their technical ability. Tricia Conway and the other women who'd come aboard in Norfolk two weeks earlier were hot pilots, as good as any rookie Tomcat drivers Tombstone had seen. With seasoning, with experience in the form of a few hundred more hours flying off the *Jefferson* day and night, in all weathers and in all types of seas, they'd be as good as any man in CVW-20. In time, he supposed, they'd be real aviators and accepted as such by the hitherto all-male fraternity of naval fliers.

His real problem with women serving aboard ship was on a different level entirely.

Tombstone's destination was the Dirty Shirt Mess, so called because officers could show up there for a bite to eat at almost any time without having to change from working clothes to

19

clean uniform, as was expected in *Jefferson*'s more formal officers' wardroom. He'd missed the regular mess call because he'd been tracking the evening's CAP in worsening weather, first from CATCC, *Jefferson*'s air traffic control center, and then from up in Pri-Fly. Now that Conway and her girls were safely down, he realized that he was hungry and wanted something to eat.

Conway and her girls. Every sensitivity session on women in the military that Tombstone had sat through during the past several years had emphasized that you don't call an adult, professional woman a "girl." It was demeaning, sexist, *insensitive*. . . .

Yeah, right. Like it was demeaning for Tombstone to talk about his "boys." Conway herself referred to her people as her "girls," though some of the female Naval Flight Officers bristled when a man called them that. The semantic distinction seemed less important to the enlisted personnel on both sides of the line, but the whole issue had the air wing's male complement so on edge they sometimes seemed positively tongue-tied. Morale was being affected, and since Tombstone, as CAG, was responsible for the fighting trim and efficiency of CVW-20, that made it *his* problem.

The line to pay for his meal at the Dirty Shirt wardroom was a short one. An enlisted man sitting at the door punched his meal ticket, and Tombstone went straight in. Fluorescent lighting gleamed from metal surfaces and white tables. A handful of NFOs, all male, sat in small groups amid the clatter of silverware and the low-voiced murmur of conversation. Tombstone picked up a tray and started through the chow line. Fried chicken was on the menu this evening, left over from the regular mess hours and kept hot for people coming in off duty.

Tombstone didn't resent the women. No, if he resented anyone, it was the politicians and bureaucrats back in Washington who continued to use the entire U.S. military as a test bed for their experiments in social reform.

The first experiment with women aboard ship had taken place as far back as 1972, when Admiral Zumwalt, then Chief of Naval Operations, had issued one of his famous "Z-grams." Among other innovations, Z-gram 116 had called for 424 men and fifty-three carefully screened Navy women volunteers to report aboard the hospital ship U.S.S. *Sanctuary* for a four-hundred-day test at sea.

Officially, the test was an enormous success. Unofficial leaks to the press, however, as well as the Navy's own classified reports, told a different story. Despite regulations, there'd been romantic relationships between members of the crew, and several pregnancies. PDAs, Navyese for "Public Displays of Affection," had been common, and there'd been a number of fights. "The situation was becoming serious," read a memorandum from *Sanctuary*'s commanding officer to the CNO, "and was definitely detrimental to the good order and discipline of the ship's company."

Perhaps the most obvious proof that the experiment had been less than totally successful could be found in the fact that the *Sanctuary* returned to port after only forty-two days at sea. She spent most of her next several years tied to a dock, before being unobtrusively decommissioned in 1975.

In 1978, after Watergate's Judge John S. Sirica ruled in Federal District Court that banning women at sea violated their 14th Amendment rights, the Navy tried integrating the sexes aboard ship again, assigning a mixed crew to the repair ship *Vulcan*. Even before she left port, several pregnant personnel had to be put ashore, and the media began referring to the U.S.S. *Vulcan* as "the Love Boat."

Eventually, Sirica's decision was overturned by the Supreme Court in 1981, a ruling that feminists decried as tragic and the ACLU called "a devastating loss for women's rights."

But the matter had not ended there. Women continued to be stationed on some auxiliary, noncombat vessels. In the early nineties, the destroyer tender *Samuel Gompers* had become the next Navy ship to be known as the Love Boat when three sailors, two men and a woman, videotaped themselves having sex. One of the men was caught passing the tape around to his buddies, precipitating court-martial proceedings and yet another Navy sex scandal.

But there was another side to the larger issue of women in combat than pregnancies and PDAs. During the Gulf War of 1991, women had served with distinction, including helicopter pilots operating at the front. The death of one female pilot in a helicopter crash, and the capture and sexual mistreatment of another, had been widely reported. Several women had died in one night when a barracks of the 14th Quartermaster Corps at Dahran had been hit by an incoming Iraqi SCUD missile.

Finally, the Clinton Administration, coming to office in 1993, ruled once and for all that there should be no barriers whatsoever to women serving aboard ship or in combat aircraft. The Air Force, first to admit women cadets to their academy as far back as 1976, had swiftly integrated women pilots into front-line aviation, but implementation of the new policy in the other services had been slow. The Navy's first female combat aviators had begun feeding into shore-based fighter squadrons by the mid-nineties, but it wasn't until now that a serious attempt had been made to fully integrate women into carrier-based units.

The official story was that *Jefferson*'s squadrons had suffered severe combat losses in the Battles of the Fjords, and qualified women had been needed to bring the carrier's squadrons back to full strength. That played well on CNN, but Tombstone knew that there were still plenty of male NFOs available for duty. The situation was being used by the politicians back home who were eager for the support of women's groups such as NOW.

As he took his tray to a vacant table and sat down, he couldn't help wondering what tune the radical feminists would be singing if the Russian situation deteriorated far enough that a draft became necessary, a draft that would put women in front-line foxholes next to men.

He thought again of his conversation with Barnes up in Pri-Fly. If war erupted again between the resurrected Soviet empire and the West, there would be no way to contain it. Conway and her "girls" would be right in the thick of what promised to be a long, bloody, gruesome war.

"Hello, CAG. You look about as chipper as a man on the way to his own execution. Surely the chow's not *that* bad."

Tombstone looked up. "Hey, Batman. Secure a chair."

Lieutenant Commander Edward Everett Wayne, wiry, dark-haired, and irrepressible, was VF-95's Executive Officer. He was also one of Tombstone's most experienced flight officers. The two men had known each other for better than four years now.

"So why all the unrestrained hilarity?"

"What?"

"Actually," Batman said, stabbing a fork loaded with mashed potatoes at the empty space above Tombstone's head, "it's that little black cloud above you that worries me. I'm going to have to report that thing to the Met office, you know. They take a dim view of micro-thunderstorms going off loose aboard ship. Plays hell with their obs. Makes 'em look bad."

Tombstone chuckled, the bleak spell of his thoughts broken. "Okay, Batman. You can rest easy. Right after chow, I'll trot up to Scott's office and get my cloud registered."

Lieutenant Scott was head of *Jefferson*'s OA division, the Meteorological Office. An "ob" was one of Met's weather observations, taken once each hour when *Jefferson* was underway, and every thirty minutes during flight quarters.

"That'll do it," Batman opined, nodding and chewing. "Now tell Dr. Batman what triggered that LBC in the first place."

"LBC?"

"Little black cloud, of course. Aren't keeping up with our official navy acronyms, are we?" He shook his head. "Obviously, CAG, you're slipping, suffering deeply from the strain of command."

Tombstone sighed. "You got that right. I'm concerned about our nuggets. Our *female* nuggets."

Batman grinned. "Woman trouble, Tombstone? That's not like you. What would Pamela say?"

Pamela Drake was Tombstone's fiancée, a network anchor for ACN news. "Leave Pam out of this."

"I suppose we should. Although I imagine she's just *thrilled* by the news that we have girls serving aboard the *Jefferson* now. Her and about six thousand other Navy wives and sweethearts who have to stay behind while their men sail off into danger."

"I've had some letters from worried wives already," Tombstone admitted. "God, this female aviator thing is nothing but one big headache. As if we didn't have headaches enough already."

"Ah, don't sweat it. Be like me. I *love* the women's movement!"

Tombstone eyed his friend warily, sensing a trap. "You do?"

"Yup. Especially from behind!"

Tombstone closed his eyes, groaning. "You, Wayne, are a hopeless degenerate."

Batman nodded vigorously. "A Neanderthal male chauvinist pig, that's me."

"Yeah, and you're probably the last person aboard this boat I should talk to about this. I still remember that incident in Bangkok."

"Incident?" Batman's eyes widened into blank innocence. "What incident?"

"The Thai International Hotel? Skinny-dipping with a couple of stewardesses in the hotel's pool, with God knows how many civilians watching from the lounge through a big underwater window?"

"I'm sure I have no idea what the captain is talking about," Batman said with sore-wounded dignity. "I would certainly have remembered the incident in question had I been the alleged perpetrator involved. Sir."

"Save it. You never did track that one stew down again, did you? What was her name?"

"Which one? Becky or Arlene? Besides, I still don't know what you're talking about."

"I rest my case. I can't talk to you about the problems I'm having with women on board ship. You're too busy chasing them."

Surprisingly, Batman didn't answer right away, and when he did, the bantering tone was gone. "I know I used to be a skirt-chaser, Stoney," he said. "Used to be I had just one use for women. That's not true anymore."

Tombstone regarded his friend for a moment with a level gaze. "I know. I was out of line, Batman."

He'd heard the story from Batman himself. Several years back, during *Jefferson*'s deployment to Thailand during an attempted military coup in that country, Batman had been shot down by rebels along the Thai-Burmese border. Chances were he would have ended up dead . . . but he'd been found instead by a young Karen woman named Phya Nin, a sergeant in the Karen National Liberation Army. He almost certainly owed her his life. Ever since, Batman had continued to maintain the traditional facade of the swinging, predatory, womanizing naval aviator, but it was clear that nowadays his manner *was* a facade.

Perhaps he'd learned something about women while hiking through the Thai jungle.

"Hey, no biggie," Batman said. "But in case you were wondering, I'm *not* bedding the Amazons. Not that the idea doesn't have a certain appeal, but it's too damned hard to manage any privacy on this bird farm!"

" 'Amazons?' "

"The DACOWITS Amazons. What the guys are calling Conway's people. Strictly unofficial, of course."

DACOWITS was the Defense Advisory Committee on Women in the Services. Founded in 1951, the organization had for years been in the vanguard of the fight to secure women the same opportunities in the military as men. Since the late 1970s, though, the committee had frequently been used as a political front for the radical feminist agenda. Some people had claimed that its more extreme members actively sought the draft for women, if only to deliberately expose more American women to a non-traditional lifestyle, forcing change for change's sake.

Tombstone had no opinion on such charges, but he hated the political shenanigans that were turning the U.S. military into some kind of social testing program. The Clinton Administration had forced the women-in-combat issue, just as they'd forced another controversial issue by lifting the military's ban on homosexuals. Damn it all, between the gargantuan budget cuts and the social engineering, it was as though the White House had been *determined* to torpedo Navy morale and efficiency.

"So what's eating you about 'em?" Batman prodded.

"Now that I think about it, I'm afraid the problem is more with me than with the situation. I was up in Pri-Fly tonight, watching while they brought Conway and Hanson down. Hanson trapped okay, no problem, but the weather was getting dicey by the time Conway charlied. She boltered once, and her fuel was getting tight."

"She made it?"

"Yup. Second pass."

"Happens to the best of us, man."

"Sure. The point is, I was up there with the Air Boss about to have a cow, hoping Conway wouldn't have to ditch and praying she wouldn't slam into the roundoff. Damn it, I worry about any of my men when they're in trouble, but this was different. Worse."

"The fact that Conway's a woman made it worse?"

"I guess that's what I'm saying." Tombstone took a deep breath. "I was brought up in a pretty traditional family, Batman. A Navy family. I was always taught that the womenfolk back home were part of what we were fighting for. You know, civilization. Family. Motherhood."

"Mom in the kitchen baking apple pie."

"God damn it, Batman—"

"Hey, chill out, CAG. I'm not making fun of you. But it sounds to me like you're having some trouble adjusting to the times that are a-changin'."

"You got that right." He shook his head. "Another dinosaur, blundering off to extinction."

"Another male chauvinist pig dinosaur." Batman took a bite of chicken and chewed thoughtfully for a moment. "But you're worried about more than just your response to female aviators."

"How perceptive."

"That's why they pay me the big bucks, man. What's the matter, then? Afraid one of 'em'll go on the rag and bleed all over the seat of one of your airplanes?"

"Jesus, Wayne!"

"Sorry. Bad joke. Okay, how's this. You're afraid Conway's people can't cut it, is that it? That they can't handle the pressure?"

"Well, I used to wonder about how hard they'd push. Aggression's supposed to be a male thing, you know. Then I realized that any woman who'd fought her way to the top of the pyramid in naval aviation sure as hell didn't have anything lacking in the aggressiveness department."

"I'd say that's an understatement."

"I'm worried about the wing's morale. The men as well as the women. Damn it, we're about to go into combat. People are going to be making split-second decisions where a half second's hesitation is the difference between living and dying. People are going to *die*, Batman." He closed his eyes for a moment and saw again the horror aboard the *Jefferson* after the last of the Battles of the Fjords.

Modern, high-tech warfare carried its own peculiar intensity. Four Soviet Kerry missiles had struck the carrier at the height of the battle, and fuel and munitions in the hangar bay had been set ablaze. The fires had nearly claimed the ship. He could still remember the scene on her flight deck, just after he'd returned to the *Jeff* aboard an SH-3 helicopter. The wounded had been lined up on stretchers in ranks, waiting their turn to evacuate. Kids, most of them, with hideous burns over faces and arms.

Could he watch something like that happen to a woman?

"The morale and the efficiency of this unit are my responsibility," he continued. "I think having them aboard is hurting our morale, and I think it's going to get worse the closer we get to Russian airspace. The closer we get to battle."

Batman didn't answer right away. "How do you feel about it?" Tombstone prompted him.

"Oh, my morale's just fine, thank you. And I'm not aware of anyone else in the Vipers with a problem. Well, Arrenberger, maybe."

"Slider? What's with him?"

"Bad attitude, mostly. He's one of those 'the woman's place is in the home' types. And there're a few others who may like having them aboard too much, if you know what I mean."

"The question is, what's that going to do to our combat efficiency when we go one-on-one against the Russians?"

"There's not a lot we can do that we're not already doing. You make sure your people are the best trained, the best motivated there are, like always. Shouldn't be hard. You've got good material to work with. I think you're just shook because you reacted to a situation tonight like a *man* instead of like a commanding officer."

"Yeah. And I can't help what I am, can I? I'm also wondering if that's going to be a problem for other men in this wing. What about these guys you say like having the women aboard too much?"

"Hey, CAG. I named no names."

"I'm not interrogating you. But is it a problem? PDAs? Fraternization?"

"I'm pretty sure some of the guys have something going with some of the gals, yeah. You know Navy guys."

"And aviators."

"Right. But they're doing their jobs. They're professionals, Stoney. They wouldn't be here if they weren't."

There was no way, Tombstone knew, to stop men and women from *being* men and women, certainly not when they were locked up together for month after month in an unrelieved confinement that could make life in a prison seem liberal by comparison. The question was whether the issue of sex aboard ship could impair *Jefferson*'s fighting ability. There was nothing he could do but, as Batman had suggested, rely on his people's own professionalism and good sense.

He wondered, though, about Conway. As the senior female aviator aboard, she was de facto the women's CO, though she and all of the women in turn answered to him, as commander of the wing.

Was she having the same worries about her girls as Tombstone was having with his boys? Maybe it would be a good idea to talk to her about it.

CHAPTER 3
Tuesday, 10 March

2215 hours (Zulu −1)
O-2 deck
U.S.S. *Thomas Jefferson*

Lieutenant Commander Tricia Conway knew it was going to take her quite a while to familiarize herself with more than a tiny fraction of the *Jefferson*'s miles of corridors, compartments, and companionways. She'd gone through numerous briefings on carrier layouts and shipboard life, of course, but after two weeks aboard she still carried the small map they'd given her the first day she'd reported aboard. By now she had the main routes memorized, the ones she needed to use every day between flight deck and hangar deck, say, as well as important spaces like VF-95's ready room, the officers' wardroom, and the collection of ship's exchange, stores, and services that was popularly called *Jefferson*'s "main mall."

Jefferson's female personnel couldn't approach that area, of course, without risking comments about "mall dolls," but then it was difficult to find any aspect of life on a carrier that couldn't be twisted to humorous, salty, or racy double meaning by the men who served aboard her.

Aboard an aircraft carrier, the vast and cavernous, steel-walled space called the hangar deck marks a kind of dividing line in shipboard numbering conventions. The hangar deck is on the O-1 level; decks above this level are numbered in ascending order, O-2, O-3, all the way to the O-9 deck, high up within the carrier's island. Below the hangar deck, levels are numbered in descending order, first deck, second deck, third

deck, and so on, plunging deeper into the bowels of the ship far
beneath the waterline.

Jefferson's complement of male aviators was quartered on
the O-3 deck, which extended uninterrupted from bow to stern
and lay directly underneath the carrier's "roof," or flight deck.
During launch operations, the steel-on-steel clatter of chains
and cat shuttles just overhead, the tooth-rattling *whump* of
steam catapults hurling thirty-ton aircraft off the carrier's bow,
made sleeping or even simple conversation a chancy proposi-
tion at best.

Jefferson's women, both enlisted personnel and officers, had
been given a block of compartments one level down on the O-2
deck just beneath the officers' wardroom. It was considerably
quieter there than up on the O-3, though during launch ops it
could still get noisy enough to interrupt conversation or wake
you from a sound sleep. There were other disadvantages,
however, and one was the fact that the O-2 level was divided
fore and aft by the hangar deck, which was a full two decks
high and took up something like two-thirds of the carrier's
entire 1,092-foot length. In a classic case of you-can't-get-
there-from-here, it was necessary to cut past the men's quarters
up on O-3 to reach the women's quarters from points farther
aft.

At times, that could be like running the gauntlet.

She was coming from the VF-95 ready room, making her
way down one of *Jefferson*'s endless passageways on her way
to her own quarters and bed. She was passing the male flight
officers' area on the O-3 level, taking each raised frame
opening or "kneeknocker" with a practiced stoop-and-step,
when a man's too-familiar voice called to her from behind.

"Hey, Brewski! Little trouble getting down tonight?"

She turned in the passageway. Lieutenant Commander Greg
"Slider" Arrenberger caught up to her, a toothy grin showing
beneath his thick black mustache.

"Nah, no big deal, Slider," she said. "Boltered once. It's a
shitty night out."

"Cold too. Cold as a witch's starboard tit." He winked
broadly, clucking twice. "Anything the ol' Slider can do to
warm you up?"

She was too tired to banter with the man, or to think of
something clever enough to verbally slap him down. In her

present state of mind, Arrenberger was just one more petty annoyance. Crossing her arms, she leaned back against the bulkhead. "Fuck you, Slider," she said.

"Hey, great idea! Anytime you say, baby. Make a hole!" He squeezed past her in the passageway, taking up just a bit more space than he had to to get by, contriving to lightly brush against the tips of her breasts with his body as he passed.

Slider was a real pig, the source of the worst of the sexual harassment Conway had endured since she'd come aboard. Most of Conway's fellow flight officers treated her with complete courtesy, acceptance, and respect, but there were always a few . . .

Starting at Annapolis, and continuing through flight training and assignment to a RAG at Pensacola, Conway, like every woman now aboard the *Jefferson*, had suffered through class after class on dealing with everything from verbal harassment to forcible rape. The best way of handling that sort of thing, of course, wasn't taught in sensitivity classes or role-playing sessions.

With a small glow of inner warmth, she recalled again the first time she'd encountered that kind of harassment. She'd been a new recruit at Annapolis, twenty years old and brimming with fire, ambition, and a positively fierce determination to make good in this alien world that still, after over a decade, was run for and by men. Hurrying with an armful of books on her way to her next class, she'd squeezed past a group of five fellow cadets loitering in the passageway, all male. Just as she passed, one of them had muttered a low-voiced, "Christ, that one looks like she gives *great* head," speaking just loud enough that she could hear without having the comment directed to her.

She could have ignored it. She could have reported it. Neither course would have been satisfactory, not if she didn't want more of the same and worse. Instead, she'd stopped, turned sharply, and picked out the kid who'd spoken, selecting him by the gleam in his eye and the expressions on the faces of the others. His name tag, she remembered, had read "SHAZIN-SKY," and he'd been big, a muscular guy who towered over the others in the group like a football player at a meeting of the school math club.

"Well gee, Shazinsky," she'd said sweetly. "I wouldn't know from personal experience, 'cause I'm not equipped for it, y'know? But I heard the other night *you* gave the best head in Lehman Hall!"

She'd puckered a pretend kiss in his direction, and Shazinsky's face had flushed scarlet as his companions dissolved into hooting gales of laughter. She'd had no more wise-ass crap out of Shazinsky during her whole time at Annapolis. In fact, she'd not had much trouble out of anyone after that. Word had gotten around that she could play the guys' game on their terms, and win.

That was the way to handle verbal harassment—to give better than she got. She'd slapped Slider down a couple of times already, but so far he'd just kept coming back for more.

What to do about him? She could report him to CAG. In fact, going by the regs she probably should. But what good would it do? The man would get a lecture, maybe a slap-on-the-wrist reprimand, and the next time the squadron was gathered in the VF-95 ready room she would still be sitting next to him. Worse, the next time they were up, he might be on her wing. The jerk just thought he was being funny; that, or it was the only way he could think of to catch her attention. Report him, and things could get nasty, maybe nasty enough to lead to him getting court-martialed or grounded. Hell, she didn't want to wreck the guy's career, even if he *was* a pig.

Besides, proving sexual harassment in a situation like this was hard, verging on the impossible. After all, what had he actually said or done? Asked if there was anything he could do to warm her up, in a tone that only *suggested* something sexual? Agreed with her when she'd thoughtlessly given him a classic straight man's line? Called her "baby," or grinned as he told her to "make a hole"? That last expression had been a part of every sailor's lexicon for generations. It meant, "Get out of the way," or, "Let me through." Only on the lips of someone like Slider, and when directed at a woman, did it take on a different, salacious meaning.

What she disliked the most was Arrenberger's twisting of her call sign. She was Brewer, damn it, not "Brew" or "Brewski."

Among the popular myths of the history of American arms, the story of Lucy Brewer was one of the most enduring. She'd been a prostitute who, during the 1800s, had published a widely read series of pamphlets describing how she'd passed herself off as a male Marine serving aboard the U.S.S. *Constitution* during the War of 1812. Lucy's claims had long since been disproved by Marine Corp historians. Her accounts of battle were *too* precise, drawn nearly word-for-word in some cases from the captain's published after-action reports or from newspaper accounts at the time.

In any case, Lucy's claims that she'd escaped detection for *three years* in cramped quarters occupied by 450 men, where the toilets were a couple of open-air perches at the ship's beakhead, and where the regulations of the day required all Marines to strip, bathe, and dress in the presence of a commanding officer responsible for checking frequently on their physical condition, were patently ridiculous. There *were* cases of women serving aboard ship during that era, usually prostitutes or wives smuggled aboard without the officers' knowledge. "Jeannette," the wife of a seaman aboard a French warship who was plucked from the sea after the Battle of Trafalgar in 1805, was a well-known example. The story of Lucy Brewer, however, was almost certainly a complete fabrication, one given new life only recently by books with feminist agendas and titles like Jeanne Holm's *Women in the Military: An Unfinished Revolution.*

That hadn't stopped Conway from adopting "Brewer" as her call sign. She'd read Holm's book while she was in flight training at Pensacola, and that had led her to research Lucy's history, as well as accounts of other American women in combat, from Molly Pitcher serving a cannon at Monmouth to the now-nameless Confederate girl who, dressed like a man, had died by her husband's side during Pickett's Charge. If Lucy Brewer's story hadn't really happened the way she said it had, it still could have, even *should* have, for it reflected the attitudes of other Americans who felt that women ought to have the same right to defend their homes and loved ones as men.

Not many of the men Conway had served with knew the origin of the call sign. Most, typically, assumed it had something to do with beer, which explained why a few like Arrenberger twisted it into "Brew" or "Brewski." Usually, she didn't mind, not really, not when she'd long ago learned that fighting every *possible* slight, put-down, or innuendo did nothing but wear her own nerves to a frazzle.

Conway was fond of claiming that she was not a militant feminist, but a *military* feminist; she referred to herself and

others as "girls," just as she sometimes called the men she
served with "boys" or "the guys," and she'd laughed as hard as
any man the first time she'd heard the story of the sailor, the
Marine, and the admiral's daughter. Thirty-one years old, with
eleven of those years in the Navy, she was in every sense a
professional, intensely proud of who and what she was, and of
her success in what for so long had been an exclusively
male-dominated bastion. All her life, since long before the
notion of women serving in combat units had been seriously
addressed, she'd wanted to be a Navy aviator. Her older brother
had been a Tomcat driver in VF-41, the Black Aces, stationed
aboard the *Nimitz* during the late eighties, while her father had
flown Navy F-4B Phantoms off the *Forrestal* in Vietnam.

The day she'd first stepped onto the flight deck of the U.S.S.
Thomas Jefferson had been a dream come true.

Now, just two weeks later, she was wondering if the dream
hadn't already begun to take on the shades of nightmare.

Her defenses, she told herself with a sigh, were way, way
down. As she turned a corner and entered a companionway,
quick-stepping down a ship's ladder to the O-2 deck, she
thought that the worst of it was the environment, the tight,
gray-bounded shipboard atmosphere that was part of life at sea
and stretched on unchanging for day after day after day.
Privacy next to zero; regulations governing everything from
when she could take a shower to how she took that shower to
where she could use a toilet; the inevitable presence of a few
bastards like Arrenberger, who insisted on turning each exchange of pleasantries into a hormone-charged sexual encounter of some kind; the language, God, the language . . .

It wasn't that she minded the profanity; if she did, she'd
definitely made one hell of a bad career choice. Shit, she'd
stopped being shocked by mere words sometime during her
first week at Annapolis. No, for Conway, the worst aspect of
the language used by Navy men came from the *accidental*
verbal harassments, the expression on some guy's face when he
slipped and said something he thought he shouldn't have said
in her presence. Things like, "He's got real balls," or, "It just
went tits-up," or, "Make a hole."

She'd only been aboard the *Jefferson* for two weeks and it
was starting to get to her.

Hell, if she was this stressed out already, what would it be like in a month? In three? In seven? This was a war patrol, and no one knew when they'd be setting course for Norfolk again. Smart money said the cruise would last at least six months . . . and eight or nine was far more likely.

"Girl," she murmured to herself, "it is just barely possible that you have made one hell of a big mistake."

Turning right at the next cross passageway, Conway reached the block of compartments that had been set aside for women officers aboard. A female electrician's mate third class, a stocky, plain-faced girl wearing the bright silver police badge of *Jefferson*'s MAA force pinned to her uniform blouse, stood guard. "Evening, ma'am."

Conway eyed her name tag. "Hey, Shupe. How're they hangin'?"

Shupe's eyes widened. "I . . . beg your pardon, ma'am?"

"Nothing. Forget it. I'm just tired." She reached the compartment she shared with Lieutenant Commander Joyce Flynn and walked in.

Flynn, call sign "Tomboy," was a petite redhead, a radar intercept officer who'd served with a reserve squadron flying out of Oceana before being transferred to VF-95. She was sitting at the room's tiny wall desk, reading a Hughes factory manual on the F-14's AWG-9 radar weapons control system. "Ho, Brewer. Glad you made it. Some of us thought you were going to have to swim back."

"Shit, Tomboy, did everyone on this bird farm see me pull that bolter?"

"Only the ones on duty, and just about everybody else aboard who wasn't asleep at the time. You put on quite a PLAT show."

"I'll just bet."

"What's the matter, Brewer? You okay?"

"Nah. Just feeling unusually bitchy tonight."

"The PMS blues?"

"Navy blues is more like it. I came *that* close to cashing in on a real-estate deal for me and Damiano both tonight. I guess I'm just a little shook, is all." She plucked at her uniform blouse, feeling it cling unpleasantly to her skin. The inside of her flight suit had been soaked with sweat when she'd changed to her uniform up in the ready area a few minutes ago. "God,

Tomboy, I stink. You're going to make me sleep in the passageway."

"I can stand it if you can."

All she really wanted right now was a scalding hot shower and bed . . . and she couldn't even have that shower tonight because *Jefferson*'s women had to share the shower head with the men, rotating with them according to a posted schedule. It was damned inconvenient, though not, she reminded herself, as inconvenient as it would have been to redesign and rebuild the entire aircraft carrier just to include separate and private plumbing for women. In any case, water discipline was strictly enforced aboard the carrier for all hands, and showers could only be taken at specified times during the day. With the women sharing the facilities on the O-3 deck forward, shower times for female personnel were from 1800 to 2000 hours each evening, and again from 0500 to 0600 each morning.

Since she'd been on CAP until well past 2100, she'd missed her chance at a shower tonight. True, there was a small shower up by the ready room for the use of aviators with the duty, but someone had been in there when she'd been changing out of her flight suit and she hadn't felt like waiting. There was also a small head down the passageway outside, reserved for women only. If she wanted, she could give herself a sponge bath from the sink.

Too much trouble. Unbuttoning her blouse, she pulled it off, then tucked it in with her dirty laundry. She'd grab her shower in the morning during the 0500 to 0600 slot.

"You sure there's nothing the matter?"

"Ah, I ran into Arrenberger up on O-3."

"The guy's an asshole."

"This is news?"

"Hardly. He's been hitting on me a lot lately too."

"You going to report him?"

Tomboy shrugged. "Hardly worth the hassle, is it? Counterproductive. Especially if I get assigned as his RIO someday. You can bet I will if he gets too far out of line, though."

Stripped down to her panties, Conway pulled on the oversized T-shirt she liked to sleep in, working her head through the hole. "Sometimes I want to kick the bastard in the nuts so hard they pop out his ears. So much for the camaraderie of men at war, right?" She climbed into her rack and flicked out the reading lamp attached to the bulkhead nearby.

Tomboy watched her from the desk. "Am I going to bother you if I stay up and read a bit?"

"Flynn, right now Valentin Krasilnikov and the entire KGB could break down that door in pursuit of my maidenly virtue and I don't think I'd hear a thing. Stay up as long as you want."

But sleep didn't come immediately. As Conway lay there, feeling the corkscrew pitch of the carrier plowing through worsening seas, she wondered about this test-case role she found herself trapped in. Women serving aboard ship. Women in front-line combat. These were causes she'd passionately believed in ever since she'd first made up her mind to be a naval aviator like her dad and like Robert. Did she still believe?

Wrong question. The real question should be, was she going to let a few horny sewer-brains like Arrenberger kill that dream?

No . . . no way. She could handle Slider. She'd flame his ass if she had to. Again she considered following the regs to the letter and reporting Arrenberger to CAG. She had that right and that responsibility, and he'd definitely been breaking the rules. It wasn't so much any single exchange of words or unwanted touching with that guy, but his overall pattern of behavior. He *always* acted like an asshole . . . except when he strapped on an F-14. She hated to admit it, but that son of a bitch could *fly*.

Besides, there was no way to regulate or legislate against anybody's God-given right to be an asshole.

Eventually, she fell asleep.

CHAPTER 4
Wednesday, 11 March

0930 hours (Zulu +2)
Tretyevo Peschera
Near Polyarnyy, Russia

Admiral Ruslan Zakharovich Karelin stood on the dockside, his coterie of staff officers and guards clustered at his back as he surveyed the bustle of activity echoing and re-echoing throughout the length and breadth of the vast, rock-hewn chamber. Workers clustered everywhere, and the piercing gleams of a dozen welder's torches dazzled and hissed from the flanks of dark, quiescent monsters. Steel clashed, and an officer bellowed orders, the words ringing from rock and hull metal, then swiftly vanishing into the steady background rumble of heavy machinery. High overhead, the massive tackle of a traveling bridge crane crawled ponderously along its lattice-work tracks beneath the rough-hewn rock of the ceiling, casting weirdly shifting shadows from the banks of fluorescent lights as it moved.

They called the place *Tretyevo Peschera*, the Third Cavern, but such a colorless name scarcely seemed adequate to describe the thrilling, Socialist workers' glory of this place. It had taken an army of engineers, construction workers, and levies of forced labor imported from the mining camps beyond the Urals seven years to pierce this granite sea cliff, tunneling into solid rock for hundreds of meters. Though that initial construction had been complete by 1984, work on the deeper chambers and storerooms continued to this day. During the past decade, construction on this and three other, similar caverns scattered along the rugged western coast of the Kola Inlet between Polyarnyy and Sayda Guba had been interrupted only intermittently during Russia's brief flirtations with democracy.

"Is the work here proceeding on schedule?" Karelin demanded of his host.

"*Da, Tovarisch Admiral,*" a short, dark-haired man with the epaulets and insignia of a *kapitan pervovo ranga,* a captain first rank, snapped back with military precision. Every man at each base he'd visited, Karelin reflected, had been eager to show his zeal.

And well they might. Karelin's retinue included two men in civilian clothing, anonymous, yet obvious in their anonymity as agents of the Third Directorate, that arm of the KGB responsible for guaranteeing the loyalty of military units all the way down to the company level. Around them were eight men in standard, green-camouflaged army uniforms, but with peaked caps and the collar tabs bearing the Cyrillic "VV" identifying them as *Vnutrennie Voiska,* the MVD's interior army. All had the flat, expressionless faces of Central Asians, men favored for MVD assignments because, as one Soviet army officer had once observed, they were "known for their obedience, stupidity, and cruelty."

They particularly enjoyed hurting Russians for some reason, which was why they were so useful for internal security work. The AKM assault rifles they held were not carried slung or held at port arms. Instead, the weapons' muzzles seemed to probe restlessly in all directions about the tight-knit group, finding and tracking each potential threat.

Clasping his hands behind his back, Karelin let his eyes run the length of the nearest of two titanic mountains of steel rising like islands from the sea cave's oil-black water. "Excellent, excellent," he said. Despite being completely enclosed, the cavern air was cold, especially here by the water. Karelin's words launched puffs of white vapor before his face. "And what is their current status, Comrade Captain?"

"*Leninskiy Nesokrushimyy Pravda* is ready for sea now," the officer replied. He gestured across the dark water toward a more distant island identical to the first. A hammerhead crane was positioned above it, a blunt-tipped, white cylinder sixteen meters long dangling from its tackle. A crew was positioned on the long deck beneath, guiding the cylinder past an open hatch in the deck. "As you can see, Comrade Admiral, *Slavnyy Oktyabrskaya Revolutsita* is still taking missiles aboard. It is his captain's intent to work through the night and have him ready to deploy to sea by this time tomorrow." As a Russian, he referred to ships with the masculine pronoun, rather than the feminine.

"They are true monsters," Karelin said. It never failed. Each time he saw these black-armored behemoths, especially within the confines of one of the caverns, he found himself a boy again, gaping up at their rounded flanks and towering sides like the greenest raw recruit. These were the centerpiece of the Motherland's defense, the very embodiment of her technical and nuclear might: *Tyfun.*

One hundred seventy-one meters long, an imposing twenty-four meters wide, with a submerged displacement of almost thirty thousand tons, Typhoon was by far the largest submarine in the world. There were eight in all, two home-based at each of four specially designed and constructed underground shelters along the Kola Inlet.

Quite apart from their size, Typhoons were unlike any other submarine in the world. They were designated as PLARBs—*Podvodnaya Lodka Atomnaya Raketnaya Ballisticheskaya*—a nuclear-powered ballistic-missile submarine, what the Americans called a "boomer." Each carried twenty SS-N-20 missiles in two rows down the long, long deck forward of the squat, two-tiered sail. Each missile, in turn, mounted six to nine independently targeted MIRV warheads and had a range of 8300 kilometers. If her captain so ordered, *Lenin's Invincible Truth* could slip through the nuclear-proof blast doors at the west side of the cavern and into the Polyarnyy Inlet beyond. From that spot, just a few kilometers north of Murmansk, he could reach across the pole to strike targets as far south as San Francisco or the Americans' big nuclear-missile sub base at Kings Bay, Georgia.

Or, with different orders, he could reach any target at all anywhere across the broad sweep of Asia. No renegade army, no traitorous city, no nationalist-minded republic in all the vast sweep of the neo-Soviet empire from Odessa to Dushanbe to Vladivostok was safe.

"You are Captain First Rank Anatoli Chelyag," Karelin said, as if he were speaking the name for the first time. He gestured

toward the nearest black metal cliff rising by the concrete pier.
"This is your vessel, is it not?"

"He is, Comrade Admiral." Chelyag stiffened with evident
pride. "It is my great honor to command *Lenin's Invincible
Truth.*"

At thirty-nine, Chelyag was young for such an important
command, but his father was Vice Admiral Gennadi V. Chelyag, a senior staff officer serving now with the Baltic Fleet and
a personal friend of the Minister of Defense. Such was the
time-honored way of patronage within the fleet.

"Hmm. Where are you from, Comrade Captain?" Karelin
asked, suddenly curious. Having studied the dossiers of all
command officers in the division, he knew precisely where
Chelyag had been born and raised, but he wanted to hear what
the man would say with his own ears.

"Kuybyshev, Comrade Admiral." The man sounded suddenly defensive, cautious, as though the question masked some
unseen trap. His eyes turned private and flicked once to the
KGB men and the MVD guards. "But . . . I've not been back
there for a long time."

"Kuybyshev? I thought the city's name was now Samara."

"*I* still think of it as Kuybyshev, sir."

"Ah, I see." Kuybyshev, named in the 1930s for a leader of
the October Revolution, was one of the hundreds of former
Soviet cities and towns that had resumed their old, Czarist
names during the Soviet collapse of the early 1990s. "The city
is deep within rebel territory, Captain. And they persist in
calling it Samara."

"Y-yes, Comrade Admiral. But I assure you that my total and
complete loyalty is to—"

"Tell me, Captain. Were I to give you the order to incinerate
Samara now, this moment, what would be your response?"

"I would instantly and without question carry out my orders,
Comrade Admiral. I have trained all my life in the service of
the *Rodina*. My home now is Party, Motherland, and Navy."

"The proper answer, Captain. But what would you *feel* about
such an order, eh?"

Chelyag had difficulty meeting Karelin's eyes. "I . . . I
would be unhappy about it, of course. Kuybyshev is a
magnificent city, and an important port on the Volga. It has a
population of almost a million and a half people, and I

sincerely doubt that more than a fraction of them are Blue counterrevolutionaries. I certainly would not want them all to die. But I *would* follow orders. Sir."

"And your family?"

"My wife and child," Chelyag said slowly, "live in Severomorsk. Both my parents are now in St. Petersburg . . . in Leningrad, I mean. There is nothing to tie me to Kuybyshev, or to any other rebel city."

Relenting at last, Karelin reached out to clap the young PLARB captain on the shoulder. "Relax, Anatoli Gennadevich. I was not doubting you."

Chelyag looked as though his knees were about to give way, and his face was pale. "Thank you, Admiral."

"Nor would such a terrible burden as the destruction of your own home be laid upon your shoulders. But the destruction of our enemies, of the *Rodina*'s enemies, will demand the utmost in loyalty and dedication from every one of us."

Now it was Karelin's turn to glance briefly at the stolid, central Asian faces of his escort. Few Asians in the MVD even spoke Russian, but Karelin was not about to jeopardize the unit's morale with the information that their home cities were about to become nuclear targets.

Somehow, he did not think they would understand.

Chances were, they'd not even been told that Kazakhstan, Turkmenistan, and the other Asian republics had sided with the rebels . . . as had been inevitable from the beginning, of course. They were barbarians, fighting with one another incessantly, hating only the Great Russians more than they hated one another. If Moscow decided to loose nuclear-tipped missiles against her own territory, the Union would be well rid of dissidents' hives like Tashkent and Alma-Ata.

"So, Captain, if you will," he said, gesturing toward the back of the cavern. "Let us proceed to your Operations Building. I have important business to discuss with Rear Admiral Marchenko."

"At once, Comrade Admiral. This way, if you please."

The party made its way deeper into the cavern, leaving the waterfront and dock area, passing fenced-off clusters of machine shops, ordnance stores, foundries, and open buildings housing heavy industrial equipment. Everywhere he looked there were soldiers, overseeing the workers, standing guard on

metal catwalks and before each building, marching in small
groups along the macadam roadways that ringed the subterranean harbor. Many were MVD troops assigned to protect this
and other PLARB bases. Others were regular army troops, or
Soviet Naval Infantry with their flat caps and blue-and-white
striped shirts showing beneath their uniform blouses. Some
even, Karelin knew, were Spetsnaz, Russia's elite army special
forces, though those units had originally been under the
command of the GRU and so were now suspect. Those Spets
forces that had remained loyal to Moscow were all carefully
screened for Blue sympathizers, as carefully screened as
Chelyag and his brother PLARB captains. In addition, each
formation had its own secret cadre of KGB Third Directorate
watchdogs, working undercover.

The Operations Building was located clear to the back of the
cavern opposite from the blast doors. It seemed to grow from
the black rock, a blocky, four-story structure bearing the
traditional emblems of Soviet might: five-pointed star, hammer
and sickle, and an enormous bronze profile of Lenin. A banner
above the door repeated Lenin's image, together with the
motto: PROGRESS, MIGHT, VICTORY THROUGH SOCIALISM. In many
parts of the Russian military, the spirit and dedication of
Communism had never died, even during the worst excesses of
the democratic revolt.

In fact, Communism was as dead now as it had been in 1991,
when the Congress of People's Deputies had first disbanded the
Soviet Union. Today, Russia and her empire were ruled by the
military, by tough, practical men who had both the courage to
make hard decisions and the might to carry them out.

Inside, the Operations Building was host to a bustling swirl
of activity, gleaming, brightly lit, and modern in comparison
with the scene in the cavern outside, which might have been
lifted from some industrial center or major shipyard early in the
century. In each open office, men leaned over computer
terminals and keyboards, while in the Primary Command
Center, wall-sized monitors displayed electronic maps of all the
former Union, with color-coded symbols marking the units
mobilizing now on one side or the other from Belarus to the Far
East. Elevators in the back led up through fifty meters of solid
rock to the surface. Armed MVD troops stood guard at every
intersection, every checkpoint.

Rear Admiral Viktor I. Marchenko occupied an enormous suite of offices on the fourth floor. Karelin announced himself to Marchenko's personal secretary, a young and pretty blond corporal who, Karelin decided when she smiled up at him, owed her formidable position to talents other than her skills at typing and stenography. Her uniform blouse was unbuttoned farther than regulations allowed, and as she moved behind her desk he suspected she was not wearing a bra.

After a brief exchange with Marchenko over the intercom, the secretary ushered Karelin into the inner sanctum. Only Karelin's chief aide, a captain third rank with a leather briefcase chained to his wrist, accompanied him. The rest of the entourage, including Captain Chelyag, remained in the outer office.

The inner office was luxuriously furnished, featuring a massive wooden desk the size of an aircraft carrier, and a broad window overlooking the cavern outside. Marchenko was a small, rotund man whose red-nosed, fleshy face looked more like that of a bartender or shopkeeper than the commander of one of Russia's most secret and most vital military installations. Like others, like Karelin himself, he owed his present power to connections in Moscow. His uncle was a member of the neo-Soviet Parliament, a man wielding considerable power.

"So, Viktor Ivanovich," Karelin said cordially, exchanging busses with the base commander. "You still have an excellent eye for picking out efficient and highly motivated personnel, I see."

Marchenko hesitated, then laughed, a booming, jolly sound. "Ah! You mean Yelana! She's something quite special, yes? Easy to look at, as they say, and a dynamo in bed! I'll let you try her, if you like."

The idea disgusted Karelin, who had already decided that Marchenko was too comfortable with this post, too willing to enjoy the perquisites of his position without exercising the responsibilities that went with them. Using his secretary as his personal whore . . .

Karelin knew that the practice was common enough in the higher ranks of the Red Army. Unlike the United States, where better than ten percent of its active military was composed of women, and contrary to the widespread myth of total equality for Russian women in every field of economic, military, and political life, only ten thousand of Russia's 4.4-million-member army were women, and the vast majority of them served in clerical and medical positions. Women, especially compliant women willing to use their bodies to advance their own fortunes, were cherished throughout the upper ranks of the Soviet hierarchy, traded back and forth for favors, even assigned to officers as rewards for service well done, like a bigger office or apartment or a bump up to a higher pay grade.

Though he'd often tried to imagine it, Karelin could not picture what it must be like in the American military, where women were even now being actively integrated into front-line units. Several weeks earlier he'd read a report about female aviators assigned to American carriers and he'd laughed out loud. Women aboard ship? Flying combat aircraft? Absurd! The military was the domain of men, and women's roles there were and should be sharply restricted.

As for Marchenko, well, he'd about lived out his usefulness at the Third Cavern. A younger, more aggressive man was needed here, one who would not let luxury interfere with good judgment. For the time being, though, Russia's ruling junta desperately needed the support of men like Marchenko's uncle. The fat whoremaster would keep his command for a short time longer, at least until a way could be found to ease him up the ladder to some less sensitive command.

"Thank you, Comrade," Karelin said. His eyes shifted toward a gleaming samovar in one corner of the office. "But for now I would settle for some tea."

"Of course. Of course. Have a seat, Comrade Admiral." Marchenko spoke briefly over the intercom, directing Yelana to come in and pour tea. Karelin, meanwhile, snapped his fingers at his aide, who produced a key to unchain the briefcase from his wrist. The secretary strutted in a moment later and, as she poured tea for Karelin, bending far enough forward to allow him a glimpse down the front of her uniform blouse, she gave him a secret smile that nearly made him regret his refusal of her boss's offer. His earlier suspicions had been correct. She was not wearing a bra.

Later, with both the girl and the aide gone from the room, the door locked, and glasses of tea steaming on Marchenko's desk, Karelin opened the briefcase and extracted the heavy sheaf of folders, papers, and maps inside.

"You are to be congratulated, Comrade Rear Admiral," he told Marchenko smoothly. "Of the four caverns, yours is the only one even approximately on schedule."

Marchenko glowed beneath the praise. "We only do our duty for the Revolution, Comrade Admiral."

"This means, however, that more will be expected of you. Kashirin and Golovanov report that their Typhoons will be another week in preparation at least."

It was frustrating that, despite direct military rule of the nation's supply and transport nets, the inefficiencies of the old regime remained. Of the other six available Typhoon PLARBs, two were laid up in the yards at Severodvinsk, their repairs held up by shipments of parts that were already months overdue. Three more were at the other three Polyarnyy Caverns, still waiting for the torpedoes, food supplies, and missiles that made them more than inert steel mountains tied uselessly to their docks. Knowing how the system worked, Karelin suspected that Marchenko had received *his* missiles and other supplies by mentioning his uncle's name.

The fleet's last Typhoon, *Blestyashchiy Krasnyy Pabeda,* was on station at her bastion beneath the Arctic ice, but Karelin could not use him. While it was possible to communicate with the vessel through ELF radio transmissions—how else to give the order to fire?—the *Magnificent Red Victory*'s crew had not been screened against the possibility that they might be ordered to direct a nuclear attack against their own homeland.

The burden of *Derzkiy Plamya*, Operation Audacious Flame, would of necessity rest entirely on Marchenko's blocky shoulders.

"This plan is certainly audacious," Marchenko said, leafing through a binder filled with loose-leaf pages, each marked SOVERSHENNO SEKRETNO at top and bottom. He looked shaken. "To deliver nuclear fire upon our own cities, our own people . . ."

"To deliver 'nuclear fire,' as you call it, on traitors, dissidents, and rebels. In war, especially in a war such as this that shall determine the character and heart and mind of this nation for the next thousand years, there is no room for half measures. Besides, if Leonov and his cronies take us seriously, there will be no need for an actual launch."

Karelin was surprised at how calmly he could sit in this office, sipping tea as he discussed the use of nuclear weapons—or at least the *threat* of nuclear weapons—in Russia's worsening civil war.

As the battle lines were drawn between neo-Soviet forces in the north and the so-called democrats in the south, it had become increasingly clear that the bulk of the former Soviet Union's ICBMs, including the vast missile fields of Kazakhstan and Ukraine, would eventually fall into rebel hands. Most were still under the control of Strategic Rocket Force commanders loyal to Moscow, but they were isolated and under siege. Worse, the rebels now held the launch codes for the land-based, long-range ICBMs.

But Moscow still controlled a number of short- and intermediate-range missile batteries, and perhaps most telling of all, she controlled the Northern Fleet . . . including the eight Typhoon submarines based near Polyarnyy. Those eight Typhoons alone carried unimaginable potential firepower, 160 ICBMs, mounting a total of over twelve hundred warheads of one-hundred-kiloton yield apiece.

The deadly threat posed by a single Typhoon, Moscow believed, would be enough to cow the rebels. They would dare not launch a nuclear strike of their own, even if they had managed to come up with the necessary codes, not when a launch would devastate the entire country. The leaders of the military command in Moscow believed, frankly, that while *they* could afford to vaporize cities like Samara or Tashkent, Leonov could not possibly contemplate the destruction of Moscow or Leningrad, the combined heart and central nervous system of the entire Russian empire.

And if Leonov did not surrender, if it proved necessary to launch, then it would be "Audacious Flame" indeed, an audacious, *cleansing* flame scouring the rebels from the earth, leaving a purified remnant once again under the order and discipline of a unified and central authority.

Everything depended on the Northern Submarine Fleet—in particular upon the eight Typhoon submarines hidden in their shelters along the Polyarnyy, Sayda, and Kola inlets. Nearly one hundred ballistic-missile submarines were deployed with the fleet, from the Typhoons themselves to thirteen aging, diesel-powered relics the West called Golf-IIs. Another seventy-odd attack submarines carried as their primary warloads cruise missiles mounting nuclear warheads. But of that entire number, perhaps a third were in Black Sea or Far East ports, and the loyalties of their captains and crews were suspect. Over half of those in the Northern Fleet were laid up for repairs or maintenance, or were waiting for deliveries of supplies. Many of the rest were at sea, maintaining Russia's posture of strategic defense.

Those in port and combat ready were standing by, but Karelin was convinced that a single Typhoon would be enough to do the job. Typhoon was the very image of the Fleet's nuclear strength. The mere thought of one loosing its nuclear payload at the rebel forces would be enough to bring about their utter capitulation.

"Will it work?" Marchenko asked at last. "Can it possibly work?"

"Moscow believes so, yes," Karelin told him.

"But if their belief is wrong. If Leonov is able to arm even a few missiles and retaliate . . ."

"The rebels have everything to lose through a nuclear exchange. And nothing to win. We have only one immediate problem."

"Yes. The possibility that Leonov is crazy enough to consider launching missiles of his own!"

"Leonov is a politician, Comrade Rear Admiral, not a madman. He will not seriously contemplate the destruction of the Union's industrial and transportation infrastructure. No, our problem, Viktor Ivanovich, is the Americans. As always."

CHAPTER 5
Wednesday, 11 March

"The Americans!" Marchenko looked up from the papers. "You believe they will interfere with Operation Audacious Flame?"

"It is possible. The Military Council in Moscow believes that once there is a clear threat of a nuclear exchange in our civil war, American intervention in our affairs is a certainty. Already they move to blockade our fleet from the open sea." Karelin pulled a set of maps from among the papers, spreading them out on the desk. His finger came down on a group of symbols clustered off the Norwegian coast north of the Arctic Circle. "Here. *Eisenhower* and her battle group." His finger traced the coastline south to Denmark. "The *Kennedy*. Blocking our access from the Baltic." The finger moved once more, coming to a group of symbols east of Iceland. "And the *Jefferson*, returning to the Norwegian theater after her battle damage repairs and refit in the United States. Other American battle groups are reported to be on the way as well, some to the North Sea, others to the Mediterranean."

"What can they do?" Marchenko scoffed. "Even the Americans, with their vaunted technology, cannot shoot down an ICBM in flight. They abandoned their Star Wars program years ago."

"Perhaps they cannot shoot down our missiles," Karelin countered. "But they can dog our PLARBs with antisubmarine aircraft and with the Los Angeles attack submarines attached to their battle groups. They can blockade our ports and challenge our submarine forces as they deploy. They could even track our PLARBs to their strategic bastions, moving quietly and unobserved, with orders to open fire should they hear the missile tube hatches on our submarines open. If they think it in their interests to prevent a launch, they will not hesitate to fire first in such a confrontation."

"Are . . . are we at war with the Americans then?"

"Bah!" Karelin made a dismissive gesture. "What does it matter? Officially, no, we are not at war. Not since the last units of our Scandinavian expeditionary force surrendered and the Blues invited the UN bastards to occupy our cities. But then, if you examine the record, you will find that we were not officially at war with the Americans when we invaded Norway either. The entire episode was characterized in the UN as an 'incident,' a 'peacekeeping action.' The Western governments, you see, fear even the admission that a state of war exists between East and West. Oh, there have been threats from Washington and the various Western puppets since Marshal Krasilnikov's coup, of course, the bellows and head-tossings of angry bulls. But no decisive action . . . beyond this threatening deployment of these carrier groups of theirs.

"It is our plan," he continued, "to attack first, to hit them before they can hit us."

Marchenko drew in his breath with a sharp hiss.

Karelin looked up sharply. "This frightens you?"

"It occurs to me, Comrade Admiral," Marchenko said with great deliberation, "that one reason the Fascists lost the Great Patriotic War was their decision to attack Russia while still fighting England. Later, at the moment the Hitlerites were getting their first taste of General Winter, they added the United States to their list of enemies."

"Be careful, my friend. Your words could be seen as dangerously revisionist." Even yet, senior Red Army officers did not admit that the *Rodina* had received substantial help from the West during the Second World War. Still, Karelin was impressed, and pleased. He'd not pegged Marchenko as one who would venture any opinion contrary to the Party line. Perhaps there was hope for the man yet.

"I only state the obvious, Comrade Admiral." His shoulders

slumped, and he turned in his chair for a moment to stare through his office window at the bustling work in the shipyard below. "I wonder if future historians might regard our decision to attack the United States while we are fighting the Blues as, ah, somewhat less than tactically sound."

"It is a gamble certainly. But you must remember that while the Americans like to make big noises, they will be unwilling to involve themselves deeply in our internal problems."

"They fought willingly enough in Norway."

"An entirely different case. There, they came to the aid of an old ally. As it was, they sent but a single carrier battle group, and that was very nearly too little, too late. I assure you, they will look at our civil war, and their politicians will remember Vietnam . . . *another* civil war within the living memory of most Americans. They will recognize the fact that they cannot possibly intervene on one side or the other with any hope of success."

"But for us to deliberately *attack* them . . ."

"Calm yourself," Karelin said. "So far as Washington is concerned, our nation is disintegrating into anarchy and civil war, yes? They see dozens of factions, and the possibility of renegade officers, rebels, dissidents. That, after all, is why they fear our nuclear forces. When we strike them, it will be in such a way that they will be unable to fix the blame. Perhaps one faction mistook the approaching American carrier group for a rival Russian group." Karelin spread his hands, and shrugged. "In the fog of war, regrettable mistakes happen.

"In any case, believe me, Viktor Ivanovich, when I say that the Americans have no stomach for a lengthy or expensive involvement in our war. They will harass, even sink our submarines if that is in their best interests, but they will not risk a major war. *Especially* a nuclear war now, as their news media likes to put it, that the Cold War is over."

"What will we do, then?"

Karelin shuffled through the papers, producing another map. This one showed the Kola Peninsula, from Russia's borders with Norway and Finland in the west to the landlocked waters of the White Sea in the east. The region was peppered with military bases—airfields, SAM sites, command control centers, radar installations. And, of course, the major naval facilities at and around Polyarnyy, Severomorsk, and Murmansk.

"Our intelligence indicates that one of the American carrier battle groups—either *Eisenhower* or *Jefferson*—will enter the Barents Sea within the next few days. They are expected to take up a patrol station within easy observation range of our submarine facilities at Polyarnyy." He picked up a red pencil on the desk and circled an area two hundred kilometers north of the narrow border between Norway and Russia's Kola Peninsula. "Approximately here."

"Close enough to project ASW patrols beyond Polyarnyy Inlet," Marchenko observed, "while maintaining the option of sheltering within the Norwegian fjords."

"Exactly. They can also draw on additional air support and ASW assets land-based in Norway. We intend to strike before they can take up their patrol station.

"Moscow has named the operation *Ognevoy*," he continued. The Russian word meant Curtain of Fire, and Karelin thought it apt. "Primary responsibility is being handed to Frontal Aviation units deployed from these airfields—Zapolyarnyy and Pechenga near the border. Kirovsk, Alakurtti, Vaga Guba, Monchegorsk inland. Overall control will be exercised through the district command facility at Kandalaksha. None of these airfields, you will notice, lies closer than one hundred kilometers to our naval facilities here at Polyarnyy."

"So that the Americans, if they retaliate, will not attack our submarine bases."

"Correct. Moscow will disavow any connection with the attack, claiming that it was mounted by a small clique of anti-military Blues seeking to discredit the legal government. If the Americans retaliate, it will be against the airfields where the attack originated.

"In the meantime, you will have both of your Typhoons, *Lenin's Invincible Truth* and *Glorious October Revolution*, ready to put to sea at an instant's notice. If possible, you will deploy them under cover of bad weather, but the key factor will be to get them out of Polyarnyy Inlet while the Americans are still shocked and disoriented by our strike against their battle group."

"How will I know when—"

"I will inform you. I will be at the Kandalaksha Command Center. When I see that the attack has been successful, that the American carrier is sunk or, at the least, that the enemy forces are concentrating their attention on their own defense, I will send you a coded signal. Upon receipt of that message, you will deploy the Typhoons at once. At *once*. It is imperative that you keep both of them ready to leave at a moment's notice."

"Understood, Comrade Admiral."

"I will be relying on you utterly, Viktor Ivanovich," Karelin said. "Everything depends on the Typhoons reaching deep water safely and undetected. Other PLARB submarines will be dispatched as they become available, but your two Typhoons offer us our best chance. They are the quietest submarines in the fleet and the most reliable. If any vessels can evade the American blockade, it is they."

"The Americans will have their attack submarines positioned off the mouth of the Kola Inlet, waiting for them to come out."

"That has been allowed for. ASW forces will sweep the entire area during the attack. As will our own attack subs out of Severodvinsk."

"I see." Marchenko hesitated, still studying the map.

"There is something?"

"Only a small question. Why must the Typhoons break out at all?" He gestured toward his office window, at the massive blast doors beyond. "They could launch on any city in the Union from right outside those doors."

"Because they will need time, Comrade Rear Admiral, while we deliver our ultimatum and while Leonov considers his options. And sea room to maneuver while that time is passing. Since the Blues now have the necessary launch codes, if they are insane enough to launch, then we can expect the facilities here to be their first target."

"I . . . see." It was obvious Marchenko had not thought of that possibility.

"These submarine shelters were designed to withstand a nuclear blast, of course," Karelin went on, "but that would not help us if the mountain over our heads collapses across the entrance. If they can reach their strategic bastions, however, safely beneath the Arctic ice . . ."

"As in the grand game we've played with the Americans all these years," Marchenko said, completing the thought. "Leonov and his people will not know where they are, or when they might surface and fire."

"Leonov will be forced to surrender or see his major cities, staging areas, and transportation hubs incinerated one by one. Order will be restored to a Soviet Union reborn."

"Tell me one thing more, Comrade Admiral," Marchenko said, leaning back in his chair with a thoughtful expression on his face. "Just between you and me."

"If I can."

"Back at the Naval Academy, and later at various staff planning exercises, we ran endless war games covering precisely this sort of situation, an attack by Frontal Aviation against an American carrier battle group approaching Russian waters. I always had the impression that the results were cooked. To keep the officers handling the Russian side from looking bad."

"That sort of thing happens. I hear they have the same problem at the Pentagon."

"I wouldn't be surprised. But tell me, what do you think? Can an attack of this sort destroy a carrier battle group? Their defenses are . . . formidable."

Karelin thought about it for a moment. "I will tell you, Viktor Ivanovich, I'm not sure. In this case, of course, it is not necessary to destroy the Americans . . . but only to disorient them long enough for our PLARBs to get away."

"Of course. But I was curious about your estimation of the outcome of the engagement itself. It should be a test of a classic war-gaming scenario."

"Key to a Yankee carrier battle group are two vessels," Karelin said, "and two vessels alone. The aircraft carrier itself, naturally, which is the group's whole reason for being, and the group's Ticonderoga-class Aegis cruiser, which serves as a command and control ship for the formation, coordinating its maneuvers and antiair defenses.

"Operation Ognevoy will muster some two to three *hundred* aircraft, including advanced heavy bombers armed with anti-ship cruise missiles, as well as surface-attack aircraft. Combined with these will be cruise-missile attacks both from shore installations and from submarines.

"What do I think? I think that the battle group's brain—the Aegis cruiser—and its heart—the aircraft carrier—will both be overwhelmed, completely obliterated in the first wave. The survivors—the destroyers, frigates, and submarines—will flee, or be mopped up at our leisure.

"And our Typhoons will be free in the Barents Sea, ready to carry out their orders."

"And those are, Comrade Admiral? Will they be told to launch without warning, or will they threaten first?"

"Their orders will be to make history, Comrade Rear Admiral," Karelin said. "To make history, and to secure ultimate victory for the legitimate government of the Russian Union."

1330 hours (Zulu)
CAG's office
U.S.S. *Thomas Jefferson*

There was a sharp rap on the door, and Tombstone looked up from the expendables report he was working on at his desk. "Door's open."

Brewer Conway walked in. She was a tall, lean, athletic-looking woman, her silver-blond hair kept mannishly short. She was wearing her undress blue shirt and slacks; the Navy woman's traditional blue or white skirt had been replaced by slacks for all but formal dress occasions some time ago. Having women in skirts negotiating the nearly vertical ladders of shipboard companionways had proved to be too much of a distraction for the sailors who, alerted by the almost psychic communications system that stretched from stem to stern on every Navy vessel, tended to congregate at the bottoms of those ladders just as the women began their descents.

"Good afternoon, CAG," she said. Since she was uncovered, she didn't salute, but she came to attention in front of Tombstone's desk. "You wanted to see me?"

"Brewer," Tombstone said, rising. "At ease. Grab a chair."

"It's not necessary for you to get up for me when I enter a room, Captain," she said, moving a chair out from the bulkhead and perching herself on the edge. She seemed tense, Tombstone thought. Or upset.

"Old habits die hard, Commander," Tombstone said, settling back into his own seat. "My apologies. I was raised the old-fashioned way. Thanks for coming in."

"It would be best, sir, if you not treat us any differently from your men. That, after all, is what integration is all about, right?"

"Thank you for the lecture, Commander."

"Sorry, sir. I meant no disrespect. What did you want to see me about?"

He sighed. "I want your impressions, Brewer. Your honest evaluation. How are your people settling in aboard the *Jeff*?"

Her expression was guarded. "Well enough, CAG."

"No problems with privacy? The shower head schedules? Any instances of harassment or unwanted attention?"

"None worth mentioning, sir."

"But there have been incidents."

"It would be pretty strange if there weren't, sir." She hesitated, and for a moment Tombstone thought she was about to say something more. Then she pursed her lips and shook her head. "No problems, CAG. None that my people can't handle on their own."

"That's the best way, of course." Tombstone selected a paper from the several scattered on his desk. "I have a request here, though, from Lieutenant Kandinsky. She wants to be assigned with another aviator."

Brewer's eyes widened. "She should have talked to me about that, CAG. I'll have a word with her."

Tombstone considered this. Lieutenant Thelma Kandinsky, call sign "Sunshine," was a B/N, a bombardier/navigator, the flight officer who rode right-seat in the A-6E Intruder. Normally, she flew with Lieutenant Commander Bruce "Willis" Payne, in Jefferson's VA-89, the Death Dealers. Intruder crew assignments were no more permanent than pilot/RIO assignments in Tomcats, though good teams that worked well as a unit tended to stick together. To have a B/N specifically request a change, however, suggested that there was something wrong.

"Is there some kind of trouble between Sunshine and Willis?"

"Commander Payne can be pretty overbearing at times," Brewer replied. "He's made it abundantly clear that he doesn't think female NFOs can hack it. Nothing overt, really, but he'll be talking to some men about how he feels, and pitch his voice just loud enough that a woman nearby can overhear."

"Hmm." His fingers drummed on the desk. "What do you think the solution is here?"

"I wouldn't grant that request, if that's what you mean. Not unless there's something seriously wrong. They ought to learn how to get along themselves, and not come crying to Mamma. Or Papa, in this case."

"I agree completely. If I start shuffling crew assignments, a lot of people are going to get pissed, not just Willis and Sunshine. You'll talk to Kandinsky?"

"Yes, CAG."

"Don't come down on her for going around you with this. Her request is perfectly within her rights. But see if you can find out what the problem is with Willis. Specifics. Meanwhile, I'll have a talk with Willis, get his side of the story. Okay?"

"Sounds fair, sir."

"What about Slider Arrenberger?"

She shrugged. "He's . . . opinionated. There've been no problems I'm aware of."

"No friction?"

"Nothing that can't be handled informally, sir."

"Okay." Tombstone clasped his hands together on his desk. This next was the hard one. "Commander, I've heard . . . scuttlebutt. About sexual liaisons between the men and the women in the wing."

She bristled. "Are you suggesting we hold bed checks, CAG? Like they do for enlisted personnel?"

"No. But I'm worried about the problems those types of relationships could cause aboard ship. Jealousy. Hurt feelings. Lovers' quarrels . . ."

"Captain, the personal lives of the officers in this wing is not my concern. They are adults, and they are professionals. I don't—"

"They are adults and they are professionals, yes. But sexual activity aboard ship is still strictly against regulations, Commander. It's our responsibility to uphold those regulations, even though you and I both know that they're going to get bent or broken whenever there's temptation and opportunity."

"There's precious little opportunity for hanky-panky aboard ship, Captain. And to answer your question, I've heard the same scuttlebutt but I don't know anything as fact. You can be sure, sir, that I will uphold Navy regulations to the best of my ability. But I am not going to start demanding chits from my girls every time they want to leave their compartment to go to the head. Sir."

"I wasn't suggesting that you should, Commander." He unclasped his hands, then looked Conway in the eye. "And you don't have any other gripes? If you got 'em, I want to hear 'em."

"No, sir. No gripes."

"Okay. That'll be all, then. Dismissed. Thanks for coming in."

But after she left, Tombstone was sure that there was a problem. He just didn't know what it was that was bothering her.

One thing was certain. This sexual integration nonsense was taking up one hell of a lot of man hours—yes, and woman hours too—just to make it work. Instead of working like a smoothly functioning machine, the air group's personnel were experiencing friction . . . and inefficiency. With the chances that the *Jefferson* would soon be in combat growing greater every day, that friction was becoming dangerous.

Tombstone had only one question at the moment, though.

"What in God's name would the Russians think of all this if they could see us now?" he asked the bulkheads of his office.

With no reply forthcoming, he returned, scowling, to the waiting expendables report. A moment later, his phone rang. "CAG."

"This is Lieutenant Commander Delano," the voice said. Delano was on Captain Brandt's staff. "The Captain's compliments, and he wonders if you could join him for an ops briefing in Flag Plot at fifteen hundred hours."

"Very well, Commander." Tombstone checked his watch. Despite the polite wording, this was not a request. "I'll be there."

"Very good, sir. I will inform the Captain."

Tombstone sighed. If it wasn't one thing, it was another. He decided he just might be able to complete the expendables report before he had to be up in Flag Plot.

CHAPTER 6
Wednesday, 11 March

Tombstone leaned over the plot table, studying the cryptic symbols and geometric shapes marked with wax pencil onto the glass top overlying the navigational chart of the North Cape–Murman Coast area. "But what's it mean, Admiral? Is Washington actually giving us a shoot-first order?"

"Hell, no. You know it's never that simple with them." Admiral Douglas F. Tarrant, tall, slender, and aristocratic-looking with his head of silver hair, was the carrier group's commanding officer, and he was holding court in *Jefferson*'s Flag Plot. His uniform, as always, was immaculate and razor-creased. "The orders are to shadow neo-Soviet fleet units, particularly their ICBM subs. Starting Friday when we reach our patrol station, gentlemen, we are going to begin making Class-A nuisances of ourselves."

"Off the Kola Peninsula?" Tombstone said. "That's going to be like taking on the whole damned Russian military!"

"CAG's got a point, Admiral," Captain Jeremy Brandt said. Brandt was *Jefferson*'s captain. As hound-dog ugly as Tarrant was good-looking, he was short and fire-plug-built, with his blond-to-gray hair shaved to a stubble.

The three of them, Tombstone, Brandt, and Tarrant, were standing about the plot table, hemmed in by a number of senior aides and staff officers. Tarrant and his entourage had arrived by helicopter aboard the *Jefferson* a few hours earlier from the

Shiloh, the Aegis cruiser Tarrant used as his headquarters, and the lot of them had crowded into the carrier's Flag Plot to consider the latest set of orders from Washington.

Reaching out with the stem of an unlit pipe, Captain Brandt pointed out a line of red symbols on the map stretching down the jagged slash of the Kola Inlet. Sayda Guba, Polyarnyy, Severomorsk, Murmansk. "Wasn't it some CNO who called this stretch the single most valuable piece of real estate on Earth? Hell, the Russian SAM operators alone must be tripping over each other there."

"Secretary of the Navy John F. Lehman said that," Tarrant replied. "He was referring to the whole Kola Peninsula, and he was dead right. Over here, in this strip of what was Finland before World War II, is Pechenga, just eighteen miles from the Norwegian border. It's both a commercial and a military port. And down here, just above where the Tuloma and the Kola rivers come together, is Murmansk. That's the largest city north of the Arctic Circle. Population about a half million. Ten miles further northeast is Severomorsk, headquarters for the whole Russian Northern Fleet. Enormous naval support facilities, shipyards, ammunition depots, that sort of thing."

"There was a big explosion there a while back, wasn't there?" Tombstone asked.

"Correct. May 1984. Most of the Northern Fleet's missile reserves went up in one big fireball. We never did learn the number of casualties, but the damage was extensive.

"Anyway, the Tuloma River starts to open up here, becoming the Kol'skiy Zaliv, the Kola Inlet. Eight miles north of Severomorsk is Polyarnyy, on the Polyarnyy Inlet. It's a major base for both surface ships and submarines. Nine miles further to the northwest is Sayda Guba. Important submarine support facilities there.

"Right here in this region, between Polyarnyy and Sayda Guba, are four massive, underground facilities, tunnels cut right into the solid rock, with blast doors thick enough to protect what's inside from a nuclear blast. The first was completed, we think, in the early 1980s. Satellite photos show enormous structures against the hillside, with obvious submarine support facilities outside. Our submariners call them 'the barns.' "

"Typhoons," Brandt said.

"That's right. The Polyarnyy complex is their primary Typhoon basing facility. They don't keep them all in one basket, of course. Way down here, a good one hundred sixty miles east along the Kola Peninsula from Polyarnyy, is Gremikha. They base and supply Typhoons there too, as well as at ports in the White Sea, but their main PLARB center is at Polyarnyy. The Russians, remember, like a tight, centralized administration, especially when it comes to their nukes, and the Polyarnyy complex is nice and handy to Severomorsk.

"Altogether, the Russians have some forty air bases on the Kola Peninsula, as well as hundreds of SAM sites, radar installations, supply depots, bases for two motorized rifle divisions, and the headquarters, barracks, and training center for the Northern Fleet's Naval Infantry brigade. All of that is not counting their fleet facilities on the White Sea, at Arkhangel'sk and Severodvinsk."

"So where the hell does Washington get off telling us to 'close with and shadow neo-Soviet fleet units,' eh?" Brandt shook his bulldog head. "What do they think, that CBG-14 is going to scare the Russkis into being peaceful?"

"After the Battles of the Fjords, I imagine they'll be a bit more circumspect," Tarrant said, his eyes twinkling. "And we'll be backed by CBG-7, the *Eisenhower* and her group, as well as Navy and Air Force squadrons coming out of Norway. But we're first-string this time. If the Russkis want to play, we'll be up to bat first."

"Just like last time," Tombstone said. "When we were up first against *two* Soviet carrier groups. Does someone in Washington have it in for us?"

"Political, Tombstone," Brandt said. He made a sour face. "DACOWITS wants a report on how their girls—excuse me, their *women*—stand up to combat."

Brandt had fought bitterly against the decision to use *Jefferson* as a test case for female flight officers, Tombstone knew. He'd lost, though, because the *Jeff*, in Norfolk for repairs, was the only carrier immediately available when the decision was made. Tombstone had heard rumors that Brandt had threatened to resign over the issue. If they were true, he was glad the skipper hadn't carried out the threat. He was a damned good officer, and a good ship captain. *Jefferson* was almost certainly his last command at sea—how did a naval officer top command of a CVN?—and it would be tragic if he was forced to go ashore under a cloud.

"I doubt that DACOWITS had anything to do with this, Captain," Tarrant said gently. "*Jefferson* is up to full strength with the new units brought on board at Norfolk. She also has the best combat record in the fleet. I'm sure that was quite enough to recommend us to the CNO."

"Don't get me wrong, Admiral," Brandt said. "I'm not trying to wiggle out of this. But merciful God in heaven . . ." He surveyed the map, as though in amazement. "One CBG can't possibly blockade the entire Murman coast!"

"We won't have to, Captain," Tarrant said. "Washington already has it blocked out."

Tombstone listened intently as Tarrant laid out the plan as proposed by the Pentagon in their latest orders. It was simple and direct, but required considerable support from other fleet elements.

Jefferson and the other surface ships of the battle group would take up a patrol station north of the Russian-Norwegian border, far enough east to maintain their surveillance of the nearest neo-Soviet bases, far enough west to be able to head for shelter in Tanafjorden or to run for the Norwegian Sea if the Russians came out in overwhelming strength. The *Eisenhower* group would move further north, toward the edge of the Barents ice pack.

Galveston and *Morgantown*, meanwhile, the two Los Angeles–class attack subs attached to CBG-14, were already off the Kola Peninsula. They would probe ahead, deep into Russian territorial waters, taking up position right off the Kola Inlet itself. CBG-7's subs would take up station fifty miles behind them, to catch any big ones that got away. Other American SSNs were already in the area. They would cover Gremikha and the mouth to the White Sea and would serve as backups for the subs of the two carrier groups.

Submarines, Tombstone thought, would definitely prove their worth in this situation. Air strikes and showing the flag both had their place, but the superbly quiet SSNs could sneak right up to Ivan's front porch, stay as long as was necessary, and slip silently away again.

The submarines would be the CBG's advance scouts, monitoring Russian subs and other vessels as they entered or left port—especially at Polyarnyy. Backing them would be *Jefferson*'s ASW squadrons—the Vikings of VS-42, the King Fishers, and the SH-3H Sea Kings of HS-19—using air-dropped sonobuoys to weave a net across the southern reaches of the Barents Sea. Any sub contact would be shadowed, by air or by submarine. Russian PLARBs would be identified; if necessary, the hunters would deliberately reveal themselves and thereby warn the Russian sub skippers that the Americans had them in their sights.

"We will not give the weapons-free order," Tarrant explained, "unless the PLARB is clearly about to launch despite our interference."

"And if he tries to launch anyway?" Tombstone asked.

"Then we drop him."

Brandt scratched at one fleshy jowl. "What about their Northern Fleet?"

"Still licking their wounds after the Fjords," Tarrant replied. "Latest satellite intel suggests that at least ten capital ships were sunk or dinged up pretty bad, and that doesn't count both the *Kreml* and the *Soyuz* getting deep-sixed. A lot of ships are laid up in drydock, or rusting on their moorings. Some of their nuke subs have become hazards, no longer seaworthy, too hot to break up. God knows what they're going to do with them. Morale in their Northern Fleet is wretched. What's worse, they've been having a bad time getting supplies for the fleet."

"I bleed for them," Brandt said.

"There will be a chance, of course, that the Russians will sortie their fleet, or as much of their fleet as they can get to sea, either to threaten us or to actually mount an attack. The fact is, we don't have a clue as to how they're likely to react to our provocations. Everything we've seen indicates that there's total chaos over there. Leonov's forces have launched a major offensive in the south, and Red units have invaded Ukraine and Belarus. That should work in our favor; the Moscow faction will have more than enough to occupy them in the south without having to worry about the Kola Peninsula."

"Maybe," Brandt said. "But I'll tell you right now they're not going to take kindly to us parking a CBG in their backyard. Hell, what would we say if they planted the *Kiev* battle group twenty miles off Hampton Roads and dared us to make something of it?"

"Well, that's why we're going to have to be damned careful on this one, gentlemen. One mistake could ruin our whole day.

"Our worst problem, of course, is going to be their submarines. Half of all the Russians' subs are based up here, and that means things are going to be frantic for the ASW departments. As I said earlier, though, we'll be drawing heavily on support from Norway. That includes three squadrons of P-3 Orions, and a Brit Nimrod group. They should be able to let us stretch our assets a bit.

"CAG, your people are going to be running shy on sleep, I'm afraid. You'll not only be handling the brunt of the close-in ASW patrols, but I'm going to want heavy CAPs up at all times. In addition, it would be a good idea if you had at least two attack squadrons fueled, armed, and ready to go on short notice, in case we have to engage Russian surface units. I'd like at least one of those attack squadrons to be F/A-18s."

"They'll be ready, Admiral."

"You have two days to make damn sure of that. How are your people getting on so far?"

Tombstone knew the admiral was asking obliquely about the air wing's ongoing sexual integration.

"Some teething pains, Admiral. Nothing we can't handle."

"Your people are going to be in a real pressure cooker, son. Word from Washington is that the *Ike* and the *Jeff* battle groups are going to be pretty much on their own for at least a week. It'll be that long before the *Nimitz* gets here to reinforce us, and Washington is keeping the *Kennedy* stationed off the Skagerrak."

"We'll get the job done, sir."

"I know, son. You've got the best people in the Navy. That's why I'm counting on you. Captain Brandt? Any problems?"

"We're not going to get that week, Admiral. You know that as well as I do."

"I know. If they're going to pull something, it'll be sooner. A lot sooner."

"We'd just better pray to God that we're ready then. Because when those bastards come out of their hidey-holes, it's going to be full strength, fangs out, and ready for a major rumble."

"With your permission, Captain, I'd like to tape a broadcast for your TV station. Let the men know what's going on, how we're counting on them."

"Of course, Admiral."

Tarrant's face looked terribly grim. "God help us if we drop the ball on this one, people. We're *not* going to get a second chance."

**1720 hours
Crew's lounge
U.S.S. *Thomas Jefferson***

The crew's lounge, located far aft aboard the *Jefferson*, throbbed faintly with the suppressed thunder of the ship's four propellers, each twenty-two feet wide. It was a utilitarian space, occupied by round tables and plastic chairs, and decorated with framed prints showing scenes out of naval history.

It was a popular place for *Jefferson*'s enlisted men and women to gather when they went off duty. There were the usual collections of games to be checked out—decks of cards, military board games, and classics like Scrabble or Monopoly. There was a Coke machine, and a jukebox that played pieces ranging from country to hard rock. One bulkhead was taken up by a collection of arcade-type video games, most with names like MiG Blaster and Torpedo Alley.

Photographer's Mate Second Class Tom Margolis sat at one of the tables with four of his shipmates, and he was getting mad.

"Hey, Marge!" As he pulled up a chair and joined the group, FTG2 Roy Kirkpatrick puckered his lips, making a loud smacking noise. "How's about a kiss, sweetie?"

Margolis winced at the familiar taunt. How were you supposed to fight something like this?

"Fuck off," he said. Angrily, he picked up his can of Coke and took a swig. "I'm not queer. I *like* girls! I've got a girlfriend back in the States!"

"Sure, sure," Gunner's Mate (Missiles) Third Class Enrique Hernandez said, a toothy grin lighting his swarthy face. "That's what they all say!"

"I'm not a homo!"

"Yeah, well, your boyfriend Pellet's one, ain't he?" Radioman Third Class Mike Weydener said. "I thought all you queers hung out together."

"Yeah!" Kirkpatrick said, giggling. "How's Pellet hung?"

"Frank's a nice guy."

"Oh, I'll just bet he is!" Fire Control Technician Larry Jankowski mimed a kiss and the others howled with laughter.

"How nice *was* he?" Hernandez asked.

Margolis could feel his face getting red. He never knew how to answer these guys when they started making fun of him. He took another swig of Coke, desperately hoping to cover his embarrassment.

"Hey, look at Margie's face!" Kirkpatrick said, slapping the table. "I never seen a guy get so red!"

"Matches his hair," Radarman Third Class Reidel observed. Harold Reidel looked like a recruiting poster: surfboard blond, health-club muscular, and as handsome as a teen movie idol. "You must've hit a major nerve, Big-K."

PH2 Margolis was twenty-one years old. He'd joined the Navy the day after he'd graduated from high school; his parents were divorced and life at home with an alcoholic mother was no picnic. The sea had seemed the perfect escape.

But after three and a half years in the Navy, he was ready to call it quits. *Six more months*, he thought, *and I'm out of here, a civilian again and free at last, free at last, thank God Almighty I'm free at last!*

It wasn't that he disliked the Navy. He'd gotten by okay, on the whole. Going to photographer's school after boot camp had taught him a trade, and when he got out he wanted to pursue a career as a professional photographer, maybe for a newspaper.

The problem was that Tom Margolis was not exactly the athletic, macho type, not big like Kirkpatrick, not hard-muscled like Reidel. He was intelligent and his speech showed it. He liked to read, he wore glasses, and his pale, freckled skin—legacy of his hated red hair—seemed to betray every intense or unpleasant emotion. He stood out in a crowd, especially in a crowd of jock types like Kirkpatrick and Reidel, and that made his chronic shyness worse.

So he was different from the other sailors of the group he'd fallen in with lately. As for the issue of his being gay, he wasn't . . . at least as far as he knew. He'd heard that you could be homosexual and not be aware of the fact, but he'd done a lot of pretty heavy petting with Doris in the backseat of her father's car during his senior year in high school, and he was pretty sure he was all right in *that* department at least.

Gays in the military, *especially* in the Navy, aboard ship, had remained a controversial issue long after President Clinton had lifted the ban on recruiting them. Margolis had never had much of an opinion one way or the other. He'd heard scuttlebutt that Fire Control Technician Third Class Frank Pellet was gay, but as far as Margolis knew from personal experience, Pellet was just a friendly, bright, and outgoing guy who shared Margolis's love of photography. Pellet had never made a pass at him, never said or done anything to betray his sexual orientation. Margolis had decided early on to ignore the rumors and enjoy the friendship.

And that was when the rumors had started about *him*.

"I'll tell you, Marge," Hernandez said. "If you *are* gay and we find out, your ass is grass, you get me?"

"Yeah," Reidel added. "We don't want no fags on this ship."

"Oh, *Mama*!" Kirkpatrick said, licking his lips. His eyes had strayed across the room to a pair of female enlisted personnel who'd just entered the lounge. One was a rather plain-looking girl who worked in personnel, but the other was a brunette bombshell from Disbursing who filled her too-tight uniform blouse with wondrous, bobbing motion. "You know, guys, it just ain't fuckin' fair. They went and made it legal for queers to join up in this man's Navy. I mean, there they are, right? Sleeping in our compartments. Crowding in with us nuts to butts right there in the shower heads. Well, I'll tell you one thing, and no shit. When they let *us* shower with the girls on this ship, I'll stop bitching about them letting fags take showers with *me*! I mean, am I right? It's the same thing, right?"

"Fuckin'-A, Big-K," Hernandez said. "Man, oh, man, lookit that nice ass. Betcha *that* looks Grade-A prime in the shower, huh?"

"It'd look better in bed," Jankowski volunteered. "With her legs spread apart like this." He demonstrated, rubbing his crotch suggestively, and the others agreed with moans and laughter.

There had always been gays in the Navy. Always. Until the early nineties, however, they'd kept their presence secret for the most part, for anyone who admitted to being gay was immediately discharged from the service. Sometimes the discovery ended tragically. In October 1992, a young seaman aboard the U.S.S. *Belleau Wood*—a ship with a fleet-wide reputation for being especially rough on gays—had had his face brutally smashed against a urinal in a restroom in Sasebo, Japan, until he was dead. There had long been dark rumors of other, similar incidents, men reported missing overboard in a storm or AWOL in some foreign port.

Not until the abrupt liberal shift in the government with the Clinton Administration had the official ban on gays finally been lifted. Recruiters were no longer allowed to ask prospective recruits about sexual orientation.

Unfortunately, lifting the ban had not solved the problem. Relatively few gays had come out of the closet, for there was no way to change the embedded prejudice of their shipmates, not overnight. Kirkpatrick's complaint was a common one: If we can't shower with the female sailors, why should gays be allowed to shower with us?

No civilian could imagine the closeness of the quarters, the complete lack of privacy aboard ship. Even aboard a floating city like the *Jefferson*, with most of her thousand-foot length reserved for her aircraft and the gear and supplies that kept them flying, space was at a premium. When morale was poor, when stress was high, slights, attacks, or harassments, real or imagined, could explode like a magnesium flare in an avgas fuel-storage tank. More than four years after the ban on gays had been lifted, there were still far too many suspicious "accidents" at sea.

Margolis was scared. As the rumor that he was gay had spread, he'd been getting more and more harassment— shipmates banging into him in the passageways or the chow line, apparently by accident but *hard*. Once his sheets had been stolen from his rack. He'd even received a couple of threatening letters telling him to get off the ship or else.

But Margolis had been working on a plan for two weeks now, a way to fight back. He had the necessary equipment. All he needed was some help. And if he managed to pull it off, he'd prove that he was a red-blooded guy just like the rest of them. He'd *show* them!

"All right, guys," he said. He crushed his Coke can for emphasis, then let the crumpled husk clatter on the tabletop.

"I've got a little scheme going, and you're going to help me. It'll prove to you, once and for all, that I'm no queer."

"Yeah?" Kirkpatrick asked. "How you gonna do that, Marge?"

"Just listen up," Margolis said. He snickered. "You're gonna love this!"

CHAPTER 7
Thursday, 12 March

1330 hours (Zulu +1)
CAG's office
U.S.S. *Thomas Jefferson*

"Come in."

Master Chief Mike Weston, *Jefferson*'s Chief of the Boat, entered Tombstone's small office. "Afternoon, CAG."

"Hi, COB. What can I do for you?"

"Well, this is kind of the way of an informal invitation, if you know what I mean."

"I'm afraid I don't."

"Well, there's gonna be a little, ah, get-together. Fourteen hundred hours, O-1 deck aft of the hangar bays, across from the paint locker. I know it's kind of unusual, but some of the boys told me they'd be honored if you could come. Unofficial, like."

Tombstone leaned back in his swivel chair, considering Weston's invitation. The big man appeared almost embarrassed, something Tombstone had never seen as long as he'd known him.

He also knew now what this was all about. "My nose is already blue, Master Chief."

"I know, sir. But it'd help morale if you could come. A lot."

"You think so?"

"One airman told me this morning, 'Hey, COB! We *gotta* invite Captain Magruder. He's the best officer on the boat!' "

Tombstone smiled. "I'm flattered."

"Between you and me, CAG, morale on the *Jeff* just struck bottom. This business with having women on board, well, it's got the whole crew pretty damned tight. Especially since the word is we're likely to see combat soon. Now, this shindig this afternoon'll be strictly contra-regs, but I can't see that it'll hurt anything. And having some of the officers there'll let the guys know the brass hasn't just decided to torpedo them."

"I can't get away right this moment, COB." He waved at the paper protruding from the platen of the IBM Selectric resting on his desk. "I have these quarterly personnel evaluations to finish, my XO's on CAP, and the skipper'll keelhaul me if they're not on Commander Parker's desk this afternoon. But save me some cake. I'll come down the second I'm free."

Weston grinned back. "That'd be fine, sir. Thanks." He reached for the door, then hesitated. "Oh . . . just one thing. I'm afraid this here do will *not* be squared away on the Papa Charlie front. Do you take my meaning?"

"Perfectly. I'll be down . . . oh, make it fifteen-thirty."

"Good enough, sir. See you there."

He left.

Tombstone stared after him for several long moments, and wondered how it had come to this. "Not squared away on the Papa Charlie front" meant not PC, not "politically correct." No women. And there was a damned good reason for that.

Sometime during the night, the *Jefferson*, continuing on course toward the northeast, had crossed the Arctic Circle. The fact had been duly recorded in the ship's logs, of course, and announced over the carrier's closed-circuit television, but not officially celebrated as time-honored custom demanded. Tombstone was well aware that there'd been grumbling all day, and that morale, within the air wing and the ship's company both, had plummeted.

The immediate cause of the gloom, it appeared, was the peremptory official cancellation of the initiation ceremony to the ancient and honorable Noble Order of Blue Noses.

Long seafaring tradition had established and perpetuated certain shipboard ceremonies. Most famous, of course, was the Order of Neptune, conferred on officers and sailors alike the first time they crossed the equator. There were other fraternities, less well known to landlubbers: the Domain of the Golden Dragon for crossing the 180th meridian; the prestigious Order of the Golden Shellback for crossing the equator *at* the 180th meridian.

And there was the fraternal Order of the Blue Nose for men crossing the Arctic Circle for the first time.

That was the problem. *Men* crossing the Arctic Circle. The attendant ceremonies consisted of some fairly grotesque hazing of the "cherries" being initiated, usually on the flight deck with all free hands in attendance. Tombstone well remembered his own initiation. He'd seen frat parties that were worse . . . but a gathering of several hundred men, shivering in their skivvies and with their noses painted blue, kneeling one by one before the Chief of the Boat in his guise as King Neptune as they swore to do various improbable and usually obscene tasks, then bobbing for green apples in tubs of ice water and blue-colored whipped cream, was not exactly a ceremony Navy women could be expected to attend.

At least that was the thinking back in the Pentagon, where the CNO himself had issued an order suspending all such festivities aboard ships with mixed crews.

It wouldn't do, Tombstone thought glumly to himself, to let the women see how men *really* acted while they were at sea. It might shatter their illusions . . . or worse, confirm them.

And women sure as hell couldn't be expected to strip to their underwear, promise the COB to perform anatomically improbable acts, or bob for apples at the center of a screaming, chanting mob of half-dressed men, not with the current hypersensitivity to sexual harassment pervading the service. There'd been serious discussion in Washington, he knew, about holding some kind of alternate ceremony that included men *and* women, with no hazing of the cherries and no indecent exposure, but in some ways that would have been worse than cancelling the thing completely. While silly, the ceremony served a serious purpose, binding the men together, old hands and nuggets, in a fraternity of the sea older than the navy in which they served. To substitute some watered-down congratulations-and-welcome-to-the-club claptrap would only insult the guys who'd already been through it, and render the whole concept meaningless.

So the ceremony was officially proscribed . . . and yet inevitably, some of the men, at least, were going ahead with the initiations anyway. By tradition, the ship's captain—and by extension, a carrier's CAG—usually pretended ignorance of any Domain of Neptune proceedings. Aboard *Jefferson*, the pretended secrecy had just become a bit more true-to-life; the people involved in this could technically be brought up on court-martial charges. In theory, the gathering on the O-1 deck could constitute a mutiny.

But they wanted him to attend, and he'd be damned if he'd let them down, even if it meant he got tailhooked for it.

Tailhooked. The expression had become widespread in the Navy after the notorious Tailhook scandal of 1991, when Navy aviators just home after Desert Storm had gone ballistic at the Tailhook Convention in Las Vegas. The partying that year had been . . . spirited. Some of the women present—including several Navy officers—had been made to run a gauntlet in which they'd been groped, fondled, and undressed. Such goings-on had typified other Tailhook Conventions, but somehow, this one had gotten out of hand. The charges of sexual harassment and threatened lawsuits had rocked the entire Navy establishment. Several careers had been wrecked in the scandal's aftermath, promotions for hundreds of junior officers had been held up just on the possibility that they'd been involved, and the rounds of male-female sensitivity training for all hands had begun in deadly earnest. The term "tailhooked" had quickly come to mean any potential scandal or hassle involving women and the Navy.

Tombstone couldn't escape one glaring contradiction, though. If he winked at breaking Navy regs here, even condoned it with his presence, how could he object to sexual activity in defiance of those same regulations?

The initiations were being held to bolster sagging morale. Which would hurt worse, sex aboard ship, or draconian regulations forbidding sex aboard ship?

There was no easy answer. "Women and salt water don't mix" ran the ancient maritime saw, and Tombstone was beginning to agree, Papa Charlie or no Papa Charlie.

He returned to his typewriter, read what he'd already written to remind himself of his place, then continued typing.

The COB was right. Having the ceremony, even if it was against regs, would do the ship's company a hell of a lot of good.

1745 hours
Aviators' shower head
0-2 deck forward
U.S.S. *Thomas Jefferson*

"God damn it, Marge, watch where you're putting your feet!"

PH2 Margolis clutched at a metal joist, then reached inside for a water pipe, his head and shoulders already through the hole created by removing one of the soundproofing tiles in the overhead. "Hey, man, get outa my face! I'm no damned acrobat! Gimme a leg up."

He felt Kirkpatrick's hand steadying his left foot as he boosted himself off the top step of the ladder. His head came up, whacking into the pipe and eliciting a muffled curse.

"You okay up there?" Kirkpatrick asked.

"Yeah, yeah." Margolis flattened himself out, looking around the narrow crawl space. There wasn't much room here, and most of that was taken up with wiring and the water pipes feeding the shower. But there was room enough, and the boards they'd already shoved up there took his weight without knocking the insulation tiles out.

Looking down through the opening in the tiles, he could see Kirkpatrick's anxious face, looking up at him from the top of the ladder. Like Margolis, he was clad in dungarees. On the tile deck below, a mop and a large bucket filled with dirty water rested by the lockers and benches outside the showers. Margolis and Kirkpatrick were *supposed* to be in here on a cleaning detail—the only possible excuse for their presence in a head reserved for officers—but they had something more in mind just now than shipboard routine.

"Okay," Margolis called down. "Gimme the stuff."

Kirkpatrick handed him a canvas bag, and Margolis hauled it up. He'd have to work fast to assemble the gear.

"Psst! Hurry it, you guys!" That was Hernandez, standing watch at the shower head's entrance. He was scared about their being caught. It wasn't likely anyone would be coming in here for a while, though. A fair number of the aviators were still at the strictly unofficial and unauthorized Blue Nose initiations aft; those who weren't were on duty or were scheduled to fly tonight and were asleep now.

"Stay frosty, man," Kirkpatrick called back to Hernandez. "We're almost there." He raised the ceiling tile they'd removed, fitting it carefully back into place. Margolis helped guide it home.

"Everything look okay from out there?" Margolis asked.

"Yeah." Kirkpatrick's voice was muffled. "Just like new."

"No bits of insulation or shit on the desk?"

"All clear."

"Here goes, then."

They'd already used an awl to pierce the soft, white material of the insulation panel, cutting a small, sharply angled hole. Now Margolis took a pencil-thick, silver tube with a complex-looking attachment at one end from the canvas bag, carefully fitted the small end of the tube into the hole, then used duct tape to secure the tube in place. Next, he removed a Nikon 35mm SLR camera from the bag, unfastened and carefully stowed its lens, and attached the body of the camera to the attachment end of the tube. Squinting through the SLR's viewfinder, he found he now had an excellent, camera's-eye view of the inside of the head. He could clearly see Kirkpatrick folding up the stepladder and checking again to make sure that no sign of their activities was left lying on the deck.

"Hey, Kirkpatrick!" he called. "See anything unusual up here?"

Kirkpatrick's face turned up, facing him. "Nah. I can just see the tip of that fancy lens of yours, man, but I wouldn't notice it unless I was lookin' for it. Hey, it's almost time. I'm outa here."

"Okay. You guys promise to come back for me now, y'hear me?"

"Don't you worry, Marge," Kirkpatrick said with a laugh. "We'll be back! Shit, we're gonna want to see what you get!"

"Well, this'll prove what I said, man," he said, instantly ashamed of the whine he heard in his own voice. "I ain't no fag!"

"Hey, I never said you was, man! Some of the guys, they just get carried away, y'know? They don't mean nothin' by it."

"Ha! Just you wait till you get an eyeful of what I'm going

to be lookin' at!" Margolis said. "Pussy, man! Miles and miles of soft, sweet pussy!"

"My mouth's watering, my man. See you in a couple hours!" Gathering the ladder under one arm, and wheeling the mop and bucket with the other, he left the field of Margolis's view. The bucket's wheels gave a mournful *squeak-squeak-squeak* on the deck tiles. Then he heard the head's door slam and he was alone.

The air was dusty up here, and he rubbed a tickle in his nose that might have led to a sneeze. Rocking the camera back and forth slightly, he felt his heart hammering in his chest. He had a real good view of the lockers and benches, right there on the fifty-yard line. Should he have set up facing the other way, looking toward the showers? he wondered. No, from this high up, at this angle, he wouldn't have been able to see that much. This was a lot better. He pulled his face back from the camera and checked his watch. It was pitch dark in the crawl space, but his watch had a touch-light feature.

Hot damn. It wouldn't be much longer now.

2210 hours
Junior officers' quarters
U.S.S. *Thomas Jefferson*

A thump sounded at the door, and Chris Hanson reared up, snatching at the blanket crumpled at the foot of the bunk. The mattress was so narrow that she and Steve Strickland more than filled it in a tangle of bare arms and legs. Both of them were naked, and if someone did walk in, there sure as hell was no place in the tiny compartment to hide.

Her heart raced, and she felt herself blushing.

"Hey, Lobo, it's okay," Strickland told her. "Relax. Just someone going down the passageway."

"What if someone comes in?"

"No one will. I told you, my roommates know to give us some space. They're hanging out down in the Dirty Shirt Mess and aren't going to come back until 2400 hours. We've got until then, okay?"

She turned in the bunk, clutching the blanket to her chest and looking down at him with wide, brown eyes. "Good God, Steve, you didn't tell them what we're doing, did you?"

"I told them I needed some time to be with you." He slipped his hand between her thighs, squeezing her gently. "They can form their own opinions about what we're doing in here. Does it matter?"

She sighed. The small, digital clock on the compartment's tiny desk read 2211. "I guess not."

Lieutenant Chris Hanson did not think of herself as a shy person. She'd joined the Navy, quite frankly, hoping to meet a man, the right man . . . someone like her father, who'd been a Navy chief with twenty years in.

But something like this . . .

She caught the chime of someone's laughter in the passageway and voices, too low for her to make out. "I'm not sure why I let you talk me into this, Steve," she said, her voice a husky whisper.

"Hey, I thought you wanted this, babe! As much as I did!" Reaching up, he tugged the blanket from her fingers, letting it slide off the rack and onto the deck. With one hand, he touched her left breast, lightly circling the nipple with his finger. She closed her eyes as a warm shiver rippled down her spine.

"I don't know," she said. "Maybe I should just go—"

"Aw, c'mon, Chris," Strickland said smoothly. "This'll really relax you. You've been working hard these last couple of weeks. You should let your hair down and unwind a bit, okay?"

"But if we're caught . . ."

"Ah, nobody cares! I mean, everybody knows it's gonna happen, right? You can't crowd grown men and women together aboard ship for months at a time and expect them to just ignore each other! It just ain't natural!"

She laughed, and leaned into his hand a little more.

"Of course," he continued, still stroking her breast, "if they sound General Quarters right now, we're gonna look damned silly charging around starkers in the crowd trying to find our stations."

They both laughed at that, and Hanson felt her fear evaporating. She knew that several of the other women in the department were making it with various guys. Rose Damiano for one. And Cynthia Thomas. It was all well and good to talk about professionalism and staying aloof and concentrating on the job at hand, but damn it, people were going to act like people, no matter what. In fact, it seemed like the more extreme the situation—with danger, overcrowding, and a continuing, no-holds-barred tension that would put any high-powered business executive to shame—the more they tended to act like . . . well, like people. The rules, the lectures, even the difficulty in finding an hour's privacy aboard ship, didn't seem to deter them a bit.

Besides, there was something delicious about that danger, the thought that at any minute Steve's roommates could walk in and catch them in the act. Just thinking about it made her feel warm and tinglingly aroused. She'd always had a crazy, unpredictable streak in her; her handle, "Lobo," had been short for "lobotomy" back at Pensacola.

Strickland's ministrations grew rougher as he moved his face to her breasts, taking first one nipple into his mouth, then the other, sucking them to bullet hardness. His hand kept probing restlessly between her thighs, and she gave a small, involuntary gasp, then allowed herself to be drawn back down onto the bunk.

God, she thought, but she needed this, needed the closeness and the warmth of one special man in this crowded, floating city of men. When she'd first volunteered for carrier duty she'd thought it would be a real kick, but the novelty of being one of a handful of girls among six thousand guys had swiftly worn off.

She slipped her hand between them, running it down his belly. Urgently, needfully, she touched him, cradling him. "Fuck me, Steve," she murmured in his ear. "Fuck me *hard*. . . ."

CHAPTER 8
Friday, 13 March

Sometimes the boredom seemed to mount like the pressure on the outer hull, building pound upon crushing pound until it seemed that mere flesh and blood, like the strongest steel, must finally crumple and collapse. Of course, the boredom had ended five hours ago, when the *Galveston* first began penetrating the Russian coastal submarine defenses.

Commander Richard Montgomery was captain of the American Los Angeles–class submarine *Galveston*, SSN 770. He was new to the boat, having taken her over just two months earlier. Though still officially attached to Carrier Battle Group 14, during the past few weeks *Galveston* had been on patrol here, north of the Kola Peninsula, monitoring the Russian giant and its slow, bloody suicide.

Nearly ten hours earlier, the sub had come to periscope depth, extending the slender tip of a radio mast long enough to pick up a set of coded messages relayed by satellite from the Aegis cruiser *Shiloh*, even now approaching North Cape in company with the *Jefferson* and five other warships. The transmission had included a verification of his operating orders: work as close into the Kola Inlet as possible and watch for the departure of Russian boomers, their big, nuclear missile boats.

"Bridge, Sonar."

Montgomery picked up a microphone. "Bridge, aye. Go ahead."

"Sir, sonar surface contact, Sierra Two, bearing one-seven-five. Twin screws, making slow revs. Sounds like a skimmer coming out of the slot."

"Skimmer" was a submariner's slang for any surface vessel. "Sonar, this is the captain. Can you make him?"

"Not yet, sir. We're running it through the library now. But my educated guess would be a sub-hunter. A Riga, or possibly a Mirka II."

"Stay on him, Ekhart. Engineering! Come to dead slow."

"Engineering, aye, sir. Come to dead slow, aye, sir."

"Diving Officer. What's the depth under our keel?"

"Depth to keel eight-zero feet and shoaling, sir."

"Steady on the helm. Take us down to four hundred twenty feet, nice and gentle."

"Steady on the helm, aye, aye, sir. Planesman, give me five degrees down bubble. Make our depth four-two-zero feet."

"Five degrees down bubble, depth four-two-zero, aye, sir."

The nuclear sub's crew, thirteen officers and 120 enlisted men, functioned with an effortless precision that was almost machine-like, through a litany of orders and orders repeated. Admiral Hyman Rickover, the father of the American nuclear navy, had laid down each detail of the procedure of multiple echoes of each order almost forty years before, a guarantee against that one mistake that could kill the boat and everyone on her.

Four hundred twenty feet would put *Galveston* within a scant few feet of the bottom. With her single screw scarcely turning and riding at a precisely balanced neutral buoyancy, she was relying on her forward momentum to carry her down, leveling off when her keel was just skimming the cold black mud a few miles off the Kola Inlet.

Montgomery felt the slight cant to the steel deck beneath his feet, then felt the submarine leveling off.

"Depth four-two-zero," the enlisted man at the diving planes forward announced.

"Very well. Captain, depth now four-two-zero. We have ten feet beneath the keel."

They spoke in hushed voices, scarcely louder than whispers, observing silent routine. All personnel not at battle stations were in their bunks, partly to avoid unnecessary noise, partly to help maintain trim fore and aft, which could be affected by men moving about the boat. Men on watch wore rubber shoes, and unnecessary machinery—the ice maker in the galley and the soda machine in the mess among others—had all been shut down.

"Very well, Diving Officer," Montgomery said. "Maintain depth and trim."

"Maintain depth and trim, aye, sir."

Four hundred twenty feet seemed like a lot of water, but in fact that depth was only sixty feet deeper than the *Galveston* was long. She was capable of diving to twelve hundred feet or more, and working this far inshore always posed extraordinary difficulties for a submarine. The chances for discovery were increased a hundred fold, and if they were discovered, there was no place to run or hide. Somewhere astern, perhaps ten miles off, was a new addition to the carrier battle group, another improved Los Angeles attack sub, the *Morgantown*. Together, the two nuclear subs had been steadily working their way toward the Murman coast, moving with extreme stealth through one of the deadliest arrays of antisubmarine defenses on the planet.

They were now far inside the twelve-mile limit claimed by Russia as her territorial waters. The Kola Inlet was opening up directly ahead, and the small island called Ostrov Kil'din was less than seven miles to starboard. Their position was complicated by the fact that they were moving south down one of the busiest shipping channels of the former Soviet Union, the sole shipping lane to the busy ports of Murmansk, Severomorsk, and Polyarnyy.

Attack subs were arguably the single most useful tool in the U.S. Navy's inventory . . . though aviators or skimmer crews would never have admitted the fact. When something went wrong with diplomacy anywhere in the world, sending a carrier battle group was a great way to send a message, a very *loud* message, to the offending party: "Behave or we'll flatten you." Time after time, as regional conflicts and brushfire wars had broken out across the face of the globe, the planners in Washington had repeated that time-honored phrase, "Where are the carriers?"

But far more often it was necessary to take a more diplomatic tack—or a more covert one—and an aircraft carrier with ninety planes sitting off the coast in question was not exactly a

comfortable statement in the language of diplomacy. If a CBG
penetrated this far into foreign territorial waters, it was an act
of war.

But a submarine, on the other hand . . . that was different.
A Los Angeles attack sub could slip silently into enemy waters,
listening to radio traffic, counting ships and radar sources and
aircraft, then slip away without anyone knowing it'd been
there. Throughout the Cold War, American attack subs had
repeatedly penetrated such closely guarded Soviet fortresses as
the Shelikhova Gulf, the Tatarskiy Strait, the White Sea, and
the Gulf of Finland. The nature and specifics of those penetra-
tions were all still highly classified.

"Control room, Sonar."

"Control room. What is it, Ekhart?"

"I've got an ID on Sierra Two. Riga-class frigate. Still at
one-seven-five. Estimate he's making turns for one-five knots."

A Riga-class frigate, a sub-hunter for sure. She'd be a hair
under three hundred feet long, with a displacement of about
twelve hundred tons. Either a Herkules or a Pegas high-
frequency sonar mounted in the hull. ASW weapons including
RBU-2500 rocket launchers, depth charges, and 533mm torpedoes.

Ping!

Every man in *Galveston*'s control room froze, eyes turning
toward the overhead.

"Control room, Sonar. Sierra Two has gone active on sonar."

There were two types of sonar, passive and active. With
passive sonar, a ship or submarine simply listened for noise
produced by the target—the sound of its screws, the machinery
in its engine room, the pumps circulating water through its
nuclear reactor, the clang of a carelessly dropped tool. Active
sonar, on the other hand, transmitted a pulse of sound, then
listened for the echo from a solid target. Far more accurate than
passive listening—through pinging, a sonar operator could get
an accurate measurement of the range to the target—active
sonar had the single disadvantage that it gave the transmitting
vessel away. Submarines nearly always preferred to use passive
sonar only.

Destroyers and other ASW surface ships, however, rarely
cared whether their quarry heard them or not. This one was

almost certainly sweeping the Kola channel, searching for intruders precisely like the *Galveston*.

Ping!

They were getting closer. Montgomery could hear the gentle *chug-chug-chug* of the ship's screws now, gradually growing louder.

Ping!

Just because *Galveston*'s crew could hear the active sonar of the approaching surface ship, it didn't necessarily mean they'd been spotted. Sonar was more complicated than simply making a noise and waiting for the echo; discontinuities in the temperature and salinity of the water could refract sound waves in odd ways, and a submarine as close to the bottom as *Galveston* was now could be lost in the background clutter. Shipping channels such as this were usually littered with wrecks or with debris dumped from surface ships, and near naval bases they were sown with undersea hydrophones, remotely activated mines, and various types of detection equipment. Even if the Russian sonar operators heard an echo, they might easily misinterpret it. Getting any information at all out of a sonar return was an arcane and mysterious art.

Ping-ing!

The throb of the ship's propellers sounded almost directly overhead. Had they spotted the American submarine, now lying directly beneath their keel? Throughout the control room, every eye not focused on a specific readout or instrumentation was fastened on the compartment's overhead, as though trying to pierce the double hull and the darkness and the water, to see the looming presence of the Russian ship as it came closer . . . closer . . .

. . . and then the sound of the *Riga*'s engines was dwindling . . . fading into the distance somewhere astern.

And it was gone.

Slowly, Montgomery let out a sigh of pent-up breath. Though the temperature throughout the boat was always maintained at a comfortable seventy degrees, Montgomery realized his khaki uniform shirt was sopping wet beneath his arms and down his spine. His left hand was gripping a handhold on the attack periscope mounting so tightly his hand had cramped.

"Just routine," he said, letting go of the handhold and

massaging his fingers. "Cakewalk." Several of the men in the
control room chuckled nervously. "Engineering Officer, Captain. Make turns for five knots."

"Make turns for five knots, aye, sir."

Galveston continued her creep toward the south, penetrating
still deeper into the Kola Inlet.

0615 hours
Tomcat 201
U.S.S. *Thomas Jefferson*

Lieutenant j.g. Kathleen "Cat" Garrity sat in the rear seat of the
F-14 Tomcat, which was parked on the starboard side of
Jefferson's flight deck. The long pins, each tagged with a red
flag, that safed her ejection seat mechanism had already been
pulled. In front of her, the Viper Squadron CO, Commander
Willis E. Grant, better known aboard *Jefferson* by his call sign
"Coyote," was going through the last of his pre-flight.

"Canopy coming down," Coyote told her over the Tomcat's
intercom system, or ICS. The transparent plastic bubble descended slowly over her head, locking in place with a reassuring thump. "Starting engines."

Cat's heart was pounding beneath the tightness of her seat
harness and G-suit, and she could hear the rasp of her own
breathing, thick behind the rubber embrace of her oxygen
mask, hissing in her ears. The Tomcat D's twin F110-GE-400
engines spooled to life, their whine penetrating the cockpit like
rolling, high-pitched thunder. She concentrated on finishing up
her own pre-flight: WCS to STBY; wait for the Weapons Control
System light to come on, then flip the liquid cooling switch
from OFF to AWG-9.

"AWG-Nine light's out," she said. That was as it should be.

"Rog," Coyote replied.

Next she flipped the Nav Mode switch left of the radar
display from OFF to NAV, set IFF to STBY, and turned the radio
knobs to BOTH and ON. On the console just above her left knee
was a keypad. Carefully, reading from the penciled notations
on a pad strapped to her thigh, she keyed in *Jefferson*'s current
longitude and latitude for the Tomcat's on-board computer:
22°05'15" East, 71°00'35" North—which translated as about

eighty miles off the northern coast of Norway. Finally she began checking circuit breakers, by eye for those on her side consoles, and by reaching up behind her head and feeling for the set behind the seat. None had popped. Good. "Breakers all go."

A loud thump from outside the aircraft startled her. The blue-shirted deck crewmen were beginning to break the Tomcat down, removing the chains and chocks that secured the thirty-ton aircraft to its place on the flight deck. A plane director in a Mickey Mouse helmet and a stained, yellow jersey moved past the starboard wing, hands raised, signaling like a cop at a busy intersection. Every man in the deck crew wore a color-coded jersey that identified his section: yellow for plane directors, blue for aircraft handlers, green for maintenance personnel and for the hook-and-cat men, brown for plane captains, purple for fuel handlers, red for firefighters and ordnance men, white for safety monitors, black-and-white checks for inspectors and troubleshooters.

"Here we go," Coyote said. "Gold Eagle Two-oh-one, rolling."

Guided by the Yellow Shirt, the Tomcat rolled smoothly across the flight deck, nosing up behind the vertical wall of a jet-blast deflector raised from the deck. Forward of the JBD, another Tomcat had just screamed off the bow and into the sky, and steam was swirling past the deck like low-flying clouds. The JBD dropped into its recess in the deck, and Coyote guided the Tomcat forward, aligning it with precision along the rail-straight slash of the starboard bow catapult.

From her vantage point high up off the steel deck, Cat had a glorious view of the sea and sky around her. It was minutes before dawn, which came at 0640 hours at this latitude and this time of year. The sky was completely clear save for a rim of purple clouds along the horizon. Aft and to port the sky was still a deep, midnight blue; ahead and to starboard, toward the east, it had already lightened to a dazzling blend of cerulean and gold, and the tops of the clouds were catching the first orange touch of the hidden sun. A dazzlingly bright star—actually the planet Venus—gleamed like a beacon low in the southeast. In every direction, the sea was a deep, deep blue-green shadowed to near-invisibility by the last remnants of night.

With a thunderous, shuddering roar, the engines of Tomcat 206 on the catapult to her left rose to a shrieking crescendo, the aircraft trembling against that twin-mouthed fury. The launch officer performed his ballet of movement, swinging his arm up to point off the carrier's bow, then dropping to touch the deck. At the signal, the catapult officer in his enclosed cockpit on the deck off to one side pressed his button. Tomcat 206, Lieutenant Bruce "Mustang" Davis at the stick, whooshed down the catapult and off the bow, its engines glowing like twin orange eyes in the twilight. Steam fumed from the catapult track as deck crewmen dashed from their standby positions, preparing to receive the next Tomcat in line.

Other crewmen, meanwhile, were making the final preparations on 201. Red-shirted ordies yanked the safing wires from the F-14's armament stores: four AIM-54C Phoenix missiles, two AIM-9M Sidewinders, and two of the new AMRAAM radar-guided missiles that were only now slowly coming into service as a replacement for the old, less-than-satisfactory Sparrow. One of them held a handful of wires up so that Coyote and Cat could verify that all of the weapons were now ready to fire. A Purple Shirt, a "Grape" in the lexicon of carrier deck crews, held up a signboard with the numerals 65000. That was the weight in pounds of the Tomcat, its stores, and its fuel. A cross-check with Coyote was necessary to verify the figure, so that the launch crews could set their catapult to fire with the proper strength. Green-shirted hook-and-cat men crawled beneath the aircraft, attaching the catapult shuttle and making certain all was ready for launch.

"Father, Son, Holy Ghost, Amen" sounded over her headset, a murmured litany. Coyote was running through the old naval aviator's ritual, "wiping" the Tomcat's rudder and ailerons by moving his stick forward and back, left and right, then moving the rudder pedals with his feet.

"Harness set?" Coyote asked her.

"Ready to go," she said. Could he hear her heart hammering through the ICS? Her mouth was dry, her palms inside her flight gloves were wet. She heard the Air Boss speaking to Coyote over the radio, giving him clearance. A light shining from the island and visible over her right shoulder showed green. They were ready for launch. Leaning her helmet as far back into her headrest as it would go, she braced herself, fighting the tension building in her gut. Suddenly, it was as though perspective had changed for her. The length of track from the Tomcat to the bow, just visible past the console and the back of Coyote's seat in front of her, seemed now impossibly short, a few feet at most. The deck officer was making revving motions with his wands, and she felt the F-14's engines coming to full power, a volcanic blast of power shrieking scant feet behind the small of her back. The Tomcat trembled now at the head of the catapult, like a great, gray eagle poised for flight.

How many times had she been hurled from the bow of an aircraft carrier? She'd long ago lost count . . . but the excitement and the fear and the adrenaline rush were always the same for her.

Coyote saluted the deck officer, indicating he was ready. The deck officer swung his arm up in that graceful point, dropped, touched the deck . . .

WHAM!

The Tomcat accelerated from zero to 170 mph in two seconds, thundering off *Jefferson*'s bow in a dizzying rush of raw power. Had something gone wrong, had the catapult failed to provide the necessary thrust, they would have plunged off the carrier's bow toward the sea . . . with a scant second or two to grab their ejection rings and blast themselves clear.

"Wheeooo!" Coyote shrilled from the forward seat. "Good shot!"

And then they were climbing . . . her seat tipping back as the nose came up . . . up . . . *up* . . . and the Tomcat rocketed into the dawn. Golden light exploded over the eastern horizon as they passed five thousand feet, a mile up and still climbing. The sky above was pure glory.

And *this* was why Kathy Garrity had become a naval flight officer, despite the protests of her parents, despite the grueling training and study she'd put herself through for the past four years.

"Oh, God, this is beautiful!" she cried over the ICS, unable and unwilling to suppress the joy.

"Amen to that," Coyote replied. "Let's tuck 'em in and see what this crate'll really do."

The Tomcat's wings, extended straight out to achieve maxi-

mum lift for takeoff, were folding back now, turning the
Tomcat into a sleek spearhead designed for speed.

Accelerating now, they kept climbing into blue-gold glory.

The E-2C Hawkeye had roared off *Jefferson*'s number-two
catapult hours earlier, taking up station in advance of the carrier
group as it made its way northeast along the Norwegian coast.
One of four E-2Cs in VAW-130, the Catseyes, the Hawkeye
was a carrier-based AEW, or early warning aircraft, thought by
many to be the most capable radar-warning and aircraft-
control plane in service anywhere in the world. In an age of
high-performance jets, it was driven by two Allison turboprops,
which gave the plane fuel efficiency enough to manage a
two-hundred-mile patrol radius with six hours of loiter time on
station. By far its most distinctive feature was the saucer-
shaped radome, twenty-four feet in diameter, circling at a
leisurely six revolutions per minute on its mounting above the
aircraft's fuselage. The saucer provided lift enough to offset its
own weight, and housed the powerful APS-125 radar that
allowed the E-2C to track targets out to a range of 240 nautical
miles.

On board was a crew of five: two pilots, a combat information center officer, an air controller, and a radar operator.
Though it was now past sunrise, the aft part of the aircraft was
shielded from outside light, and the only illumination came
from the green-glowing screens that were the Hawkeye's entire
reason for being. On the radar operator's main console, the
sweep line painted smears of liquid light, stage-lighting the
man as he noted the appearance of unidentified blips just
entering the E-2C's range.

The CIC officer and the air controller stood behind him,
peering over his shoulders at the screen. "My Lord in heaven,"
the air controller said. "They must be standing on each other's
shoulders."

"Let's flash it," the CIC officer said. He picked up a

microphone, keyed it, and began speaking in rapid, urgent tones.

"Home Plate, Home Plate," he said, using *Jefferson*'s call sign. "This is Echo-Tango Seven-six-one. We have multiple contacts, repeat, numerous multiple contacts, from one-zero-zero to one-five-zero, range two-four-zero nautical miles. . . ."

The radar operator was Radarman First Class Richard Lee. Twenty-four years old, he'd been in the Navy for seven years and he had never, in all his life, seen such an array of aircraft except, possibly, for simulations of a mass Russian attack.

The Hawkeye was flying well in advance of the *Jefferson* and had now reached its patrol station twenty miles off Norway's North Cape. From that vantage point, and at the aircraft's ceiling of just over thirty thousand feet, he could see well into Russia's Kola Peninsula, painted on his display in crisp lines of light. Nothing was happening around Polyarnyy or Murmansk, but the sky must be thick with aircraft over the airfields at Titovka, Pechenga, Zapolyarnyy, Nikel.

This couldn't be happening. . . .

"Sir," he said, pointing. "They're crossing the line."

It was true. Aircraft from Nikel and Pechenga, already practically on Russia's narrow border with Norway, were moving across the demarcation line between the countries. More aircraft were arriving too, from further to the south and east, from Kola airfields not yet within range of the E-2C's radar.

"Home Plate, Home Plate," the CIC officer said. How could the man keep his voice so steady? "Echo-Tango Seven-six-one. We have a fire. I repeat, we have a fire. Bogies are assuming intercept vectors, bearing on Home Plate."

A fire—the current code phrase meaning a possible attack in progress.

As far as Lee could tell from his radar screen, every aircraft in Eurasia was on its way.

And their destination appeared to be the *Jefferson*.

CHAPTER 9
Friday, 13 March

Batman had already been on his way to the Viper Squadron's ready room from morning chow when the alert came over the 1-MC speaker mounted on the bulkhead. "Now General Quarters, General Quarters. All hands, man your battle stations. . . ."

Before the announcement ended, Batman had broken into a run, forcing his way through passageways and up companionways suddenly filled with young men—and a few women—each of them bent on getting somewhere in the least possible time with the greatest possible efficiency. The scene was at first one of chaos, but it was soon clear that each person had a place to go and a task to perform, and there was actually very little confusion or wasted effort as six thousand people turned out in this ship-wide evolution.

Batman banged through the door to the Viper ready room at a fast jog, just ahead of half a dozen other VF-95 aviators and RIOs. Attached to the main ready room area, with its rows of wooden desks like some 1950s-era schoolhouse, was a dressing area with lockers and a small shower head, where the squadron's NFOs could stow their uniforms and don the flight suits that helped keep them from blacking out in the high-G maneuvers of aerial combat.

As he swiftly unbuttoned his khaki shirt and pulled it off, Batman was marginally aware of the fact that several of the

people crowded shoulder to shoulder into the dressing room
with him were women. Normally, VF-95's flight officers had
shared the dressing area through an unspoken agreement,
taking turns and allowing fellow members of the squadron who
happened to be of the opposite sex some small measure of
privacy, but in an all-hands evolution, where seconds counted,
there was no time for such civilized niceties. A few feet to his
left, Cynthia Thomas was just shrugging out of her bra. On his
right Chris Hanson bumped against his hip as she wiggled into
the lower half of her tight-fitting, cold-water survival suit, a
rubberized garment worn under the flight suit, always an
awkward maneuver even when there was space enough to
move around.

The room was crowded, noisy, and tense, but no comment
was made by anyone at the display of skin, no lewd wisecracks,
not even a peremptory "Keep your eyes to yourself!" In
minutes, Batman was tugging the last zipper on his flight suit
shut, grabbing a clipboard with its attached checklist, pen, and
notebook, and heading back to the ready room proper.

A large television monitor was suspended from the overhead
at the front of the ready room next to the PLAT monitor, and
someone had already switched it on. The PLAT screen was
showing one of VFA-161's Hornets preparing to launch off the
angled flight deck from one of the carrier's waist catapults, but
the big TV showed only the crest insignia of the U.S.S. *Thomas
Jefferson*, a stylized CVN seen bow-on, with the motto
"COMBAT READY."

Batman slumped into a seat next to his usual RIO, Lieutenant Commander Ken Blake, a sandy-haired guy from southern
California who went by the handle "Malibu." Seconds later,
Jefferson's insignia on the TV screen was replaced by Tombstone's face.

"Good morning, Air Wing Twenty," he said, speaking
directly into the camera. "I'll keep this short and sweet. A few
minutes ago, our AEW patrol picked up a large number of
Russian aircraft taking off from military fields in the north-
western regions of the Kola Peninsula. The figures go up every
time a new update comes through, but at this point we are
estimating at least one hundred twenty aircraft. Several flights
have already crossed the Norwegian border and are on a direct
intercept course with the carrier group."

Tombstone was addressing all of *Jefferson*'s squadrons simultaneously from the TV studio up in the Carrier Intelligence Center, the CVIC, or "Civic" for short. Batman knew him well enough to know he must wish he were here, with the Vipers, but as CAG his responsibility was for the entire wing, from the two squadrons of Tomcats to the HS-19 squadron of SH-3 helos.

"The battle group has already assumed a defensive posture along the threat axis," Tombstone continued. "Admiral Tarrant has ordered that all radar and radio traffic aboard *Jefferson* be shut down. CATCC will go back on the air only when we have to start bringing you in for rearming. All combat communications and command control will be handled through the *Shiloh*."

That particular ploy had been worked out back in the early eighties and had been used successfully on numerous occasions since. As large as it was, an aircraft carrier could virtually disappear if all of the radar and radio transmissions that could light it up on the enemy's screens like a New York City skyscraper at night were shut down. The Aegis cruiser would take over all radar and combat command control duties, making itself a target in the process, of course . . . but it would be a very well-defended one.

"*Shiloh*'s call sign for this op will be Hotspur," Tombstone continued. In concise, rapid-fire words, he outlined the entire wing's deployment. Four VF-95 Tomcats were already aloft on CAP and were being deployed into an advance BARCAP, or Barrier Combat Air Patrol, positioned 250 miles ahead of the *Jefferson*, squarely between the approaching enemy aircraft and the carrier. Four aircraft from VFA-161, the Javelins, that had been on Ready Fifteen, set to launch within fifteen minutes, were now being sent aloft in their air-interceptor role, leaving bombs and ground-attack rockets behind for Sidewinders and AMRAAMs.

The rest of VF-95 would launch next, moving forward to reinforce the BARCAP. It was vital to get as many Tomcats in the sky as possible since out of all the aircraft aboard, only the F-14s could carry the AIM-54C Phoenix. The second Tomcat squadron, VF-97, was being armed at that moment with full Phoenix warloads, six AIM-54s on each aircraft. More of the Javelins' Hornets would be launched until VF-97 was armed and ready, and then the catapults would begin putting them up.

Ultimately, both of *Jefferson*'s Tomcat squadrons would be in the air, positioned to launch their long-range Phoenix missiles against the approaching Russians. Once they had expended their munitions, they would return to *Jefferson* and recover for rearming, while the two Hornet squadrons moved in to take on the surviving Russians close-up. The carrier's EA-6 electronic warfare planes would be thrown far forward, to scramble the enemy's radar and communications. Her sub-hunting Vikings would be deployed to maintain an ASW screen around the battle group; her ground-attack A-6 Intruders, useless in a fight such as this one, would stand down and stay out of the way.

"I must emphasize," Tombstone said, "that we still don't know for certain whether the Russian deployment constitutes a full-scale attack, or if they're just making a feint, warning us off from their coast. BARCAP will be positioned to test them, and by the time the rest of you get airborne, we ought to know one way or the other. Until we do, however, weapons will be locked, and released only upon direct order from the Combat Information Center. Once it has been determined that the Russian force is intent on hostile action, weapons-free will be issued by the *Shiloh* CIC."

Tombstone concluded with several more items about deployment, and a report from the Met Office—sky clear, ceiling unlimited, winds from the northeast at ten knots.

"That's it," Tombstone said at last. "Good luck, men. And God go with you."

Amused, Batman wondered if Tombstone's use of the word "men," obviously an oversight in the pressure of the moment, had bothered any of the women. None of them appeared to have noticed.

Good. This was no time to let petty sexual politics interfere with the smooth operation of the squadron.

"Okay, people," Batman said, raising his voice to blanket the room. As the Viper XO, he was squadron commander in Coyote's absence. "You all heard the man. Let's go kick ass and take names!"

"Yeah!" Slider Arrenberger yelled back, punching his clenched fist at the overhead. "Today we kick Russki ass!"

Arrenberger hadn't been aboard on *Jefferson*'s last deployment, during the fiercely fought battles over Romsdalfjord or off the Lofoten Islands. The chances were all too good that, while the American aviators were kicking Russian ass, the Russians would be kicking their share of American ass as well. Some good people were likely to die today.

Batman was no more superstitious than any other naval aviator, but he suddenly remembered the date—Friday the 13th. Bad luck for who, the Americans or the Russians?

As the squadron rose with a scraping and squeaking of chairs, Batman noticed Striker—Lieutenant Strickland—reach out and grab Lieutenant Hanson's arm. When she turned, he leaned over and gave her a quick, hard kiss on the mouth.

No one said anything, but Batman felt a small twist in his gut. Any PDA—public display of affection—was both inappropriate at the moment and strictly contra-regs. He'd already heard scuttlebutt about those two and hoped they didn't get into trouble for it.

He remembered Tombstone's concerns about sexual relationships between members of the squadron, though, and thought he understood. It was embarrassing to admit it, even to himself.

Twenty-nine years old, and Edward Everett "Batman" Wayne was unmarried. At the moment, he didn't even have a girlfriend, though he was notorious for his skill in acquiring attractive dates when he was ashore. Ever since his experiences in Thailand a few years ago, however, he'd found himself increasingly dissatisfied with his lifestyle and unable to pinpoint the cause.

Now he was beginning to think it was time to settle down, maybe even get married.

Well, maybe he wouldn't go that far. But he recognized a certain small, sharp pang each time he saw a couple who obviously shared a deep, mutual affection. It wasn't jealousy, not really, but it was an awareness, a reminder that his life wasn't complete.

Sometimes it hurt.

"Let's go strap on an airplane, Batman," Malibu said, punching him in the arm and jarring him from less-than-pleasant thoughts. "Betcha Chief Leyden's already got Two-oh-two opened up and warming for us." Leyden was the crew chief for Tomcat 202, Batman's and Malibu's aircraft.

The passageways and decks between VF-95's ready room

and *Jefferson*'s flight deck were still crowded as the carrier's crew proceeded with their assigned battle station duties. Out on the flight deck, the scene was one of frantic, purposeful activity; of steam and thundering, brawling noise; of dozens of men in color-coded jerseys carrying out their assigned duties in surroundings that might have been lifted from one of Dante's hells.

Moving this many of *Jefferson*'s complement of combat aircraft to the proper place at the proper time was a fantastically complex operation, one requiring split-second timing and precision to carry out. At any given time, roughly half of the carrier's aircraft were stowed on her hangar deck, and these had to be fed up to the flight deck in just the proper order and at just the proper times to replace the aircraft that were even now shrieking skyward off *Jefferson*'s catapults.

Jefferson had four catapults and could hurl aircraft aloft two at a time, one off the bow, the other from the waist. However, it took nearly thirty minutes to ready most aircraft from a standing start, and space both on the flight deck and below on the hangar deck was sharply limited. Though the launch order for today's operation had been worked out previously in painstaking detail, *Jefferson*'s Deck Handler and his crew in Flight Deck Control would have their work cut out for them.

The "Mangler," as the Handler was called, was responsible for moving aircraft from the hangar deck up to the flight deck by way of just four elevators, mapping out each movement with the aid of large maps of both decks, plus precisely scaled plan-view silhouettes of each aircraft. Getting the right aircraft to the right place at the right time, without creating bottlenecks at the elevators or while feeding into line, without brushing against another aircraft in tractor-towed maneuvers carried out with scant inches to spare, always seemed nothing short of miraculous.

Sprinting across the flight deck to Tomcat 202, Batman and Malibu saw that Chief Leyden already had the aircraft hooked up to external power cables and the "huffer," a small tractor that injected air through a hose directly into each engine's turbine fast enough to allow the engine to run on its own. Though Leyden and the blue shirts working with him had already inspected the aircraft, Batman gave it a quick external, checking the fuselage for obvious damage or open access hatches, tugging on the deadly, white darts of the AIM-54Cs to make sure they were secured and wouldn't drop off during the stress of a cat launch. He traded a jaunty thumbs-up with Leyden, then climbed up the Tomcat's access steps and settled into the cockpit. He felt the aircraft rock as Malibu dropped in behind him.

Quick check . . . donning helmet and O_2 mask, checking oxygen lines and electrical connections, removing safing pins from the ejection seats, fastening seat belt and chest harness. He brought the canopy down.

As Batman began flipping console switches and bringing the F-14's engines on line, he thought again about Tombstone. When he'd first come on board the *Jefferson*, Stoney had been all but an object of worship for the young Lieutenant Wayne, despite the royal ass-chewings the younger officer had received from him a time or two for hotdogging. Now, Stoney was a friend, and he was carrying one hell of a burden on his captain's epaulets. It would be especially rough today. As superCAG, he normally would direct the operation from *Jefferson*'s CATCC rather than fly with his pilots, and Batman knew that was hard on the man. Worse still, today's battle would be run from *Shiloh*'s CIC, leaving Stoney in a more or less supernumerary position.

Batman decided that he didn't want to be in the CAG's shoes for anything.

His engines were running, the blue shirts had broken down 202's chains and chocks, and a plane director was signaling for him to come ahead. Gently, Batman eased his thirty-ton charger forward, maneuvering toward the catapults.

0710 hours
Tomcat 201
Over the Barents Sea

Coyote put the F-14 in a gentle starboard bank. The BARCAP was on station now, at an altitude of 32,000 feet. Early morning sunlight sparkled off an ultramarine sea. His wingman, Mustang Davis, was holding Tomcat 206 some fifty feet off Coyote's starboard wingtip. Nightmare Marinaro's 204, and his wingman, Slider Arrenberger in 209, were about ten miles behind and to the north of Coyote and Mustang, positioned to get maximum information from their powerful AWG-9 radars.

The Russian force was close enough now to track. When set to pulse-doppler search, or PDS, the F-14's AWG-9 radar could determine range and speed on a five-square-meter target out to a distance of 115 nautical miles—over 130 standard miles. Their radar was now showing a heavy clot of blips, crossing the Norwegian coast near North Cape and still heading toward the CBG. The nearest targets were already within sixty miles of the orbiting Tomcats.

"Hotspur, Gold Eagle One," Coyote said, calling *Shiloh*'s Combat Information Center. "Request weapons free."

"Gold Eagle, Hotspur. Negative on weapons release. Situation still confused. We need confirmation of hostile intent."

"How much confirmation do they need?" Cat asked from the back seat.

"Yeah," Coyote replied. "They've already crossed Norwegian airspace, and that doesn't look like the formation for a welcoming parade."

"Uh-oh," Cat said. "I've got . . ."

"What?"

"Wait one. Okay, we're reading J-band pulse-doppler. Coyote, I think we've got some Badger-Gs out there."

"Shit," Coyote said. "Okay, send it."

This did not sound good.

0712 hours
Hawkeye 761
Twenty-five miles north of North Cape

The E-2C Hawkeye was still following the massive aerial deployment of aircraft, now crossing the Norwegian coastline near Tanafjorden, less than one hundred miles to the southeast.

"Echo-Tango, this is Gold Eagle One" sounded in the air controller's headset . . . a *woman's* voice. Gold Eagle One must have a female RIO.

"Gold Eagle, Echo-Tango Seven-six-one. Copy."

"Echo-Tango, we're picking up attack radar from the bogies. I've got steady J-band transmissions. Sounds like Shorthorn."

Shorthorn was the NATO code for a particular type of Soviet

weapons/navigation radar. It was carried by naval aircraft armed with AS-5 and -6 antiship missiles.

The Hawkeye's radar operator flicked a dial, narrowly watching several of his dials. "That's confirmed, sir. J-band, weapon control radar. I think we're tracking Badger-Gs."

"Send it," the CIC officer said. Holding his headset mike to his lips, he said, "Gold Eagle, Echo-Tango Seven-six-one, we confirm Shorthorn. BARCAP is clear to go to Tango-Whiskey-Sierra. Let 'em know you're there."

TWS—shorthand for track-while-search—was the AWG-9 radar mode that allowed the F-14 to track enemy targets. When switched on, it would light up Russian threat warnings up to ninety nautical miles away.

On the radar display, meanwhile, the blips marking approaching Russian aircraft began to spread out, to resolve into clusters of three and four separate targets in tightly grouped formations. Suddenly, the radar operator leaned forward, eyes narrowing. "Sir! I have a launch!"

The CICO had already seen the same thing, smaller blips detaching themselves from the larger ones.

If the firing aircraft were Badger-Gs, the missiles slung under their wings were AS-5 or AS-6 air-to-surface missiles, ship-killers with one-ton HE warheads.

"Hotspur! Hotspur! Echo-Tango!" he called. "Launch, we have cruise-missile launch!"

"Ninety-nine aircraft" came the call back from the Aegis cruiser *Shiloh*, using a code phrase meaning all aircraft. "Ninety-nine aircraft, Hotspur. Weapons free. I say again, weapons are free!"

The message was instantly relayed via data link through the E-2C to every American plane already in the air.

The Battle of North Cape had begun.

CHAPTER 10
Friday, 13 March

0713 hours (Zulu +2)
Tomcat 201
Over the Barents Sea

"Let's go with a Phoenix launch first," Coyote told Cat. "We've for damned sure got targets enough to choose from."

"Definitely what they call a 'target-rich environment,' Boss," Cat replied. "We're tracking on four."

In all the arsenals of all the world's powers, even in the arsenals of other U.S. military services, there was nothing like the ΛIM 54C Phoenix. A 985-pound missile with a range of over 120 miles and a speed of better than Mach 5, the weapon could be fired only by the F-14 Tomcat with its advanced AWG-9 radar guidance system, and was therefore available only to the U.S. Navy. The Tomcat's radar, set to track-while-scan, could lock onto six separate targets while simultaneously guiding six missiles at once.

Coyote was carrying only four AIM-54s, so Cat had selected four targets, tagging them on her radar screen in the back seat.

"Let 'er rip, Cat," he told her.

"That's fox three," she replied, using the aviator's code for a Phoenix launch.

Cat hit the launch button and the Tomcat lurched higher as it was freed of nearly a half-ton weight slung beneath its belly. Igniting beneath the F-14, the missile speared forward into a crystal-blue sky, a cotton-white contrail streaming astern.

"And firing two," Cat said. "Fox three!"

"Gold Eagle One, Eagle Two." That was Mustang Davis, Coyote's wingman. "We've got track-and-lock. Fox three!"

One of Mustang's white Phoenix darts dropped clear, ignited, and *swooshed* into the distance.

"Hey, Coyote!" Mustang called. "What about those cruise missiles?"

"We'd have to backtrack to get a lock," he told him. "We'll leave them for the follow-up crew. Or *Jeff*'s CIWS."

"Okay, copy. Here's another fox three."

The sky was rapidly becoming filled with the twisting white streamers of missile contrails arcing toward the southeast.

0715 hours
Off North Cape

The basic tactics of modern aircraft carrier warfare had been laid down in World War II, when Admiral Chester Nimitz took on a far larger Japanese force with three aircraft carriers, their air groups providing both offensive strike capability and defensive CAP over the fleet, plus eight cruisers and seventeen destroyers dedicated to providing close-in antiaircraft defense for the carriers. His tactics—and the luck that blesses or curses every plan of battle—won the Battle of Midway, and the concept of hard-hitting, well-protected carrier groups quickly became the guiding combat doctrine for the U.S. Navy's Pacific War.

During the next fifty years, the aircraft became larger, faster, and farther-ranging; the weapons became smarter, more destructive, and capable of superb accuracy across ranges unthinkable in 1942. The Nimitz doctrine, however, remained essentially the same.

The modern aircraft carrier battle group, variously called CBG or CVBG, was built around the supercarrier. Some, like *Jefferson* or *Eisenhower*, were nuclear-powered. Others, like the *Kennedy* and the *America*, had originally been designed for nuclear power but, thanks to Congressional budget cuts, were driven instead by conventional, fuel-oil-fired boilers. Depending on their class, their flight decks stretched from 990 to 1,040 feet long, just six feet less than the height of New York City's Chrysler Building. Their full-load displacement ranged anywhere from 80,000 to 96,000 tons—compared to the 19,900 tons of the U.S.S. *Enterprise* at Midway.

The rest of the battle group was devoted to protecting the carrier and consisted of one or two guided-missile cruisers, a mixed force of four to seven frigates and destroyers, and one or two Los Angeles–class attack submarines. As it approached its patrol area off North Cape, *Jefferson*'s battle group included the Aegis cruiser *Shiloh*; three guided-missile destroyers, *John A. Winslow, William B. Truesdale,* and *Alan Kirk;* four Perry-class guided-missile frigates, *Dickinson, Esek Hopkins, Stephen Decatur,* and *Leslie;* and the attack subs *Morgantown* and *Galveston.*

It was a powerful force. CBG-14, already understrength by the time it reached Romsdalfjord nine months before, had been badly hurt during the Battles of the Fjords, and the decision had been made to reinforce it big-time. The *Truesdale, Kirk, Dickinson, Leslie,* and *Morgantown* all were new additions to the battle group.

In modern warfare, a carrier battle group is deployed across an incredibly vast stretch of open ocean. If CBG-14 could have been magically transported to the eastern seaboard of the United States, with the *Jefferson* herself planted on the Mall in downtown Washington, D.C., her escort ships would have been ranging as far afield as central Pennsylvania, southern Virginia, and West Virginia; her defensive air units would have been patrolling the skies over Maine and South Carolina, Kentucky and Michigan; and her attack subs and S-3 Vikings would have been searching out enemy submarines somewhere in Ohio. Her attack planes, meanwhile, could have struck targets as far off as Chicago.

As the first wave of Russian bombers entered *Jefferson*'s outer defensive ring, Tomcat-launched Phoenix missiles drew the first blood. Russian long- and medium-range bombers— Bears, Badgers, and Backfires—began exploding in flames as far off as the Russia-Norway border.

As Tomcat after Tomcat locked on and fired, the losses within the approaching Russian horde mounted. In the first five minutes of the battle, eighteen Tomcats launched ninety-six AIM-54Cs. The Phoenix had a reliability rating of about ninety percent, meaning that in ideal conditions, nine out of ten would hit what they were aimed at.

In warfare, conditions are never ideal. Badger-J electronic-warfare aircraft were accompanying the bomber formations, and they were able to kill or blind a number of AIM-54s before they reached their targets.

Seventy-eight struck, however, all but annihilating the first wave of bombers.

0718 hours
Tomcat 201
Over the Barents Sea

All four Phoenix missiles were gone, but Coyote still had two Sidewinders and two AMRAAMs slung beneath the wings of his Tomcat. Pushing his throttle forward, feeling the click of each detent as he went all the way to zone-five afterburner, Coyote hurtled toward the southeast. His F-14's computer automatically slid the aircraft's wings back, adjusting drag and lift for maximum speed. A moment later they slipped past the sound barrier with scarcely a shudder in the big Tomcat's airframe.

"That's . . . a . . . kill!" Cat called from the back seat, her words and breaths coming in short bursts as she labored against the transverse-Gs pressing her back against her seat. "Splash . . . *four!*"

"Send it," Coyote told her, cutting back the F-14's power and dropping below Mach 1 again. Ahead, the ragged gray coastline of Norway was stretched along the sea at the horizon. Numerous threads of white crisscrossed the blue sky, Phoenix contrails from a dozen F-14s. "Mustang, where the hell are you?"

"Coyote, Mustang. I'm on your five at six miles. Going for Phoenix launch!"

"Okay. Dump your load, then close up. I'm naked up here."

"Roger that, Two-oh-one. Here we go. Lock and . . . fox three!"

Coyote switched to ICS. "Cat! Gimme a vector! Gimme something to shoot at!"

"Shit, Coyote, take your pick. Ah . . . come right five. Looks like a large target at angels ten, range four-two miles."

He picked out the target on his own display. "Got it. We'll take it with AMRAAM."

The AIM-120A, also called the Advanced Medium-Range

Air-to-Air Missile or AMRAAM for short, had been a long, long time in coming. With Phoenix to hit targets up to a hundred miles away, with the Sidewinder heat-seeker to take on close targets out to ten miles or so, a medium-range missile was needed to fill the gap between the two extremes. Since the 1950s, the Navy's medium-range missile had been the AIM-7 Sparrow.

For the men who'd had to rely on them, the AIM-7 had never been entirely satisfactory. They were SARH-guided—semi-active radar-homing—which meant they homed on radar energy reflected off the target by the firing aircraft. That meant that the aviator who locked on to an enemy target and fired a Sparrow at it had to keep his aircraft flying straight and level, continuing to paint the target while his missile completed its flight—as much as sixty-two miles in later versions of the AIM-7.

And while he was doing that, he was vulnerable, unable to maneuver without breaking the radar lock and wasting his shot.

Coyote switched his heads-up display to medium-range-missile mode, selecting an AIM-120. On his HUD, a small rectangle drifted across his field of view, the target designator. To the left, beneath the vertical line of his airspeed indicator, ARM M2 appeared, showing he had two missiles ready, while to the right, just inside the altitude scale, a vertical line gave the target's closing speed and range. The target was twenty-five nautical miles away now, closing at 512 knots.

Dragging his stick over, he merged the designator box with the target pip; the letters ACQ let him know that the target had been acquired by the missile's radar. There was a beat as computers calculated firing conditions, angles, and probabilities . . . and then the rectangle blinked to a circle embracing the letter M.

A tone shrilled in his ear. "Radar lock!" Cat called from the RIO's seat.

"Fox one!" Coyote answered, and he squeezed the firing trigger.

AMRAAM represented a whole new type of air-to-air missile, carrying its own radar-guidance system as well as extremely sensitive infrared sensors for terminal homing. Cost overruns and unexpected technical difficulties had delayed the missile's production for the better part of a decade, and with the first production models going to the Air Force, the new missile had been slow to reach Navy combat units.

With a roar, the AIM-120 detached itself from the Tomcat, boosting on a trail of flame to Mach 4 in seconds. On Coyote's HUD, beneath the altitude scale, the characters IN RNG and 28 glowed in silent affirmation. The AMRAAM would reach the target in another twenty-eight seconds.

With the missile away, Coyote immediately brought his stick hard to the right, dropping into a starboard turn away from the target that would have been impossible with the old AIM-7.

"I've got a target," CAT told him. "Bearing one-eight-five at three-one nautical miles."

Coyote pulled back on his stick, easing out of the turn. "Got him!" he said. "Set the next one for AMRAAM."

0719 hours
Off North Cape

At first, as the long-range Phoenix missiles streaked in from the U.S. fighter screen, the Russian fighters escorting the bombers couldn't even hit back. The best air-to-air missile they possessed was the semi-active radar-homing AA-9 "Amos," carried as a stand-off interceptor by the MiG-31 and having a range of about eighty miles. Production of the AA-9 had been plagued by problems even worse than those endured by the AMRAAM, however, and they were not as reliable as the AIM-54 Phoenix they'd been designed to emulate—especially in a hostile ECM environment.

Nor were there as many of them. Most of the air-to-air missiles protecting the Russian bomber force were big AA-6 "Acrids," carried by MiG-25 Foxbats and having a lock-on range of about sixty-two miles, and the modern AA-10 "Alamo," with a thirty-mile range.

As the two air armadas closed with one another, more and more of the Russian weapons began coming into play. But if the Russians were beginning to concentrate their forces, so too were the Americans. While the basic unit of naval warfare was the carrier battle group, a common strategy involved combining two or more CBGs into a carrier battle force, or CBF. During the Gulf War of 1991, four separate carrier groups had united in the Persian Gulf, forming a single battle force of unprecedented firepower.

Now, off the northernmost tip of Norway, two carrier battle groups were in the process of joining forces. Though the surface elements of CBG-7 and CBG-14 had not yet merged, the moment orbiting Hawkeyes had spotted the approaching Russian air armada, the *Eisenhower* had thrown her defensive cordon of Tomcats and Hornets into the sky along *Jefferson*'s threat axis, combining and bolstering the defenses for both carrier groups. Tomcats from the *Eisenhower* loosed their AIM-54Cs at targets still deep in the Kola Peninsula; Hornets vectored in to provide air protection for *Jefferson* Tomcats that had already expended their missiles.

Despite the reinforcements, however, the battle was still so scattered that it was in reality a large number of separate, isolated clashes between tiny groups or even individuals, all fighting for their lives.

0719 hours
Tomcat 201
Over the Barents Sea

"Tone! Fox one!"

Their second AMRAAM slid from its launch rail, tracking a Russian bomber that had already passed Tomcat 201's position and was now almost thirty miles ahead, between Coyote and the fleet.

There were more aircraft in the sky now. All of *Jefferson*'s Tomcats were in the air, and more and more of the Hornets from her two F/A-18 squadrons were arriving in the battle zone.

In addition, new Tomcats were vectoring in from the northwest, F-14s launched earlier from the U.S.S. *Eisenhower*.

Coyote was glad to see the extra talent arrive, but there was scant time for celebration. Seconds after his second AMRAAM struck home, Cat cut in over the ICS.

"Coyote," she said, sounding worried. "I've got a threat tone here."

He glanced down at his own console and saw the glowing light on his threat-warning receiver. A radar-guided missile had just locked onto his aircraft, was tracking them now from astern.

"I see it. Do you have it on your TID?"

"Wait one . . ." She was checking her Tactical Information Display, the round screen centered on her NFO's console. "Yeah! Got it. Bearing zero-nine-five, range four-two and closing . . . shit, Mach three point five. Coyote, I think we've just picked up an Amos."

"Stay on it. We'll let it get closer."

"It's close enough for me right now."

"Yeah, but if we break, it'll break with us. Stay frosty."

"I'm so frosty I'm freezing to death."

"Mustang! You there?"

"Right here, Coyote. Loose as a goose on your four." Navy aviators tended to fly in widely spaced, flexible tactical formations, referred to as "loose goose," rather than the tight wing-and-wing approach used by most of their opponents.

"Rog. Let's go ballistic before that thing kicks us in the ass."

At this range, the incoming missile might be tracking either of them. There'd be no way to tell until it got a lot closer.

"Affirmative."

"Going to zone five." He rammed his throttle forward.

"Right with you."

At their current altitude of just over twenty-thousand feet, the Tomcats could manage about Mach 2.3. The missile following them, now forty miles away, was traveling at Mach 3.5, which meant that even at their top speed it would continue to overhaul them with a closing rate of almost eight hundred miles per hour.

With luck, the air-to-air missile would run out of fuel before it reached them.

If it didn't, it would catch up to them in another three minutes.

0719 hours
Off North Cape

The CICOs in the American line's E-2Cs reported thirty Amos air-to-air missiles incoming during the first few minutes of the exchange. EA-6B Prowlers, flying in their electronic-warfare/electronic-countermeasures role off both the *Jefferson* and the *Eisenhower*, targeted the missiles with intense bursts of radar energy designed to burn out their delicate SARH receivers. Other AA-9s were decoyed by chaff or knocked out by RIOs using their Tomcats' own ECM assets.

In all, only eleven American aircraft were hit, and of those, four were only damaged by the detonation of the AA-9's radar proximity fuze and were able to make it back to their respective carriers.

Against such odds as they were facing now, however, the Americans could not afford to lose a single plane.

0722 hours
Tomcat 201
Over the Barents Sea

"It's coming fast, Coyote! Range five miles . . ."

"Mustang! When I give the word, break right. I'll go left."

". . . four miles . . ."

"Roger that, Coyote!"

". . . three miles . . ."

"Now! Break!"

Coyote pulled the stick hard to the left and forward, going into a dive to pick up extra, crucial speed. Stealing a look back over his shoulder, he could see the onrushing missile now, a pinpoint trailing an endless thread of white scrawling across the eastern sky. As Mustang slipped off to the right, the missile tracked left.

It was after him and Cat.

He'd dropped out of afterburners to avoid guzzling up his remaining fuel, but he kicked them in once more, fighting for every possible extra measure of speed. The G-forces piled on top of his head and chest and gut, squeezing the air from his lungs, clawing at his eyeballs in their sockets.

". . . one . . . *uh!* . . . mile . . . still . . . *uh!* . . . with . . . us!" Cat was having to force each word out, punctuating them with savage grunts to literally force the air out of a diaphragm nearly paralyzed by almost nine Gs.

"Chaff!" Coyote yelled. Rapid-bloom chaff exploded from the Tomcat's tail, myriad slivers of aluminum-coated mylar cut to precise lengths blossoming in an expanding cloud astern. The missile, now a few hundred yards away, automatically tracked for the middle of its radar target as it traveled left to right, aiming at the so-called "centroid of reflected radiation." When the radar image suddenly smeared into a far larger, longer target, the AA-9's aim shifted to the right . . .

. . . and then Coyote snap-rolled the F-14 into a hard, reverse turn, climbing now and breaking out of its turn. The missile flashed into the still-scattering cloud of chaff, its simple-minded proximity fuze decided that it had reached the target, and it detonated with a thunderous roar. Bits of metal pinged and clattered off the Tomcat's hull, but no warning lights winked on in response.

"Coyote, this is Mustang! Are you okay?"

"Copacetic, Mustang. Still here!" Coyote stared up through his canopy at that deep, impossibly blue sky, crisscrossed with the lacy weavings of aircraft and missile contrails. It struck him suddenly that he'd been engaged in a life-and-death struggle for the past ten minutes, killing or damaging a probable total of six enemy planes and damned near getting killed himself.

And in all that time, he'd never been close enough to even once see a Russian aircraft.

"Mustang, Coyote," he called. "We're down to two AIM-9s and coming up on bingo fuel. I'd say it's time to RTB."

"RTB" meant "return to base." Time to head back to the *Jeff* and rearm.

"That's a major roger, Skipper. Lead the way."

Coyote switched his HUD back to NAV MODE and picked up *Shiloh*'s directional beacon. With *Jefferson* off the air for the moment, he'd have to home on the *Shiloh*, then when he got in close enough, find the *Jeff* by Mark-One eyeball.

He was now less than 120 miles from the center of the battle group. He cut back on his throttle to take them down closer to the water and eased onto the new heading.

They should be in shouting distance of the *Jefferson* in another twelve minutes.

0725 hours
Off North Cape

Russian naval tactics, like their tactics for land warfare, depended on saturating the enemy's defenses, piling on so much raw power in such huge numbers that sooner or later those defenses began to leak. Their bombers, the survivors of the Tomcats' Phoenix assault plus those that managed to get close enough to launch before being shot down, had managed to release a total of ninety-three ship-killers, most of them AS-5 "Kelt" and AS-6 "Kingfish" antiship missiles. Over thirty feet long, weighing over five tons apiece, and traveling at better than Mach 3, these missiles hurtled across the Barents Sea at wave-skimming height. Some were programmed to go all the way in at low altitude; others were set to pop up during the last few miles of their approach, attacking the carrier group from almost straight overhead. The mix of approaches was designed, like the dive-bomber/torpedo-plane tactics of World War II, to confuse, divide, and overtax the target's defenses.

0726 hours
Tomcat 201
Over the Barents Sea

"Shit! Where did *he* come from?"

Coyote peered past his fighter's HUD, trying to pick out details against the sun-sparkle off the ultramarine sea. He was at five thousand feet now, but the bandit was below him, skimming at damn-near wave-top height on a direct course for the center of the battle group. His low altitude had provided excellent cover, masking him in the back-scatter from the surface of the sea. He was definitely a "leaker," a Russian bomber that had managed to slip unobserved deep inside the CBG's defenses.

"Range two miles," Cat told him.

"Rog. I'm setting him up."

They were close enough now that Coyote could recognize the back-swept wings, the twin turbojets set close along the fuselage. It was a Tu-16 Badger, almost certainly the Badger-G missile-strike variant. Flying off each wing was a smaller aircraft, indistinguishable at this distance but almost certainly a fighter escort. Coyote edged his stick to port and pushed it forward, nudging the F-14 into a better firing position. The Badger grew rapidly behind the pale computer-graphic symbols and data lines on his HUD. Its attendants, already breaking from their larger consort and swinging around to face him, were a pair of Sukhoi-21 interceptors, Flagon-Fs painted in a tactical green-and-brown camouflage scheme.

But Coyote glimpsed something else in that blurred instant of approach. Beneath each wing of the Badger-G was the slim fuselage and pointed nose of an AS-6 "Kingfish" antiship missile. As he watched, locking his target designator onto the hot IR glow of the bomber's twin engines, first one, then the other of those sleek and deadly darts dropped from their hardpoints, igniting tails of orange flame and unraveling contrails of white smoke.

"Launch! Launch!" Coyote yelled into his radio. "Hotspur, Gold Eagle One, I have confirmed launch of two Alfa-Sierra six . . ."

Two more cruise missiles were now streaking at Mach 3 toward the center of the fleet.

And they were now less than one hundred miles out.

CHAPTER 11
Friday, 13 March

"Fox two!" Coyote yelled, and a Sidewinder *whooshed* off the rail beneath his starboard wing. Unlike Phoenix or AMRAAM, the AIM-9 Sidewinder was IR-guided, homing on the heat given off by the target, especially the heat thrown off by a jet engine.

Too late, he realized he probably should have retargeted on one of the Sukhois. Its warload dropped, the Badger-G was already clumsily turning to port, moving onto a heading that would take it back toward the Kola Peninsula. The Flagon-Fs, however, were thundering up from the sea, their targeting radars already locking onto Coyote's Tomcat.

Thinking fast, Coyote veered left, dropping his targeting pipper across the closer of the two Flagons. His last missile's IR warhead locked on and he squeezed the trigger. "Fox two!"

Head-on shots with IR-homers were a lot riskier than sending one up the tailpipe; such a shot would have been impossible with earlier models of the Sidewinder, but the AIM-9M was an all-aspect heat-seeker, able to lock on to and track the heat radiated from any part of a target aircraft, front or rear.

With his last missile away, he broke to the left; at the same moment, his first Sidewinder arrowed up the starboard engine exhaust of the Badger and detonated.

Ten pounds of high explosive did not make that big of a

117

bang. There was a puff of white smoke and a scattering of debris, but the Badger continued to fly, still turning gently away from the center of the American fleet.

Coyote, meanwhile, dove for the deck, forcing the two Flagons to break their climb in order to maintain their radar lock.

Standard operating procedure for the Su-21 was to fit it out with two AA-3 "Anab" missiles, loading a heat-seeking version on the port side, a SARH-guided version to starboard. By ripple-firing the two, the pilot better than doubled his chances of a kill. The Sukhoi also carried several smaller AA-8 "Aphids," highly maneuverable dogfighting missiles for close-in work.

At a range of about a mile now, Coyote decided, the Flagons would probably try to take him with Aphids. By going onto the deck and coming up underneath or behind them, he would keep them from getting a solid lock.

"Warning tone!" Cat yelled. "He's going for a fox one!"

Damn! They'd opted for a radar lock rather than infrared . . . or else they were going to try to nail them with both.

"Hang on to your lunch!" he warned Cat, and he kicked in the afterburners.

Their second Sidewinder slammed into one of the Flagons; from Coyote's viewpoint, it looked as though the nine-foot missile had smashed straight through the Sukhoi's cockpit and detonated in a shattering cascade of glittering fragments. At almost the same moment, first one, then another missile blasted clear of the second Sukhoi, tracking on the hurtling Tomcat.

The Badger had been circling to the left during those past few seconds, smoke streaming from its damaged starboard engine. Coyote had been cutting to the left as well and was now dropping toward the Badger on a collision course.

There'd been no conscious planning on Coyote's part, only the instinctive and near-instantaneous reactions of a Top Gun–trained aviator in combat. As the two Anab air-to-air missiles circled around toward the fleeing F-14, Coyote slammed the Tomcat past the Badger so close he felt the airframe shuddering as it carved through the bomber's slipstream. For a split second, he could look up and to the right, seeing every detail of the Tu-16—the greenhouse-type canopies over cockpit and nose, the deadly probe of a 23mm cannon extending from the starboard side of its fuselage forward, the back-swept wings each tagged by a bright, red star. Almost, he imagined, he could see the startled faces of its pilot and crew.

Then he was beneath the Tupolev and past it, still shrieking toward the sea. The Badger was firing at him with its twin 23mm tail guns—he could see them twinkling—but without effect.

A moment later, the bomber exploded in a ball of flame.

"My God!" Cat said, and there was something like awe in her voice. "You . . . you suckered that SARH into the Badger!"

Coyote twisted in his seat, looking back over his right shoulder. The Badger was falling toward the sea, its fuselage a mass of flame that was picked up and reflected by the water as a brilliant orange glow. Fire and glow rushed to meet one another.

"If the Flagon had a radar lock on us," he said, "we broke it by slipping into the Badger's shadow. The SARH lock transferred to the Badger and the Flagon driver didn't have a chance to break it . . . or else he didn't realize he'd started tracking the Badger."

"You make it sound like you didn't know what was going to happen," Cat said. "But *I* know better! That was sheer genius!"

"Coyote, this is Mustang!" a voice called over his headset. "Did you see that Flagon score an own goal?"

"Rog," Coyote replied.

"Looks like that last Flagon's called it quits. He's running."

"What about those cruise missiles?" Cat asked.

"Nothing we can do about them now. That'll be *Shiloh*'s headache."

"Coyote, this is Mustang. Listen, Skipper, I'm down to fumes. Let's head for the farm. I think we're gonna need to find a Texaco before we start hunting for the *Jeff*."

"I'm with you, pal. Let's do it!" The two Tomcats vectored back toward the fleet.

0730 hours
Off North Cape

The battle group's cruisers, destroyers, and frigates had but a single purpose in life: to protect the CBG's carrier. To accomplish this, the surrounding area was divided into three distinct defensive zones.

The outermost zone, between one hundred and three hundred miles from the carrier, was patrolled by the air wing's interceptors—F-14 Tomcats and F/A-18 Hornets—which with their look-down, shoot-down radar capability could take on any target from a Backfire bomber to a sea-skimming cruise missile. The middle zone, from ten to one hundred miles out, was covered by the frigates and destroyers, firing Standard missiles designed to lock on to incoming cruise missiles and take them down. The inner zone, out to ten miles from the carrier, was protected by surface ships firing both Standard missiles and short-ranged RIM-7 Sea Sparrows.

Of course, with so many aircraft and missiles in the sky all at once, confusion—even deadly mistakes—was always possible. Key to handling so many ships scattered across so much empty water was the Aegis cruiser and its remarkable SPY-1 radar.

0732 hours
Combat Information Center
U.S.S. Shiloh

Admiral Tarrant sat in the Aegis cruiser's Combat Information Center, surrounded by the subdued green glow of a dozen large radar screens and electronic displays. From his post at one of four huge multi-colored consoles, the unfolding course of the battle could be followed on those screens, which separated sea from land and pinpointed both the IFF-tagged blips of friendly ships and aircraft and the far larger number of approaching hostiles. The SPY-1 radar had a reach of 250 miles, nearly to the limit of the carrier group's defensive patrol range, but it could also take data fed through an electronic data link from

E-2Cs or other far-ranging eyes of the fleet, extending its personal space even farther, tracking everything on and over the sea. The system was called *Aegis* after the magical shield of Zeus in Greek mythology.

At the reductions necessary to compress so much data onto a single screen, however, detail was lost . . . with potentially deadly results. Usually, the Battle Group Commander's screens were set to show ranges of either thirty-two or sixty-four miles from the cruiser. For the moment, Tarrant had set his primary display for 128 miles, a necessary compromise between accuracy and what Tarrant liked to call "the big picture." The Battle of North Cape was sprawling across thousands of squares miles now. Several enemy bombers had penetrated to within eighty miles before releasing their deadly cargoes. Most, fortunately, had launched much farther out. The farther away from the carrier group a missile could be killed, the better.

As Tarrant and his battle staff watched the incoming missiles, they spoke in low, measured tones to communications and weapons officers over their radio headsets, identifying missiles and assigning them to specific ships. With so many shooters and targets, there was a real danger that in the confusion of battle, ships might gang up on some targets with more firepower than was necessary to destroy them . . . but allow other targets to pass through the CBG's perimeter unchallenged. *Battle management,* it was called, but Tarrant was terribly afraid that no one human could keep track of all of the variables, all of the moving graphic symbols on those screens, and do more than nudge the unmanageable conflict along in one stumbling direction or another.

"Tally Six, Hotspur King," Tarrant said. "Designating Alpha Sierra Five-three at one-one-eight. He's yours."

"Hotspur King, Tally Six, roger that. Alpha Sierra Five-three at one-one-eight. Range six-three miles. Confirm lock-on. Firing number one."

A new blip appeared, separating from the radar return marking the *Leslie* and closing silently with a fast-traveling blip just crossing the one-hundred-mile mark. Moments later, the two blips merged, grew fuzzy, then faded from view. A Standard missile had just killed a Kingfish.

There were no cheers, however, no celebration, though he thought he heard a ragged cheer transmitted from the CIC aboard the *Leslie*, hastily cut short. Tarrant and the battle staff were already detailing another missile to another ship, and there was no time for anything but curtly worded orders and equally curt message repeats and acknowledgments.

0735 hours
Off North Cape

Tomcats and Hornets, interceptors still deploying from both carriers toward the front line of battle, ate away at the cruise-missile threat by locking on to them one by one with their look-down, shoot-down radars, then tagging them with AMRAAMs or Sparrows. Cruise missiles that closed to within one hundred miles of Carrier Group 14's center began to take fire from the frigates posted in *Jefferson*'s outer defensive zone. Normally spread across thirty thousand square miles or more, the CBG's escorting surface ships had redeployed along the "threat axis" before combat, concentrating the group's defensive fire between the carrier and the approaching ship-killers. One after another, shipboard radars locked on, missile mounts pivoted, elevated, then loosed their deadly warloads in billowing contrails lancing into the sky. Explosions detonated across the sea, some direct hits, others near-misses that sprayed thin skins and delicate electronics with white-hot shards of shrapnel. In minutes, the number of incoming cruise missiles was reduced to seventy-six . . . then sixty-four . . . then thirty-eight. Circling Hawkeye E-2Cs tracked the survivors, plotted their courses, and vectored in additional Tomcats and Hornets to add to the mid-zone defense.

The surviving missiles kept coming.

0738 hours
Combat Information Center
U.S.S. *Thomas Jefferson*

Jefferson's CIC was similar to the combat center aboard the *Shiloh*, but far less elaborate. The carrier's several radar systems—SPS-49 air search, SPS-64 surface search, SPS-65 threat detection, and the fire-control systems for her missiles and Phalanx CIWS—had a much shorter range than the SPY-1, adequate for tracking ships and aircraft throughout *Jefferson*'s area under most circumstances, but insufficient to deal with the complex threat of a massed Russian air assault. That, after all, was why the Navy had Aegis cruisers.

Tombstone was in CIC, watching the computer displays, listening to the chatter of his aviators as they continued to press the oncoming mass of Soviet bombers and their fighter escorts. A dozen separate dogfights had broken out so far. Tomcats such as those flying BARCAP, after they expended their loads of AIM-54s, still had Sidewinder and AMRAAM missiles and were closing eagerly on the Russian formations. The F-14s that had gone aloft with a warload of six Phoenix missiles had only their guns to fall back on in a dogfight and were vectored out of the fray by the all-seeing Hawkeyes, but the F/A-18 Hornets moved in close to cover their withdrawal.

As far as he could see from here, the battle was quickly degenerating into blind, random chaos.

And Tombstone could do nothing to help. *Jefferson*'s CIC was "off the air," her radio and primary communications networks shut down to avoid detection and tracking by radar-seeking missiles. The data displayed on the combat center's screens were being transmitted via data link from the *Shiloh* and from the orbiting Hawkeyes.

All he could do was stand in the eerie semidarkness, watching this clash between anonymous points of light that had all the ferocity and blood-lust of a video game. It was difficult to attach faces and names to the voices he heard relayed over the room's speakers.

"*Rodeo Eight, Rodeo One. Come left three-five and goose it!*"

"*Ah, roger, roger. We've got Alpha Sierra Two-one in our sights. Goin' for fox one.*"

"*Easy . . . almost on him. Lock! Fox one!*"

"*Echo Tango, Rodeo Eight. Splash Alpha Sierra Two-one . . .*"

"*Shit-fire, what was that?*"

"*MiGs! MiGs! We got four . . . no, five MiGs, coming down fast!*"

"*This is Echo Tango Seven-six one. Repeat last and identify.*"

"Echo Tango, this is King Three! We just got buzzed by a wing of MiG-29s. That's MiG Two-niner. Goin' to burner!"

"Yah, we're turnin' and burnin'!"

"Rock and roll!"

Tombstone turned to the CIC officer at his side, a young, black commander named Frazier. "Who're 'King' and 'Rodeo'?" he asked.

The officer glanced up at a plastic board where a petty officer was marking up additions to the order of battle.

"King'd be VF-142, CAG," he said. "Rodeo is VF-143. The Ghostriders and the Pukin' Dogs, off the *Ike*."

Carrier battle force. Combining *Jefferson's* fighter squadrons with the squadrons off the *Eisenhower* gave the American task force a fighting chance. Tombstone moved to one of the big repeater screens, showing the location of each CBG element, ships and aircraft, identified by circling Hawkeyes and compiled and transmitted from the *Shiloh*.

Several of CBG-7's outer defensive zone pickets were already showing on the board, 150 miles north of *Jefferson's* position, the frigates *Blakely, John C. Pauly,* and *Simpson*, and the Arleigh Burke–class destroyer *David D. Porter*. All four ships had already added their Standard missile firepower to the battle and were knocking down incoming Russian cruise missiles as fast as they appeared on the screen.

As he kept listening to the bursts of radio communication between the men and women in the fighters, however, Tombstone knew that the real brunt of the fighting was being borne not by the CICs of the surface ships involved, but by the aviators. As minute dragged after minute, the Tomcats and Hornets from both CBGs continued to claw at the neo-Soviet aircraft formations pressing in across *Jefferson's* eastern combat perimeter. One wave had largely been wiped out of the sky by the long-range AIM-54Cs; there'd been a brief pause, but now a second wave had appeared, and the Hawkeye radar pickets indicated that still more aircraft were beginning to appear in the skies above the Kola Peninsula air bases.

Sooner or later, the repeated Russian assaults, crashing like storm-driven waves across the CBF's slender defenses, would break through.

When that happened, the water would come crashing

through the breach, and there would be nothing left with which to stop it.

0740 hours
Tomcat 105
Over the Barents Sea

"Low Down!" Bouncer cried in his ear. "Watch it! We got two dropping in from our five o'clock!"

Lieutenant James Stanley Lowe, call sign "Low Down," was a new arrival aboard the *Jefferson*. A member of the carrier's other Tomcat squadron, the VF-97 War Eagles, he'd come aboard during *Jefferson*'s refit at Norfolk some two months before, having flown before that with a reserve squadron at Oceana.

He'd brought his RIO with him, Lieutenant j.g. Beth Harper. After she'd thrown an abusive drunk out the door of a squadron watering hole in Norfolk, everyone had called her Bouncer.

They worked well together, and he'd enjoyed the notoriety of being one of the first in his reserve group to team with a female NFO.

Glancing back over his shoulder, he spotted the slim, nose-on silhouettes of the MiGs following the Tomcat into a long right turn. Damn . . . a pair of MiG-29 Fulcrums, flying welded-wing. They were still perhaps a mile off. He pulled the stick farther to the right, tightening his turn.

"Keep . . . watching . . . 'em . . ." he called back, battling the increasing G-forces of the turn.

This was bad. Fulcrums were hot . . . as fast and as maneuverable as the F-15 Eagle they'd been designed to combat, and in some ways better. Worse, Lowe and Harper had launched with a warload of six Phoenix missiles. They'd expended them all at long-range targets and been on their way back to the *Jeff* to rearm when these jokers had slipped through the perimeter and jumped them.

Trading altitude for speed, Low Down straightened out of the turn to starboard; the two MiGs, still flying in tight side-by-side formation, punched across his flight path a good mile to the rear. With twin stabilizers and large underslung intakes, they looked a lot like U.S. Air Force Eagles.

"They're turning," Bouncer told him. "They're coming right and following us down!"

He'd lost sight of them behind the aircraft. "Are they still turning?"

"Yeah! Still coming! Turning our way!"

Lowe went into a reverse turn to the left that made the Tomcat shudder in protest. He'd practiced this stunt a lot, had even pulled it once on a couple of F-15s during Navy–Air Force "Red Flag" maneuvers. Standing on his port-side wing, he watched sea and sky wheel past his canopy until the two tiny, distant shapes swung past his left shoulder and dropped behind his HUD. One of the MiGs had turned smartly and was coming down Lowe's path virtually in his footsteps, too close and too far to the right for Lowe to engage. The other had had trouble with the hard left turn and drifted away from his wingman. As he pulled out of his turn, he was a mile beyond his companion and almost directly in the center of Lowe's HUD.

This would be the time for a heat-seeker shot, but he didn't have any. "Going to guns!" he called, and he flipped the selector. His HUD showed the drifting circle of his aiming reticle, as well as the rectangle marking the target. Just beneath the vertical airspeed indicator on the left side of his HUD was a discrete reading ARM 675, showing his gun ready, with a full load of 675 rounds of 20mm ammo. Pulling up slightly, he dragged the reticle across the rectangle, squeezing the trigger when the one encompassed the other.

The F-14 mounted the M61A1 Vulcan, a six-barreled, high-speed cannon recessed into the left side of the fuselage, just below the cockpit. That gun screamed now, hurling 20mm shells toward the MiG as it angled toward him almost nose-on.

The other MiG flashed past him on the left. He ignored it and kept holding down the trigger. Firing six thousand rounds per minute, the Vulcan would eat 675 rounds in less than seven seconds. He held the trigger down for two full seconds, watching the flicker of yellow tracers as they whipped off his Tomcat's nose, then slowed in accordance with the laws of perspective, floating, nearly stopping as they converged on the MiG. He imagined he saw debris breaking off the target but couldn't be sure.

Yes! The MiG was trailing smoke. There was a puff of

smoke, and something separated from the aircraft, now less than half a mile away. The Russian pilot had just ejected.

Bringing his stick back to the right and kicking his rudder over, Low Down rolled to starboard, cutting away from the oncoming aircraft. Burning now, it held its long, straight descent toward the sea.

"Splash one Fulcrum!" he called over the tactical channel.

"Low Down!" Bouncer warned. "The other MiG's reversed. He's coming in on our five again!"

Twisting in his seat, he picked up the enemy aircraft over his right shoulder. *Damn*, this guy was good! His wingman must have been a rookie to let himself get pulled out of formation like that, but this man was matching Lowe turn for turn, and then some, getting full value out of the Fulcrum's superior turning and maneuverability.

While he was looking at the MiG, he saw a yellow spark ignite beneath its wing. Missile! With no radar warning, it would be an IR homer, probably one of the Russians' AA-8 Aphids.

"Missile launch!" Bouncer called. "Incoming!"

"Flares!" he snapped. He rolled hard to the right, turning into the attacker, hoping to break inside the missile's turn radius. He could already tell, though, that he was too late.

Next choice. He throttled back, way back, pulling the Tomcat's engines nearly to idle. More hot-burning magnesium flares scattered into the sky behind his aircraft. With the engine throttled back, the IR homer might choose the flares instead of his exhaust.

A second missile was in the air now, and the first was hurtling toward his six with appalling speed. He let the F-14's nose fall way off. The ocean spun across the front of his canopy, filling his view forward in a spinning blur of ultramarine . . .

The first missile slammed into his starboard engine and exploded, sending white-hot fragments ripping through avionics, combustion chambers, turbine blades, and fuel tanks. In that same instant, Low Down knew that the aircraft was doomed. He could feel the plane tearing itself to pieces around him.

"Punch out, Bouncer!" he yelled. "Eject! Eject!"

He grabbed his own red-and-white-striped ejection ring and

pulled, hard. The canopy exploded away from the falling aircraft, and a second later, an angry giant slammed his boot into the base of Lowe's spine, flinging him clear of the Tomcat in a shrieking cacophony of wind and rocket motor.

For a few seconds, Low Down was suspended in blissful silence. He saw his Tomcat—what was left of it, anyway— disintegrating into flaming, tumbling fragments as it dropped toward the sea.

And then his chute opened, jerking him upright with a jolt that nearly knocked the breath from his lungs. Reflexively grabbing the chute's risers, he dangled there, surveying his surroundings.

Low Down was alone in a wide, open sky. He couldn't see the MiG that had killed him, though the snarled white contrails of other aircraft and missiles in the distance gave the skyscape a strange, surreal look. Twisting in his harness, he tried to spot Bouncer. Had she gotten clear?

He couldn't see her chute anywhere. Minutes later, he plunged into the frigid waters of the Barents Sea.

CHAPTER 12
Friday, 13 March

"We've just lost Low Down and Bouncer," the CIC officer said. "They've routed an SH-3 for search and rescue."

"It'll have to be quick," Tombstone replied. "That water's damned cold."

He felt numb. He'd heard Lowe's exultant cry of "Splash one Fulcrum" over the tactical channel and hoped the kid might be able to shake the second MiG. Obviously, the Fulcrum had stuck with him.

This, Tombstone thought, was what had been bothering him a few days before, now made diamond hard. Lowe's RIO, Beth Harper, was the first of Jefferson's female aviators to get shot down in combat. Had she survived? *Could* she survive, given that even in her survival suit and with her life raft she would live only minutes in the cold Arctic water?

And yet, Tombstone surprised himself with the agility with which his mind shifted to other things, more pressing things. The rest of the fighters from *Jefferson* and the *Eisenhower* continued in their one-sided struggle against superior numbers . . . and the Russian missiles were starting to leak through the middle defensive zone. There was an exclamation from several sailors at one of the consoles. *Blakely*, one of the *Ike* battle group's frigates, had just taken a missile amidships, a big one. Reports were coming in that the FFG was already heeling far over to port, furiously ablaze.

"I think the Russkis are trying to flank us," Frazier said. "We're having more leakers coming around from the northeast. God *damn!*"

The CICO's exclamation was in response to another report. A radar-homing missile had just struck the *Gettysburg,* the *Eisenhower* group's Aegis cruiser. It would be minutes yet before a clear picture of the damage could be transmitted, longer still before it could be assessed.

"CAG?" A sailor handed a telephone to Tombstone. "CATCC."

Tombstone took the call from the carrier's air traffic control. Many of *Jefferson's* Tomcats were heading back now for rearming. He acknowledged the information and suggested that permission be secured from the *Shiloh* for air ops to go back on the air again.

Handing the receiver back to the sailor, he turned to Frazier.

"We're going to have to start taking aircraft aboard pretty quick," he said. "Wind's still from the northeast, so we won't need a course change, but we'll need to break radio silence for approach control."

"We'll be able to start recoverin' if those Russian Kingfishes don't burn our ass first." The CIC officer paused, listening to something over his headset. "Damn," he said. "*Dickinson's* playin' hero!"

At one end of the darkened CIC was a row of consoles manned by enlisted men, watched over by a chief petty officer. The consoles controlled *Jefferson's* CIWS.

"Chief Carangelo!" Frazier called. "*Dickinson's* about to pass close aboard to starboard. Make sure the starboard CIWS is on standby."

"Starboard CIWS on standby, aye, aye, sir."

"Better wait a sec on the recovery ops, CAG," he added. "We got trouble comin' in from starboard, big time, and we're gonna be kinda busy."

0745 hours
Off North Cape

Any attacker that made it through the carrier group's three tactical zones had one final barrier to hurdle: the carrier's Phalanx CIWS, or Close-In Weapons System, computer-directed Gatling guns firing depleted-uranium shells at the incredible rate of three thousand rounds per minute. With a maximum effective range of only 1,500 yards, CIWS, called "sea-whiz" by the men it protected, was definitely a last-ditch defense against any attackers that managed to penetrate to what counted for knife-fighting range in modern warfare.

The count of incoming missiles was still dwindling fast, but at the ten-mile mark, the beginning of *Jefferson*'s inner defense zone, twenty-three remained in the air, still boring in on their target with deadly, single-minded purpose. With *Jefferson*'s own radar shut off, the cruise missile threat would be scattered across a wide area, and many must be tracking the *Shiloh*. All such missiles, however, could be programmed to reach a given area through inertial guidance alone, and then begin searching with their own on-board radars for the largest target they could find.

A few of them were bound to spot the *Jefferson*.

Meanwhile, one of *Jefferson*'s escorts, the guided-missile frigate *Dickinson*, had been providing close fire support from a position nearly half a mile astern of the carrier and to starboard. Now, however, as the enemy cruise missiles closed from starboard, *Dickinson*'s skipper had ordered his ship to full speed ahead, racing up alongside the *Jefferson* in an attempt to block the incoming missiles.

0745 hours
Combat Information Center
U.S.S. *Thomas Jefferson*

Fire Control Technician Third Class Frank Pellet was scared to death.

It wasn't the battle. The drift of colored lights, the remote buzz of voices from the speakers, the chirp and warble of various consoles of data-linked electronics did not *feel* like what he had imagined combat to be. He knew there were cruise missiles out there, inbound, but that information seemed curiously second-hand, remote, even unimportant.

No, Pellet was scared because of what had happened last night.

The fact that FCT3 Pellet was homosexual had nothing to do

with his skills as a sailor. He'd been in the Navy for almost three years now, had learned his job well, and had consistently pulled in marks of 3.6, 3.8, and even 4.0 on his quarterly fitness reports.

He was under a hell of a lot of stress, though. The official ban against gays in the military had been lifted a good many years ago, but Pellet and tens of thousands of others like him continued to keep their sexual preferences hidden, or tried to, *especially* aboard ship. The *Jeff* wasn't bad as Navy ships went—not like the *Belleau Wood* or a few others he'd heard about—but in any assembly of thousands of people there were always a few who detested gays no matter what the brass or the Navy Department or the White House itself had to say.

He'd done his best to keep his secret. He'd approached none of his shipmates, never made a pass, kept his eyes to himself in the showers, and generally tried to maintain a low profile.

Of course, that meant he also hadn't made many friends. When the *Jefferson* had been laid up in Norfolk, he'd quartered aboard but gone ashore three nights out of four. Usually, he hadn't gone with his shipmates, though, because they'd often ended their drinking binges with a visit to one or another of Norfolk's whorehouses, and he found the very idea of doing *that* with some girl, well, disgusting. One memorable night, he'd been practically shanghaied into going with some of the other weapons techs and gunner's mates. Unable to get out of it, he'd ended up paying the woman to let him sit with her in the room and just . . . talk. He'd told her everything and she'd been understanding and really nice about it. Afterward, she'd even endorsed his sexual prowess in front of the guys, telling them what a stud he was and how he'd done her until she could hardly walk.

That incident should have made things safer for him, but despite what she'd said, the story that he was gay had been spreading through the carrier like wildfire. Some straight, he was pretty sure, must have followed him one night when he'd donned his civies, taken liberty, and headed into town and the Pink Slipper. That was a notorious gay bar, and his secret would sure as hell be out if he'd been seen going in there. Or maybe that whore had told the truth to one of his shipmates.

Last night, though, his secret had been blown for good, and now he was just waiting for the ax to fall.

Damn it all! He'd been so careful not to give himself away by making a pass at someone or being too friendly, but he'd not thought that being careful meant he had to stay celibate! *Jefferson*'s small gay community had a pretty closely knit organization aboard, what was still sometimes called a "daisy chain" by the straights. Its members met whenever possible and used an elaborate ritual of code phrases and passwords to screen possible new members when they came aboard. The relief, the sheer *joy* just of knowing that there were others like him in this floating city was indescribable. Harold was one of his favorites. He'd had good sex with him on a number of occasions.

Last night, though, they'd met at their usual place, in a linen storage locker down on First Deck. Pellet had taken his pants off, but the two of them hadn't been doing anything, not really, when there'd been a rattling at the compartment door . . . and then the door had flown open and a first class boatswain's mate named Arbogast had walked in on them.

It had been awful. Turning sharply, Harold had slammed Pellet across the compartment with a sudden, backhanded smash. *"You faggot!"* he'd bellowed, and then he'd advanced on Pellet like an avenging fury, fists clenched, face screwed up in hideous, black-cloud rage.

Arbogast had restrained him, telling him to settle down. Harold had claimed that Pellet had made a pass at him, which seemed pretty silly afterward. Pellet, after all, stood five-seven and weighed 148, while Harold was over six feet tall and as powerful as a body builder.

Screaming and red in the face, Harold had threatened to put him on report . . . for sexual harassment, no less. Arbogast had threatened to put them both on report for fighting. Stunned, Pellet had made his way back to his quarters, tried to sleep, and failed. If gays were no longer banned in the military, gay *behavior* was, just as it was against regs for Navy men and women to have sex with each other. He could get captain's mast . . . or a court-martial and a BCD. Damn it all, he *liked* the Navy! He didn't want to get thrown out!

But worst of all was the terrible, sick-in-the-stomach knowledge that Harold Reidel, his lover, had betrayed him.

"Pellet! Wake up, goddamn it!" Chief Carangelo was standing several feet behind him, bellowing in his ear.

"Uh . . . yeah, Chief?"

"I said CIWS to *standby*, damn it! Move your ass!"

"Yes, Chief!" His hand snapped out, grabbing the knob marked CIWS #1, twisting it hard from STBY to AUTO.

He didn't catch his mistake for another two tragic seconds.

0746 hours
Off North Cape

The Phalanx CIWS is controlled by an extraordinarily sophisticated computer, one able to read the radar returns from a target that may be approaching at better than three times the speed of sound and the radar returns from the weapon's own bullets departing at one thousand feet per second, computing gun angle, direction, and trajectory to bring the two together. A completely self-contained system, the Phalanx can operate independently of any outside control, a necessity in modern warfare since computers and high-speed weapons can appear, close, and strike before a human could react. Phalanx is capable of opening fire within two seconds of acquiring a target.

But it is also vital for humans to maintain control of their high-tech war toys—the so-called "man in the loop" so often discussed in any debate over computer-controlled weapons.

Phalanx has two operational settings. On standby, it cannot fire without a direct command from a human operator in the ship's CIC; on automatic, it is controlled entirely by its computer, tracking and firing on any radar contact in range that it perceives as a threat.

The U.S.S. *Dickinson* was an Oliver Hazard Perry–class FFG, a guided-missile frigate. Four hundred forty-five feet long, with a full-load displacement of 3,650 tons, Perry-class frigates had originally been designed as merchant escorts charged with defending America's sea lines of communication, or SLOC. After budgetary cutbacks in other shipbuilding programs, however, they'd found an uncomfortable niche as replacement destroyers, providing ASW and antiair protection for convoys, task forces, amphibious forces, and carrier battle groups. Lightly armed, lightly armored, and with only a single shaft driven by two gas turbines, Perry FFGs had struggled valiantly to fill their new budget-conscious roles. Four were currently assigned to CBG-14.

Detecting the cruise missiles coming in from the southeast on his vessel's SPS-49 air-search array, *Dickinson*'s skipper, Commander Randolph Conde, had ordered flank speed, sending the frigate lunging ahead some 1,200 yards off *Jefferson*'s starboard side. By putting *Dickinson* between the missiles and the *Jefferson*, by "standing into harm's way" in the grandest tradition of the U.S. Navy, Conde hoped both to shield his vastly larger consort from sea-skimming missiles and to add his antiair assets to the carrier's defense against any pop-up targets.

Dickinson had already begun loosing her Standard RIM-66C missiles at any targets within their range of about ninety miles and had scored several kills. When the nearest oncoming cruise missile was within twelve miles, *Dickinson*'s single Mark 75 gun, mounted amidships on the ship's superstructure, began banging away, hurling 76mm rounds at the rapidly approaching target at the rate of eighty-five per minute. Her single Phalanx CIWS, mounted aft atop her helicopter hangar, was set on standby and was ready to fire if a missile penetrated to within one mile.

As *Dickinson* passed less than eight tenths of a mile off *Jefferson*'s starboard beam, Pellet, in the carrier's CIC, accidentally switched his CIWS from standby to auto. Under computer control, the six-barreled Gatling gun slewed sharply, tracking the frigate . . . then classified it as a friendly surface vessel.

An instant later, as three more missiles penetrated the CBG's ten-mile inner defense zone, *Dickinson*'s skipper gave the order to fire the frigate's super-RBOC launchers.

Rapid-blooming off-board chaff, fired from tubes mounted on the superstructure just aft of the bridge, was packed into cylindrical cartridges. Each was four feet long and designed to arc high into the air before exploding for maximum dispersal of their radar-confusing payloads.

Dickinson's port-side launcher fired three chaff canisters toward the *Jefferson*. The carrier's number-one CIWS, mounted to starboard on the flight deck, outboard of the island and just below and abaft of the bridge, detected the chaff containers and reacted with superhuman speed . . . exactly as it had been designed to react.

The Phalanx's six barrels, spinning with a high-pitched whine, slewed to the right, then fired, the burst sounding more like the scream of a chain saw than the firing of a gun. The first few rounds missed, but the gun, still tracking cartridge and bullets, corrected the aim in a fraction of a second, tearing the chaff container in two. The CIWS then slewed left, tracking a second cylinder as it approached the *Jefferson*, firing once . . . then again.

At that moment, the mistake had been detected in *Jefferson*'s CIC, and the selector switch hastily set back to standby mode. The Phalanx abruptly fell silent with a dwindling moan . . . but the damage had already been done. *Dickinson* had been squarely in the line of fire.

A similar incident had occurred during the Gulf War, when the FFG *Jarret* accidentally fired into the battleship *Missouri*. That time, there'd been no casualties and minimal damage. This time, however, the frigate was on the receiving end of the friendly fire. Each CIWS round was a depleted-uranium penetrator two and a half times denser than steel, shrouded in a discarding nylon sabot that imparted a stabilizing spin to the projectile. Fifty of those rounds, the salvo fired by *Jefferson*'s Phalanx in just one second, smashed into *Dickinson*'s port side, slashing through her superstructure like bullets through paper.

The frigate's vital spaces were protected by anti-frag-mentation armor—six millimeters of steel over her engineering compartments, nineteen millimeters of aluminum over her magazines, and nineteen millimeters of Kevlar over her com-mand and electronics spaces—but much of the ship was virtually unarmored. Four sailors were cut down in her galley by hurtling splinters of aluminum and uranium, and another was killed in a crew's quarters' head. Six rounds penetrated the helicopter hangar aft, punching through thin aluminum and tearing into the SH-2F helicopter parked there. Avgas in the helo's tanks spewed into the compartment; fumes came in contact with severed electrical leads . . .

The explosion tore the hangar wide open, vomiting a column of orange flame and oil-black smoke boiling hundreds of feet into the air. Flames and blast killed seven more men and wounded twenty-five; *Dickinson*'s Phalanx was ripped from its mounting and hurled eighty feet aft into the sea. Wreckage spilled across the fantail helo deck as flames engulfed the aft part of the superstructure.

The U.S.S. *Dickinson* wallowed heavily as the fire began to go out of control.

0746 hours
Combat Information Center
U.S.S. *Thomas Jefferson*

Jefferson's CIC fell dead silent for one stunned instant. To Tombstone, it felt as though someone had thrown a switch, cutting every sound in the compartment. The chief at the CIWS console broke the spell an instant after he'd snapped the Phalanx selector back to standby.

"Pellet!" he barked. "You're relieved! Get the hell out of there!"

"Chief, I—"

"Out, mister! You're confined to quarters until further notice! Newell! Get in there! You have CIWS One!"

"*Dickinson*'s falling off abeam," Frazier snapped, staring at a television monitor that showed the burning frigate. "Let's get on those missiles!"

The FFG's missile launcher and main gun had both stopped firing when the helicopter hangar exploded. As *Dickinson* dropped astern, *Jefferson*'s starboard-side defenses opened up with renewed fury. Sea Sparrow missiles burst from their boxy eight-tube mounts in clouds of smoke and sprayed shards of plastic packing material. One after another, the Sea Sparrows arced low across the water, homing on incoming cruise missiles as they passed the ten-mile mark. Moments later, a bright blue flash lit the eastern horizon . . . then another.

Several men in *Jefferson*'s CIC cheered, but discipline returned almost at once. On the main screen display repeated from *Shiloh*, eleven missiles had crossed the ten-mile point. Even here, deep in *Jefferson*'s CIC, the thud-*whoosh* of Sea Sparrows sprinting toward the horizon could be felt as a faint trembling in the deck, transmitted through the carrier's hull.

Watching the gathering force of the avalanche, Tombstone found he was holding his breath.

CHAPTER 13
Friday, 13 March

Two AS-6 Kingfish missiles streaked low across the water toward *Jefferson*'s forward quarter. The carrier's number-one CIWS, released by the man in CIC, tracked on the nearer Kingfish and opened fire, sending a brief burst, correcting the angle of fire, then firing again. Nine hundred yards off *Jefferson*'s starboard quarter, the missile's one-ton warhead detonated with a savage bang that scattered glittering metallic fragments across three thousand square feet of sea, lashing the water to white frenzy.

The second missile flashed across the intervening space in an instant; the CIWS slewed to meet it, fired, and uranium penetraters slashed into its body. Liquid fuel burst into flame, and the missile, tumbling now and furiously ablaze, hurtled low across *Jefferson*'s flight deck, scant yards above a row of A-6 Intruders parked with wings folded along the starboard side. Deck personnel engaged in launching a Hornet and a KA-6D tanker off the bow catapults dropped flat; for one agonized moment, it appeared that the burning wreckage was going to slam into the tanker loaded with over 21,000 pounds of jet fuel.

Then the burning Kingfish had passed, hurtling into the sea off *Jefferson*'s port beam, striking the water with a thunderous detonation that sent a geysering white pillar hundreds of feet into the air, lashing the flight deck with spray.

Flight deck operations continued without letup. Minutes later, the fully laden tanker slammed off *Jefferson*'s catapult,

climbing aloft to rendezvous with those of the carrier's
Tomcats that were returning now low on fuel. Meanwhile, with
the immediate threat from enemy missiles ended, the carrier's
air traffic control center went back on the air.

0752 hours
Tomcat 201
Over the Barents Sea

"*Dickinson*'s been hit," Cat reported over the Tomcat's ICS.
"Sounds like she's got a fire on her helo deck."

"Too damned many Russian leakers," Coyote replied. Glancing out his canopy to his left, he saw a black smudge against
the horizon and knew with cold certainty it marked a burning
ship.

"Coyote, our fuel state's getting critical."

"Affirmative, Cat. I see it. Give me the latest vector on our
Texaco."

"Come right three-five degrees. Another twenty miles."

"Sounds good."

Throughout the battle, *Jefferson* had kept at least one KA-6D
tanker orbiting north and astern of the carrier, available for
returning aircraft that might need some extra fuel for the
inevitable loiter time in the Marshall Stack before recovering
on the flight deck. Popularly called a "Texaco" by naval fliers,
the aircraft was a modified A-6 Intruder, fitted with five-
hundred-gallon drop tanks and with some of its avionics pulled
from the after fuselage to accommodate the refueling reel.

Minutes later, Coyote was slipping the F-14 in behind the
tanker, holding back for a moment while a Hornet already
hooked up to the refueling basket drank its fill. Then the Hornet
detached from the KA-6D and dropped out of the way, and
Coyote eased in closer. Flicking a switch on his console
extended the Tomcat's refueling probe from a compartment just
below and to the right of the cockpit. Ahead, his target dangled
in midair, a metal-woven basket suspended on the end of a
fifty-foot hose extruded from a protrusion beneath the tanker's
tail.

"Gold Eagle Two-oh-one, Tango-Romeo One-two" sounded

over his headset, a man's voice. "What can we fix you up with today?"

"Tango-Romeo One-two, Eagle Two-oh-one," Coyote replied. "Set us up, barkeep. We're running on fumes."

"Approach looking good, Two-oh-one. Come and take us, guys. Our legs are spread in a proper military fashion, and we're ready for some good ol' I&I."

The almost blatantly phallic imagery of an aircraft's fuel probe attempting to penetrate and lock into the tanker's basket had inevitably given rise to numerous lines of standard dialogue traded between pilots and tanker crewmen, ranging from the mildly ribald to the sexually explicit. I&I was a graphic replacement for the military's R&R, standing for "Intercourse and Intoxication."

"Ah, roger that, Tango-Romeo," Coyote said. "Here we come."

He felt mildly embarrassed. Until that moment, he'd actually forgotten that the officer in his back seat was a woman. The KA-6D operator's coarse banter had managed to remind him. He didn't know Cat that well yet, and he wondered what she thought of this.

Both aircraft, now separated by scant yards, were traveling at better than 370 knots. Creeping in now, with a closing rate of a foot per second, Coyote was attempting to slip the thread of his Tomcat's fuel probe into the eye of the tanker's basket. Since he needed to concentrate on his instrumentation, the looming presence of the tanker's tail just above and ahead of his cockpit, and his flying, he could not keep watching the relative positions of fuel probe and drogue basket only a few feet beyond the plastic of his canopy. That was his RIO's job, and Cat called second-to-second course adjustments to him over the ICS with clarity and precision.

"Come right one foot," she said. "That's good. You're four feet from contact, and a little low. Come up . . . more . . . more . . . that's it. Hold that. Forward now, easy . . . three feet . . . two . . ."

Coyote was battling the tanker's slipstream now, with no room for error. The drogue basket jittered ominously in the airflow just beyond the tip of the probe. He eased forward a bit more . . .

"Contact," the tanker crewman called, and Coyote felt the

thump of a solid connection, followed by a small jolt as locking catches snapped home.

"Ready to receive," Coyote said.

"Ohh . . . that feels *soooo* good, Two-oh-one."

"Tango-Romeo, be advised there's a lady aboard."

"Ah, copy that, Two-oh-one. Capture confirmed. Whatcha want?"

"Make it a thousand pounds of high-test," Coyote replied, trying to keep his voice light. "Check the oil, clean the windshield, and put it on my Visa."

"Here it comes."

For several moments there was silence, as the tanker transferred a thousand pounds of fuel to Coyote's tanks. Then: "That's a thousand, Two-oh-one."

"Roger, Tango-Romeo. Ready to disengage to starboard." He snapped the switches that closed off the probe.

"Clear to starboard."

"That was so very, *very* good for us," Cat said suddenly, breaking in on the frequency in a sultry, sexy voice that Coyote had never heard her use before. "Was it good for you too?"

There was a momentary silence from the tanker, a stunned silence, Coyote thought.

"Uh, roger, Two-oh-one," they replied finally. "Why don't you come on up and see us again some time?"

Coyote backed clear of the refueling drogue, then let the Tomcat slide gently to the right until it was out from beneath the tanker's tail.

"Coyote," Cat said over the ICS. "I'm a big girl. I *can* take care of myself."

"You certainly can, Cat. I stand corrected. Now, how about finding us a bird farm before we have to go through that again."

"You got it, Boss. Come right to one-nine-five. They've put CATCC back on the air now, so I guess the welcome mat is out."

Coyote could already see the *Jefferson* on the horizon, close alongside that smudge of fuzzy black. He began to line the Tomcat up for insertion into the carrier's Marshall Stack.

He noticed that the radio traffic between aircraft groups had died down quite a bit. It sounded as though the worst of the fighting might be over.

Batman and Malibu were already in the Marshall Stack, waiting for their turn to head back in for recovery. After launching, they'd taken up a reserve position south of the *Jefferson* for several minutes, then been vectored by a Hawk-eye to a forward area from which they'd launched their six Phoenix missiles, one after another. After that, with all missiles expended and with plenty of fuel remaining, they'd been routed back to the carrier's Marshall Stack.

"I'm not sure I care for this modern warfare stuff," Batman told Striker, who'd been flying as his wingman in Tomcat 211. "Up, fire, and down again. Whatever happened to the knights of the sky, jousting in mortal one-on-one combat?"

"Roger that," Striker replied. "This push-button crap is for the birds."

"How about that, Pogie?" Brewer Conway's voice broke in over the channel. "Pogie" was Conway's RIO, Rose Damiano. "Sounds to me like the poor dears can't handle high-tech mayhem."

"Ah, you know how it is, Brewer," Pogie's voice replied. "They prefer to wade in with a club the old-fashioned way, mano-a-mano."

"What have we here?" Batman replied. "Kibitzing from the nuggets? Definitely contra-regs. How many kills did you girls rack up today?"

"We girls did just fine, Batman," Brewer said. "Five for six, and another probable. How about you?"

"Six up, six down. Hardly fair, though. The poor bastards never knew what hit 'em."

"Actually," Malibu interrupted, "we're only being credited with four kills. Two of our shots couldn't be confirmed."

"Hey, Malibu, whose side are you on anyway?" Batman said, sounding hurt.

"All in the interests of fair play and honesty in advertising, dude."

"I make it five to four then," Brewer said. "You guys buy the beer."

"This engagement isn't over yet, Brewer," Batman replied. "We'll see who buys the beer when it's over, right?"

"You got yourself a bet, XO. Only let's make it interesting . . . beer *and* dinner next time we're in port. Your crew against mine. Deal?"

"Hey, they're going big-time on us, Batman. I don't know if we can afford this."

"Ah, show some backbone, Malibu. We can't let these women think they've got us where we want 'em, right?"

"Two-oh-two," another voice cut in. "Home Plate. Charlie now."

"They're playing our song," Malibu said.

"Roger. See you back at the farm, Brewer."

He banked into his approach to the carrier.

0830 hours
Off the Kola Inlet
U.S.S. *Galveston*

The Los Angeles submarine *Galveston* continued to make her stealthy way along the muddy bottom at the mouth of the Kola Inlet. Since her first encounter with a Riga-class sub-hunter early that morning, four more surface ships had exited into the Barents Sea, each time pinging loudly with active sonar. *Galveston*, apparently, had not been spotted. Unlike their World War II predecessors, modern submarines cannot rest on the bottom, but *Galveston* was creeping just above the muddy and uneven surface that tended to confuse the echoes reflected back toward the listening warships.

She was further helped by a strong inversion layer that tended to trap sonar waves in a deep channel and carry them away from the skimmer hydrophones. The cities of Murmansk and Severomorsk poured quantities of industrial waste, cooling water from nuclear reactors, and raw sewage unimaginable in any Western country directly into the waters of the Tuloma River; this made the upper water layers much warmer than in the deep of the central shipping channel, creating a sharp-boundaried thermocline beneath which *Galveston* lurked. The situation was further aided by the huge quantities of organic and inorganic waste particles collecting along the boundary layer. Sound waves passed through from the surface, but they became trapped in the deep channel, unable to echo back to the surface and reveal *Galveston*'s presence.

At least, that was Sonarman First Class Rudi Ekhart's theory. When he'd told Commander Montgomery his idea, the skipper had laughed and said, "So you're saying we're hiding under a layer of Russian shit?"

An inelegant way of putting it, but essentially true. Soon after that, Montgomery had taken *Galveston* even deeper into the inlet's mouth, taking advantage of this man-made sonar blind.

Safe, perhaps, from surface sonar, the U.S. attack sub was still running a fearful risk penetrating so far into Russian territorial waters. The seabed here was littered with hydrophones and compact undersea listening devices, not to mention encapsulated torpedoes set to fire at an electronic command from naval listening posts ashore. The slightest mistake—a wrench dropped on the deck in engineering, a piece of gear adrift in a berthing compartment, or a loose pan in the galley—would give away their presence to the listening Russians, calling down upon the American submarine a fusillade of deadly mine and torpedo fire. Every man aboard wore rubber shoes or went barefoot; the official order was "silence in the boat."

Rudi Ekhart remained at his post in *Galveston*'s sonar compartment, a long, narrow room where several sonar operators sat side by side, heads embraced in padded earphones, their eyes on the cascades of flowing light on their displays where sound was made visible. There, the silence was dragging out in an ongoing and unendurable test of skill and will. Through his headphones, he could hear the susurration of the river's current flowing past *Galveston*'s hull and across the uneven bottom, the far-off boom of some kind of heavy machinery, transmitted through the water. There were precious few "biologicals," the sounds made by sea life, here, for the Tuloma was dead, and in the process of poisoning the sea for scores of miles beyond the mouth of the inlet.

And he could also hear . . . something else, something very, very faint but definitely mechanical.

Ekhart was one of the best sonar technicians in the U.S. naval submarine service. Like many other sonarmen, he had a special love for classical music—especially Baroque—which he claimed sharpened the ear, and a complete disdain for rock, which could actually damage hearing. His shipmates found him distant sometimes, and a bit standoffish, and it was well known that he had a large ego.

But such character flaws could easily be overlooked, because he was very good at what he did. A Navy man for the past ten years, he would be going up for chief soon. His likeliest career option at that point would be to take a post as a sonar instructor at the Navy sub school at Groton, Connecticut.

He was also homosexual.

Rudi Ekhart was a man of strong will and strong purpose. He'd long ago decided that sex was not only a distraction aboard ship, it was a definite threat. *Especially* aboard a submarine, where a man's only privacy was the curtain he could draw to wall off his rack from the eight others stacked three-high in his tiny berthing compartment. Just getting into one of those backbreakers took a certain amount of gymnastic skill, and the headroom was so small it was all but impossible to turn over.

No, there was no room for sex aboard a submarine. Worse, because of the crowding and also because of constant occupational pressure that each man felt from the moment the boat first submerged, there was no tolerance for gays in the submarine service. Anyone in a sub crew who'd admitted openly to being homosexual would have been harassed unmercifully and might even have had some sort of "accident."

Perhaps the single saving grace there was that the victim could not fall overboard while the sub was submerged.

Those mechanical sounds were growing slowly louder. He concentrated a moment, closing his eyes, willing the sounds he was hearing to take shape in his mind. Yes . . . it was the *throb-throb-throb* of a ship's screws, two of them, turning slowly. Whatever it was was making revs for only a few knots at best.

"Control room, Sonar," he said, speaking barely above a whisper into the mike attached to his headset. All submarine ICS had been set to be barely audible at the other end. For a moment, he wondered if the skipper had heard him.

"Sonar, Captain. Whatcha got, Ekhart?"

"Definite submerged contact, Captain. Designate Sierra Nine. Sounds like something big coming out of the barns."

"Submerged, you said?"

"Yessir."

"You got a make and model yet?"

"Wait one." Ekhart adjusted the gain on his console, still listening. On the screen inches in front of his face, he was getting the peaks and troughs of low-frequency sounds now. That thumping just behind the beat of the screws had to be a reactor pump. And there was a sharp, thuttering sound that puzzled him for several moments. Then he got it. There was some weed or a length of rope, possibly a ship's painter, trailing from the approaching vessel's deck.

He sensed a presence at his back. Captain Montgomery had stepped in behind him. "Let me hear, son." Montgomery was from south Texas, and in times of stress his accent and country mannerisms grew pronounced.

Ekhart passed Montgomery the headset, then leaned back to run the sound through *Galveston*'s library. All American submarines maintained digitized collections of sounds from a staggeringly vast number of sources, everything from fish love-calls to the running sounds of specific submarines. Often, *Galveston* herself could identify not only a given class of submarine, but a specific individual. Ekhart liked to compete with the boat's library, coming up with an ID before it did.

This time, it was a tie. "My guess is a Typhoon, Captain," he told Montgomery. "Twin screws, and big as Godzilla. Can't tell you which one."

"That's what the *Gal* says, sir," Sonarman Second Class Harrington said, checking the computer display. "Typhoon, no ident."

"This must be one of the ones we haven't heard before," Montgomery said. "Any guess on the range?"

While active sonar could give an exact range to target, the same was not true for passive listening. Still, a good sonar man could make a shrewd estimation, based on local conditions and a lot of experience.

"He's moving damned slow, Captain. Cautious like. Given the current, and the channeling effect of the sludge above us, I'd guess he's within ten or twelve miles."

"Good enough. I want you to stay on his ass, Ekhart. Stick tight like a tick on a hound dog's ear and don't let 'im go. Tell me the moment you pick up an aspect change."

"We're gonna tail him, Skipper?"

"You bet. That's what our orders say. We'll come about real nice and easy, until we're pointed out of this pocket, then wait. When Sierra Nine passes us, we'll just slip in behind him, right square in his baffles."

"What if he's heading straight for us, Captain?" Harrington asked.

"Then we try to get out of his way, son. I don't plan to ram the sumfabitch. You need any help, Ekhart?"

But Ekhart had taken back the headset and was already lost in the black, watery world beyond *Galveston*'s double hull, his eyes closed, imaging the approaching monster in his mind.

He could almost *see* her. . . .

CHAPTER 14
Friday, 13 March

Captain First Rank Anatoli Chelyag was furious. "Idiots! I can have you shot for this! I should have you shot for this, this blatant and irresponsible destruction of the State's property!"

The eight seamen standing on the *Pravda*'s mess hall deck glanced uneasily at one another, each looking as though he expected someone else to step forward and accept the blame.

"Get below!" Chelyag concluded. "I will deal with you later, when I have the time!"

The sailors filed from the mess hall, but Chelyag had the feeling he'd not made that much of an impression. While they all shared the responsibility for the accident—himself included, he was quick to admit—it was virtually impossible to make rankers accept the responsibility for their own actions. It was, Chelyag thought, one of the flaws in the Soviet system, though he knew better than to admit that to anyone less trustworthy than himself. Russian submarine crewmen were usually assigned rather than being volunteers, and they tended to be indifferent seamen. Mistakes were inevitable, especially when the men were under pressure.

But could Russia's most modern, most deadly high-tech instrument of war actually be crippled by a thirty-meter length of ten-centimeter wire rope?

The two great Typhoon ballistic-missile submarines, his own *Leninskiy Nesokrushimyy Pravda* and Captain First Rank

Dobrynin's *Slavnyy Oktyabrskaya Revolutsita*, had been lying
side by side at their subterranean moorings, ready for sea,
awaiting only the order from Admiral Karelin before proceeding with *Derzkiy Plamya*, Operation Audacious Flame. Save
for the ground-line communications link with Kandalaksha, the
cavern was cut off from the outside world. Chelyag had no way
of knowing whether or not the diversionary operation *Ognevoy*
had gone off as planned, whether or not the American carriers
had been destroyed or damaged, whether or not American
ASW aircraft or submarines might be waiting in the area off the
Kola Inlet.

Then at 0740 hours, the awaited word had come. American
and neo-Soviet aircraft were engaged over the Barents Sea off
North Cape; the Yankee carriers were on the point of being
overwhelmed by waves of Russian aircraft and missiles.

Pravda and *Revolutsita* were to leave their shelter at once,
make their way north from the Kola Inlet to their assigned
strategic bastion beneath the Arctic ice, and await final orders
via ELF communications from Kandalaksha.

The *Glorious October Revolution* had pulled away from her
moorings almost at once, the line-handling parties on her fore-
and afterdecks cheering and waving as the great submarine
slowly chugged past *Lenin's Invincible Truth*. Chelyag had
bellowed at his own line-handling parties. *"Cast off astern!
Move yourselves! Do you want the* Revolution *to show us his
ass as he leads us into the channel?"*

It was a common practice to exercise naval crews against
one another in good-natured competition, to accustom them to
working under pressure, and to instill camaraderie and team
spirit among the men. The afterdeck line-handlers had signaled
"lines clear" even as the men on the pier were still slipping the
huge loop on the stern line clear of its bollard and tossing it
toward the waiting *Pravda* sailors. One man had grabbed the
line, overbalanced, and fallen into the water between submarine and pier, dragging the stern line with him.

Unaware that his men aft were taking some strictly nonregu-
lation shortcuts with proper naval procedure, Chelyag, in
Pravda's weather cockpit high atop the sail, had ordered one
quarter ahead on both engines. *Pravda* had churned slowly
ahead, drawing away from the pier . . .

. . . and then the trailing stern line had fouled around the

Typhoon's port screw, wrapping itself tightly about the shaft. Chelyag had felt the change in the vibrations coming through the deck, a hard, unpleasant shudder like the rasp of the keel going aground . . . and then the *Pravda* was swinging toward the pier, propelled now by her starboard engine alone.

Chelyag had bellowed the order "All stop!" Too late. *Pravda* had caught the pier on her port side midway between bow and sail, the collision hard enough to make Chelyag grasp the cockpit railing. The pier had crumpled like styrofoam, splintering with the impact and sending the dockside line-handlers scattering in every direction.

That had been an hour ago, and only now had the final word come up from damage control. There was a possibility that one of the blades on the Typhoon's port screw had been bent ever so slightly out of alignment. If true, it might be enough to cause significant cavitation. Cavitation, the creation of momentary pockets of vacuum behind a turning propeller that then collapsed with a distinctive sound, was the bane of all nuclear subs, which relied on absolute silence to remain undetected by their hunters within the ocean depths.

It would take at least twenty-four hours—and more likely forty-eight—to clear the propeller shaft and check the blade alignment. If the blade was bent, it would be another several days before it could be repaired or replaced. It was God's own luck—and Chelyag said that to himself as a devout atheist—that the shaft had not been bent or the turbine's bearings burned out. Something like that could have put the Typhoon out of commission for a month, longer if the spare parts were slow in arriving.

Meanwhile, the *Revolutsita* was already on his way out of the Kola Inlet.

Chelyag was not looking forward to informing Admiral Karelin that he was still in port.

1230 hours
Flag Plot
U.S.S. *Shiloh*

Gradually, it became clear that the attack was over. At least three separate waves of Russian planes had hurled themselves against the American battle force off North Cape, a total of at least three hundred aircraft. One hundred fifty cruise missiles of various types had been launched, both from aircraft and from bases on the Kola Peninsula.

But the battle force had survived. The clear victor in the engagement had been the Americans with their AIM-54C Phoenix, coupled with the remarkable Phalanx CIWS covering the last-ditch ship defense at knife-fighting range. Tombstone was still adjusting to the idea that they'd actually come through the attack relatively unscathed.

Of course, there *had* been losses. . . .

This time, the battle ops meeting was being held aboard the *Shiloh*, which had taken over coordination for the entire carrier battle force. Coyote was back aboard the *Jefferson* and running things for the wing as Deputy CAG, freeing Tombstone to join Admiral Tarrant's planning staff. He'd flown across less than an hour before, aboard one of *Shiloh*'s two SH-60B LAMPS III ASW helos, dispatched by Tarrant especially for him. All of *Jefferson*'s helos were still engaged in SAR work—marine search and rescue for the aviators still lost somewhere at sea.

Tombstone was just wrapping up his after-action report. Tarrant, as always crisply attired in a spotless uniform, rested with one leg hitched up over a corner of the chart table, listening attentively. Nearby, another rear admiral, John H. Morrisey, the commanding officer of CBG-7 just arrived off the *Eisenhower*, leaned against a bulkhead. Bald and bulldog-ugly, he too was neatly attired, the rack of colored ribbons on his left chest gleaming in the compartment's overhead fluorescents like peacock's plumage. After a long, active morning and a crowded helicopter flight, Tombstone felt conspicuously rumpled.

"We've also begun coordinating all air ops with the *Eisenhower*," Tombstone was saying. He glanced at Admiral Morrisey, who smiled slightly and nodded. "That way, both air wings can share the grunt work. Both carrier wings are still at flight quarters. Both carriers are maintaining four aircraft on Alert Five, and four more on Alert Fifteen." An aircraft on Alert Fifteen could be put into the air in fifteen minutes. An Alert Five aircraft had the pilot suited up and strapped in, ready to launch on five minutes' notice.

"We're maintaining extra-strength CAPs, of course," Tombstone continued. "And at any given moment, we have two

EA-6B Prowlers up and running recon flights along the Russian coast, just outside their twelve-mile limit, plus at least two Hawkeyes, positioned to give us AEW deep inside the Kola Peninsula. In the last three hours, there have been no further air strikes. In fact, there's been no hostile activity from the other side at all." Tombstone glanced down at the briefing notes he'd scrawled for himself on a clipboard legal pad during his flight across to the *Shiloh*. "Combat losses. Carrier Air Wing Twenty lost seven aircraft this morning. The breakdown was four Tomcats, two Hornets, and one Prowler. Of those crews, fourteen people, eight were recovered. Four other aircraft were pretty badly shot up, but they managed to get back to the *Jeff* and trap. They've already been shoved over the side in order to clear the deck. I don't have a final report from *Eisenhower's* CAG, but a first estimate gives them combat losses of three Tomcats, one Hornet." He consulted his clipboard once more. "That's all I have at this time, sir."

"Very good, Stoney," Admiral Tarrant said. He slid off the table and looked at the other officers in the room. "Anyone have questions? Comments?"

Admiral Morrisey stirred. "Enemy aircraft losses were—what? One hundred forty, you said?"

"That's the estimate, Admiral. Most of those were knocked down by F-14 Phoenix strikes, though, and many were not confirmed."

"Still not bad . . . a kill ratio of twelve to one."

"Nine to one if you count our junkers," someone else pointed out.

"Yeah, but we don't know how many Russkis were junkers by the time they made it back to base." Morrisey looked pleased. "I'd say our boys are holding to the old Top Gun balance sheets."

During the Vietnam War, the U.S. Navy's kill ratio had averaged two or three enemy planes downed for every one of their own lost. Then the Navy Fighter Weapons School—better known as Top Gun—had opened at NAS Miramar, near San Diego. A grueling, five-week course in Air Combat Maneuvers that pitted naval aviators in realistic mock combat against *better* aviators, Top Gun had literally changed the course of the air war in Vietnam almost overnight. As soon as Top Gun graduates had begun flying combat missions—and passing on their training to their fellow aviators—the Navy's kill ratio had rocketed to thirteen to one.

"Good combat ratios are all very admirable," Tarrant said, "but they don't help us in this situation. The Russians, remember, can always ferry in more aircraft. It will be some time before we have that luxury. In other words, this command cannot afford to lose even one aircraft, not even if we trade it for fifteen of the enemy's."

"I should also point out, sir," Tombstone added, "that from now on exhaustion is going to be a factor. Some of my people have been up three times so far this morning. Most have been up twice. With the heavy patrol schedule, I expect that by dawn tomorrow every NFO I have will have been up at least four or five times, and that's going to start wearing them down fast. Same goes for the deck crews, turning around that many aircraft, round-the-clock refueling and rearming. Those guys're going to be dead on their feet soon. Exhaustion means mistakes, accidents, and downtime when equipment fouls or bits of metal get scattered across a flight deck."

"Understood," Tarrant said. "All I can tell you is that we're going to have to play this one as it's dealt to us. Other questions?"

"Yeah," a tall, gangly commander next to Tarrant said. "Why the Sam Hill'd they do it?"

"Not my department, Dan," Tombstone said with a tired smile. "I'd say the answer's more in your line of work."

The tall commander was Daniel Sykes, and he was Tarrant's chief intelligence officer. It was his responsibility to know what the Russians were doing, and why.

Sykes shook his head. "So far, we just don't have the data to go on. The Russians lost . . . call it fifty percent casualties. Plus one hundred fifty cruise missiles, not counting the ones on bombers that got clobbered before they could launch. Nearly all of them shot down or decoyed into the sea."

Only three cruise missiles had made it through the carrier group's defenses, but those three had hurt, Tombstone thought. The *Blakely* had rolled over and sunk in five minutes, taking 201 of the 205 men aboard with her. There'd simply been no time for her to lower boats, and no time for helicopters to rescue more than those four before the rest succumbed to hypothermia. In *Ike*'s battle group, besides minor damage to the

Gettysburg from an antiradar missile, the frigate *John C. Pauly* had taken a half-ton warhead from a Kingfish amidships, while in CBG-14 both the DDG *Truesdale* and the FFG *Dickinson* had been badly mauled. All three of those ships were again under way, the fires aboard under control, the wounded air-evaced to the *Jefferson*, where they were being made ready for a series of medevac flights to Narvik, then Lakenheath, and finally the States. It had been touch-and-go aboard the *Dickinson* and the *Pauly* for a while, though.

And of course, *Dickinson* hadn't been hit by a missile. Friendly fire, obviously, could be no less deadly than hostile fire.

"The point is," Sykes concluded, "that this was one hell of an expensive adventure for them. They wouldn't have started it without a damned good reason."

"Radio intercepts have been talking about a rebel group grabbing control of some of the Kola airfields," an intelligence officer with Morrisey's staff pointed out. "The word from Washington is that Moscow is claiming the attack was mounted either by Blue forces, or by mutinous Reds with anti-American feelings."

"Does anybody seriously believe that?" Tarrant asked. There were no takers, only a number of heads shaking slowly back and forth. "The Reds could be trying to discredit the Blues, of course. But I can't see that what they hoped to win in propaganda points was worth one hundred forty of their front-line aircraft."

"They gambled and they lost," Captain Maxwell, Tarrant's chief of staff suggested. "If they'd managed to sink even one of our carriers . . ."

"They came damned close to doing just that," Tarrant said. "But—"

There was a knock on the door, and a first class yeoman poked his head in. "Excuse me. Admiral Tarrant?"

"Yes."

"Two priority messages, sir, FLASH URGENT."

"Give 'em here." Tarrant took the dispatch flimsies, which had obviously just come up from *Shiloh*'s decoding shack. He scanned each briefly, then passed them around. "It's just possible, gentlemen," he said, "that we have here the reason for the Russian attack."

Tombstone read the messages when they came to him. The first was a repeat of a message from the *Galveston*, with header information indicating that it had been relayed by satellite to Washington, where it had been re-coded and transmitted to the *Shiloh*.

The body of the message was curt and to the point.

TIME: 0848 HRS, ZULU+2
TO: COCBG14
FROM: COSSN770
       PLARB TYPHOON DEPARTED KOLA INLET 0830 HRS. SSN770 IN
PURSUIT. REQUEST ORDERS, SCHED-3/ELF.
MONTGOMERY SENDS.

Routing the message through D.C. accounted for the four-hour delay in *Shiloh*'s receiving it. The Joint Chiefs, maybe even the President and his advisors, must still be mulling this one over, because the second message, from the commanding officer of the Atlantic fleet, was even more curt.

TIME: 0515 HRS, ZULU–5
TO: COCBG14
FROM: COMLANT
       STAND BY FOR FURTHER ORDERS.
HAMPTON SENDS.

In other words, take no action until you hear from Washington, or your ass is in a sling.

And they had good reason to be thinking this one over carefully. A Typhoon ballistic-missile sub had put to sea during the height of the air battle over the carrier battle force. The timing was indeed suspicious. "How was this transmitted?" Tombstone asked, holding up the message from *Galveston*. Submarines normally refrained from risking any communication that might give their positions away.

The yeoman, still standing by the door, explained that *Galveston* had extended a UHF antenna above the surface and zip-squealed the message, coded and packed into a compressed digital format that allowed it to be transmitted to a military comsat in a burst less than a hundredth of a second long. There was still the danger that the message would be picked up by

Russian eavesdroppers—or that the antenna would be tagged by their radar for the few seconds it was above the surface, but in this case the risk was acceptable.

Obviously, though, Montgomery wasn't yet aware of the air battle that morning, cut off as he was from routine communications with the outside world. All he knew was that he had a Russian PLARB by the tail, and he wanted to know what to do with it. His orders were to track them if they appeared, to destroy them if they prepared to launch. They said nothing about how long he was to maintain his covert reconnaissance. "Sched-3/ELF" referred to a timetable for *Galveston* to receive messages by extremely low-frequency radio. At 1400 hours, and every six hours after that, she would rise to within a hundred feet of the surface where she could receive ELF communications.

"Thank you, son," Tarrant told the yeoman. "You're dismissed." After the sailor had left, he turned to the planning staff again. "Well? Opinions?"

Morrisey frowned. "Possibly the Russians are just taking advantage of the confusion to get their PLARB boats clear of Polyarnyy. If there is trouble with rebel forces in the area, they'd want their boomers out of there, and fast."

"But there hasn't been, Admiral," Sykes said. "All of our intelligence indicates that Leonov's Blue forces have taken up positions in the south."

"Still, some dissidents or mutineers—"

"Would be unable to mount an attack of the sort we've witnessed this morning," Tarrant said. "My guess is that the attack was precisely to keep us busy, off balance while they slipped one or more of their boats to sea. The question is, why?"

"Nuclear attack on the United States?" someone asked. There was a deathly hush in the room after that.

"Or nuclear blackmail," another voice added. "Telling us to stay out of their fight, or they nuke New York."

"They've already attacked us," a junior staffer pointed out. "They're afraid we're going to retaliate."

"More likely, they plan to blackmail the Blues," Morrisey suggested.

"Would they fire on their own cities?" somebody asked.

"They might," Tarrant conceded. He sighed. "In any case,

this one's already been bucked up the chain. It's way too hot for us to handle at this level." He paused, looking at the others. "But while we're waiting for Washington to make up their minds, I'm going to send off a status report, and I'm going to include a strong recommendation that they give *Galveston* the order to sink that PLARB. Just in case the target *is* New York."

The meeting broke up shortly after that, with no firm planning beyond carrying out a modified version of the original orders. The carrier battle force would take up position at a point sixty miles north of the Norway-Russian border, called Bear Station, and wait. The planning staff would meet again when word one way or the other came through from Washington.

"By the way, Stoney," Tarrant said, as the others were already leaving the room. "After I make my report, I expect to be deluged with questions from the Pentagon about the Great Experiment. The Washington press corps is going to be all over their ass and ours."

"The women."

"That's right. Were any lost this morning?"

Tombstone nodded slowly. "Yes, sir. One. An F-14 RIO in VF-97. We pulled the pilot out of the drink a couple of hours ago. He's going to be all right, but he doesn't think she ejected."

"Ejection seat failure?"

"Maybe. Or she just wasn't found. We still have SAR helos out, looking for all our MIAs, of course, but in water this cold, even if she *did* make it down in one piece . . ."

"I understand. What was her name?"

"Lieutenant j.g. Elizabeth Harper."

"Okay. I'll pass that on. Thanks."

"Lieutenant Lowe told me that she performed extremely well. He asked me about recommending her for the Navy Cross."

"Hmm. We'll have to see about that. Okay, CAG. Thank you."

Aboard the helo, on his way back to the *Jefferson*, Tombstone found time to think of Harper—and the five other naval officers off the *Jefferson* who'd not been recovered. He'd not known any of them well—all had been relative newcomers to CVW-20—but they would be missed.

The mourning would come later, however, once they got through this.

If they got through it. Right now, it was not at all certain that they would.

CHAPTER 15
Saturday, 14 March

Jefferson's quarterdeck was on her starboard side forward, between the number-one and number-two elevators, a bulge extending out from the ship's hull beneath the flight deck and connecting inboard with the hangar deck. When *Jefferson* was in port, this was the carrier's "front door," with a gangway extended to the dock. VIPs and officers entered the ship here, and the space was used for some ceremonial occasions such as piping flag officers or captains aboard.

Now, the day after the Battle of North Cape, *Jefferson*'s quarterdeck was being used for a very specific ceremony, one with its roots in the age of sail, when offenders were called to give an account of themselves before the captain at the foot of the ship's mizzenmast.

Even today, long after masts had given way to screws, it was called captain's mast.

"I am getting damned sick and tired," Captain Brandt said evenly, "of the problems generated by the raging hormones aboard this ship." He looked up at the four men facing him from across the podium before him. Front and center was a young second class, a kid with thick-rimmed glasses and buck teeth that gave him the look of a skinny, frightened rabbit. "How old are you, son?"

"Twenty-one, sir," the kid replied, standing stiffly at attention and managing to look as awkward in his dress blues as a boot at the start of recruit training. He was a photographer's mate from the carrier's OP Department, a PH2 named Tom Margolis, and he looked scared.

"Old enough to know better, in other words." Brandt glanced at the men flanking Margolis. Master Chief Charles Michener, to his left, was a powerfully built tower of ugly black muscle who had been the *Jefferson*'s Master at Arms for the past six months. His badge of office, like a police officer's badge, gleamed in the overhead lights against his dress blues. Master Chief Mike Weston, on the kid's right, was just as big, just as powerfully built. Where Michener was the closest thing the supercarrier's city-in-miniature had to a chief of police, Weston was that indispensable go-between who ran interference between the enlisted men and the officers, the COB or Chief of the Boat.

Standing off to the right was a chief warrant officer, CWO2 Kimball Dupuy. As head of *Jefferson*'s OP Division, or photographic services, he was Margolis's boss. Brandt had also asked Tombstone Magruder to attend, because the charges against Margolis involved people in the air wing. Tombstone was standing behind the captain, at parade rest.

"Photographer's Mate Second Class Margolis," Brandt continued, "the charges against you are serious enough that they *could* warrant summary court-martial. I am of a mind to deal with this as a mast offense. However, it is your right to request a summary court, if you prefer, where you can either request legal representation, or have legal representation appointed for you by the court. What is your preference?"

"Uh, no, sir," Margolis said. His Adam's apple bobbed as he swallowed. "I mean, I'll go with the mast. Sir."

"Very well," Brandt said. "That's a wise decision on your part. A court-martial could award far heavier punishment than I, under the articles of the UCMJ, am allowed to give you." He paused, giving his words time to sink in. "Son, you've made a very, very bad mistake here."

Brandt turned his attention to the top of his podium. There was a slender, silver tube there, as thick as a pencil and perhaps eighteen inches long, with a complex assembly attached to one end. Next to that was a manila folder. Pulling the folder to him, he opened it up. He'd already seen the photographs earlier, but he leafed through them again now, slowly, and he could feel the kid trembling as he turned them over one by one.

The top two were contact prints, 8"x10" sheets on which strips of pictures had been pulled straight off the negatives, without enlargement, and the figures there were so tiny a magnifier would be necessary to make out the faces. Twenty-eight more photos, though, were enlargements of some of the contacts, crisp and beautifully detailed black-and-white photographs. All appeared to have been shot from the same position, inside the junior flight officers' shower head and from a high angle, probably from up close to the ceiling.

Each picture showed one or more women, all of them flight officers, all of them revealed nude or only partly dressed. One photo showed someone at the far end of the locker area—he thought it might be Lieutenant Damiano—bending over, her buttocks toward the camera as she picked her panties up off the deck. Another, at much closer range, revealed a dripping Lieutenant Commander Conway with one foot up on a bench as she toweled off her crotch, and another apparently taken moments later showed Conway pulling her panties up past her knees. There was one spectacular full frontal shot of Lieutenant Flynn as she walked toward the showers and the camera, carrying a washcloth and a bar of soap and wearing nothing but her sandals.

"Okay, Chief," he told the MAA. "You want to tell me about this?"

"Yes, sir. Last night, one of my men, Boatswain's Mate First Class Motely, was making his rounds in the enlisted berthing compartments when he noticed two men, PH2 Margolis and one other, looking at something and acting in what he considered to be a suspicious manner. As he approached, the second sailor, who could not be identified, hurried away, while Margolis attempted to hide something under his blanket at the foot of his rack.

"Upon further investigation, PH2 Margolis was found to have in his possession a manila envelope containing five black-and-white photographs, all showing various female officers aboard this ship in the nude. Obviously, the photos were taken in the junior flight officers' shower, and during times when the shower area and head were restricted to female personnel only. Margolis was placed on report and the photographs confiscated."

"I see." He looked at the Chief of the Boat. "Master Chief?"

"The MAA and myself were brought in on this last night, Captain. When we questioned Margolis, he admitted to having a number of other, similar photographs in his possession. When asked to do so, he opened his locker and turned over to us seventy-two negatives and twenty-five additional eight-by-ten photos.

"He confessed that he thought it might be fun to get what he called 'skin pics' of female officers while they were in the shower. He told me that last Thursday afternoon he entered the shower area before it was secured to male personnel, and gained access to the piping and electrical spaces above the locker room by removing an overhead insulation panel and pulling himself up, then replacing the panel behind him.

"As a photographer's mate in the carrier's OP Department, he had routine access to both necessary equipment and the developing and enlarging facilities aboard ship. He says that he processed the photographs in the ship's darkroom during his free time. Developing pictures, incidentally, is one of his regular duties." Weston reached out and picked up the pencil-slender tube on the podium. "To take the pictures without the ladies' knowledge, he used this. It's called an endoscope, and it's a special lens attachment for his 35mm camera. As you can see, it has an extremely narrow bore, allowing him to take photographs through a thumbnail-sized hole poked through an overhead panel without the subjects' knowledge."

Brandt held out his hand, accepting the endoscope from Weston. "Chief, is this thing government property?"

"No, sir. It's a surveillance device sometimes used by the police or FBI personnel ashore, but it is not illegal for other people to own them. He says he got this one from a friend in Norfolk. He was keeping it in his locker."

"I see. Go ahead."

"Margolis told me that he lay hidden in the overhead crawl space for the two hours while the shower area was secured to male personnel, watching the women and taking pictures of them. He says he shot two rolls, seventy-two shots in all, but that since then he's only had time to make these twenty-eight enlargements."

"I see." To give himself time to think, Brandt returned his attention to the photos in the folder once more. None of the shots, not even that one of Flynn, had the same erotic quality as, say, a photo spread in a typical man's magazine. All were simply hidden-camera pictures of naked or half-dressed women in a locker room, and there was nothing seductive or sexy about their expressions or their poses. Hell, Brandt had seen more exciting stuff in *Playboy*, and there were certainly plenty of copies of *that* publication already aboard.

The real excitement, he thought, and the worst aspect of the problem, was generated by the fact that these photographs were not of some anonymous pretty face and body in the pages of a magazine but were all-too identifiable images of real people, of women literally living and working right next door. Any of *Jefferson*'s men who saw Margolis's pictures would *know* that it was, say, Lieutenant Joyce Flynn that they'd seen naked . . . and that could only increase the titillation for them. Hell, every time they met her in a passageway, they'd be thinking about that damned photo.

It made this violation of the women's privacy that much worse, a kind of sneaking, nonphysical rape.

Disgusted, he closed the folder with a snap. "Do you think you got 'em all, Master Chief? Could he have made more?"

"That's all we found in his locker, Captain," Weston replied. "The negatives from two rolls of film, two contact sheets, and twenty-eight enlargements. We checked the prints against the negatives. He could've made additional prints, of course, but there are no enlargements in that stack that aren't accounted for among the negatives."

"How about it, Margolis? Are these all of the photographs? Or did you already sell some of them to your buddies?"

"Th-those are all, sir. I swear! Two rolls of thirty-six. And I wasn't gonna sell them, sir. They were just . . . just—"

"Just for the amusement of you and your 'buddies.'"

"That's right, sir."

"Did your friends put you up to this?"

Margolis looked uncomfortable. "No, sir. Not really, sir. It was all my idea."

Brandt suspected he was lying, or at least shading the truth a bit. Margolis didn't fit the profile of the typical shipboard troublemaker, and from the look of him he must have been scared to death throughout the time he was up there in the overhead. He *could* have done it all alone, but it would have helped to have someone to help boost him up into the crawl space, and to come in and tell him the coast was clear afterward.

Chances were, though, he'd never admit to having accomplices. He wouldn't want to be seen as a guy who would rat on his shipmates. Brandt doubted that it would be productive to question him further along those lines.

He tapped the folder with an ominously slow meter for emphasis. "Son, this had damn well better be all of these. If there are any more, negatives or prints, or if any of your buddies already have some of these, you tell me right now. You won't be in any worse trouble than you already are."

Margolis hesitated, then swallowed. "There aren't any more, sir."

"If I find out that there are more of these floating around this ship, I am going to smack you down so hard that when you look up, whale shit's going to look like shooting stars to you."

"I swear, sir! Really! That's all there are. Two rolls, and I didn't have time to make up any more than those prints you have right there. I gave everything to the COB when he asked me."

"Very well. What do you have to say for yourself?"

"Uh . . . no excuse, sir." The standard Navy all-purpose statement for when you were caught red-handed. Attempts to make excuses in such circumstances generally backfired.

"You sure, son? I'm not sure you realize just how much trouble you're in because of this."

"I . . . uh, sir, I mean . . . I didn't mean any harm by it, sir. Honest to God I didn't!"

Brandt looked at the officer behind Margolis. "Chief Warrant Officer Dupuy? Do you have anything to add in this man's defense?"

"Sir, PH2 Margolis has been in my department since he came aboard. He does what he's told, and he's never given me any trouble. Three-eights and four-ohs on his last fitness report. He does his work with a minimum of supervision and he does it well."

"A little *too* well in this case," Brandt said. "I'd feel better if these things weren't so damned professional-looking. If he'd just cut their heads off or overexposed them or something."

Michener coughed suddenly, and Brandt looked up. He caught a tightening of Weston's jaw, a narrowing of his eyes, and realized the COB was rigidly stifling a laugh. Same with Dupuy. He replayed what he'd just said in his mind, then groaned inwardly. Overexposed! Yeah, these women were overexposed, all right, though his pun had been completely unintentional. *Damn* it all, there were aspects of this mess that were hilarious, but it could lead to bad, bad trouble aboard his ship.

Turning slightly, he waved Tombstone closer. "What do you say, CAG? These are your people involved. Should we talk to them? Show them the pictures?"

Tombstone caught his lower lip between his teeth, then shook his head. "Hard call, Captain. But I think maybe not. It wouldn't help anything, and it might hurt morale if the women involved know about this."

"They won't feel like victims if they don't know they've been victimized, that it?"

"Something like that, Captain."

Brandt sighed, then turned back to Margolis. He picked up the folder. "Son, needless to say, I am confiscating these. MAA, you will see to it personally that these are destroyed at once."

Michener accepted the folder. "Aye, aye, sir."

Brandt picked up the endoscope. "I am also impounding your toy here. It will be locked up in the MAA's office for the duration of the cruise."

He leaned forward over the podium, facing the kid square-on. "Margolis, the men and women who serve together aboard the *Jefferson* form a community far more closely knit than any similar community ashore. Such a community works only through the establishment of certain social customs, responsibilities, and most important of all, through the mutual *trust* between the members of that community.

"By taking these photographs and by attempting to distribute them among your shipmates, you have betrayed your responsibilities as a photographer's mate in Chief Warrant Officer Dupuy's division, and you have betrayed the trust of the people serving aboard this ship with you. Let me ask you something,

Margolis. You know it's wrong to rob your shipmates, don't you?"

"Huh? I mean, yeah, sure!"

"Say 'yes, sir,' " the MAA rumbled at his side.

"Yes, sir!"

"The women aboard the *Jefferson* are our shipmates, Margolis. They deserve our respect and our consideration. By your actions, you have robbed them of their dignity and their privacy. By passing those pictures around, you make your friends thieves as well. What you have done is reprehensible. It is conduct that cannot and will not be tolerated aboard this vessel." He paused for a moment, watching Margolis. The kid's face was pinched and white, his eyes quite round behind his glasses. He was obviously terrified.

Brandt took a deep breath. "Photographer's Mate Second Class Margolis, you are reduced in rate one pay grade, to Third Class. You will be taken immediately to the ship's brig, where you will be confined on bread and water for two days. Since you seem to have an excess of time on your hands, upon your return to duty you will report to your division officer for two hours' extra duty each day for the next forty-five days. You will also, at the earliest time your duties allow, report to the Chaplain's Office, where you will enroll in Commander Ferris's next available sensitivity training session on sexual harassment. You will attend all of those classes on pain of further and harsher punishment. Do I make myself quite clear?"

"Uh, y-yes, sir." His voice was scarcely above a whisper. His eyes looked haunted.

"I didn't hear that, son. Sound off!"

"Yessir!"

"If there is a repeat of this incident, if I find out you're holding out on us regarding how many of these prints you made or distributed to your friends, I swear by God that I will bounce you in front of a summary court so fast you won't know what hit you. You'll find yourself in jail back Stateside, and after that you'll be out on the streets with a BCD. Do you think the chance to play Peeping Tom in the girls' shower is worth a bad-conduct discharge?"

"No, sir!"

"I will not tolerate voyeurs, I will not tolerate harassment of the women under my command, and I will not tolerate grown men acting like giggling, sex-crazed adolescents instead of as professionals!

"Margolis, I am not assigning harsher punishment because your record has been exemplary up until now. I also strongly suspect that some of your shipmates put you up to this. I think you've just been listening to the wrong people, and I hope this episode will teach you to be responsible for your own actions.

"At the same time, I'm making your punishment as severe as I am because it is clear that you regarded this escapade as a prank, something that could harm no one. I gave you brig time because I want you to have some time to think about that 'prank' and maybe to think about just how precious a commodity privacy can be aboard ship. Understand me?"

"Yes, sir." The voice was firmer now, though still low. The bread and water, Brandt thought, had jolted him hard, like something out of another time, another world.

The fact was, under the Uniform Code of Military Justice, Brandt could have hit him with up to three days in the brig *and* broken him by two pay grades *and* fined him half of his pay for the next two months, or given the nature of the man's offense, even recommended a summary court. Something like that would wreck the rest of the kid's Navy career.

"Very well," Brandt said at last. "Dismissed."

For a long time after they led the kid out, Brandt stared after them. The only part of the punishment he'd just meted out that he really regretted was the sensitivity counseling, but that was mandated by current Navy regulations. Back in the '70s, when the Navy's reputation had been blackened by several ugly race-related incidents, all hands had been required to attend consciousness-raising programs intended to stop prejudice and bigotry. Seminars and programs to fight sexual harassment among naval aviators had been instituted in the wake of the infamous Tailhook scandal.

Today, all officers and men were routinely put through such programs. Hell, Margolis would have gone through one in boot camp and another upon his arrival aboard the *Jefferson*. Unfortunately, Brandt had yet to meet any Navy man who admitted that he'd learned anything from such sessions, and most regarded them as a complete waste of time. Men went into them with their attitudes and prejudices already fully

formed. Increased awareness? Brandt grimaced at the thought.
Too often, what increased was their resentment against women
for the additional burden of bureaucratic micromanaging and
official harassments collectively and colloquially known as
"Mickey Mouse." In two centuries of American naval history,
the government had yet to find an effective way to legislate the
way people thought, and attempts to try always made things
worse.

"Never mind the Russians," Brandt told Tombstone. "God
save us from adolescent hormones."

"Yes, sir."

Weston returned to the quarterdeck.

"Okay, Master Chief. What's next?"

"Fire Control Technician Third Class Frank Pellet, Captain,"
the COB said, handing another folder to Brandt. "Charged by
Commander Frazier with negligence and inattention to duty."

"The *Dickinson*."

"Yes, sir." He looked like he was about to say something
more.

"Well? What else? Spit it out, Master Chief."

"Captain, it has come to my attention that FTC3 Pellet is gay,
and that there was an, um, incident the night before the battle.
It was reported to me unofficially by a first class in the MAA's
division."

Brandt closed his eyes. "*Sex* again. God damn it, sex and salt
water . . ." He stopped himself, then slapped the folder down
on the podium. "Master Chief, this one gets held over for a
court. We may have to wait until a full inquiry into the
Dickinson incident is complete. Understood?"

"Yes, sir."

"In any case, this'll be a matter for the CID. Pellet is
confined to quarters until we can get him the hell off my ship."

"Aye, aye, Captain."

"Criminal investigation?" Tombstone asked, one eyebrow
raised. "I was there in CIC when it happened, sir. The kid got
confused and threw the wrong switch."

"Seventeen men died aboard the *Dickinson*, Tombstone. Can
we tell their wives, mothers, and sweethearts that they died
because a twenty-year-old kid got confused? Forty-three men
were wounded. What do I tell them? The *Dickinson* is now
barely afloat and limping back to Narvik at a time when this

battle force needs every antiair and antisubmarine asset it can muster. That kid's inattention nearly cost us a ship, and it might have cost us a battle. In any case, any time lives are lost, there has to be an inquiry . . . and criminal charges. It's out of my hands."

"Yes, sir."

"The hell of it is, even if he gets shipped back to the States for trial, we still won't be off the hook. You know, I've got a very unpleasant feeling that we haven't heard the last of either one of these affairs . . . Margolis or Pellet."

Tombstone nodded slowly. "I'm afraid I have to agree, sir."

CHAPTER 16
Saturday, 14 March

Admiral Thomas Magruder took his seat in the White House Situation Room. As a special Presidential Advisor on military matters, he'd been here plenty of times before. Ordered constructed by President Kennedy right after the Bay of Pigs, the carpeted, concrete-walled room in the White House basement was not as large, as glamorous, or as high-tech as popular fiction usually described it. There were hidden television screens behind wood-paneled cupboards, yes, and the room next door was filled with telex machines, a crypto unit, facsimile machines, and secure telephones.

For most high-level briefings, though, the President used a second Situation Room located in Room 208 of the Executive Office Building, the same room, in fact, from which Secretary of State Cordell Hull had ejected the Japanese envoys on December 7, 1941. Variously called the Crisis Management Center and the Situation Room Support Facility, it was large enough for all of the President's principal officers and their aides.

As a matter of course, however, the President's senior aides and cabinet officers used the original White House basement Sit Room to discuss specific strategies before going upstairs to brief the President. The current President, while not as anti-military as some of his more liberal White House cabinet officers, was less than fully knowledgeable about military

173

affairs. Rather than sitting in on military and intelligence briefings, the President preferred to have his National Security Advisor, Herbert T. Waring, chair the meeting instead, then brief him afterward.

Magruder leaned back in his chair, glumly studying the American and Presidential flags flanking a curtained screen at the far end of the room. There'd been a lot of changes in the U.S. military during the past few years, and in his opinion, none of them were good.

Since 1991, the military had been called upon to fill a rapidly expanding role in policing a world that reverberated with the ongoing death throes of the old Communist empire. There'd been the Gulf War with a state originally armed and trained by the old U.S.S.R., a war possible only because the Soviets under Gorbachev had been willing to turn a blind eye to what was happening in Iraq in exchange for a free hand in suppressing the popular revolutions in the Baltics. Then had come the coup, and the breakup of the Soviet Union despite the Black Berets' attacks against Baltic nationalism. By the end of the year, the Communist flag had been lowered above the Kremlin for the last time . . . or at least, so everyone had thought. The Cold War was over, and the calls to drastically pare back an unnecessary American military had begun.

Somehow it hadn't worked out that way, though. There'd been Somalia and Bosnia and continued trouble in Iraq. A Marine foray into North Korea to rescue the crew of a Navy intelligence ship taken hostage. A coup in Thailand backed by renegade Chinese Communists. A war between Pakistan and India that might have gone nuclear without intervention by an American carrier task force.

And finally, the year before, there'd been the neo-Soviet coup and the invasion of Scandinavia.

Both the press and the U.S. government were carefully avoiding calling that bloody fracas World War III. The neo-Soviets, needing a war to secure their own power base at home, had tried to snap up Scandinavia in a quick military adventure while a fragmenting NATO argued about what to do. The heroic stand by the U.S.S. *Jefferson* and her CBG had stopped the Russians in their tracks off Norway, but *still* the Russian giant was threatening to drag the rest of the world into final Armageddon.

Now it was a civil war being fought on a ragged line all the way from Minsk to Vladivostok, one that already had engulfed Belarus, Ukraine, and Kazakhstan and might well soon involve China, North Korea, and most of Europe as well . . . and if *that* wasn't a world war, Admiral Magruder didn't know what was.

Yet during these past few years, the budget cuts to the U.S. military had kept coming. Worse, though, far worse, had been the wholesale mismanagement of the armed forces by blatantly anti-military congressmen in positions such as head of the Armed Forces Appropriations Committee, and the wildly leftist swing by the Clinton Administration beginning in 1993. Those had done unspeakable harm to America's defense establishment. Too, scandals had rocked the services . . . especially the Navy, which had suffered through Tailhook, the murder of a gay sailor in Japan and the subsequent cover-up, the videotape scandal aboard the *Gompers*, and others. Finally, the twin, dynamite-charged issues of gays in the military and women in combat and aboard ship had savaged the morale of everyone from ordinary enlisted personnel, male and female alike, all the way up to the Joint Chiefs of Staff. Admiral Magruder himself had reached the point where he was seriously considering taking an early retirement, even if it meant losing some of his benefits.

Hell, the grind just wasn't worth it anymore. He hadn't seen such liberal, anti-military hysteria since Vietnam . . . and this was from the people in the *government*! He still remembered the day he'd held a door open for a female White House staffer and had her jump down his throat with a viciousness that must have been well-practiced and rehearsed. "I don't need help from anyone," she'd sniffed. "Especially from a trained, uniformed *killer!*"

"I'm no trained killer, ma'am," he'd said genially. "I *lead* trained killers." But the episode had soured him, convinced him that the gulf between those who defended America and those who governed her had widened to the point that understanding—or compromise—was impossible.

He thought again of his nephew, Matthew Magruder, now a captain and CAG aboard the *Jefferson* off the Kola Peninsula. "Damn, Matt," he murmured to himself. "What the hell are we getting you into out there?" He was plagued by the fear that the

present administration would respond to neo-Soviet provocations with too little too late, then pull back and cut its political
losses when the first offering, in this case CBG-14, was
snapped up. Sometimes he had nightmares. Last night he'd
dreamed he was talking to Matt, trying to explain why the
Jefferson was being left in Murmansk while the rest of the fleet
came home. *"Sorry, Matt,"* he remembered himself saying in
the dream. *"They've cut the Navy's budget for aircraft carriers.
We just can't afford to run the damn things anymore, so we're
trading you to the Russians for two million dollars and a crate
of White Sea caviar. Oh, and Pamela says to dress
warm. . . ."*

The other attendees at today's meeting were taking their
places about the large wooden table. Vincent Duvall, the CIA
Director, was there, as were Secretary of Defense George Vane
and the white-maned Admiral Brandon Scott, Chairman of the
Joint Chiefs. Magruder knew what Scott thought of using the
armed forces as a social test platform. Rumor had it he'd
threatened to resign several times, and each time been refused.
Robert Heideman, the Secretary of State, was also present, a
stuffy, lifelong politician who had little love for the military.
All four men were attended by several aides.

There was a stir at the back of the room, and Herbert Waring
and White House Chief of Staff Gordon West walked in. "Sit,
sit," Waring said as the others started to rise. "Sorry to drag you
all in on a Saturday, but I'm sure you recognize the importance
of what's breaking now in Russia." He glanced at his Rolex.
"This meeting today has got to be a quickie, by the way.
Gordon and I are due upstairs in The Man's office in thirty
minutes to brief him on this new Russia thing. So let's get the
ball rolling. Bob? What kind of input do you have for us?"

The Secretary of State shifted in his chair. "Frankly, Herb,
there's been little new hard data since our meeting yesterday.
Moscow is still insisting that the attack on our carrier groups
was the work of dissident forces that had seized certain airfields
in the western half of the Kola Peninsula, and has promised to
punish those responsible. That's on the official diplomatic front.
Unofficially, well, the picture's a lot murkier."

"Leonov flatly insists that the Reds are behind the attack,"
the CIA director said. "He thinks they're trying to discredit

him, to block U.S. recognition of his side as the legitimate government of Russia."

"I'm not sure we can trust Leonov," Heideman pointed out. "Actually, the new bunch in the Kremlin, Krasilnikov and his people, seem to be more stable, more interested in the long-term outlook. They're devoted to reorganizing Russia's economy, revitalizing their industry, getting food supplies moving to the cities again—"

"Making the trains run on time," Duvall put in.

Heideman looked surprised. "Why, yes. Exactly. They're working hard to get all public services working again. Once the situation stabilizes in Russia, we should have no trouble doing business with them."

"Admiral Magruder?" Waring said, staring at him from across the table with his hands carefully folded. "You look impatient. Do you have something to add?"

"With all due respect to the Secretary of State, sir, now is not the time to be discussing doing business with the Russians. The situation has not changed since our meeting here yesterday, but we cannot allow things to drift any further without specific attention." He glanced from face to face at those watching him from around the table. "Gentlemen, ladies, the Russians attacked us yesterday, deliberately and without provocation. We *must* respond."

Gordon West frowned. "Are you saying we should attack them, Admiral? Maybe start a war?"

"I submit, sir, that the war has already started. This is an outgrowth of the Scandinavian invasion last year. If you like, it is a direct outgrowth of the coup in '91. These things don't happen in a vacuum. They are part and parcel of an overall body of events, decisions, and acts carried out by Russia's current batch of leaders. They are trying to secure power for themselves. Historically, the best way to do that is to get into a war with someone else. It takes the people's minds off empty bellies, boosts industrial productivity, and creates employment. It seems to me that it was inevitable that the Russians would attack us."

"Nonsense," Heideman said. "They already have a war . . . their own civil war."

"Not the same thing, Mr. Secretary. Not the same thing at all. A war with foreign enemies helps them get their people to pull together, while civil war divides them. Case in point: Revolutionary France in the 1780s and '90s. They were weak and divided, but they went on to declare war against most of Europe. United their own country, and eventually got an emperor, Napoleon. Or there's revolutionary Iran in the late 1970s—"

"We're not here to discuss history, Admiral," Waring said. "We're discussing the Russian problem."

"Perhaps Admiral Magruder is suggesting that we can better understand our own times if we understand the lessons of history," the Chief of Staff said. "Certainly, I would have to agree with the premise that we cannot count on the, um, good will, the respect and good intentions, of Krasilnikov and his gang of thugs."

"So, Admiral," George Vane said. He gave an uncomfortable glance in Heideman's direction. *"Are* you suggesting that we attack them? An escalation at this point . . ."

Magruder sighed. They'd been over this set of arguments countless times since the crisis had broken late Thursday night—Friday morning in the Kola Peninsula. "My personal recommendation, Mr. Secretary, would be to sink that Typhoon that slipped out of Polyarnyy during the battle. Admiral Tarrant seems to believe the two events are connected, that the air strike could have been providing cover for that Russian PLARB. If so, hitting the sub would be a valid, measured response to their attack against our carriers."

"But they didn't *hit* our carriers, Admiral," Heideman said, sounding exasperated. "We must not overreact!"

"It was by God's grace alone they didn't blow both the *Eisenhower* and the *Jefferson* clean out of the water, sir. They did sink one ship and damage several others. Hundreds of lives have been lost, most of them on the *Blakely.* Several of our aircraft have been shot down, and if they missed the carriers, it was thanks to our people's vigilance, not for lack of the Russians trying!"

"But to just go out and sink their submarine . . ." Vane began.

"Okay, sir," Magruder said, spreading his hands. He was having more and more trouble containing his impatience. "If you don't like that, another response would be an alpha strike, a bombing raid against the airfields from which those air attacks were launched. We know which ones were involved. If you want to pretend to believe that mutineers launched that attack, fine. Hit the bases that launched the planes and missiles. Knock out the radar and SAM sites. Send them a message that we're not going to stand for this kind of provocation."

"And be guilty of greater provocation ourselves!" West pointed out.

Magruder shrugged pointedly. "I must also point out that we have Resolution 982 to consider. Our response to the Russian attack could incorporate the UN mandate as our moral imperative for involving ourselves in the Kola."

Resolution 982 had been passed by the UN Security Council a month earlier, just after the violent coup that had ousted Leonov. It condemned any use of nuclear weapons in Russia's civil war and called for UN control of all of Russia's nuclear weapons, including her ICBM submarines. Needless to say, all parties in Russia had flatly rejected the idea, and so far, the resolution had served only to further isolate the bloodily fragmented nation.

Still, Resolution 982 provided the legal framework for any future intervention in Russia's affairs.

"Until we have more, um, decisive backing from the UN," Waring pointed out, "Nine eighty-two is little more than pretty words. We must consider the Russian response to our presence off their coast."

"Indeed," West said. "It is possible that Moscow is simply responding to our provocation. We, after all, are the ones who sent two carrier battle groups into their waters. We should remain sensitive to their perceptions of the situation."

Magruder sighed and settled back in his seat. Clearly, this was going to be a long and bloodthirsty session.

CHAPTER 17
Sunday, 15 March

1340 hours (Zulu +2)
Barents Sea
U.S.S. *Galveston*

Galveston was cruising toward the edge of the ice pack at a depth of eight hundred feet, still on silent routine, still dogging the wake of the Typhoon submarine that had set out from Polyarnyy over fifty hours earlier.

The Typhoon had been traveling slowly, barely making ten knots, sometimes slowing or suddenly reversing course as if checking for shadows, a maneuver American submariners referred to as "Crazy Ivan." *Galveston* followed cautiously, silently, remaining in the Russian sub's baffles, quick to go dead in the water at each Crazy Ivan, remaining nearly motionless as the Russian Typhoon slowly, like a self-propelled island, rumbled past, once passing only a few hundred yards to starboard. The Typhoon was half again as long as the *Galveston* and was over four times more massive. A collision would have crumpled the Los Angeles attack sub's hull like tinfoil.

Faithful to Schedule-3, *Galveston* rose every six hours to within three hundred feet of the surface, unreeling a long antenna cable in her wake capable of receiving extremely low-frequency radio waves, or ELF. For over fifty hours, no new orders had come through, and each time, *Galveston* returned to her hiding place within the sheltering cone of turbulent water spun off from the Typhoon's twin screws.

Through most of that time, Sonarman First Class Ekhart had

led the chase, sitting in the sonar compartment, ears encased in
the sonar headset, a faraway glaze to his eyes as he followed in
his mind the movements of the giant ahead. For the past hour,
the target, Sierra Nine, had been probing the edge of the
Barents Sea ice pack, rising gradually until her conning tower
was brushing just beneath the rugged white ceiling of the ice.

Though *Galveston* was some ten to twelve miles south of the
ice pack, Ekhart was still having to rely on every trick in the
book—and several that weren't in the book as well—to make
sense out of what he was hearing. Sound was curiously
distorted beneath the ice, where sounds reflected from the
surface as though from a wall, and the ice itself filled the
depths with crackling, popping, and rasping noises that masked
the stealthy sounds of soft-gliding submarines.

Suddenly, he snapped upright, every muscle taut. "Control
room! Sonar!"

"Captain. Whatcha got, Ekhart?"

"Flushing noises, Captain, followed by ice breaking. I think
Sierra Nine has just come up under a *polynya.*"

Flushing sounds meant ballast tanks being blown. Sierra
Nine was surfacing. *Polynya* was Russian for a lead in the ice,
either an open pool or an area where the water was only thinly
iced over. A ballistic-missile sub could not fire its warloads
through the ice. It would have to surface first before launching.

Which appeared to be precisely what Sierra Nine was doing.

1345 hours
Kandalaksha Command Center
Kola Peninsula

"Message from Captain First Rank Dobrynin, Comrade Admiral," the aide said, handing Karelin the message flimsy.
"*Slavnyy Oktyabrskaya Revolutsita* is in position."

Karelin glanced at the message, then handed it back. "At
last," he said. "It is time."

He would have been happier if both of Admiral Marchenko's
Typhoons had made it out to the open sea, but one should be
enough. His principal concern was American attack submarines
in the area. Russian naval planning for her nuclear missile
boats called for placing them in so-called "strategic bastions,"

secret regions of the Barents and White seas and in the Arctic Ocean where a few PLARBs could be protected by a large number of fast and powerful attack boats, the submarines the West called "Alfas," "Akulas," and "Victors."

Karelin hadn't dared work his Typhoons into regular Northern Fleet planning, however. If it had become known before the fact that Krasilnikov's faction was planning a nuclear strike against the *Rodina* herself, even if it was targeted against Leonov's rebels, there could have been mutiny throughout the fleet, perhaps even an attempt by dissidents to stop the *Revolutsita* before Dobrynin could carry out his orders. A Typhoon could be sunk by an Alfa as easily as by a Los Angeles.

But Operation Curtain of Fire appeared to have been successful in blocking the Americans from the Kola Inlet approaches. Dobrynin's message made no mention of unknown sonar contacts. He appeared to have reached his firing position midway between Spitsbergen and Nova Zemlya undetected.

Taking a notebook from his pocket, Karelin opened to a blank page and carefully printed the words "Crimson Winter Fire," tore the sheet out, and handed it to the aide. "Transmit this to the Kremlin," he said. "Priority One-One, Urgent."

Krasilnikov would receive it within minutes. Then the critical phase of Audacious Flame could truly begin.

1428 hours
Control room/attack center
Russian PLARB *Slavnyy Oktyabrskaya Revolutsita*

Captain First Rank Vsevolod Nikolaevich Dobrynin leaned over *Revolutsita*'s primary communications console, listening to the voice of Marshal Valentin Krasilnikov coming through the speakers.

"We fight for the future of our people, of our Motherland, of our revolution," Krasilnikov's voice said, faint but discernible through the blasting white noise of static. This far north, atmospherics frequently played havoc with radio broadcasts. "Sacrifices must be made if we are to secure our place in history as saviors of the Socialist Republic, even sacrifices made in fire and blood."

Most holy God, Dobrynin thought . . . and he had to savagely repress the urge to cross himself. *He's actually going to do it. . . .*

Dobrynin had not had a religious thought for years. He'd been a good Communist ever since his years in the Leningrad *Komsomolets.* He'd even been a good Communist during the hard, lean years of Yeltsin's treason, though he'd kept a low profile and been careful not to call undue attention to his beliefs.

But Krasilnikov's words had shaken him so badly that somehow the hated religious instruction pressed upon him in secret by his mother had surfaced like some broaching sea monster. He felt ashamed.

"Traitors have betrayed our Motherland, allowing her to be taken hostage and raped by foreigners and capitalist opportunists. They have taken up arms against the people and against the government which at long last offers hope and stability in a time of economic chaos and ruin. We offer you, who have taken up arms against our sovereign Motherland, one hour in which to recant your capitalist heresies, one hour to seize the traitors who have betrayed our country, Leonov and his cronies, and lay them and your weapons before the forces of the People's Red Army.

"If Leonov is not surrendered within the hour, if the forces of division and counterrevolution continue to defy the forces of lawful government, one SS-N-20 missile with six independently targeted warheads will be launched from a submarine at targets in rebellion against Moscow's authority. . . ."

One hour. Krasilnikov was giving them one hour! It was as though he *wanted* to incinerate Chelyabinsk—for that was the identity of the rebel city in the orders now locked in Dobrynin's personal safe. That city of a million people in the eastern fringes of the Urals had been chosen as a demonstration site, for there were several major rebel troop and armor concentrations in the area that could also be taken out by the same strike.

"If, after the first target is destroyed, the rebel forces do not surrender the traitor Leonov, a second target will be destroyed one hour after the first. . . ."

Alma-Ata was the second target on the list, the capital of the sprawling republic of Kazakhstan. The revelation that Moscow was willing to sacrifice one of its own cities, like Chelyabinsk, would make the republics supporting Leonov eager to change sides. No one seriously believed that a second missile would need to be fired. While Chelyabinsk was still burning, Alma-Ata, Kiev, Minsk, and the rest would be scrambling to be the first to swear eternal loyalty to Moscow. Even the Baltic states might fall into line.

Just in case, though, Dobrynin's orders listed twenty targets, from Minsk in Belarus to Khabarovsk in the Far East.

For at least the hundredth time during the past sixty hours, Dobrynin examined his feelings about the orders he had sworn to carry out.

In a little over one hour, he would give an order and as a direct result, some one million of his countrymen would die, some in a single, searing instant, their shadows burned into the sidewalks and walls of their city, others in lingering pain ten years hence, as cancers rotted their bodies. Could he possibly carry out such orders?

Even as he asked the question though, he knew—for the hundredth time—that he would. He believed in Krasilnikov's vision for a new Russia and had accepted the premise that suffering in the short term was needed to win a future security. Like Chelyag, his counterpart aboard the *Pravda*, he'd undergone countless meetings with Karelin before this mission—and even one interview with Krasilnikov himself. They'd screened him carefully, gauging the depth and the conviction of his belief in Communism. They knew him, he was convinced, better than he knew himself.

And besides, there was Strelbitski.

Kirill Borisovich Strelbitski was the *Revolutsita*'s political commissar, a civilian assigned to the *Revolutsita* by Karelin "to maintain the political fervor of the crew." Maintaining political fervor, Dobrynin knew, meant keeping an eye on the Captain. If Dobrynin failed to carry out his orders precisely as they were written, he would be relieved of his command and Strelbitski would take his place, and there was no doubt at all that *that* mean-eyed, thin-lipped reptile would carry out the orders . . . and even enjoy doing so. As for Dobrynin, his wife Tanya, in Murmansk, his son fighting with the 12th Red Guards at Voronezh, his daughter, a thirty-year-old doctor working in Moscow, all would be rounded up within the hour.

And then . . . well, he didn't want to think about the ultimate cost of his defection.

Yes, when the time came, he would give the proper order.

0730 hours EST (Zulu –5)
Situation Room Support Facility
Washington, D.C.

It had been another long, working night.

They'd reconvened here, in Room 208 of the Executive Office Building, sitting around a long, highly polished table that gleamed in the morning sunlight spilling through the huge windows along the east wall. It was a lot airier here than in the White House Situation Room, with more light and more space. Hours before, the Sit Room had proved inadequate for the task, as more and more advisors, aides, and staffers had been brought in to ride herd on what clearly was becoming a crisis of mammoth proportions. This room, its nineteenth-century decor masking a wealth of hidden electronics, television monitors, and computers, was large enough to accommodate sixty people.

Some fifty men and women were gathered here at the moment. Officially designated the Presidential Crisis Management Group, they weren't managing so much as they were floundering in a veritable sea of information coming through from the worsening Kola situation. At the moment, Admiral Scott had the podium at the front of the room, as he ran down the list of American and British assets in the region . . . and the possible Russian response.

Admiral Magruder leaned back in his chair, his attention less on Scott—he'd helped the head of the Joint Chiefs prepare his briefing so he already knew its contents by heart—than it was on the wall at Scott's back.

There, the richly ornamented wood paneling had been rolled back to reveal a giant computer screen. Run by three VAX computers hidden in the room beyond, a digital information and display system, or DIDS, could project on that screen complex maps, graphic representations of data received from around the world, or displays repeated from the National Military Command Center.

Currently, the screen showed a computer-generated map of the northern half of the Kola Peninsula, the Russian coast as far east as Nosovaya, and most of the Barents Sea. Bear Station was a bright blue racetrack oval north of the Norwegian border, but dozens of other U.S. and NATO assets were displayed as well. P-3C Orions, big, four-engined ASW aircraft, were patrolling the entire area from Svalbard to Nova Zemlya and south almost to the Murman coast. Fifteen American attack subs, plus four British Trafalgar-class SSNs, were already in the area, though their exact positions could not be known with certainty. And II MEF was racing northeast just off the Norwegian coast, its ASW air and sea pickets spread across ten thousand square miles.

As many red graphics dotted the map as blue. The forty air bases in the Kola Peninsula were all tagged with data lines indicating that they were on full alert. Fortunately, all of the Russians' Northern Fleet was in port, except for some of their submarines. Over thirty of their subs, however, dotted the waters of the Norwegian and Barents seas . . . and those were just the ones that had been picked up by Western ASW forces. During the past ten hours, the British, Norwegian, and American sea and air sub hunters had been dogging the Russian subs, pressing them, rattling their hulls with active, high-frequency sonar, letting their captains know that the NATO forces knew where they were and could kill them at any time. It was a deadly game. The Russians—or rather, *some* Russians—had already attacked American forces, and no one could say for sure how their subs would act, what their orders were or which side of their country's civil war they'd joined. There'd been one incident already, when a Russian Alfa off Iceland had launched a torpedo at the *Bolan*, a Perry-class frigate dogging its wake. The frigate had been blown up and sunk with terrible loss of life in those frigid waters; five minutes later the Alfa had been hit by two Advanced Lightweight Torpedoes dropped from the *Bolan*'s SH-2F Seasprite helicopter and was listed now as a probable kill.

It was beginning.

Admiral Magruder was dead on his feet. He'd been up for most of the past two days, briefing aides, reviewing intelligence updates, even going over computer graphics data with the Crisis Management Group staff. Most of the men and women in the room with him had been keeping similar hours, snatching naps when they could on office sofas, or going home, only to be called back a few hours later by another twist in the ongoing crisis.

His primary duties as a senior military aide attached to the White House consisted of acting as liaison between the White House staff and the Joint Chiefs. Technically, he still worked for the Pentagon—that "six-sided squirrel cage across the river," as he liked to call it—but in practice he worked out of an office in the White House basement.

God, but he wanted to go home.

As he studied the array of colored lights on the DIDS map, Magruder felt trapped between two opposing fears, two extremes of government in its relation to the military. On the one hand, there was a tendency by the government, by the various bureaucracies in particular, to waffle this way and that on any given foreign policy question. As a result, all too often a crisis best met either by a decisive application of military force or *no* military force at all was met instead by half measures and tokens. Then, when American boys had already died, the powers-that-be in Washington frequently lost a clear vision of where they were going—if they'd ever had one in the first place—and either froze or changed their mind. Magruder was continually haunted by the possibility that the carrier battle force already at Bear Station might be sacrificed, with anything it might have won thrown away by inaction, indecision, or incompetence. The best example Magruder could think of was the terrorist bombing of the U.S. Marine barracks in Beirut in 1983.

On the other hand, there was a constant tendency by Washington to micromanage, to second-guess commanders in the field while attempting to run military operations from W^3, an in-joking reference to the White House West Wing. Carter's step-by-step control of the failed Iran hostage rescue mission in 1980 was an example of this opposite extreme.

The temptation toward this end of the military management spectrum was especially strong with the advent of technology such as the DIDS screen he was studying now. Real-time satellite photography and high-altitude Aurora transmissions, computer links with the NSA and with diplomatic stations around the globe, the sense of you-are-there immediacy provided by CNN, ACN, and the various other news networks all contributed to a feeling of almost Godlike power, anchored, somehow, in this building.

If Matt and the rest were to have any chance at all, the people in this room had to steer a careful course between the two extremes of not paying enough attention to the Kola crisis . . . and of paying it too much.

"At the moment," Admiral Scott was saying, "much of our attention is focused here, at the edge of the Arctic ice pack." The symbols marking the SSN *Galveston* and the Typhoon it had been tracking flashed obligingly on the DIDS. "The Russian sub appears to be running through a ballistic-missile launch drill, which in itself is provocative enough. *Galveston*'s skipper was originally ordered to stick close, and to open fire if it appeared that the Typhoon was actually going to launch. There's a certain amount of guesswork involved, of course, and—"

At the back of the room, tall, double doors boomed open and an aide walked in, his footsteps echoing slightly in the high-ceilinged emptiness. The man made his way swiftly to Robert Heideman's side, spoke to the Secretary in urgent whispers, then handed him a manila folder.

After glancing through the contents of the folder, the Secretary of State rose, his long face made longer by some ominous news.

"Mr. Secretary?" Scott said from the podium. "You look like a man with something important to say. You have news, sir?"

"Bad news, I'm afraid." He gestured with the paper in his hands. "I have here a translation of a speech just delivered by Marshal Krasilnikov at the Kremlin. My people are printing up copies for each of you, but I can summarize it now." Briefly, tersely, he told them of Krasilnikov's ultimatum, of the threat to destroy a rebel city within the hour if Leonov was not surrendered.

"Clearly," Heideman concluded, "the situation has changed, becoming more urgent. We cannot allow the Russians to launch that missile."

"Why not?" the White House Chief of Staff asked. "If it's just Russian against Russian . . ."

"Bob's right," Secretary of Defense Vane said. "If the civil

war over there goes nuclear, we're going to have serious
problems containing it."

"I might also point out something else," Duvall, the CIA
head, said. "A nuclear war is going to affect everyone on this
planet, not just the people fighting it."

"Nuclear winter?" someone asked.

"Possibly. And you'll recall that after the nuclear plant
disaster at Chernobyl, radioactivity was detected in cow's milk
as far away as Sweden. There's also going to be the problem of
vastly increased numbers of refugees fleeing across the border
into Eastern Europe. Even *one* nuclear detonation in this war
could set off repercussions that frankly, ladies and gentlemen,
we're just not equipped to deal with."

"Admiral Scott? What do you recommend?" the National
Security Advisor asked. He sounded subdued.

Scott extended a collapsible pointer, reached high, and
tapped the DIDS screen twice, close by the graphic symbol
marking the *Galveston*. "I think we have only one option open
to us," he said. "But we're going to have to move damned fast
to exercise it."

1439 hours (Zulu +2)
Control room/attack center
U.S.S. *Galveston*

Commander Montgomery pressed his eyes against the rubber
light shield of *Galveston*'s number-one search periscope. The
attack sub was at a depth of one hundred feet, creeping north
toward the edge of the ice. Underwater visibility was superb.
Though still submerged, the sub's periscope gave Montgomery
a view of shifting lights and darks; he could see the white
shimmer of the ice less than a mile ahead, brighter where it was
thin, deeply shadowed where pressure ridges plunged into the
aquamarine depths like inverted mountain ranges. The periscope view was repeated on a television monitor on the attack
center's bulkhead, showing open water overhead giving way to
a ceiling of ice.

"Captain, comm shack."

He reached for an intercom mike. "Captain here."

"Sir, we've just had an ELF ring the bell. Message decodes

as 'Priority FLASH, stand by for VLF communications, comply immediate.' That's the end of the transmission, sir."

"Very well." He turned from the periscope, catching the eye of *Galveston*'s XO. "Mr. Harris, come about to one-eight-zero. As soon as we're well clear of the ice, come up to fifty feet."

"Course one-eight-zero, aye, sir," Harris repeated, following the correct control room procedure. "Come to five-zero feet when we're clear of the ice, aye, sir." He then turned and repeated the orders to the helmsman and diving planes operator, who sat side by side at the front of the control room.

As he listened to the litany of multiply repeated orders, Montgomery wondered what Washington was so anxious about. It was almost forty minutes past the last Sched-3 contact window. It had been sheer luck *Galveston* was still trailing her ELF antenna and had been close enough to the surface to pick up that first priority flash.

Transmitted from enormous antennas at remote shore stations, extremely low-frequency signals, broadcast at from 300 hertz to 3 kilohertz, could penetrate the ocean to a depth of about three hundred feet, far deeper than any other form of radio communications. The drawback was that the laws of physics dictated that information could be transmitted on ELF channels only very slowly, at a rate of about ten bits per minute; it took fifteen minutes to transmit a three-letter code group, enough to, say, order the sub to the surface to receive new instructions according to a pre-arranged code, but not enough to transmit new and detailed orders. Such code groups were called "bell ringers."

Minutes later, *Galveston* was traveling slowly south away from the edge of the ice. Once the long ELF antenna wire had been reeled in, Montgomery ordered the shorter VLF antenna deployed, trailing it astern from the top of *Galveston*'s sail. The very low-frequency band, broadcast at between 3 and 30 kilohertz, could only penetrate the top fifty feet or so of the ocean. By rising to such a shallow depth, *Galveston* was dangerously exposed to any Soviet ASW aircraft that might be in the area.

"Captain, comm shack."

"Yeah. Go ahead."

"Message coming through, sir. Code group Red-Charlie-One."

"On my way."

The message would be in code, of course. Red-Charlie-One was the current designation for a launch-condition message, flagged urgent.

Montgomery had a chilling premonition about what might be in such a message.

1449 hours (Zulu +2)
Control room / attack center
Russian PLARB *Slavnyy Oktyabrskaya Revolutsita*

Surfaced, the *Revolutsita* had no trouble picking up the satellite-relayed communication from Kandalaksha. Krasilnikov's address to the Russian people was still ringing in Dobrynin's ears when the call from Karelin had come through.

"Are all systems in readiness, Comrade Captain Dobrynin?" Karelin's voice was curiously flattened after being scrambled at the fleet headquarters, then descrambled aboard the *Glorious October Revolution.*

"Yes, Comrade Admiral. All missile guidance systems have been programmed with the appropriate coordinates. We are ready to fire the first on two minutes' notice."

"Very well. In the name of the Ruling Council, I hereby direct you to fire missile number one at precisely 1530 hours, Moscow time."

"But, might not the rebels capitulate, Comrade Admiral? Surely—"

"They will not surrender, not so long as they assume we are bluffing. Once a city dies, they will know that we are in deadly earnest. Frankly, I suspect that the surrender will come through within ten minutes of the destruction of the target . . . just long enough for Leonov's people to receive confirmation that the city is gone. Then they will come around."

"Yes, sir." Dobrynin felt sick. He showed nothing, however, in his face. Strelbitski was standing close by his side, and the

193

eyes of every man in the communications compartment were on him. "Of course. It will be done according to your orders."

"Excellent." Karelin's voice nearly purred. "I am counting on you, Comrade Captain. Do not let me down."

1502 hours
Control room/attack center
U.S.S. Galveston

"The order decodes as . . . 'Sink the Typhoon,' sir."

Montgomery nodded. It was as he'd feared. "God in heaven."

"There's more . . ."

"What is it, son?"

"It says, 'Radio intercept indicates Typhoon will launch on own city about 1530 hours local time. Prompt action necessary to prevent Russian conflict going nuclear.' It's signed 'Scott,' Captain."

"I concur, sir," a second communications chief said. The message had been decoded, as required, by two different men in the communications suite. It was now being presented to the Captain and the XO.

Montgomery looked at Harris expectantly. "Bob?"

"Authenticated, Captain."

"I concur. Well, if the Chairman of the Joint Chiefs says so, we'd better get on with it. God damn, but that's fast action for Washington, though. They must be shook to have acted that fast on this thing. Okay. Reel in the cable. Let's clear for action."

"Aye, aye, Captain."

Backing out of the communications shack, Montgomery strode forward to his accustomed place in Galveston's control room/attack center. "Mr. Harris, what is our weapons status, please?"

"Tubes one through four loaded and ready to shoot, Captain. ADCAP Mark 48s, primed, hot and ready."

"Very well. Bring us onto a heading of zero-zero-five. Make depth one hundred feet. Bring us ahead slow."

"Come to bearing zero-zero-five, make depth one hundred feet, ahead slow, aye, sir."

"Weapons officer!"

"Yes, sir."

"I'll have the bow doors open, Mr. Villiers. But quietly. Crank 'em open by hand."

"Aye, aye, sir."

Montgomery felt the deck tilt beneath his feet as *Galveston* swung around in a great, slow circle, then began descending once again into her element. For most of his adult life, Richard Montgomery had trained for this moment, had dreamed about it, wondering whether he would be able to meet the test if and when the time finally came. He was an attack boat skipper, and one of the best. The Los Angeles attack submarine had been designed to handle many missions, but her most important, the one she'd been built for above all others, was to track and kill Russian boomers. In a nuclear war between East and West, America's survival might well depend on whether a few men like Dick Montgomery could take down monsters such as that Typhoon out there under the ice before they could target New York or Washington from their Arctic bastions.

As the threat of global nuclear holocaust had receded, Montgomery had assumed that his particular skills and training in tracking Russian PLARBs would never be called into play. Submarines had been employed in numerous military actions through the last decade, from the Gulf War to the scrape last year with the Russians off Norway, but he'd thought the old game of stalking their boomers was over.

Evidently, he was wrong.

Would the Russians really launch on one of their own cities? Washington seemed to think so, and it was not part of his job to question his boss's orders. Not long ago, a cruise missile from the *Galveston* had helped sink the Indian carrier *Viraat*, part of an action fought to stop the Indo-Pakistani war from going nuclear. The *Gal*'s skipper then had been Gerry Hawkins. What had he thought of his orders at the time?

There were 150 men aboard the Typhoon out there, as opposed to thousands aboard the *Viraat*. Their deaths might save tens of thousands, even millions of lives if that PLARB could be killed before it loosed its deadly arrow.

But submariners share a special bond, no matter what flag they sail under. The shared experience of patrolling, month upon month, in the cold and unyielding night of the oceans where the slightest mistake can expose the entire crew to the implacable wrath of the submariner's real and constant enemy, the sea, somehow bypasses national boundaries, alien cultures, and even politics.

But not loyalties. *Never* loyalties. The submariner's devotion is to his boat, his shipmates, and his captain; the captain's devotions are to his boat, his men, and to the trust invested in him by the government he serves.

There was no question of disobeying those orders.

"Bow doors are open by hand, Captain," the weapons officer announced. "We are ready to fire."

"Very well. Stand by." He took his place at the search periscope. "Let's take her in nice and smooth, gentlemen. Under the ice."

1505 hours
Bear Station
Radio shack, U.S.S. *Shiloh*

"Admiral Tarrant, sir? This just came out of decoding."

Tarrant accepted the flimsy from the communications officer, scanning it quickly. It was from Admiral Scott, head of the Joint Chiefs of Staff. In a few terse lines, it described Krasilnikov's radio broadcast, explained that the Russians were expected to launch a nuclear missile into their own homeland at or about 1530 hours, and said that the U.S.S. *Galveston* had been ordered to intercept and sink the Russian sub before it could launch.

Tarrant glanced at his watch. Less than thirty minutes. This was bad, very bad.

"Says here this broadcast from Moscow took place half an hour ago. Why the hell didn't we pick it up?"

"We got something, Admiral," the communications officer replied. "Recorded it. Intelligence's got it now, but it might take a while to translate."

"God damn. The world could blow up around our ears while we're trying to translate a damned radio program. Okay." He picked up a nearby telephone handset and punched in a number.

"CIC," a voice answered. "Officer of the Watch Wilkins speaking."

"This is Admiral Tarrant. What's our current defense posture?"

"Alert state three, Admiral."

"Come to full alert. Pass the word to the rest of the battle force."

"Yes, sir. Uh . . . what is it, Admiral? An attack?"

"Son, we're just about to shove a stick square into the middle of a hornets' nest. Inside of thirty minutes, they're gonna be coming at us all out, and they're going to be looking for blood."

1510 hours
Control room/attack center
U.S.S. *Galveston*

"Control room, Sonar."

"Captain here. Go ahead."

"Ice-breaking noises now at zero-one-eight. No target motion. Range now within forty thousand yards."

"Very well. Helm, come right to zero-one-eight. Increase speed to ten knots."

"Steering right to zero-one-eight, increase speed to ten knots, aye, sir."

"Bring us up to two hundred feet."

"Coming to two hundred feet, aye, sir."

Montgomery did some fast calculations in his head. Extreme range for a Mark 48 Advanced Capability torpedo running at its top speed setting of fifty-five knots was seventeen and a half nautical miles, thirty-five thousand yards. That would give it a running time of just under nineteen minutes. He glanced at the clock on the attack center bulkhead. *Damn!* If he launched right now, it would still be a squeaker.

To delay longer would mean the torpedoes could not arrive until after the 1530 hours deadline. Would the Russian boomer launch anyway as soon as it heard the sound of the approaching ADCAP? That depended on its orders. It was equally possible the Russians would break off their missile run in order to maneuver.

As long as they didn't fire that damned nuke . . .

"Weapons officer!"

"Weapons, aye."

"Fire one."

Lieutenant Villiers slapped the heel of his hand across a red button on the torpedo firing console in front of him. A green light shifted from one side of a status display to the other, and a hollow-sounding *shush* echoed faintly through the control room. Unlike earlier submarine classes, a Los Angeles sub's torpedo tubes were mounted amidships, two to either side of and just below the attack center, and the sound was easily transmitted through the inner hull.

"Torpedo one fired. We have positive guidance."

The Mark 48 ADCAP torpedo was wire-guided, at least for the first part of its run. It was being steered by an enlisted man at the weapons board, who tracked it through its own passive sonar relayed down the unraveling wire that connected it with the *Galveston*. Responding to those signals, the crewman could in turn send steering instructions back down that same cable, using a small joystick on the console before him.

Silently, Montgomery ticked off twenty seconds.

"Fire two."

The second ADCAP lurched from *Galveston*'s number-two tube. Shots under the ice were always risky, the sonar picture obscured by reflections from the "roof." Montgomery wanted to make certain of his kill.

"Number two away. Running on positive guidance."

Montgomery glanced at the clock on the bulkhead. It now read 1511 hours. How long would it be before the Russians heard *Galveston*'s approaching torpedoes?

1525 hours
Control room / attack center
Russian PLARB *Slavnyy Oktyabrskaya Revolutsita*

"Captain! Sonar! High-speed screw, bearing one-nine-five!"

"What!"

"Confirmed, Captain! Torpedo in the water! Range, estimate less than eight thousand meters. Speed fifty to fifty-five knots."

Damn the Americans and their superbly silent submarines!

How had a Yankee attack sub managed to slip to within a few miles of the *Revolutsita*?

Or . . . could the attacker be another *Russian* sub? One loyal to the Leonov faction and attempting to halt the firing of the *Revolution*'s missiles? Dobrynin at once discarded that possibility. Some of the recent Soviet submarine designs, building on technology liberated from the West, were extremely quiet. Typhoons, for example, were among the most silent submarines in the world's oceans. But if this was a Russian attack sub it was most likely what the West called an Alfa, a small boat designed for high-speed interceptions . . . and the pumps for an Alfa's liquid sodium—cooled reactor were distinctive, and extremely noisy. There was no way that the *Revolution*'s sonar officers could have missed an Alfa's approach!

So the torpedo was an American one, probably one of their wire-guided ADCAPs, with a range of less than twenty miles at fifty-five knots, and carrying a 300-kilogram high-explosive warhead.

Why had they fired? Possibly, they feared an ICBM launch on the continental United States. Whatever their reasoning, there was no time to analyze it. Dobrynin was faced now with a critical tactical decision. Should he stay put and carry out the launch sequence already begun, hoping to get the missile aloft before the torpedo hit; or should he button up and dive, seeking maneuvering room beneath the ice in an attempt to avoid the torpedo and keep his options open for a launch later?

"Sokolov!" he yelled. "Abort the count! Secure missile hatch and prepare to dive!"

"At once, Comrade Captain!"

"Is this wise, Comrade Captain?" Inevitably, Strelbitski was there, at Dobrynin's elbow, his thin lips tight with disapproval. "We could still carry out our orders before the torpedo reaches us."

"Damn you, Strelbitski. I have a duty to this vessel and to these men. We will fire the cursed missile . . . *if* we survive the next five minutes!" He snatched up a microphone. "Torpedo room! This is Dobrynin!"

"Torpedo room here, Captain."

"Torpedo status!"

"Eight tubes loaded, Comrade Captain. One through four with Type 65! Five through eight with Type C1!"

The Type 65 was the largest and deadliest torpedo in the world, a 650mm-thick, nine-meter-long wake- or active-sonar-homer that could travel twenty-seven nautical miles at fifty knots, or fifty-four miles at thirty knots. Type C1s were older, smaller torpedoes with smaller warheads and a range of eight miles. Typhoons mounted tubes for both sizes, arrayed four-over-four across the huge submarine's broad, bluntly rounded bow.

"We will use the Type 65s," Dobrynin ordered. "Set running speed at fifty knots."

"Comrade Captain! The missile hatch is secure. The submarine is ready to dive."

"Then dive him, damn you! Dive!" The Typhoon's deck trembled as water thundered into the sub's ballast tanks. "Set depth to . . . set depth at twenty meters. Come to one-eight-five, speed fifteen knots!"

Strelbitski stared at him, open-mouthed.

"We still have a few tricks in our weapons locker, Comrade Commissar."

The man's face was pale. He looked frankly terrified. "What is it you intend to do?"

Dobrynin did not reply. He was staring at the attack center's overhead, focusing on the faint, far hum of the American torpedo, audible now, and swiftly growing louder.

1527 hours
Control room/attack center
U.S.S. *Galveston*

Sixteen long minutes had passed since the torpedoes had been fired.

"Torpedo one has acquired the target, Captain," the weapons officer announced.

"Cut it loose."

Freed of the wire connecting it to the *Galveston*, the torpedo went to active homing, sending out a stream of sharp *pings* that reflected from the hull of its slow-moving target and returned like a radar echo, guiding the ADCAP torp toward its prey.

"Torpedo two has acquired."

"Release it."

Now two Mark 48s howled through the water, skimming a few yards beneath the jagged, downward thrust of the ice-roofed surface. The target was less than two miles ahead. . . .

1528 hours
Control room/attack center
Russian PLARB *Slavnyy Oktyabrskaya Revolutsita*

"Now!" Dobrynin roared. His eyes were squeezed shut as he pictured the shifting relative positions of submarine, torpedoes, and ice. "Full speed ahead! Come right, to three-five-zero! Engineering! I want one hundred ten percent on both reactors, now! *Kick* his ass!"

Slavnyy Oktyabrskaya Revolutsita shuddered, heeling sharply to the right as the helmsman swung the giant sub into a hard starboard turn. Strelbitski grabbed for a brass stanchion and clung to it, his eyes very large as he stared up past the attack center's fluorescent lights.

Ping!

The sound of the torpedoes actively hunting the *Revolutsita* echoed through the sub's double hull like a hammer blow.

Ping!

Just a little farther into the turn . . .

WHAM!

The Typhoon, already heeling a good twenty degrees to starboard, slewed even farther onto the beam, flinging men, clipboards, loose papers, and unsecured gear into the bulkhead. In the crews' quarters, off-duty personnel were unceremoniously dumped from their bunks; in the torpedo room one of the racked monsters burst its steel bonds and smashed across the compartment, crushing two torpedomen to death and pulping the legs of a shrieking third.

Then the Typhoon rocked back to port, hurling her bruised and battered crew back in the opposite direction, before steadying at last in a precarious balance between the two extremes.

And around the sub thundered the booming roar of echoes gone mad. . . .

**1528 hours
Control room/attack center
U.S.S. *Galveston***

"Hit!" someone yelled, as the boom rumbled through the water, caressing the *Galveston*.

"Belay that!" Villiers shouted back. "It exploded too soon!"

Then the second torpedo went off, closer to the sub. The second blast's underwater shock wave, riding close on the heels of the first, caught the attack sub and shoved her, hard. Her bow came up . . . and the sail rocked into a rugged mass of ice protruding down from the ceiling, the deepest thrust of a major pressure ridge. Sparks dazzled from a bank of electronic gear, and smoke began billowing through the compartment.

"Fire!" someone yelled as the lights dimmed. "Fire in the control room!"

**1530 hours
Control room/attack center
Russian PLARB *Slavnyy Oktyabrskaya Revolutsita***

"Captain! This is the sonar officer. I cannot get a clear picture. Wide-band noise and transients . . ."

"Never mind that. Is the sonar still operational?"

"Yes, Captain. But it will be several minutes before we have full sensitivity again."

"We don't need it. We *have* them! Helm! Bring us back around to one-nine-zero!"

The Typhoon had been shaken when the American torpedoes had struck the ice, but was otherwise undamaged. Dobrynin had acted deliberately, turning away from the torpedoes and going to full speed, a maneuver that had attracted the notice of the torpedo's passive sensors and drawn them along. He'd noticed, during his maneuvering here an hour before, the presence of several major pressure ridges, where the ice, piled high by wind and currents, thickened into inverted ranges that posed a serious threat to submarines operating close to the ice.

Or to torpedoes. He'd been taking a gamble; *Revolutsita*

could have smashed one of those ridges with her sail, damaging her periscopes or satellite-communication gear. The gamble had paid off, however, when the torpedoes had stopped tracking the Typhoon and started homing on one of those ridges. Probably, the lead torpedo had exploded on the ice, and the shock wave had thrown the second into the ice as well. In any case, *Revolutsita* was unharmed.

And now, Dobrynin had become the hunter, and the Americans the prey.

CHAPTER 19
Sunday, 15 March

Galveston's well-trained crew reacted with drilled efficiency and a complete lack of wasted motion. Rubber masks on hoses dropped from the overhead like the emergency apparatus aboard a 747 losing cabin pressure. The control room crew calmly strapped on the dangling masks and kept to their posts as men with fire extinguishers doused the small electrical fire. The compartment's blowers were still operational, and the air cleared rapidly.

"Mr. Paulson!" Montgomery yelled, his voice muffled somewhat by his mask. "What's our damage?"

"Nothing too bad, Skipper! Dinged the sail, port side. Fire in the aux comm circuitry, under control. Minor casualties, bumps and bruises . . ."

"Okay! Sonar! This is the Captain. Can you hear anything yet?"

"Still awfully fuzzy, Captain," Ekhart's voice came back. "We've got echoes off the ice and bottom. Might be fifteen minutes before we get a clear sweep. And, sir . . ."

"Yes?"

"Captain, I think we've lost one flank array. We're deaf to port."

"Okay. Stay on it. If anyone can hear that bastard through the crap, it's you!"

"Aye, sir."

Think like the enemy! Montgomery told himself. And who was the enemy? A sub driver, like him. A captain first rank, most likely, for one of their biggest and finest vessels, or even an admiral.

No, *not* an admiral. That clever bastard had dived, turned away from the Mark 48s, then suckered them into the ice, as slippery-slick as sex. The guy had balls . . . and the maneuver suggested he did this for a living, not as a reward for years of faithful service to the Motherland.

Okay, so he was a working captain, and he knew how to use the ice as cover against torpedo attack. He also knew he would have to find and kill the American attack sub before the attack sub was able to take another shot. The Russian's sonars would be deafened for the moment; he wouldn't know how badly *Galveston*'s ears had been singed, so he'd assume *Galveston* still had fully operational sonar.

He would turn onto a reciprocal course to the torpedoes, running straight down the track toward *Galveston*'s position. He'd be coming fast, to cover the distance before *Gal* could recover her hearing, and he would be skimming as close to the ice as he dared just in case she *could* hear him, making use of the confused echoes still bouncing back and forth between ice and bottom to mask the noise of her engines. He might dump noisemakers too, just to keep things lively.

"Diving Officer!"

"Yes, sir!"

"Make our depth two hundred feet. Helm, come to zero-zero-five. Make our speed dead slow. Just enough to maintain way."

"Two hundred feet, aye, aye, Captain."

"Coming now to zero-zero-five, speed three knots . . ."

Montgomery took his place at the search periscope. "Up scope!"

1610 hours
Control room/attack center
Russian PLARB *Slavnyy Oktyabrskaya Revolutsita*

Where is he?

That question had been weighing on Dobrynin's mind for nearly half an hour now. If the American had continued his approach at five or ten knots, the Typhoon should have met it by now. The echoes in the water were dying away at last, and the sonar officer reported clear water.

But no American sub. The bastard *couldn't* simply make himself invisible!

"Slow to one third," he said. "Sonar! Anything?"

"No, Comrade Captain. It is possible the American turned away after his torpedoes went active, and left the area."

"Hmm. Possible. But not likely. This American submarine captain, he is very good. He crept up on us like a wolf on a reindeer. I somehow doubt he went to so much trouble simply to loose two torpedoes, then run away again."

But Dobrynin was faced with another decision, and as he made it, he was well aware of Strelbitski's eyes boring into the back of his head from across the attack center. The man had been silent since the attack, and sullen. His arm, dislocated during the momentary turbulence after the explosions, was now resting in a sling, and his face had the pasty look of a corpse.

By now, Moscow knew that the missile had not been launched on time, that Chelyabinsk had not been incinerated. No doubt, the air above the ice was thick with coded radio messages just now, demanding that he acknowledge and explain himself.

Should he assume the American sub had left, surface, and carry out his orders? Or continue the hunt?

"Slow to five knots!" he ordered. "Ahead slow!"

Damn it, the American *had* to be here somewhere!

1617 hours
Control room /attack center
U.S.S. *Galveston*

Montgomery's face was pressed against the periscope's eyepiece. Scanning forward and up, he could see the light filtering down from the surface through the ice, a white-hazy ripple of light and shadow, growing brighter as *Galveston* slipped beneath thin-ice leads, darker beneath the pressure ridges and thicker blocks.

There still was no sign of the enemy.

"Captain! Sonar!"

"Captain. Go ahead."

"Sir, I'm getting very faint noises to starboard, on a heading of one-zero-two. Range . . . hard to make out, but I think it's pretty close. A mile. Maybe a bit more."

"What kind of noises?"

"Hard to pick it out of the background, sir. We're still getting some low-frequency stuff, and the ice has been cracking apart ever since the explosion. But my guess would be something damned big on two screws."

Bearing 102 . . . that was almost abeam of the *Galveston*. Montgomery walked the periscope around to the right. . . .

And there she was, no more than a blunt-nosed shadow against the brighter ice overhead, but unmistakable. He estimated the range off the reticle markings on the periscope image, using the Typhoon's length of 558 feet as a trigonometric key. The Typhoon was now about eighteen hundred yards to starboard, just over a mile. He'd never have seen her if he hadn't gone deeper to silhouette her against the light.

"Gently now," Montgomery said, keeping the target in his sights. "Helm, come right to a heading of one-seven-five. Dead slow."

"Heading one-seven-five, dead slow, aye, sir."

The minutes dragged as *Galveston* slowly turned, reversing her northbound course toward one heading almost due south . . . and sliding gently once again into the Typhoon's baffles. As with combat between fighter planes, the combatant who first spotted the other usually had the advantage. Montgomery was not about to lose it again.

"Mr. Villiers?"

"Tubes one through four are loaded, sir. Mark 48 ADCAP. Outer tube doors are open."

"Are you tracking Mr. Ekhart's target?"

"We're tracking."

"Fire one."

"One away. Running hot and clean, positive guidance."

"Fire two."

"Two away. Positive guidance."

"Fire three."

"Three away."

Montgomery saved the fourth torpedo against the unexpected. Running time for the Mark 48s at a range of one mile was just under one minute.

1619 hours
Control room/attack center
Russian PLARB *Slavnyy Oktyabrskaya Revolutsita*

"Torpedoes in the water! Very close! Bearing zero-zero-three, coming in directly astern!"

"Release countermeasure decoys!"

"Decoys away!"

"Come hard left! Full speed now!"

"Coming left."

"Engineering! I want one hundred ten percent! *Now!*"

"Yes, Captain!"

"Captain! Torpedoes closing! Estimated range four hundred meters . . ."

"*Move*, damn you!" he screamed at the helmsman. "Put the helm hard over! Stand the bastard on his side!"

"I knew you should have fired the missile when you had the chance," Strelbitski said "I will see to it that—"

"You are at liberty to report me to Moscow," Dobrynin said. The deck was tilting now at an angle of nearly thirty degrees, forcing him to grab a stanchion to support himself. "Assuming we survive the next few minutes."

"Two hundred meters . . ."

"Release more countermeasures!"

1620 hours
Sonar room
U.S.S. *Galveston*

Ekhart heard the increase in the pitch of the fast-pinging active sonar as the lead torp sprinted the last few yards to its target. He whipped off his headset. "Thar she blows!" he called as the rest of the sonar operators pulled off their earphones as well.

The first explosion rumbled through the water, louder than the blast that had rocked them earlier, but not nearly so damaging this far beneath the ice. *Galveston* rocked to star-board, shuddered, then tilted back to port.

An instant later, the second torpedo struck home, the detonation thundering through the water close on the heels of the first.

The third torpedo did not detonate. Either it had been seduced by the Typhoon's noisemaker decoys, or the first two explosions had damaged it. No matter. As soon as Ekhart slipped his headset back on, he could hear the unmistakable sounds of water flooding a large, empty space, a rushing, thundering sound, punctuated by startling popping noises.

Homing on her screws, striking the Typhoon in the stern, the first ADCAP must have ruptured the seal around one of her drive shafts, sending water pouring into her engine spaces. As he continued to listen, Ekhart heard a low, eerie groan building to an almost human wail of agony as steel warped under incredible stress, not from depth—the Typhoon was not nearly deep enough for that—but from unbalanced loads surpassing engineering tolerances. He was hearing the sound of the huge sub's back breaking as her after spaces flooded and started dragging her down.

"Captain, this is Sonar," he said. "Two hits. I'm picking up breakup noises."

"Pipe it over the ICS."

He flipped a switch, transmitting the death cries of the giant Russian sub throughout the boat. Ekhart had half expected the crew to break into cheering, but the *Galveston* remained death-silent. Now he could hear the rustle of air bubbles streaming into the void. The target was changing aspect too as it dropped away into blackness.

"Now hear this" rasped over the ICS speaker. "This is the captain speaking. All I can say, men, is congratulations to each and every one of you on a job very well done. The details of this mission may have to remain secret, but I can tell you that Washington had information that our target was a Russian Typhoon that had surfaced in order to launch her nuclear missiles. Your action prevented that launch, and the country and the world owes you a very large debt.

"Sonarman First Class Ekhart, I want to extend to you a very special job well done. That was good work, picking out the Typhoon's screws from the background garbage. You may have saved the boat, and you certainly contributed to the success of our mission. I'll be writing you up in my after action report, recommending you for special commendation . . ."

Ekhart did not feel like he deserved commendation. His . . . *talent*, his ability to feel out an opponent in the darkness of the ocean, had just been put to the ultimate test, and 150 people had died. True, they'd been trying to kill him and his shipmates at the same time, but it was still not something he could feel proud about.

The sonarman sitting beside him clapped him on the shoulder. "Real number-one job, Rudi."

"Yeah," another said, grinning from ear to ear. "The Old Man usually ain't none too free with his 'well dones.' Good work!"

Somehow, though, Ekhart had never felt more distant from his shipmates than he did at that moment. He felt both proud of his skill and ashamed of the fact that he'd just helped kill 150 men, submariners like himself.

He wished that he'd never joined the Navy.

1430 hours FST (Zulu –5)
Situation Room Support Facility
Washington, D.C.

The news that *Galveston* had torpedoed a Russian PLARB had everyone in the Crisis Management Group keyed to fever pitch. All expected some form of Russian retaliation, either against American submarines in the Barents Sea, or more likely, against the carrier battle force at Bear Station. Oddly, while the Kola bases remained on full alert, no new air strikes, no cruise missile attacks had been launched.

"Since that time," a military aide, a Navy captain, was saying, "there have been five additional incidents in the area. We're still checking on some of them, but it appears that at least four more Russian submarines have been sunk during the last three hours."

"What kind of subs were they?" someone in the audience asked.

"Two were PLARBs. Not Typhoons, but older models. A Yankee II and, we think, a Delta IV. We don't know that they were part of the Krasilnikov ultimatum, but they were heard to be flooding their missile tubes in preparation for launch. The other two were attack subs trying to work their way toward our task force at Bear Station."

The doors at the end of the room opened, and a close-knit cluster of men in suits and in uniforms walked in. "Ladies and gentlemen," Gordon West announced from the head of the pack. "The President of the United States!"

The people at the table stood with a rumble of pushed-back chairs.

"Be seated, please," the President said as he strode to the chair reserved for him. He took his seat as his aides and several military officers, including an Air Force colonel with an ominous briefcase chained to his wrist, took their places along the windows at his back.

My God, he looks old, Magruder thought, shocked. The President appeared to have aged years in just the few days since Magruder had seen him last. His was one job that Magruder would never want. The people on the crisis team, at least, had been managing a few hours of sleep at odd moments throughout the past three days. It didn't look like the President had been sleeping at all.

"Okay," the President said, looking at the faces around him. "I'll make this fast and to the point.

"A few minutes ago, I talked to our ambassador at the UN. This afternoon, gentlemen, in a special emergency meeting, with the Russian representative absent and China abstaining, the Security Council passed UN Resolution 984, calling on both sides of the Russian Civil War once again to surrender sovereignty over their nuclear arsenals. This time, they are authorizing military action to force compliance."

"Good Lord," Heideman said. "This could mean World War Three!"

"We may not have been able to avoid that in any case, Bob. A few moments ago, I spoke with Petrakov."

Viktor Petrakov had been the Russian ambassador to the United States under the Leonov government. Since Washington continued to recognize the Leonov government as the legitimate government in Russia, Petrakov remained America's principal diplomatic link with Russia, even if he was no longer recognized by the people currently in power there.

"Petrakov," the President continued slowly, "tells me that his government is holding their football, the nuclear codes for the Russian ICBM forces. However, he fears that Krasilnikov's people may have cracked the codes for the missiles on at least a few of their submarines."

"God in heaven," Waring said.

"People, we cannot allow this horror to begin," the President continued. "We must do everything in our power to prevent the outbreak of nuclear war in Russia. Resolution 984 gives us the legal authority to act. I might add that both the UN Secretary General and Ambassador Petrakov have formally requested our assistance, our intervention, to avoid a nuclear holocaust.

"I am prepared to give it."

There was silence in the room for a long moment after the President spoke. Magruder, finally, broke it. "Mr. President, are you telling us that we're about to enter that war?"

"To secure Krasilnikov's ICBM submarines in the Kola Peninsula, yes. It will be a limited incursion, and for the short term only. Why, Admiral? Why the long face?"

"I am, Mr. President, something of a student of history. I was just thinking of the last time we invaded Russia."

The President shook his head. "I don't think I understand, Admiral. When have we ever invaded Russia? Throughout the Cold War we—"

"This was from late in 1918, Mr. President, until 1920. Right after World War I. An Allied force landed in Murmansk and at several ports in the White Sea, ostensibly to look after Western interests, in fact to lend military support to the Whites in their struggle against the Bolsheviks. The expeditionary force included British, French, even Serbian troops, but nearly half of them were Americans, straight from the trenches in France. We also had some troops in the Far East of Russia, trying to keep the Trans-Siberian Railroad out of Japanese hands."

"I suspect you and I read different history books when we were in school," the President said, but he disarmed the words with his famous grin. "What happened?"

"They fought through a winter when six feet of snow fell on Arkhangel'sk. Most of the deaths were from frostbite or disease, but there were combat casualties as well, American troops fighting the Red Army in the heart of the Kola

Peninsula. Squabbles among the Allies and a change of heart in Washington brought the rest of them home after two years."

"So what are you saying, Admiral? Are you recommending that we stay out of Russia?"

"I'm saying, Mr. President, that we'd better be damned sure about what we're getting into over there, that we'd better be crystal clear on what we're doing and why. Otherwise, sir, we'll find ourselves neck-deep in quicksand."

"I appreciate your concern, Admiral. But I assure you that we will have strictly limited goals and objectives. I'm told that the Pentagon has been working for some time on a plan for just such a contingency as this. Now, people, let me touch on some of the salient points of this operation. . . ."

As he listened, Magruder had to concede that this was not intended as a long-term mission. It was more of a raid in force, with no plans for occupation, or even for cooperation with Leonov's forces.

The only problem lay in the certain knowledge that it was going to be a hell of a lot easier getting into Russia's civil war than it would be getting out.

2215 hours (Zulu +2)
Bear Station
U.S.S. *Thomas Jefferson*

"Come."

Tombstone opened the door, stepped past the Marine sentry outside, and entered Admiral Tarrant's office. Tarrant had transferred to the *Jefferson* earlier that afternoon, at least for the time being. *Shiloh* was better for managing a sea battle, but the *Jefferson* offered better facilities for planning bigger ops, especially those involving the carrier herself.

"You wanted to see me, sir?"

Captain Brandt was on a sofa in the corner of the room, but he said nothing.

"Yes, CAG. Shut the door and drag up a chair. Sorry to haul you up here so late. Drink?" There was a crystal decanter of scotch on the Captain's desk, and Tombstone's eyebrows rose when he saw it. The *Jefferson*, like all Navy ships, was dry, and he knew Brandt didn't drink. Tarrant must have brought his own stock.

"No, sir. Thank you."

"How's the wing holding up?"

"All right, sir. Tired, but we're keeping the CAPs aloft. Funny. There's not been much reaction out of the Russians since we sunk their sub. We've had two of their attack aircraft make runs at our perimeter, but those appeared to be probes sent in to test us rather than serious assaults. We turned one back and downed the other. I was expecting all hell to break loose."

In silent reply, Tarrant handed a message across the desk to Tombstone, then refilled his glass from the decanter.

It was a long one, signed by Admiral Brandon Scott himself, explaining in detail the parameters of a massive amphibious operation code-named White Storm. A U.S. amphibious task force, II MEF, was already en route to Bear Station and would be arriving sometime very early in the morning.

Scarcely believing what he was reading, Tombstone scanned rapidly through the message.

"We're . . . invading *Russia*, sir?"

"We are, and I quote, 'to secure certain key Russian naval facilities in order to prevent deployment of enemy PLARB forces.' The sub bases, Stoney. They want us to grab the sub bases at Polyarnyy."

"Good Lord. How are we going to pull *that* off?"

Tarrant sipped at his drink, put his head back, and closed his eyes with a sigh. "God damned if I know, CAG. But you can start with this." Reaching out with one hand, he slid a stack of paper across the desk toward Tombstone. The document was massive, inches thick and weighing several pounds. The cover page had the operational name, White Storm, and was marked top secret.

"The Pentagon has been working on this one ever since Leonov got kicked out of Moscow," Tarrant said. "It assumes we have to intervene in the Kola to stop a Russian ICBM launch by their submarine forces. They're calling it a UN peacekeeping operation. Hell, maybe they don't expect the Russians to put up much of a fight." He drained his glass and brought it back to the desktop with a sharp crack. "But fight or no fight, it's our baby. I called you here to tell you to get cracking. White Storm calls for a full Alpha Strike against all known shore positions, SAM batteries, radar sites, defensive installations, and port facilities. We're going to want to pay particular attention to the approaches to the submarine facilities on the Kola Inlet. See my Intelligence staff for whatever maps and satellite photos you need."

"Yes, sir."

"We don't have much time. It's Sunday night now. Washington wants to be putting the Marines ashore by Tuesday morning. That's not much time to pull together an operation this complex."

"We've done it on short notice before, Admiral. We'll manage. How about UNREP? The other day we kind of went through a lot of stuff. Like AIM-54s."

"Already taken care of, CAG," Brandt said from the sofa. "An ammunition ship, the *Santa Barbara*, will be joining us tomorrow. She should have most of the munitions we need."

Tombstone turned back to Tarrant. "I'm afraid to ask when you'll need my op plan."

"Sorry, Stoney. Tomorrow morning, first thing."

He groaned. It would take him that long just to go through the operational orders. "Admiral, I haven't slept more than five hours in the past—"

"Save it. One thing, though. It might be an idea to lighten up on your CAP schedule. Let your people get some more rest, so that they'll be fresh."

"Or if not fresh, at least able to find their way to their airplane. Okay, Admiral. I'll get right on it."

"Thanks, Stoney. I knew I could count on you. That's all."

Tombstone started to leave. "Stoney?" Tarrant said. "One thing more. Morale . . ."

"Yes, sir?"

"How is it? I mean, after . . ."

Tombstone nodded, understanding. "Word about Pellet seems to have spread through the boat, Admiral. All my people know about it. They're . . . subdued, I guess. I can't say that it's affected their morale that badly. At least, not yet."

But how would it hit them after they had some time to think about it? That afternoon, Pellet's body had been found in his bunking compartment by his shipmates. He'd used a length of nylon rope to hang himself from a lighting fixture.

At least, it was assumed to have been suicide. There *were* signs of a struggle, blankets rooted up on the bunks, a locker knocked over. Possibly, Pellet had been murdered . . . but surely a murderer would have at least straightened up the furniture afterward. More likely, Pellet had done the damage himself during his death struggles. His death clearly had not been an instantaneous snapping of the neck, but strangulation. Apparently, it had taken him a while to die, and he might have changed his mind and tried to save himself.

"His death will be investigated by the CID, naturally," Tarrant said. "Along with the *Dickinson* incident. That's bad enough, of course. But I'm worried about how the crew will take his death. Especially *now*."

"They'll do what they have to, Admiral. They'll come through. Like they *always* do."

He turned then and left the room.

CHAPTER 20
Monday, 16 March

Early in the afternoon, the Russians launched another air strike against the gathering American armada at Bear Station. Composed mostly of long-range bombers carrying air-to-surface missiles, the strike force included Tu-22 Blinder-B and Tu-26 Backfire-B bombers, most of them drawn from the Northern Fleet's *Aviatsiya Voenno-Morskoyo Flota*, or Naval Aviation groups.

Deadliest were the Backfires, sleek, swing-wing, supersonic aircraft originally designed specifically for missions against naval targets. Since the strikes were decidedly short-ranged and fuel load wasn't a problem, each Tu-26 carried three AS-4 "Kitchens," cruise missiles with one-ton conventional warheads and a range of 170 nautical miles. The bombers were escorted in by tight groups of MiG-25 Foxbats, Su-21 Flagons, and MiG-29 Fulcrums, some with naval markings, others in the livery of neo-Soviet Frontal Aviation.

The American defenses were tougher now, but there were also more targets to choose from. For hours, more ships had been arriving at Bear Station from the west: the amphibious warfare ships and their escorts of II MEF, a joint British-Norwegian squadron of destroyers and guided-missile frigates, and the supply ships and escorts of an American at-sea replenishment convoy. Altogether, there were some thirty Allied ships in the area, not counting the far-flung submarine assets that prowled the depths from the north Russian coast to beneath the Arctic ice. Still more ships, the *Nimitz* Carrier Battle Group, were scheduled to arrive the next day.

In a savage, one-hour running battle, ninety-two cruise missiles were launched against the task force at Bear Station, but the American air defenses, sharpened by the attacks on Friday, met each assault with practiced efficiency. Guided by *Shiloh*'s Combat Direction Center and vectored by the E-2C Hawkeye airborne control centers, the Kitchen antiship cruise missiles were downed almost as fast as they were picked up on radar.

One missile, though, skimming in at wave-top height, slipped through the American defenses and struck the Spruance-class destroyer *John Worden*, demolishing her bow clear back to the vertical-launch missile cells forward of her bridge. Watertight doors and superb damage control saved the ship, at least for the moment, but the *Worden* was left wallowing in the sea, helpless until the frigate *Talbot* took her in tow. Fifteen minutes later, a second destroyer with the *Eisenhower* battle group, the *J. L. Davis*, took an AS-4 amidships, broke in half, and sank with all 364 men aboard in less than eight minutes.

At about the same time, 250 miles to the southeast, an American SSN, the *Scranton*, was picked up on Russian seabed sonar detectors in the approaches to the White Sea, a few miles off Grimikha. Hounded by a flotilla of Krivak II frigates sortieing from Arkhangel'sk and by flights of Ka-27 Helix-A ASW helicopters from air stations ashore, it was forced to the surface after a three-hour chase that pinned it against the coast in shallow water, then sunk by torpedoes fired from the Kynda-class cruiser *Groznyy*.

Meanwhile, the interceptor squadrons flying off three super-carriers waged a desperate stand in the skies above the Barents Sea.

1445 hours
Tomcat 202
Over the Barents Sea

Batman rolled out of a split-S, pulling the Tomcat's nose up hard and extending the wings, deliberately killing his speed and bringing the F-14 to the shuddering edge of a stall. The MiG-29 Fulcrum that had been weaving in on his tail slammed past him at four hundred knots, unable to compensate for Batman's sudden braking maneuver.

And then it was too late, because Batman had rammed his throttles clear to zone-five burner, folded his Tomcat's wings like those of a stooping eagle, and slid neatly into the six slot squarely behind the Fulcrum.

The unexpected change in roles caught the Russian pilot completely by surprise. From less than one hundred feet behind the other aircraft, Batman could see the white dot of the Russian pilot's helmet bobbing frantically inside the MiG's canopy as he twisted and turned in his seat, trying to see the Tomcat and guess its next move.

"Too close for missiles," Batman told Malibu. At this range, even a Sidewinder might scoot past the target before its one-track mind could track on the MiG's exhaust and correct the missile's course, and if he dropped back for more room, the more maneuverable Fulcrum would give him the slip. "Goin' to guns!"

A flip of the selector, and his HUD flashed to the guns configuration. The target reticle drifted across the MiG-29's fuselage and Batman squeezed the trigger. The F-14's Vulcan cannon shrieked . . . but the Fulcrum was already rolling clear of the floating burst of tracers that seemed to slide past the MiG's twin tail and wing tip, missing by inches. Then the MiG was clear, falling toward the sea twelve thousand feet below. Batman rolled after him.

"Striker! Batman!" he yelled over the tactical channel. If his wingman could close in, they could squeeze this guy, one Tomcat moving in close, the other covering from behind. "Where the hell are you, boy?"

"I'm on your four, one mile," Striker's voice replied.

Strickland and his RIO, K-Bar, had become separated from
Batman and Malibu minutes before, when they'd been jumped
by a pair of Fulcrums. "I'm clear and I'm moving in."

"See if you can cut this guy off. You take the left, I'll stay on
his right."

"Rog."

Half a mile ahead and below, the Fulcrum was pulling out of
its dive and cutting to the right. Batman brought his stick over,
trying to lead the Russian with a tighter turn to starboard. A
thousand feet off the deck, the Fulcrum hurtled past an
American helicopter carrier, the huge LHA *Nassau.* Batman
had just switched back to missiles when the hurtling Russian
interceptor disintegrated in midair, silvery fragments spraying
out like a shotgun blast, then ignited in a billowing cloud of
orange flame.

"Scratch that MiG," Malibu said in Batman's headset. "I
think he just got nailed by one of *Nassau*'s CIWS."

"I think you're right." He pulled the F-14 up sharply.
Phalanx point-defense systems sometimes had trouble telling
the good guys from the bad, and Batman had no wish to fly into
its deadly, mile-deep kill zone.

Pulling level at six thousand feet, Batman checked his stores.
They'd launched with four Phoenix, two AMRAAMs, and a
pair of Sidewinders. They were down to two AIM-54s and one
each of the others. "Talk to me, Malibu," he said. "Where's a
target? Gimme some ass to kick."

"Nothing close. I think the leakers all got capped. I'll see if
I can tag a Hawkeye for a vector."

Strickland's Tomcat drew alongside to the left. Looking
across the distance separating them, Batman could see Striker
in the front seat, K-Bar in the back, the numerals 211 of the
other aircraft's modex number vivid on its nose.

"How's the score standing now, Batman?" Striker asked.

Batman shook his head. "I got four, but two of 'em were
Phoenix kills at extreme range, and we might not get credit."
With so many missiles in the air at the same time, it was
sometimes difficult to assess whose AIM-54s had killed which
enemy aircraft. "I don't know how Brewer did."

"Why not ask her?" Brewer's voice cut in. Brewer's 218
Tomcat pulled in on the right. "What, Batman? Only two

confirmed kills? You're slipping. Pogie'n me got four already! Fox threes, every one!"

"Tracked 'em all the way to target," Damiano added. "And no others anywhere close, so we know we scored."

"Nuggets' luck," Malibu said.

"Yeah," Batman added. "What's that make it now, Brewer? Nine to eight?"

"Nice try, Batman," Brewer replied. "We're still only counting confirmed kills. Make that nine to *six*!"

"Damn, Batman," Malibu said, sounding hurt. "We can't let a mere slip of a girl *do* this to us!"

"I'll 'slip-of-a-girl' you, Mal."

"Gee, I don't know, Batman," Malibu said. "What do you think? I don't feel these Phoenix kills should count, do you? I mean, come on! Would John Wayne shoot down a bad guy from a hundred miles away? We oughta just keep score on the ones that're up close and personal!"

"Uh-uh," Brewer replied, and Batman heard her chuckle. "No changing the bet. Score's nine to six, women's advantage."

"I think we're being taken, Malibu. These women nowadays. You can't—"

"Gold Eagles, Gold Eagles, this is Eagle Two oh-one," Coyote's voice said, cutting in. "Gather in, chicks. Time to head for home."

"Two-oh-one, Two-oh-two," Batman called. "Hey, Coyote! What's the gouge?"

"Batman, Coyote. We're going back in by squadrons for refuel and rearm, and we're up first in the Marshall Stack."

"On our way. Are the bad guys gone?"

"Most of 'em. But we're leaving the ones that're left to the *Ike* and the *Nimitz*. We've got other fish to fry."

"Two-oh-one, Two-one-one," Strickland called. "What fish did you have in mind?"

"The skipper's got a job for us, Striker," Coyote said. "And man, if you've been having fun so far, you're gonna love this!"

Lieutenant Chris Hanson slumped back into her chair in
VF-95's ready room, aware of the rustle and thump of other
NFOs filing in, aware of the murmuring conversations around
her, but mostly aware only of how tired she was. It seemed like
the Vipers had been on alert for years. She'd been aloft on CAP
last night until 0730 that morning, had just gotten to sleep when
an alert had been sounded, had just gotten to sleep *again* when
the Russians had launched this latest attack. She and her RIO,
Lieutenant McVey, had catapulted off *Jefferson*'s deck, and
been aloft for over an hour. They'd made two Phoenix kills,
then had a narrow scrape with a Fulcrum over the Norwegian
coast. On the way back, they'd used their last two Phoenix
missiles downing a couple of sea-skimming cruise missiles.

God, she was tired.

She looked across at the young, black-haired man slumped
in the seat beside her. Roy G. McVey was about as young and
raw as they came. Somehow, they'd all started calling him
Vader, playing on his last name. His head was back, his eyes
closed, his lips parted. He looked like he was asleep.

"Hey, Lobo."

She looked up. Striker was standing behind her, his hands on
the back of the chair.

"Hello, Steve."

He bent over, so his lips were close by her ear. "Listen," he
said, whispering so no one else could hear. "I was wondering
about tonight. . . ."

"Uh-uh," she said. "*Uh*-uh! If they let me, I am going to
sleep for about five hundred years. Call me in 2500."

He smiled. "Actually, I had the same thing in mind. This
watch-on, watch-off stuff is—"

"Attention on deck!"

The men and women in the room rose to their feet as
Tombstone walked in, Coyote close behind him. "At ease. At
ease." He took his place behind the podium at the front of the
room. "Sit down and listen up. We don't have much time."

At his back, Coyote was tacking up a large-scale map of the Kola Peninsula. Lines of bright red quarter-inch tape had been stretched across it, all starting at Bear Station, reaching along several distinct paths through several doglegs, and terminating at various points inland.

"Ladies and gentlemen," Tombstone said. "The air phase of Operation White Storm."

Chris's exhaustion faded back, replaced by intense excitement. An alpha strike, an all-out assault against Russian targets in the Kola Peninsula!

And the Vipers were going to be in it up to their necks!

"The lead attack elements will be *Jefferson*'s VAQ-143 and *Eisenhower*'s VAQ-132. They'll go in first, using HARMs to hit the radar sites at Ozerko, Titovka, and Port Vladimir. Right behind them will be our attack squadrons, VA-89 and VFA-161, plus VA-66 from the *Eisenhower*. Their targets will be those SAM sites and radar installations we've been tagging with our Hawkeyes, plus naval installations up and down the Kola inlet.

"VF-95 will fly close escort on the Intruders."

There were several groans in the room. "Aw, CAG!" Arrenberger said from the back. "Why us? We've been at full throttle for the last forty-eight hours!" Other voices chimed in, agreeing with him.

Tombstone gave Slider a long, gray stare. "You have a problem, mister?"

"Yeah, I got a problem! How long are we supposed to keep pumping at this pace?"

"We can't keep going like this, CAG," Mustang Davis put in. "The squadron's beat."

Chris held her breath, wondering just how close to mutiny the squadron might be. If everyone in the squadron just refused to fly . . .

Tombstone kept his eyes on Slider. "You want to stand down, Slider? Turn in your wings?"

Slider paled. "No, CAG."

"I don't want one man or woman up there who can't take the strain. If you can't take the heat, Arrenberger, I want to know it."

"I can handle it."

"What about the rest of you people? I'll fly this mission by myself if I have to."

Chris joined with the others in a low-voiced murmur that filled the compartment. "We can do it, CAG." "We're okay, Tombstone." "We're with you, CAG."

Tombstone waited a moment, hands on hips. Then he nodded. "Okay. That's the way professionals handle it. I know you're tired. We're all tired, right down to the thin ragged edge. But Washington thinks this one is damned important. Today, it's up to us to start hammering away at the northern Kola defenses. Tomorrow morning, it'll be the Marines' turn."

That got their attention, Chris thought. There wasn't a sound in the compartment now, save the faint, faraway *boom* of a catapult launch.

"So, let's look at the mission profile," Tombstone continued. "You can expect heavy triple-A and SAM fire. The Hornets will be tasked with opening a corridor through for the Intruders, but we all know that they're going to miss a hell of a lot. The Russians will keep lots of their stuff in reserve, switched off so they can surprise us later. With luck, though, their local fighter defenses will have been whittled down a bit by the actions of the past couple of days. Our satellite reconnaissance of their bases shows they're pretty weak in aircraft. But don't let yourselves get complacent. There're sure to be several regiments of Soviet Frontal Aviation still on tap, hidden somewhere in camouflaged casements, and you can expect them to throw everything they have against us.

"We've got the first watch. By tomorrow morning, the Marines will be going ashore. They'll be covered by the Tomcat squadrons off the *Nimitz*, and by their own Harriers. You should be able to stand down then, or at least take a little breather." He hesitated, then gave a haggard grin. "At least, we can hope so."

Chris had never seen the CAG looking this beat. Judging from the condition of his khaki uniform, he must have been up all night . . . and probably most of the previous few nights as well. Did the man have a breaking point?

Tombstone continued with the briefing, laying out the specifics of VF-95's part in the mission. The first elements of the raid would start launching within the hour, and VAQ-143's Prowlers, armed with HARM and Tacit Rainbow antiradar missiles, would make their turn toward the Russian coast at 1715 hours, launching at stand-off distance to begin clearing the way for the squadrons to follow. Mixed flights of Tomcats, Hornets, and Intruders would fly through the radar-blind corridor, accompanied by Prowlers providing ECM cover and flying "close enough to the ground to sandblast your bellies," as Tombstone put it. Each flight would be vectored in by Hawkeyes orbiting offshore, which would also warn them of enemy aircraft in the vicinity.

Combat. Lobo shook her head. She was going to be flying into *combat*.

Oh, she'd had her fill of combat flying CAP over the carrier group during the past few days. They'd all had. Somehow, though, the thought of taking the fight to the enemy, attacking him over his own territory, was intensely exciting, exciting enough to banish her fatigue in a warm flush of adrenaline. Both of her kills so far had been at a range of ninety miles; hell, she hadn't even pushed the button. Vader McVey had done that, tracking the targets and launching the big Phoenix missiles when he had a lock. That engagement with the Fulcrum had been scary, but anticlimactic; the MiG had just tagged her with his radar when Slider and Blue Grass dropped in on the bad guy's six. There'd been a confused few moments of high-G maneuvers . . . and then the MiG was dead and she and McVey were in the clear. And the cruise missiles they'd downed could hardly shoot back.

Chris loved the idea of *danger*, though she'd kept her feelings carefully hidden throughout her Navy career. Hotdogs and thrill-seekers never made it far as aviators. But—she could admit it now—it was the danger that had led her to try bungee jumping and rock climbing back when she was a teenager, then flying, and skydiving after that. She'd joined the Navy when she heard the Navy was accepting female aviators. To learn how to fly *jets* . . .

Now she was flying jets, F-14 Tomcats, and she loved it. But the thought of hitting the Russians inside their own territory left her feeling warm and weak, her heart hammering inside her chest.

This was why she'd worked and trained and fought to become a Navy aviator!

"Okay, people," Tombstone said, ending his briefing. "You

know your jobs. Fly safe, stick close with your wingmen, and don't be heroes. We don't care about you, but your airplanes are extremely expensive pieces of equipment. Your plane captains will have your heads if you get them dinged up. So bring 'em back! And God fly with you all!

"That is all."

"Attention on deck!"

He strode from the room, and Chris wondered why he looked so grim. This was what every naval aviator spent his or her whole life training for, this moment.

She joined the others as they crowded up toward the front of the room, examining the Kola Peninsula map and asking questions of Coyote.

Her aircraft, she saw, would be covering an Intruder strike against SAM batteries just west of Polyarnyy.

CHAPTER 21
Monday, 16 March

"God damn it, Ski! What the hell do you mean, 'down-grudged'?"

Lieutenant Commander Frank Marinaro was livid, and for one moment, Joyce Flynn thought the man was going to slam his flight helmet to the deck in anger and frustration.

Tomboy Flynn, Nightmare Marinaro, and their plane captain, Chief Michael Cynowski, were standing at the port-side edge of the flight deck forward of the island. Several of VF-95's Tomcats were parked there, folded wings almost touching, their maintenance crews readying them for launch.

"Sorry, Commander," Cynowski said. He had to shout to make himself heard above the scream of jet engines, the air-hammer racket of the huffers. He wore a plane captain's brown jersey, and a bulky Mickey helmet. "Your AWG-Nine's burned out. Looks like a coolant switch fault, most likely. We'll have to swap it out, and that's gonna take time."

"How much time?"

"What?"

"*I said how much fucking time!*"

"Sir, I just don't have the manpower right now!" Cynowski held up the clipboard in his hand. "My boys've been goin' round the clock here for longer'n I like to think. Hell, we've got their scheds juggled between—"

"Damn it, Ski, I don't want to hear your sob story! How long before Two-oh-four is back on the line?"

Cynowski's face hardened. "Not until we secure from flight quarters. Sir. Two days . . . and that's if the brass stays off our backs!"

Nightmare was the coolest, steadiest aviator Tomboy knew, but at the moment he looked like he was going to lose that cool completely. She could understand his anger. Right now, there were no spare Tomcats aboard save for the CAG bird, and it would take time to bring Two-double-nuts to the ready. It looked like Nightmare and Tomboy were going to be staying put while the squadron launched without them.

Nightmare looked like he was about to say something else, but at that moment an A-6 Intruder taxied past the line of Tomcats, rolling slowly toward the number one catapult. The roar of its engines was deafening, and the wash from its exhaust battered at Tomboy's face, slapping at her flight suit and forcing her to turn away. Nightmare quickly pulled his helmet on and waited until the A-6 reached the cat shuttle and the noise abated somewhat. Suddenly, he seemed to relax. "Okay, Chief. Forget it. C'mon, Tomboy."

"Where we going, Nightmare?"

"Ops. Maybe we can use Stoney's bird."

Together, they turned and strode aft toward the island.

1615 hours
Intruder 504
Catapult One
U.S.S. *Thomas Jefferson*

Lieutenant Commander Bruce "Willis" Payne was uncomfortably aware of the woman seated next to him. In an A-6 Intruder, the pilot sits on the left, with the bombardier/navigator in the narrow seat to his right and slightly below and behind his position. According to *All the World's Aircraft*, the heart of the A-6 was the AN/ASQ-133 IBM computer which controlled the aircraft's Norden AN/APQ-154 multimode radar, but any Intruder driver with more than an hour of flight time logged would insist that the real heart was his B/N, squeezed in eyeball-to-eyeball with the radarscope projecting aft from the console. But *damn!* . . .

Payne's B/N so far this cruise had been Lieutenant Thelma

Kandinsky, "Sunshine" to her shipmates. She was pretty and pert and Payne loved imagining what she'd be like in bed, but he still couldn't accept her as expert enough to find her way through that maze of indicators and electronics in her face, no matter *what* Tombstone Magruder might think. The tail-chewing he'd received a couple of days before still burned . . . and rankled.

"Damn it, Payne," Tombstone had bellowed into his face. *"These women are our shipmates and they're here to stay! They can do the job as well as any man, maybe better, you read me, mister? They've already had to work ten times harder than any man aboard just to get where they are now, and if I hear you're giving any one of 'em a bad time I am personally going to have you keelhauled . . . and on an aircraft carrier that's one hell of a damned serious threat!"*

Fuck. Women had their uses, but they didn't belong aboard ship or flying combat aircraft. Oh, sure, he'd heard all the technical shit about how they could take more Gs than men, how their endurance was higher, how they could handle multiple tasks better than men could. Willis didn't believe that bullshit for a minute. The fact of it was the Washington REMFs were out to screw the little people, again, all in the name of progress.

Payne gave the array of flight instruments in front of him a final check. What the hell was Washington playing at anyway? It seemed fitting, somehow, that the venerable A-6 was on the way out, just as all this new crap was coming on-line.

He loved the A-6. America's premier strike aircraft was coming up on forty years of service. Butt-ugly, blunt end up front, eel-skinny tail aft, with the permanently fixed refueling probe stuck on the nose like a rearing snake. The Navy had hoped to replace the Intruder with the ultra-stealthy A-12 Avenger in the 1990s, but the Secretary of Defense had scrapped the project when budget overruns had reached scandal proportions. Later, during the Clinton Administration, proponents of a streamlined military had actually suggested that, since the Air Force had bombers, there was no need for bomber-carrying aircraft in the Navy.

And there was *real* shit-for-brains thinking. Strike aircraft—the Intruder and the half-bomber, half-fighter Hornet—were the sole reason for even having aircraft carriers in the first place. *Jefferson*'s Intruders were her big guns; her Tomcats were nothing more than armed protection for the carrier group and for her strike planes. Do away with Navy bombers and there was no reason for carriers.

So far, the Navy had managed to hold off the reconstructionists, at least to that extent. Until someone came up with a replacement for the A-12, though, Intruders and Hornets would be carrying the Navy's strike-mission load. Like the A-7 Corsair before it, though, already phased out save for reserve squadrons ashore, the A-6 had about reached the end of its operational life. Pretty soon, there'd be only the F/A-18s left to carry the war to the enemy's home ground, and Payne remained convinced that Hornets were neither fish nor fowl, half-breeds that did neither job well. How could they? Even with their twenty-first-century cockpits, one man was just kept too damned busy flying the aircraft to handle all the radar-intercept and bombing work as well with any kind of efficiency.

Man, the Navy should've stuck with up-rated Intruders.

And all-male combat crews.

And screw the damned politicians.

He'd heard scuttlebutt that Sunshine had been trying to get another partner, and that suited Willis just fine. He had to admit that, so far at least, Sunshine seemed to know her shit. But now they were about to launch into combat, and her life and his would be riding on how well she performed her duties as B/N. Hell, they wouldn't even be able to find the target if she couldn't untangle that gee-whiz video-game imagery on her screen into solid coordinates and vectors.

Besides, she was a goody-two-shoes bitch. When he tried to be friendly, she acted like he was coming on to her. Once, he'd stepped aside to let her enter a compartment first and she'd given him a look to freeze a snowman's balls. And then there was the smoking incident. Willis had once been a heavy smoker. He'd been cutting back a lot lately, but he always carried an extra pack still in the cellophane tucked away in the shoulder pocket of his flight suit. The first time he'd offered Sunshine a smoke, though, just trying to be friendly, she'd looked up at him like he'd just crawled out from under a rock. "Filthy habit," she'd said. "Get those things out of my face."

The pace accelerated as they completed their final pre-flights. He glanced over at her as she completed the last of her

BIT checks, the built-in test batteries that verified the A-6's radar and computer systems were operational.

Screw her. If she wouldn't even try to be friendly . . .

"System's hot," she said. "Ready to roll."

"Roger." A green light was showing from the island as a safety officer gave a last thumbs-up. Willis was all professional now as he looked out the cockpit to where the deck officer was standing ready, and gave a crisp salute. The officer returned the salute, touched the deck, and *Jefferson*'s catapult hurled Willis and Sunshine into the sky.

1635 hours
Flight deck
U.S.S. *Thomas Jefferson*

Seaman Apprentice David James White had been aboard the *Jefferson* for less than six weeks. His entire Navy career thus far had spanned less than four months, for he'd reported aboard straight out of boot camp at NTC Great Lakes, with only a ten-days leave in between to say good-bye to his mom and to his girlfriend Judy back in his home town of Ridgely, Ohio.

He wasn't sure yet whether he liked the Navy. At eighteen, the largest social group he'd ever been a part of was his high school, and he still felt utterly lost among the miles of gray-painted passageways, the noisy horde of strange faces filling a vessel that had been described to him as being as large as an eighty-story building lying on its side. There were six *thousand* people aboard the *Jefferson*; that was twice the population of Ridgely, far more than he could possibly expect to meet and get to know personally if he stayed aboard for a full two years of sea duty. He wasn't aware of them so much as a vast crowd as he was aware of them as strange faces. The only time he saw lots of men all at once was during a flight deck FOD walkdown, but it seemed as though he would never get to really know anyone.

Upon reporting aboard, White had been assigned to the deck division. After three weeks of "P school" orientation, where he'd learned the basics of flight deck theory and been given a course in first aid, he'd been given a slot with the blue shirts, the chock and chain men who secured parked aircraft to keep them from rolling. He'd started making friends . . . and his initiation into the Ancient and Sacred Order of the Blue Noses a few days ago had opened up a whole new world to him. Only now was he beginning to see himself, not as a stranger in this bizarre and alien world, but as part of something larger than himself.

It had been a good feeling.

Then had come the battle on Friday, and moments of stark terror. And after that had come the word that some kid named Pellet had hung himself. Oh, God, how could things like that happen? What had he gotten himself into? In hours, it seemed, the good feelings of belonging and being accepted had evaporated. Most of the guys White knew had withdrawn into themselves somewhat after hearing about Pellet's death. The only antidote the officers seemed to know was work . . . work and more work. White had forgotten when he'd slept last. He was exhausted, and the exhaustion dragged at both brain and body like leaden weights.

He'd been helping a crew unchock the A-6 Intruders parked forward of the island. Someone handed him the two massive chocks that had immobilized one Intruder's wheels, and someone else had pointed across the deck at the place where they were supposed to be stowed.

Though P school had provided a kind of basic orientation to the flight deck, White's actual training so far had been strictly on the job, with various petty officers telling him what to do even when he had little understanding of what he was doing or why. Carrying the chocks, he trotted across the flight deck, toward the waist catapults across from the island and aft.

The entire flight deck was one great storm of raw noise and swirling movement. Men in colored jerseys surged back and forth in some impossible, incomprehensible ballet of motion. The noise, the noise was overwhelming, even through the ear protectors built into White's helmet. An Intruder thundered off the bow, and the jet blast whipped at his jacket. He was afraid. He'd heard time and time again that it was possible for a careless man to step into a jet blast and be hurled off the side and into the sea. In combat, the carrier couldn't stop to rescue one man overboard, and the water was so cold he wouldn't survive more than moments anyway.

I could get killed out here. Death was very much on his mind today. Why had Pellet killed himself?

Darn. Where was he supposed to go now? Someone in a yellow jersey turned and stared at him, then shouted something, his mouth working but the words unheard in the thunder surrounding him. Now he was waving at him, telling him to move *that* way.

The color codes of the jerseys were still hazy. What did yellow mean? White wasn't sure. Which way now . . . over there? An odd-looking aircraft was on one of the waist catapults. White searched his memory. Yeah, it was a Prowler, what someone had called a stretched version of the A-6. The plane was being hooked to the cat shuttle, its engines already screaming against the upright barrier of a JBD. More men were gathered around over there. He started toward them.

Now where? These people were all busy. Was he supposed to be here? He spotted someone in a blue jersey standing close to the Prowler's side and started toward him, chocks still in hand.

Someone yelled. White turned, but kept walking backward. Were they yelling at him? Several men, one in white, the others in yellow, were coming toward him at a dead run. At first, he didn't connect them with himself. He thought he was in the way and took several more steps backward. . . .

1638 hours
Air Ops
U.S.S. *Thomas Jefferson*

Air Ops, right next door to *Jefferson*'s CATCC on the O-3 deck, was a large compartment made claustrophobic by the clatter of display screens, status boards, computer consoles, radarscopes, and television monitors that seemed to fill every available space. Tombstone had the CAG seat, an office executive's chair positioned on the deck to give him a clear view of most of the consoles around him.

"Just stand easy, Nightmare," he told Marinaro, who was standing beside him. The man's dark features had taken on a demonic cast in the eerie glow of radar screens and CRTs. "We'll get you guys up later, if we can."

"I really want to go with them, Stoney."

"I know." *Damn it*, Tombstone thought. *So do I!*

Which was why he was holding back on letting Nightmare and Tomboy take the CAG bird up.

"Damn it, Nightmare," Tombstone snapped. "I've got other problems on my hands right now! If you want to make yourself useful, grab a seat over there and lend a hand with squadron communications. But get the hell out of my hair!"

"Aye, aye, sir."

Shit. He'd not wanted to come down on the guy that hard. Maybe the strain was starting to show. He rose from the chair, intending to call Nightmare back . . .

"God, look there!" another CIC officer shouted. Tombstone froze, staring up at the PLAT monitor suspended from the bulkhead.

"What's the son-of-a-bitch think he's—"

"Oh, *Christ*!"

Tombstone stared in horror at the bloody spectacle on the TV screen. For a stunned moment there was dead silence in Ops. Then the voices started up again, urgent, worried, but continuing to maintain the flow of communications traffic to the aircraft already aloft.

Operations went on, even when they were punctuated by tragedy. From the look of things on the PLAT screen, a sailor had just backed into the intake of a Prowler readying on Cat Three.

The man was dead, of course. There could be no doubt whatsoever about that. Worse—from the point of view of flight operations—though, it appeared that the accident had just killed the Prowler as well. Its starboard engine had shut down, but there was smoke coming from the exhaust and from the intake. From the look of things, a turbine blade had exploded, and that meant bits of shrapnel had just ripped through the aircraft and probably scattered themselves across the deck.

Damn!

CHAPTER 22
Monday, 16 March

1705 hours (Zulu –2)
Air Ops
U.S.S. *Thomas Jefferson*

Chalk this one up to tired men, Tombstone thought.

The flight deck of a supercarrier had often been described as the most lethal working environment in the world, a place where mistakes or carelessness routinely killed people. Thirty minutes after a chain and chock man had stumbled into a Prowler's intake, the fire was out and the aircraft safely evacuated, but hurtling fragments from the Prowler's turbine fan might have damaged some of the Cat Three equipment. Worse, those scattered fragments continued to pose a risk both for Cat Three and for Cat Four next to it. Bits of metal or other debris the size of a bottle cap might still be lying on the deck, hazards that could get sucked into the intakes of other aircraft, damaging them in turn. FOD, or foreign object damage, was the bane of all carrier operations.

In peacetime, the alpha strike would have been cancelled and further catapult launches halted until an FOD walkdown could be carried out, with hundreds of sailors walking in line abreast down the entire length of the flight deck, picking up each bit of debris they found. But this was not peacetime, and a delay now would cripple the operation. Half of *Jefferson*'s aircraft were already headed into Russia at this very moment.

Tombstone reached out and picked up a telephone, punching in the number for the Air Boss. "This is CAG in Ops," he said when Barnes came on the line. "What's your assessment, Boss?"

"Shit, Stoney. Cat Three's down until we can get that Prowler cleared away," the Air Boss replied.

"Okay. How long? What's the downtime gonna be?"

"They're working on it. Maybe an hour before we can walkdown the area."

"And Four?"

"Piece of cake. They're starting a walkdown on Four now. Call it thirty minutes."

Tombstone juggled the numbers in his head. White Storm's flight operations, as laid out in that mountain of paper transmitted from the Pentagon the day before, had allowed for the possibility of two cats going down for that long . . . but only just. They would have no additional time to spare.

"Okay, Boss," Tombstone said. "Put the Prowler over the side. Yeah, munitions and all. Do your walkdowns, but make 'em damned fast. I need those catapults at four-oh ASAP."

"We'll do our best, CAG."

"What are you talking to me for, then? Get on it." He hung up the receiver. On the PLAT monitor covering the waist catapults, deck crewmen were already scurrying across the deck, together with one of the ubiquitous tractors or "mules" used to tow aircraft.

The accident had crippled the EA-6B, but not destroyed it. Still, time was more precious now than equipment. The Prowler, and the millions of dollars' worth of sophisticated electronics aboard, would be tipped over the side rather than allow it to further delay the mission. Too long a delay in the launch schedule, and *Jefferson*'s aircraft would be returning after dark. Night landings were always far more hazardous than recoveries made during the day, and while bombing strikes were planned throughout the night, the plan called for a reduction in the number of missions in order to keep the hazards associated with night ops to a minimum. Rather than face the drastically heightened risks of a night mission, he would have to scrub the alpha strike until tomorrow, and that meant the Marine assault would be going in with a lot more enemy hardpoints and radar sites operational than would be the case otherwise.

Pilot fatigue was Tombstone's principal worry now. Tired men made mistakes, as had just been demonstrated on Cat Three. And every military officer tasked with planning long-range bombing strikes always had to keep in mind what had happened during Operation El Dorado Canyon.

El Dorado Canyon was the code name of the American bombing raid against Libya in 1986, launched in retaliation for Libyan terrorist activities. Part of the assault had been assigned to Air Force F-111 Aardvarks attached to the 48th Tactical Fighter Wing based at Lakenheath, England.

It was a large and complex mission, involving both Air Force planes out of England and Navy aircraft launched from carriers in the Gulf of Sidra, attacking five separate targets, three in and around Tripoli and two at Benghazi. In all, eighteen F-111s had been assigned to the objectives at Tripoli, and of those, nine had been slated to hit the two-hundred-acre compound of Libya's leader, Muammar al-Qaddafi.

But the planning for the El Dorado Canyon had been intense, a strain on pilots and crews that robbed them of sleep for the forty-eight hours preceding the mission. Then, Spain and France had both refused overfly privileges for aircraft participating in the raid, forcing the entire contingent out of England to go the long way around, down Europe's Atlantic coast and past the Strait of Gibraltar, a flight of three thousand miles that took six and a half hours.

That flight had been an epic nightmare, requiring multiple midair refuelings and continuous, nerve-wracking close-formation flying, a tactic designed to make several planes appear as one on enemy radar. One of the pilots became disoriented during refueling and, "flying on automatic," followed the tanker halfway back to England. By the time he realized his mistake, it was too late to rejoin his flight. Four more scrubbed the attack because of breakdowns with the aircraft's electronic systems, especially with the F-111's radar, which proved to have a disturbing tendency to break down during long flights. A sixth Aardvark went down at sea just off the Libyan coast, the only American plane lost in the operation. The cause of the crash was unknown, but pilot error was a definite possibility. A seventh F-111 aircrew probably misidentified a checkpoint on the Libyan coast, though equipment malfunction was also a possibility; whatever the cause, the bombs missed Qaddafi's compound and landed near the French Embassy. Civilians died, including French nationals, in what was ironically and with bitter black humor referred to later as retaliation for the French refusal of overflight privileges. Of the nine original aircraft tasked with the mission, only two actually hit the target. Damage to the compound had been relatively light. Adding injury to the insult, one of the casualties, unfortunately, had been Qaddafi's adopted daughter.

The bombing of the Libyan dictator's compound had not been a direct attempt to kill Qaddafi—it was known that he only intermittently stayed there—but it had been intended to deliver a strongly worded warning against continuing his terrorism campaign against the West. In that, probably, the raid had succeeded, but the poor performance of the Aardvarks in that part of the mission had been a shock. During the planning, it had been estimated that at least four or five of the nine F-111s would be able to complete their bombing runs; two aircraft had simply not been enough to ensure the raid's success.

In fairness, it was important to remember that the other elements of Operation El Dorado Canyon had carried out their parts of the mission flawlessly, causing heavy damage to the other targets.

Tombstone signaled for an enlisted man standing nearby to bring him a cup of coffee. On the PLAT monitor, the Prowler's curiously flattened stabilizer tipped suddenly into the air as its nose went over the side. It hung there a moment, suspended, then vanished below the edge of the flight deck. The deck crew were already lined up along Catapult Three, walking their way slowly aft as they searched for bits of debris. Other men were using fire hoses to wash down an area of the deck astride the rear of the cat, sweeping away mingled gasoline, oil, and blood.

He wondered if the accident had badly shaken the men of the deck crew. Coming on top of a sailor's suicide, an incident like that could further erode morale, might even cause further carelessness and more accidents.

On another PLAT monitor, this one showing activity forward at Cats One and Two, an EA-6B Prowler howled off the port catapult, while hookup men locked the cat shuttle to the undercarriage of an F/A-18 Hornet to starboard. Steam boiled across the deck, obscuring the crowds of color-coded men hurrying about their elaborate choreography of readying, inspecting, and launching aircraft. The checkers, men in white jerseys and with black-and-white checked helmets, were especially evident as they combed each aircraft for downgrudges, open access panels, and loose weapons. In the background, over a communications channel, Tombstone could hear the Air Boss bellowing radio orders from his crows'-nest perch up in Pri-Fly. From the sound of it, there'd been a fault in the "mouse" worn by one of the plane directors, the distinctive earphone headset also affectionately called a Mickoy Mouse, and the director hadn't noticed yet that he was off the air. That was another bit of human error. Every man who had one was supposed to frequently check his personal radio. It took several moments to get another deck officer with a mouse on to go over and physically grab the man and alert him to the equipment failure.

How many more were going to die before this thing was done, either from enemy action or from damned, stupid carelessness born of grinding, bone-weary exhaustion?

Maybe I've just seen too damned much of this, he thought. Pamela had been after him to give it up for a long time, though recently they'd managed to arrive at a kind of uneasy truce between his dedication to his career and their love for each other. Damn, maybe she'd been right all along.

Right now he felt tired—not physically, though that was certainly a part of it, but exhausted in spirit, in his mind. He was tired to the very core of his being, but unlike those teenagers still hard at work full-out on the deck with no sleep, he was ready to pack it in. He thought of the faces of the men and women of Viper Squadron earlier, when he'd told them that they'd be flying shotgun for the Intruders this afternoon. Slider and some of the others had looked like they were ready to mutiny there for a moment . . . but by the time he'd gotten past the initial resistance and started filling them in on their mission, the newer hands had actually looked eager, rousing from their exhaustive torpor, positively glowing when they heard they'd be spearheading an attack wave into Russian territory.

Well, he could remember feeling the same way himself once, when he'd been assigned a challenging or exacting mission. But that was a hell of a long time ago.

Had he made a mistake, ordering the Air Boss to expedite the cleanup on the waist cats? That tired hookup man had merely killed himself and delayed the launch schedule; if *Jefferson's*

CAG screwed up, a lot of people would die. He didn't like the heavy, clammy feeling that thought carried with it.

The Hornet was ready. The deck director gave the aviator a thumb's-up, and the man in the aircraft saluted. The director whirled, dropped to one knee, touched the deck, pointed ahead . . .

. . . and the Hornet screamed off the catapult on a line of steam, dipping slightly as it cleared the bow, then rising steadily into the blue afternoon sky, its landing gear folding neatly away.

Tombstone had made his decision. There was no turning back now.

1724 hours
Intruder 504
Approaching the Kola Peninsula

In tight formation with two other Intruders and a Prowler ECM aircraft, the A-6 boomed low across the water, low enough that salt spray pattered across its windscreen. It was as though they were flying through fog or a light rain, with the windshield wiper ineffectually batting away at the moisture almost as quickly as it collected.

Willis ignored the water, keeping his eyes glued instead to the glowing screen of his Kaiser AVA-1 Visual Display Indicator as he concentrated on keeping his heading and his altitude precise. At an altitude of 100 feet and at a speed of 550 hundred knots, there was no margin for error.

He still felt uncomfortable with Sunshine at his side. Damn it, if she screwed the pooch on this one . . .

Not that she'd screwed up so far. But there was always a first time, and this was when a mistake would get them both killed. Glancing up, he caught the blur of a gray shoreline coming up fast, half-glimpsed through the swish-swish of the wiper. His VDI showed the coast, painted in radar. An instant later, the land exploded around them, replacing the featureless blue-gray blur of the sea.

At his side, Sunshine keyed her radio mike with her left foot. "Terminator 1.504, feet dry, feet dry." They were over land now. Over *Russia*.

"That's Point Yellow-Delta, mark number two," she said. "Come left to zero-nine-three."

He saw the radar profile of a promontory on his screen. "I got it. Zero-nine-three it is." He nudged the stick to the left. Each Intruder had its own precisely calculated, zigzag path to its target, a path through space and time, designed to keep it clear of active enemy SAM and gun batteries, as well as letting it avoid occupying the same airspace at the same time as some other American aircraft.

"Terminator 2.500" sounded over his headset. "We're feet dry, feet dry." That was the voice of Commander John "Thumper" Hargraves, the Death Dealers' squadron leader, coming in a few miles behind 504, and a bit to the east.

"This is 3.505. Feet dry."

"Jammer 4.703." That was the EA-6B Prowler accompanying the Terminator flight, providing electronic countermeasures for the three Intruders as they made their run. "Feet dry, feet dry."

Antiaircraft fire appeared to his left, tracers rising from the ground, like gently drifting specks of orange light. They were past so quickly he didn't even have a chance to see where the fire was coming from.

"We're coming up on mark three," Sunshine said over the ICS. Her helmeted head was still pressed up against the rubber shield of her radar scope. "Point Red-Sierra."

"Okay, boys and girls," Terminator 500 told them over the tactical channel. "That's Red-Sierra, on the money. Time to break. Terminator Five-oh-four, you have the honors."

Red-Sierra was the southern tip of a long island in the mouth of a ragged-edged inlet. There was a fishing village there, Port Vladimir. Willis and Sunshine's flight plan called for a sharp dogleg to the south now, as each aircraft maneuvered independently to come at their objective from a different direction, breaking up the enemy's defensive fire and keeping him guessing about where the next strike was coming from.

Willis brought his stick to the left, veering clear of Port Vladimir and heading sharply south away from the coast. He started climbing too, rising to his attack altitude of six hundred feet.

"Roger that," Sunshine said over the tactical channel. "We're climbing to attack altitude. See you boys over the target."

"Yeah," Willis added. "You guys can eat our dust."

"Launch! Launch!" sounded over his headset. "This is Terminator Five-oh-five! I've got a SAM launch at zero-eight-five!"

"Copy, Five-oh-five," Thumper called. "I see it."

Willis saw it too, a pillar, like a telephone pole painted white, balancing skyward on smoke and flame a mile to the east.

"Looks like they're finally waking up down there," Willis told Sunshine. A threat warning lit up on his console. They were being tracked. "It's about damn time, huh? I was beginning to think they didn't care."

"Three miles to the last turn," Sunshine said, ignoring his banter. Her voice was cold, all business. The Intruder jolted once, turbulence from a near-miss. "Weapons armed. Safe off. Pickle's hot."

The miles flashed by. "Okay," Sunshine said. "Mark. Come right to one-seven-two."

"Rog." The aircraft's wing seemed to skim the blurred earth as the Intruder swung to the right.

"We're in the groove for our approach. Range twelve miles."

More seconds dragged past. Willis's hands were wet beneath his gloves. "C'mon, c'mon. You see 'em yet?"

"Negative. Ten miles."

"Christ, we'll be on top of—"

"Got it! Lots of static from jamming, but I've got a solid lock. Come right a bit. See it?"

"Yeah," he said. "Yeah, I've got it. Going to attack." His VDI changed to attack mode, the graphics now more complex, feeding him more data. He scanned it all: time to target, drift angle, steering point. Where was that missile headed? Damn, he'd lost it when they'd made that second course change, and it was behind them somewhere. Okay. The threat warning was off. The Prowler piggybacking on the Intruder flight must have jammed the thing or seduced it out of the way.

"Not all that much in the way of antiair defenses," he said. Tracers continued to flash and flicker across the ground below them, and the puffy, deceptively peaceful-looking cotton balls of triple-A were scattered across the sky. "Not as bad as I thought it would be this close in, anyway."

"Looks to me like their air defense is pretty much off the air," Sunshine replied. "Thank the Sharks for that."

The Sharks, the EA-6Bs of VAQ-143, had delivered the first blow that afternoon. Their stand-off HARM and Tacit Rainbow missiles homed on enemy radars, even targeting radar sources that were switched on briefly, then turned off. Of course, the enemy was sure to have kept a lot of his radars off the air completely, as a combat reserve.

The A-6 gave another hard jolt, slamming Willis against Sunshine's leg. "Hang on!" He keyed the tactical frequency. "Terminator Five-oh-oh, this is Five-oh-four. I've got my primary. Going in hot."

"Terminator Five-oh-four, Terminator Five-double-oh. Copy that. We'll be right behind you. Good luck!"

"Roger that, Five-oh-four," a different voice said. It sounded like Lucas, in Five-oh-five. "Don't get greedy now. Save some for us poor tagalongs."

"Copy." Willis pushed the stick over, picking up speed as the Intruder's nose dropped below the horizon line.

"Picking up some heavy triple-A here," someone said. Willis didn't catch who it was. "Aw, shit! Shit! I'm hit!"

"Abort your run, Five-oh-five! You're on fire."

"I see it. Engine light. I'm losing my starboard engine. Shit! Fire in the aircraft! Fire—"

The hiss of static chopped the transmission off in midsentence. Willis felt cold. Mike Daniels and his B/N, Frank Lucas, had been good friends.

Somehow, he managed to keep his concentration locked on his VDI. The Intruder was sometimes described as possessing a heads-*down* display, for the aircraft could be flown by an aviator who never needed to look up through his canopy. When Willis did look up, it was into nightmare. Puffs of smoke were scattered thickly across the sky ahead, mingled with the rising, twisting white threads of SAM contrails. His missile-threat warning was flashing again, coupled with a plaintive, chirping warble in his headset.

"Steady," Sunshine warned him. "Steady! You're drifting left!"

On his VDI, his targeting pipper was climbing steadily up the screen toward the release point. Something hit them, a loud thump aft like someone kicking the fuselage.

"I'm taking it in on manual," he said, flipping the selector. If the A-6 had been hit by gunfire, he didn't want to risk going in on auto-release, flying over the target, then finding out they'd failed to release.

The release pipper crawled relentlessly toward the bottom of the display. When it winked out, Willis slammed his thumb down on the pickle switch. In the same instant, the brown and gray ground outside gave way to pavement, runways, dozens of tightly clustered buildings, parked vehicles, and aircraft resting in high-walled revetments. He thought he even glimpsed men down there, dashing wildly for cover.

Then the Intruder lurched heavily upward in a series of thumping jolts. Its warload consisted of thirty five-hundred-pound retarded bombs, four groups of three clamped to A/A 37B-6 multiple eject racks beneath each wing, and two groups more mounted one in front of the other on his centerline, and they were dropping from the aircraft six at a time, in a pattern designed to scatter them across as much real estate as possible.

Relieved of some fifteen thousand pounds of ordnance, the Intruder rocketed into the sky. Willis helped it along, going to full throttle and hauling back on the stick. The shock wave struck them from behind as they climbed.

Willis twisted in his seat, trying to see aft past the Intruder's port wing. The center of the airfield was engulfed in boiling flame, and several buildings were erupting in pulsing, flaring blasts, contributing to the ongoing mass detonations as he watched. "Secondaries!" he yelled, excitement hammering at him. "We've got secondaries."

"Roger that, Five-oh-four," Thumper called. "I think you dropped one into their missile stores! Look at that sucker *blow!*"

"Goddamn!" Willis enthused. "We did it, Sunshine, we did it!"

"Did you have any doubts about that, Willis?" For the first time in long minutes, she had her face out of her radar screen and was looking at him. The eyes visible between her visor and her oxygen mask were very blue, and sparkled with something that might be amusement.

Or possibly it was just pride at a job well and professionally done.

"No!" he said, laughing. Willis felt as though a tremendous weight had been lifted from his shoulders. There was something almost magical in the shared camaraderie of combat that wiped away doubt, replacing it with trust. "*No*, God damn it! I didn't!"

He brought the Intruder around, heading north toward the coast.

CHAPTER 23
Tuesday, 17 March

Early morning hours
The Kola Peninsula

During the night the U.S. Air Force entered the fray. F-117 Stealth Fighters and F-111 Aardvarks, deploying out of Lakenheath and Upper Heyford, England, crossed the mountains above Bodø, then skimmed the forests and lake country of northern Sweden and Finland, striking the Kola military bases from the west and south instead of from the north. "Smart" weapons, first seen publicly in the Gulf War of 1991, followed invisible beams of laser light unerringly into bunker-complex ventilator shafts, aircraft hangar doors, and command-center windows, as American forces kept up a relentless pressure against Russian C^3 assets—Command, Control, and Communications.

Contributing their firepower to the assault through that long night were over two hundred Tomahawk cruise missiles fired from the wide-scattered fleet of Los Angeles–class attack subs in the Barents Sea. Skimming sea and earth at subsonic speeds, the TLAMs followed the terrain features loaded into their onboard computers. Their principal targets were communication relays and operations centers, SAM sites, and aircraft in their revetments.

Carrier strikes continued as well, but at a lower tempo as both deck personnel and aircrews were given a respite in preparation for missions in support of the Marine amphib operations. One carrier attack squadron off the *Eisenhower*, VA-66, the Waldos, participated in a long-range, nighttime strike far to the east. The Waldos' A-6 Intruders were loaded with four Harpoon missiles apiece and sent to hunt down the *Groznyy*, the Russian cruiser that had sunk the *Scranton* the day before.

Guided by Hawkeye radar pickets and by Forward-Looking Infra-Red tracking, or FLIR, they found the *Groznyy* in the mouth of the White Sea and left her burning and with her decks awash. The Waldos and another attack squadron off the *Ike*, the Tigers of VA-65, also hit other naval targets found at sea between Polyarnyy and Grimikha, sinking dozens of vessels from Osa II guided-missile boats to a destroyer, the *Nastoychivyy*. The idea was to convince what was left of the Russians' Northern Fleet to stay at home, in port and safely under the protection of shore-based antiaircraft and SAM batteries.

Meanwhile, throughout the night in the skies above the Kola Peninsula, spy satellites and high-flying Aurora reconnaissance aircraft continued to pinpoint key targets and update the Pentagon's overall intelligence picture. Microwave communications between command centers and outlying facilities were tapped by various electronic intelligence assets. Even from orbit, ELINT satellites could listen in on encrypted conversations between unit commanders and their units; as streams of intercepted communications were relayed back to its secret complex at Fort Meade, Maryland, the National Security Agency, largest and arguably the most secret of America's intelligence organizations, swiftly broke the codes on their batteries of Cray supercomputers. Even without decoding, the patterns of radio communications provided NSA, CIA, and Pentagon analysts with a clear picture of the Russians' Kola Peninsula military command structure . . . and final proof, in the form of orders from Krasilnikov himself, that the defenses were being orchestrated from the Kremlin. The idea that the attacks on the American carrier groups had been carried out by renegade local commanders was clearly a complete fiction.

That night, however, the UN's determination to enforce Resolutions 982 and 984 began taking on a new urgency.

The President sat in his high-backed chair, watching without expression the contorted face of Marshal Valentin Grigorevich Krasilnikov on one of the large television monitors in one wall of the Oval Office. Elsewhere in the room, Gordon West, his chief of staff, and Herbert Waring, the National Security Advisor, along with a number of secretaries, aides, and staffers, stood in silence as they listened to a translator's voice providing a simultaneous translation for Krasilnikov's impassioned speech.

"The United Nations has taken dangerous . . . ah . . . a dangerous course of action," the translator's voice was saying. Krasilnikov's own voice, the volume turned down but still audible, was shaking with an emotion the translator could not express. "For fifty years United Nations has provided forum for international debate, for keeping, uh, for peacekeeping activities through rule of law. . . ."

"The guy's not a bad speech-maker," the President said. "No wonder he went in for politics."

Waring, standing closest to the Chief Executive, looked up from a transcript of Krasilnikov's speech. "I wonder if he might not have some valid points here, Mr. President. After all, if we continue to act as the UN's muscle in Russia, what's to stop the UN from pulling the same tactics against us some day?"

"The alternative, Herb," the President said slowly, "is to let them start nuking each other, and anyone else who makes them mad. The UN can't afford to let that start happening. *We* can't afford to let it happen."

"Uh, oh," Gordon West said. "He's starting in on us now."

"The United States of America has embarked down dangerous road," the translator was saying. "One of military adventurism, of unrestrained and illegal meddling in internal affairs of sovereign, ah, of a sovereign world power. This, perhaps, was safe enough when confronting Third World countries like Iraq or the People's Republic of Korea, nations that could not seriously challenge American military might.

"But now, the United States, operating behind facade of bandit thugs of United Nations, has challenged a great power, one capable of most, of the most severe and devastating retaliatory response."

"My God, he's threatening us!" West said softly. "He's actually threatening to loose his nukes on us if we don't back off!"

"I hear him, Gordy," the President said. Indeed, he'd heard this speech three times that night already, as well as going over the written transcript. The key here was knowing—or at least taking a damned good guess at—what Krasilnikov was really saying beneath his bombastic phrases of you-can't-do-this-to-us hurt and outrage.

"The wanton destruction of one of Russia's most modern ballistic-missile submarines by units of the U.S. Navy operating illegally within the Barents Sea," Krasilnikov went on, "cannot swerve us from our purpose, which is the final unity and security of the Russian peoples, and the defense of our Motherland against all foreign invaders, even those cloaked in the rags of so-called United Nations mandates. The United States should bear in mind the fact that we have many ballistic-missile submarines, and that a suitable demonstration of our will could as easily be directed against the American aggressors as against the traitors in illegal rebellion against the present Russian government."

"Mr. President," Waring said. "It may be that the thing to do at this point would be to pull back, take a deep breath, and think this whole thing through. We are looking at the possibility of thermonuclear war. I don't think we've been this close to a full-scale nuclear exchange since the Cuban Missile Crisis."

The President shifted his gaze to others in the Oval Office. In one corner was a small coterie of military officers, among them the Pentagon liaison, Admiral Magruder.

"What do you say, Admiral?" the President asked.

"Actually, Mr. President, we've been eyeball to eyeball with the Russians several times since 1962. They had nuclear missiles ready to go during the Six-Day War, for instance—"

"That's not what I was asking, Admiral. How shall we respond to Krasilnikov's, ah, accusations?"

"Hardly my place to say, Mr. President. I'm a military man, not a leader of government."

"Damn it, Admiral—"

"Sir, I can point out that all of our intelligence to date suggests that the only nuclear weapons he has access to are those in the Northern Fleet. The rest are either in rebel hands or contested, controlled by loyalist Strategic Rocket Forces but cut off behind the lines in rebel territory. If he were to order a nuclear strike against the United States, it would be a sharply limited one."

"Even a single nuclear detonation in the continental United States would be devastating, Mr. President," West pointed out. "A catastrophe."

"A nuclear detonation anywhere in the *world* could be a catastrophe, Gordy," the President replied. "Especially if one followed another, and another, and another . . ."

"I can also point out, Mr. President," Magruder continued, "that if we pull back now, we achieve nothing. We've gained no ground. We haven't stopped the Krasilnikov faction from carrying out their threats. The American men and women who have died already will have died for nothing but some rather thin symbolism. 'Delivering a message,' as some of your political friends like to put it. We might even lose our whole battle force, probably will, in fact, if the shooting match goes nuclear over there. All for nothing."

"Well, good God," Waring said, angry now. "If it's a choice between losing a couple of damned aircraft carriers and losing New York City—"

"Admiral Magruder," the President said, cutting off Waring in mid-sentence. "Do you think our military forces over there have a chance, any chance at all, of carrying out their mission?"

"Yes, sir. If our intelligence estimates of the situation are correct. If they're not micromanaged into a pocket. If their mission isn't changed on them in mid-course by people back here who think they know better."

"What do you mean?"

Magruder shrugged. "Sir, right now our carrier battle force and the II MEF have clearly defined goals, a mission, a *purpose*, and the support they need to carry it out. If you or the UN decide to change or muddy their mission goals, well, there aren't any guarantees. That was a large part of the problem in Vietnam, the lack of a clear, well-defined objective."

"Point taken, Admiral. The men can do the job, so long as

the guy giving the orders tells them what to do, then gets out of the way."

"Mr. President—" Waring began.

"Herb, we're too far into this to change now. We've got to go ahead."

"God help us if you're wrong, Mr. President."

"Amen," the President replied. "Because no one else will."

0830 hours (Zulu +2)
Air Ops
U.S.S. *Thomas Jefferson*

Despite the continuing, usually good-natured rivalry between Navy and Air Force over who had the better flyers, Tombstone had been damned glad to see the new arrivals plotted on the Ops displays. While Intruders were all-weather, day-or-night-capable attack aircraft, handing off the bombing to the Air Force had let VA-84 and VA-89 stand down for a decent night's sleep, in anticipation of what would be happening in the morning.

Tombstone had been up late the night before again, going over the final planning for Operation White Storm, but he'd been able to pull down five uninterrupted hours of sleep, and when an aide had rousted him awake at 0530 hours he was feeling better rested—and more confident—than he'd felt in several long days.

At least part of his change in heart was the result of a decision he'd made the night before, a decision he implemented that morning with a change to the air wing duty roster. Tombstone had decided to put himself on the active flight list.

Years before, the CAG of a carrier air wing had been expected to fly combat missions. Hell, that was a tradition that went back to World War II, when CAGs really were commanders of air groups and were expected to lead their men against the enemy. Modern warfare, however, had become more and more a war of machines and technicians, of computers and radar-guided weapons and of unit commanders who gave their orders over secure data links. With the superCAG concept, the commander of a carrier air wing, while he still logged his hours of flight time, was expected to lead a mission from Air Ops, where he could use his training and his judgment to direct an entire battle, rather than the small part he'd be able to see from the front seat of an F-14.

By and large, Tombstone agreed with the common sense of doing things that way. It cost hundreds of thousands of dollars to train a man to be a leader; it simply no longer made sense to have an army's generals out front with the flag, the first to die as they inspired their men.

But at this point, the actual development of the battle was largely out of Tombstone's hands. He'd assembled flight lists and schedules, orders of battle and logistical needs, all based on the Pentagon's preliminary work on Operation White Storm. The targets were set, and all he could do was sit in his chair in Air Ops, watching the radars and listening to the voices of his people as they engaged the enemy.

So he'd put himself down to lead a TACCAP, a tactical combat air patrol covering a bombing raid going in over the Kola Inlet later that morning.

"Admiral on deck!"

The men at the Air Ops consoles did not stand, but Tombstone and the other officers watching the operation stood as Admiral Tarrant, flanked by his chief of staff and Captain Brandt, strode in.

"Good morning, CAG," Tarrant said. "They told me I could find you down here."

"You didn't need to come hunting for me, Admiral. I could've come up to the fresh air and sunshine."

Tarrant grinned as he glanced around the Ops compartment, red-lit and claustrophobic. "It is something like a cave down here. I can understand you wanting to get out for a change."

Tombstone suspected he was driving at something. "Sir?"

"I'm disallowing your request, CAG. I need you here, directing your wing. Things are going to get damn complicated this morning when the Marines hit the beaches, and I don't want you off over Russia somewhere. Clear?"

Tombstone's hands flexed briefly at his sides. He knew better than to argue this one. "Clear, sir."

"What kind of casualties have you been running?"

"Remarkably light so far, Admiral. We lost one Tomcat and four Intruders yesterday. We lost another A-6 during recovery."

"What, a crash on the deck?"

"Not quite, sir. Lieutenant Commander Payne had a hydraulics failure after completing his run. He took a hit from triple-A over Vladimir, and his gear failed when he hit the deck. We ditched the aircraft to keep the deck clear, but Payne and his B/N got out okay."

Tarrant nodded. "*Eisenhower* reported similar losses. Light. Suspiciously so."

"Maybe the Russians are too far extended in the south," Captain Brandt suggested.

"That's what everybody back in Washington keeps telling me," Tarrant said, "but I don't quite dare believe it. They're holding something back, and I want to know what it is."

"We had a couple of TARPS aircraft up last night, Admiral," Tombstone said. TARPS—the Tactical Air Reconnaissance Pod System—was a streamlined package flown on the belly of certain specially equipped Tomcats, containing a CAI KS-87-B frame camera, a Fairchild KA-99 panoramic camera, and a Honeywell AAD-5 infrared scanner. It gave excellent and highly detailed photographs of the terrain below, by day or night. "It looks like the bombing strikes have been hurting them pretty bad."

"No argument there. We've been getting the same story through satellites and high-altitude reconnaissance flights. The word from the Pentagon this morning was that we've been putting six out of ten of our targets out of action on the first pass, and we've already started doubling up on most of the targets that are left. Most of their major SAM sites have been knocked out, and their communications network is in a shambles. That the impression your aircrews have been bringing back?"

"Yes, sir. At this point, the biggest problem our planes face is from mobile triple-A, shoulder-launched weapons, even small-arms fire. Some of our planes have been landing with 7.62mm holes in their wings."

Tarrant glanced at Brandt, then back to Tombstone. "Gentlemen, about five hours ago the Pentagon got the final nod from the President. There was some question about how deeply the United States should get itself involved in Russia's internal conflict, but the word now is that White Storm is a go. The President has publicly declared full American support for UN Resolutions 982 and 984, and we are prepared to back them up with direct military intervention on the ground. We are going in to disarm the Russians, gentlemen. One way or another. CAG, you can pass that on to your people in your morning briefing."

Tombstone's heart was pounding in his chest. "Aye, aye, sir."

"Air Force attacks will be continuing as well, of course, so it's likely to get a little crowded over the beach."

"Are any strategic bombing runs planned, Admiral?" Brandt wanted to know.

"No, Captain. B-52s, B-1Bs, and B-2s deployed out of CONUS would all carry the risk of making the Russians think we're escalating a strictly regional conflict into global war . . . or that we might be trying to sneak in a preemptive nuclear strike.

"But anything else goes. Last night, the ships of II MEF shifted eastward to position themselves for the amphibious operation. That will begin at 1000 hours. Both *Jefferson* and the *Ike* will be joining the amphib force later today. Throughout that time, CAG, I want every aircraft you can muster in the air, hitting the Russians everywhere you find them, keeping them off balance. White Storm won't have a chance if Krasilnikov's people can catch their breath and concentrate their forces."

"The next phase of the air op calls for interdiction of the rail lines and roads connecting the Kola bases with the south, Admiral," Tombstone said. "We'll be paying special attention to Kandalaksha, at the head of the White Sea, because that appears to be the hub of the local command structure."

"Excellent. I know if anyone can carry it off, Tombstone, it's you and your people."

"Thank you, Admiral. I'll pass that along to them."

But as they continued discussing the day's operations, Tombstone felt the depression, the pressure, the spiritual tiredness that had been weighing him down for the past several days, returning. If the Russians had reserves, if they were holding something, anything, back, it would be revealed today when the Marines began storming ashore.

And Tombstone would be *here*, in *Jefferson*'s Air Ops, while his people were dying.

Never in his life had he wanted more to disobey a direct order.

CHAPTER 24
Tuesday, 17 March

The U.S. Marines were coming ashore.

During the night, II MEF had deployed for its landings. Covered by the *Eisenhower* carrier group, the Marine amphibious force had taken up a position some fifteen miles northeast of the land mass called Poluostrov Rybachiy, a near-island thirty-five miles long connected to the mainland by a slender isthmus at the head of a narrow bay called the Motovokiy Zaliv.

Within the U.S. Marine Corps, the Marine Expeditionary Force is the largest modern deployable force, consisting of a Marine division, an aircraft wing, and an MEF Service Support Group, a total of 48,000 Marines and 2,600 naval personnel. II MEF, assembled off the Murman coast under the command of Marine Lieutenant General Ronald K. Simpson, included two LHAs, *Saipan* and *Nassau*; two LPDs, *Austin* and *Trenton*; two LPH helo carriers, *Inchon* and *Iwo Jima*; the LST *Westmoreland County*; the LKA cargo ship *Charleston*; and an escort of two Perry-class frigates, two destroyers, and the nuclear-powered guided-missile cruiser *Virginia*.

The Marines' first beachhead was a stretch of low-lying dunes and tundra along the headland west of the Kola Inlet. In this part of the Murman Coast, the northern tree line ran east-to-west some twenty-five miles south of the beach. North of that line, the terrain was tundra, a region of frozen subsoil with only low-growing vegetation, dwarf shrubs, and stunted birches. Cover was scant, and tactical advantage went to the

side with superior mobility. In a lightning operation, CH-53E
Super Stallions approached behind an aerial blitz of Marine
Harriers and Intruders, touching down long enough to disgorge
their loads of fifty-five troops apiece. Close on the Super
Stallions' heels were the air-cushion landing craft, or LCACs,
troop-and-equipment-carrying hovercraft capable of traveling
twenty nautical miles at forty knots, crossing sea, surf, or the
flat, often swampy ground behind the beaches with equal ease.

Following the LCACs, rising from the water like snarling,
prehistoric monsters, were the Marines' AAVP7s, boxy, full-
tracked armored vehicles descended from the amtracks of
WWII. Each carrying twenty-one men and a crew of three, they
were capable of swimming through ten-foot surf on twin water
jets or surging across the land at up to forty miles per hour. The
Marines wasted no time on the beach, using their speed and
maneuverability to push past or over the coastal defenses and
to get into the enemy's rear.

Resistance was sporadic, though in isolated spots it was
fierce. Most of the defenders were KGB Border Guards and
Internal Ministry MVD troops, indifferently trained and disoriented by the savagery of the aerial attacks. Fifteen minutes
after the Marines began hitting their beaches and LZs, those
units were beginning to surrender in droves.

Some beach positions, however, were held by Naval Infantry, members of the 63rd Guards Kirkenneskaya Naval Infantry
Regiment, with its main base in Pechenga. These troops, the
Russian equivalent of U.S. Marines, put up a stiff fight,
refusing to surrender and clinging to their positions with an
almost fanatic tenacity.

As the fight for the beaches continued, however, additional
Marines were being ferried far behind the coastline, angling in
from the northwest toward naval and air bases scattered along
the west banks of the Kola Inlet. Local radar sites were either
in ruins or in hiding, and Marine Harriers off the *Saipan* and
Nassau flew close-support missions that cleared corridors from
the sea to the inland LZs. By late morning, Marines were
fighting a hundred separate battles, from Port Vladimir to
Sayda Guba.

Meanwhile, the attack aircraft of the carrier battle force,
protected by Navy Tomcats, were picking up the tempo in their
relentless hammering of the Kola bases.

1135 hours
Tomcat 201
Shotgun 1/1
Over the Kola Peninsula

Coyote glanced from one side of his canopy to the other, noting that the other aircraft in his flight were in position. The sky was clear, empty save for a few scattered wisps of cirrus at high altitudes. Ahead and below, skimming the barren land at three hundred feet, were three A-6 Intruders and an EA-6 Prowler, a strike force with the call sign White Lightning One. Coyote and Cat were following at one thousand feet, in tight formation with three other Viper Squadron Tomcats flying close Tactical Combat Air Patrol, or TACCAP, on White Lightning. Their call sign that morning was Shotgun One. Three miles to the west, Shotgun Two was covering White Lightning Two.

"Shotgun, Shotgun" sounded over Coyote's helmet phones. "This is Echo Whiskey Two-one. We're reading aircraft coming off the ground at Ura Guba. Could be an intercept."

"Echo Whiskey, Shotgun One-one," Cat replied in the back seat. "Copy that. I've got them."

Echo Whiskey was the Hawkeye providing battle management for the White Lightning/Shotgun strike force. Ura Guba was a small town at the head of the narrow gulf south of Port Vladimir, about twenty miles to the east of their current position. There was a military base there, one that had been hit repeatedly during the past eighteen hours.

"Talk to me, Cat," Coyote said over the ICS. "Whatcha got?"

"Two contacts, Coyote, just coming up out of the ground clutter. Range eighteen miles, bearing zero-eight-five."

Coyote opened his mike to the flight's tactical frequency. "Okay, Shotgun One. You all hear that? Sound off."

"Shotgun One-two," Coyote's wingman, Mustang Davis, called. "We copy."

"Shotgun One-three," Slider Arrenberger called. "Copy."

"One-four." That was Slider's wingman for this mission, Lobo, Lieutenant Chris Hanson. "We copy."

Coyote was well aware of the friction between Arrenberger and some of the women. He and Tombstone had discussed the matter at length several times over the past few days. Normally, Arrenberger flew wing with Nightmare Marinaro, but Marinaro's Tomcat, downgrudged the previous afternoon, was still down.

Both Coyote and Tombstone had been doubtful about assigning Lobo Hanson as Slider's wingman in Nightmare's place. Aviators flying wing with one another had to work closely, with an effortless and professional communication born of practice and mutual understanding, and Arrenberger, it was well known, had managed to irritate or outrage just about every woman in CVW-20.

But Tombstone had been running into problems with squadron assignments already. True, Coyote could have taken Hanson as his wing and let Mustang fly with Slider, but he and Tombstone had agreed that shuffling the rosters like that would cause more problems in the long run. Once people started getting the idea that either they or someone else was getting preferential treatment, morale would take a nose-dive, and there were troubles enough in *that* department already.

The only special treatment Tombstone had okayed—and that in complete secrecy—was to keep Lieutenants Strickland and Hanson in separate flights. The rumor had managed to spread throughout the wing that those two were sleeping together. While there was no meat to that rumor beyond the strictly circumstantial evidence of their PDAs, both Coyote as Squadron CO and Tombstone as CAG agreed that having them in the same flight risked the cold and professional calm, the engineer's detachment valued in combat flying. Human emotions didn't follow predictable patterns or lend themselves to graphs or flight data tables. What would happen to one if the other got into trouble? For the time being at least, Hanson would fly with Shotgun One, while Strickland was assigned as Batman's wingman in Shotgun Two.

Coyote's thoughts touched only lightly on the flight assignment problems. Right or wrong, the decision had been made. The primary problem at the moment was those aircraft taking off from Ura Guba.

"Shotgun Two-one," Coyote called. "This is Shotgun One-one. Do you copy?"

"Affirmative One-one," Batman's voice replied. "What's the gouge?"

"How about taking the reins for both White Lightnings, Batman? We'll slide east and eyeball those bandits coming up at zero-eight-five."

"Roger that, Shotgun One. We'll mind the store."

"Shotgun One, this is One-one. On my mark, break left and go to a two-by-two dispersal. Let's see if these boys want to play."

"Roger that," Slider replied. "Let's nail us some of those sons of bitches!"

"Ready then, on three . . . two . . . one . . . break!"

As one, the four Tomcats stood on their portside wings, slipping away from the Intruder flight ahead and angling off toward the east. Splitting into two groups of two, Coyote and Mustang moved high and to the north, while Slider and Lobo went low and to the south. The bandits were approaching rapidly, already at a thousand feet and coming on at better than Mach one.

"We're closing too fast to risk a Phoenix launch," Cat told Coyote. They were flying with a standard interception warload of four AIM-54s, two Sidewinders, and two AMRAAMs. "Recommend AMRAAM."

"Rog." Though if they got much closer they'd be in knife-fighting range.

"One-one, this is One-three!" That was Arrenberger. "I've got four bandits now, repeat four. Range ten miles and still coming hot!"

"Confirmed," Cat said over the ICS. "Four bandits. Coyote, I've got a threat warning."

Coyote heard it in his headset, the thin, high warble that meant an enemy fire-control radar was painting his aircraft. "I'm switching to air-to-air mode on my HUD." Damn! Adding their speed to his, the lead target was closing at over 1,500 knots, a good half mile every second.

There was no time to think . . . only to act. "Mustang! Stay with me! Going to full burner!" He rammed his throttles forward to zone five, felt the kick-in-the-seat boost of the F-14's powerful GE turbofan engines.

As he accelerated, his wings folded themselves to their sixty-eight-degree backswept configuration, and a moment later he slid smoothly through the sound barrier.

"Launch! Launch!" Cat cried. "Bandits have launched!"

But by going supersonic, Coyote had unexpectedly closed the range so quickly that he was already inside the Russians' optimum range for a head-on radar lock. He saw two of the enemy fighters as they flashed past, a pair of specks against blue sky that appeared, then dwindled astern almost too quickly to follow.

Immediately, Coyote chopped back on the throttles and went into a hard left turn. The Tomcat shuddered as he yanked it into an edge-of-the-envelope angle of attack, his wings sliding out to full extension, the G-forces squashing him and Cat down into their seats with the force of six full-grown people sitting in their laps. Spots danced in front of his eyes . . . and then his vision started to turn gray, closing in from the sides as blood drained from his head.

He grunted hard, tensing the muscles of his legs and torso in order to keep the blood from draining from his head. The practice was properly called the M-1 maneuver, though aviators simply called it the grunt. A good grunt could lessen the effects of the turn by perhaps one G.

"Where . . . are . . . other . . . two?" he said, forcing each word out past clenched teeth.

"Passing . . . on our . . . six! . . . Two . . . miles . . ."

He was taking a chance, letting the bandits get between him and the two Intruder flights, but the range had started out so tight that there'd been little else he could do. Now he was behind one of the bandit elements. Mustang, with Walkman, his RIO, was still with him, on his right.

Then they were out of the turn and squarely on the six of the two bandits. "Mustang, this is Coyote!" he called, even as he slid the targeting box across one of the targets. "I've got the one on the left!"

"And I've got the one on the right."

A buzz sounded over his headset. "I've got tone. Fox one!"

An AMRAAM slid off the rail beneath his right wing.

1138 hours
Tomcat 209
Shotgun 1/3

Lieutenant Commander Gregory Arrenberger had gotten his handle from shipboard slang during his flight training at Pensacola. A "slider" was a hamburger, as opposed to a "roller," or hot dog. Commended by his CO for the cold-blooded precision of his formation flying, he'd replied, "Hell, sir, I'm no hotdog." The nickname Slider seemed inevitable after that, especially when connected with the "berger" in his last name.

Slider was using every bit of his engineer's precision now as he pulled his Tomcat out of a hard-right turn, tracking on the second element of Russian planes streaking through the Tomcat formation. For a moment there, tunnel vision had clamped down on him and he'd felt himself wavering at the edge of consciousness, but he'd grunted away at an M-1, forcing the blood to stay in his head . . . and then he'd been in the clear, gasping into his oxygen mask with the effort but smoothly lining up on one of the low-flying MiGs displayed against his HUD.

Where the hell was his wingman . . . wing*person*, he corrected himself with a wry grin beneath his mask. Glancing left, outside the radius of his turn, he saw nothing and assumed she'd not been able to keep up with him. He had nothing against Hanson personally, of course—she seemed like a nice kid—but damn it, women had no business at the controls of a hot combat fighter.

Lock! "Blue Grass!" he called to his RIO. "I got tone! Fox one!"

The AMRAAM shrieked clear of the Tomcat, and Slider immediately pulled right, angling toward a second lock on the other Russian fighter.

"Pull up, Slider!" Blue Grass screamed in his ear. *"Pull up!"*

Instinctively he brought the stick back and eased back on the turn. A shadow blotted the light to his right, then slid beneath his aircraft.

"*Jesus*, Slider!" sounded over his headset. "Watch where the hell you're driving!"

Only then did Slider realize that Lobo must have stuck with him through the turn, had actually stayed inside his turn where the G-forces were higher . . . and he'd come a thumbnail's breadth from turning right into her.

"God damn it, Hanson!" he yelled back. "Give me some flying room, huh?" But he knew even as he said the words that he should have checked right for his wingman as well as to the left.

"Let's stay frosty, guys." That was Lieutenant j.g. "Vader" McVey, Hanson's RIO. "I've got two more lifting up from Ura Guba."

"Okay," Slider said. "But stay off my ass, lady! No more of this welded-wing shit!"

"Affirmative." Hanson's voice was tight and cold. Had she been as shook by the near-miss as him? Or was she just mad because he'd snapped at her?

There was no figuring women. He'd apologize later. It *was* his fault, after all, and Arrenberger prided himself on being fair.

Ahead, the Russian aircraft Slider had fired at was climbing hard, close enough now that he could distinguish the characteristic silhouette of a MiG-29, with its widely separated engine nacelles and flared LERX, the leading-edge roof extensions over the aircraft's intake.

"He's dumping chaff," Blue Grass announced. "He's pulling an Immelmann."

"I'm on him." He hauled back on the stick, climbing rapidly to cut the Russian off at the top of his twisting, vertical maneuver. The AMRAAM was still tracking, but Slider wanted to position himself to nail the guy if he gave the air-to-air missile the slip.

"I'm going for a Sidewinder lock," Lobo said over the tactical channel. "I've got a shot . . ."

"Get out of there, Lobo. He's mine!"

"Screw you, Slider. Fox two!" A white contrail seared into the sky ahead of Slider's F-14, swinging upward as it tracked the exhaust of the MiG.

"AMRAAM's been suckered, Slider," Blue Grass told him. "Miss!"

"Shit!" Glancing back over his shoulder this time to make

sure he was clear, he threw his Tomcat right. He wanted to maneuver into a good position to catch the MiGs still rising from the Ura Guba air base. Lobo could *have* the damned Fulcrum.

1140 hours
MiG 744
Near Ura Guba

In an Immelmann, the aircraft goes into a twisting, vertical climb, dropping chaff or flares if it's trying to break a missile lock, then rolling out at the top in an unpredictable direction. The Fulcrum pilot had already lost the American's AMRAAM radar lock; now, he could see the Sidewinder coming up after him, and his next maneuver was designed to defeat that as well. Releasing a scattering of fiercely burning flares, he rolled out of his climb coming straight back toward his attackers, deliberately swinging his twin engine exhausts away from the heat-seeking missile and throttling back at the same time.

While the AIM-9M was an all-aspect heat-seeker, its sensors were not infallible. This time they preferred the white-hot lure of burning magnesium to a target that had suddenly dwindled away to almost nothing. The Sidewinder flashed past and out of the fight, as the Fulcrum stooped from the top of its climb, diving straight toward the pair of Tomcats a mile ahead and below.

The Russian was grinning as he locked onto one of the gigantic F-14s with the huge, multi-barrelled 30mm rotary cannon mounted inside his port LERX.

The Fulcrum shuddered as the gun thundered.

1140 hours
Tomcat 209
Shotgun 1/3

Arrenberger was halfway into his turn when the tracers came searing past his cockpit, bright yellow globes of light that looked as big as grapefruit and close enough to touch.

Something hit the Tomcat in the belly hard, the *thump* rattling Slider's teeth.

"Christ, Slider!" Blue Grass was screaming, his voice ragged. "Get this turkey out of here!"

Turkey. Navy fliers reserved the name for the Tomcat, an aircraft that they loved, but which could betray them by its size and by its slow maneuvering compared to the more nimble MiG-29. Already into his turn, right wing high, Slider pulled the Tomcat into a barrel roll, sliding up and over the stream of tracers flashing toward him from the oncoming MiG.

Too late. The MiG pilot had already corrected for the changing angles between his aircraft and Slider's. Five more rounds slammed into the Tomcat with a rippling shudder of tortured metal, and Slider saw the flash of his starboard engine warning light.

"Shit!" He opened his mike to the tactical channel. "This is Shotgun One-three! I'm hit! I'm hit!"

Power in his starboard engine was dropping. Another burst of 30mm cannon fire smashed into his aircraft, and then Blue Grass was screaming, an inhuman screech of raw agony.

"Blue Grass! Blue Grass!"

His RIO wasn't operating the ICS switch on the cockpit floor, but his screams were loud enough for Slider to hear them anyway. "My legs!" And then his RIO was screaming again, a nightmare keening that went on and on as the MiG kept coming. . . .

CHAPTER 25
Tuesday, 17 March

Lobo had a split second to make the right choice. Her Tomcat was pointed straight at the oncoming MiG, and her HUD was already set to air-to-air-missile mode. With the range between her aircraft and the MiG dwindling rapidly to nothing, she could break away and circle, trying to get on the bad guy's tail, or she could extend her climb for a critical few seconds in an attempt to make a kill. It would have to be a Sidewinder launch; she didn't have time to switch to guns.

Bring it to the left . . . There! Lock! *Fire!* "Fox one!" she shouted, and her last Sidewinder howled off the rail and toward the oncoming MiG. The range was already down to a scant few hundreds of yards.

Time seemed frozen in that one, stark instant. Lobo could see the MiG just to the left of her Tomcat's nose, could see such details as the numerals 744 painted on the side of its sharply raked left intake, and the red and white helmet of its pilot inside the clear bubble canopy.

The AIM-9M lanced beneath the Fulcrum's port LERX and straight into the gaping intake. The explosion blew out the MiG's left engine, a puff of smoke and glittering debris, deceptively gentle . . . and then the Russian plane's wing tank erupted in white-orange flame, and its nose was spinning end over end and hurtling straight toward her out of an expanding globe of destruction.

Lobo jinked right, trying to avoid the deadly cloud of debris, but she could still hear the sharp *ping* and *pock* of fragments striking her wings, fuselage, and canopy. The burning nose section flashed past, seemingly close enough to touch, though it must have missed her by fifty yards. The fire reached out toward her . . .

. . . and then she was through, in blue and empty sky once more.

"Right down the throat!" Vader cried from the back seat. "God, Lobo! That was the gutsiest damn move I've ever seen!"

"Thanks. Shotgun One-three! One-three! This is Shotgun One-four! Do you copy?" There was no immediate answer. Damn! Where was he?

"Vader!" she called. "What's happening out there? Where is everybody?"

"Looks like the other MiGs were killed or they broke off, Lobo. Coyote's rallying Shotgun back behind the Intruders."

"Do you have Slider on your scope?"

"Bearing two-seven-five, range one mile."

She turned her head, searching . . . there! He was low, so low she'd missed seeing his gray aircraft against the monotonous gray terrain below. He had his wings extended and he was flying slowly toward the west, away from her.

"Shotgun One-three!" she repeated. "One-three! This is Shotgun One-four! Do you copy? Please respond!"

"One-four, this is One-three." Slider's voice sounded shaken.

"Slider! You radioed that you were hit. What's your damage?"

"Starboard engine out. Can't restart. And . . . Blue Grass is hit. He was screaming for a moment there. He's stopped now, but I can't raise him. I think he was hit pretty bad."

"Okay. Are your controls still working?" She was moving in closer now, watching Slider's Tomcat, a huge, gray, spread-winged eagle against the horizon ahead.

"Affirmative. I've moved my wings forward to maintain lift."

"I see you. Hold it steady, Slider. I'm coming up behind your aircraft, on your five and low."

"Rog."

Gently, she eased closer, inspecting the other plane. "I see some damage, Slider. Some holes in your starboard nacelle, about where your intake compressor is, and forward from there. And . . . looks like three big holes right below your RIO's seat."

"Can you see Blue Grass?"

"I see his helmet. He's slumped over, not moving. He's either unconscious or dead."

"Oh, damn, damn . . ."

"Okay, Slider. I'll tell you what. You can still fly, so let's nurse your turkey back to the bird farm, okay?"

"I'll never make it, Lobo."

"Damn it, yes, you will! Now bring her around to three-five-zero, nice and easy." She shifted to another frequency. "Shotgun One-one, this is Shotgun One-three!"

"One-one. Go ahead, Lobo."

"My wingman's been shot up pretty bad. One engine out and his RIO's hit. Permission to escort him back to the *Jeff*."

There was a brief hesitation. "Okay, Lobo. That's a roger. We splashed three of those MiGs, including your kill, and the others seem to have lost interest. You go ahead and get Slider and Blue Grass back to the boat."

"Roger. We'll be waiting for you with the beer when you get back." She shifted back to the channel she'd been using to talk to Arrenberger. "Okay, Slider. Let's see if you can get a bit more speed out of that thing."

**1144 hours
Tomcat 211
Shotgun 2/2**

Lieutenant Steve Strickland, Striker, had heard the brief exchange between Coyote and Lobo. His relief at hearing that Chris was all right had left him feeling weak and a little dizzy, enough so that he'd had to check his oxygen-flow panel to make sure his mask was still working.

He had no doubts now. His feelings for Chris Hanson had gone way beyond any merely sexual desire. Sex might have explained his initial attraction for her, that and their shared lust for the exotic and the dangerous that had led them to break the rules in the first place. But now, he knew he loved her, knew that he was going to marry her the moment *Jefferson* returned to Norfolk. The thought of anything happening to Chris . . .

He glanced to his left out of the cockpit. Batman and Malibu were just off his port wing, and beyond them, Brewer and Pogie and C.T. and Junker. None of them had been involved in that short, sharp dogfight a few moments before, and they were maintaining their position at one thousand feet, between the two White Lightning Intruder flights.

Striker still wasn't sure he knew what he thought about women flying combat jets. He'd always thought of himself as a progressive liberal, and that meant believing implicitly in a woman's right to do anything a man could do, including defend her country. Since he'd begun feeling this way about Chris, though, he'd started questioning the whole idea. Every time he thought of her going down in flames, maybe punching out over the cold, empty sea . . .

"Shotgun, Shotgun" he heard over his helmet phones. "This is Echo Whiskey Two-one. We've got more aircraft coming off the ground at Ura Guba, at least four new bogies. We're also reading four new contacts at very low altitude, heading in your direction just south of Port Vladimir."

"Copy that, Echo Whiskey Two-one," Coyote replied. "Heads up, Shotgun. We've got more company coming."

Striker was already checking relative positions on a small map of the northern Kola Peninsula he carried clipped to a pad on his thigh. Two groups of Russian planes, one just a few miles to the west at Ura Guba, the other coming in behind them, from the north. That northern group, the Russian planes at Port Vladimir . . . they must be heading straight for Chris and Slider.

Chris! . . .

"Shotgun Two-one, this is Two-two!" he called. "Batman! Those Port Vladimir bogies must be moving to pick off Shotgun One-three and One-four!"

"I hear you, Striker," Batman replied. "Hold your formation."

"But Batman! We've got to—"

"Hold your formation, Striker! If those MiGs are after anyone, it's White Lightning!"

"Hey, Striker," Lieutenant j.g. Ken Barringer called from the back seat. "Stay frosty, man! She'll be okay!"

"Stuff it, K-Bar!" he snapped back. White Lightning's target, a collection of dockyard facilities along the Kola Inlet, was less than five miles ahead. For one wild moment, he wondered what would happen if he broke formation heading north to cut off those Port Vladimir bandits before they jumped Chris.

Besides, of course, his being court-martialed the moment he got back to the *Jefferson*.

1145 hours
Tomcat 202
Shotgun 2/1

Batman glanced to his right, trying somehow to read the expression on the face of the masked and helmeted Striker, flying a few feet off his starboard wing. Could he depend on his wingman to stick with him?

"Batman, this is Coyote."

"Batman here. Go ahead."

"Take your flight high and to the north. See if you can pull an end run on those bandits coming in from Ura Guba."

"Roger. Everybody hear that?" One by one, the other three aircraft of Shotgun Two acknowledged. "Okay. Let's make our move. Break!"

The four Tomcats peeled off to the left, rolling onto an intercept course.

1145 hours
MiG 871
Ura Guba

Podpolkovnik Yevgenni Averin pulled back on his stick, lifting the MiG smoothly off the runway. Excitement burned in his heart and gut and brain. Yesterday, when the American air strikes had begun, he'd been furious at the orders his interceptor regiment had received from Kandalaksha, orders requiring them to remain on the ground in carefully hidden revetments, safely camouflaged from the spying senses of Yankee satellites or high-flying reconnaissance aircraft. It had seemed cowardly, hiding like that as bombing strikes and cruise missiles had slammed into military targets from Pechenga to Kandalaksha itself.

He and his men had followed orders, however, obeying the system even if they privately questioned the intelligence of the brass-heavy rear-echelon bastards running this colossal fuckup. Now, though, he realized that there'd been some strategic sense behind those orders after all. Everywhere, all over the Kola Peninsula, aircraft preserved from the general destruction of the past eighteen hours were rising from their airfields. Runways heavily pitted by American cluster munitions and cratering bombs had been hastily repaired during the night, by engineers dragging steel-link mats across the smaller holes, and filling in the larger ones with rubble.

It was like guerrilla warfare, but carried out with the high-tech weapons of modern air combat. American strike planes and their escorts deep inside Russian territory were suddenly being assaulted from all sides, by aircraft appearing out of bases the Americans thought had already been knocked out of action.

He checked his radar. Barely visible through the haze of jamming from enemy EA-6B Prowlers, he could make out several main groups of aircraft to the east, most of them heading toward Polyarnyy.

"*Volkodav* Eight-seven-one," he called. The flight's call sign meant Wolfhound. "Airborne."

Seconds later, detailed vectoring data from Ura Guba air control began feeding through the radio in the "Snoopy" communications cap beneath his helmet.

1145 hours
Tomcat 211
Shotgun 2/2

Striker was sticking with his wingman, holding position on 202's right as Batman lined up with the lead Russian plane coming up from Ura Guba. "Let's take it with a Phoenix, K-Bar!" he told his RIO.

"We've got a lock," K-Bar replied. "Range five miles."

Damned close for an AIM-54C, but American and Russian aircraft would be mixing it up real close in another few moments. He wanted to save his Sidewinders and AMRAAMs for close engagements.

"Fire!"

The heavy Phoenix slid clear of the Tomcat's belly. "Fox three!"

The AIM-54 arced off toward the west, drawing a razor-crisp line of white across the sky.

Moments later, a tiny flash went off against the western horizon, leaving a tiny puff of white smoke. "Hit!" K-Bar shouted. "Splash one MiG!"

But then the remaining MiGs were arrowing in at better than Mach 1. Contrails scrawled twisted trails across the sky as American and Russian planes joined in a savage dogfight.

1146 hours
Air Ops
U.S.S. *Thomas Jefferson*

"Pull up, C.T. Pull up!"

"I can't shake this guy!"

"Mustang, this is Coyote. Loose goose now. You hit him high, I'll take him low!"

"One-two! I'm clear! I'm taking the shot!"

"C'mon, Mustang! Help me out here!"

"Break left, C.T.! Fox one!"

"It's comin' . . . it's comin' . . ."

"Hit! Splash another Fulcrum!"

Tombstone stood motionless in the unnatural stillness of *Jefferson's* Air Ops. Closing his eyes as he listened to the radio calls between the Tomcat crews, he could picture the dogfight, the tangling of contrails and machines, of speed and technology and three-dimensional dynamics that Navy aviators called a furball. According to the displays repeated from the Hawkeye orbiting off Port Vladimir, two MiGs had already died, but at least eight more were now trying to brush past the fighters in an attempt to hit the two White Lightning groups—six Intruders and two Prowlers.

It was murder, listening to his people fighting for their lives, unable to help.

1146 hours
Tomcat 207
Shotgun 1/4

"On your toes, Lobo!" Vader warned. "I read two bandits coming dead on and climbing. They're after us!"

"Which way?"

"Bearing three-five-three."

Between them and the *Jefferson*. "One-three, this is One-four. Stay put, Slider. I'm going on ahead, see if I can pop these bozos one."

"Roger that, Lobo. And . . . uh . . . thanks. For saving my ass back there."

"Don't mention it, Slider. It's all just part of our courteous and dependable service. Hang on, Vader. I'm going to burner."

1146 hours
MiG 871
East of Ura Guba

Lieutenant Colonel Averin had broken away from the searing aerial dogfight when the MiG flying less than twenty meters off his right side had suddenly exploded in a dazzling flash and a fireball. Poor Yuri . . . struck down by one of the long-ranged American super-missiles before he'd even had time to acquire a target!

Averin was on the northern fringe of the battle, and as he studied the radar picture, he realized that he had an unprecedented opportunity. Two American aircraft had drawn off toward the north and appeared to be moving toward the sea. At the moment, several MiGs out of Port Vladimir had cut them off and were moving to intercept.

And Averin was in an ideal position to angle in on the Americans' rear, attacking them from the ideal set-up point off their tails while they were concentrating on the Russian forces in front of them.

He studied the images, which grew clearer moment by moment despite the jamming as he drew closer to them.

Yes . . . definitely two planes, one in the lead, the other trailing, possibly already damaged from the way it was moving. Averin selected one of his short-range R-60 missiles, the infrared homer Western pilots called "Aphid." If he could get close enough, he could send the R-60 right up the Yankee pilot's ass before he even knew he was being hunted.

1146 hours
Tomcat 211
Shotgun 2/2

"Hey, Striker!" K-Bar called. "Got a straggler, pulling off toward the north. Range about ten miles."

Striker stared at his display, trying to interpret the complex weave of moving blips. It looked like the MiGs were boxing Chris and Arrenberger in, with one lone straggler coming in on them from behind.

"Batman, Striker!" he called, going to zone-five burner. "I got a target! I'm in pursuit!"

"Damn it, Striker! Where the hell are you going?"

But Striker wasn't listening. His full concentration was focused on that lone Russian MiG, now eight miles ahead. He selected an AMRAAM and went for a radar lock.

1147 hours
MiG 871
East of Ura Guba

Lock! Averin grinned behind his oxygen mask as he squeezed the firing trigger on his stick, loosing the R-60 heat-seeker from its cradle beneath his wing. The target was still on afterburner and arrowing directly away from him, providing a target he couldn't miss.

1147 hours
Tomcat 207
Shotgun 1/4

The Tomcat slammed toward the north, twin spears of flame roaring from its engines. The air was heavy with moisture, and streamers of mist appeared, streaking aft from both wings.

"Range four miles," Vader warned. "One of 'em's got a radar lock on us."

"Selecting AMRAAM," Lobo replied. "I've got him on my HUD."

"Missile launch! Radar-homing missile is locked onto us!"

"Lock! Tone! Fox one! Now hang on! Breaking right! Hit the chaff!"

As her AMRAAM shrieked toward the north, Chris pulled into a hard, tight turn, dumping clouds of chaff to break the approaching missile's radar lock. The G-forces built, crushing her down against her seat until she'd come about a full one-eighty and was heading south once more.

"Lobo! Missile incoming, straight ahead!"

"What—"

She didn't have time to react or to analyze. For one fatal instant, she thought that Vader was referring to the radar homer fired by the Port Vladimir MiGs, a missile that was now *behind* them. As she jinked right, still dumping chaff, she realized that Vader had just picked up *another* missile, a heat-seeker, arrowing in from the south . . . now so close she could see it as a black pinpoint silhouetted against its own exhaust, rapidly growing larger. As she pushed the Tomcat farther into the turn, the new missile slid toward her left shoulder but seemed to be moving much more quickly now, curving slightly to meet her turn, leaping straight toward her cockpit with heart-pounding speed.

"Flares!" she yelled at Vader. "Pop flares!"

1147 hours
Tomcat 211
Shotgun 2/2

"Fox one!"

The AMRAAM streaked toward the Russian MiG, now only three miles ahead . . . but Striker had already seen the flash of the MiG's missile launch. Shit! Was he already too late?

1147 hours
Tomcat 207
Shotgun 1/4

Lobo knew it was already too late. Dropping flares, reversing her turn to take her toward the new missile instead of away, she knew there was nothing more she could do. The missile slammed into the Tomcat's left wing close by the engine. There was a shattering explosion, and then half of the F-14 was ablaze and she was tumbling through a dizzying spin, earth alternating with sky in her canopy. Centrifugal force pinned her for a moment against the side of the cockpit, but she was able to grope for the striped ejection ring between her legs.

"Vader!" she called. "Punch out!" There was no answer. "Vader! Eject! Eject! Eject!"

Then she yanked the ring. The canopy exploded away over her head, and then the rocket motor built into the base of her ejection seat fired, kicking her into a roaring, shrieking hell of wind and noise and flame.

CHAPTER 26
Tuesday, 17 March

1148 hours (Zulu +2)
Over the Kola Peninsula

Lobo fell through space, the roar of her ejection gone now, replaced by the eerie shriek of air rushing past her helmet. A moment later, her chute opened with a savage jerk at her shoulders and groin. Looking up, she was rewarded by the heart-filling sight of an open and undamaged canopy stretching overhead.

Where was Vader? His ejection seat should have triggered an instant after she'd cleared the cockpit, but she couldn't see him, couldn't see her stricken F-14, for that matter. There was a tangle of contrails off toward the south, where Shotgun was still battling the MiGs, but she was all alone in that wide, blue sky.

No . . . *there* was something in the distance, an aircraft approaching from the south. But was it a MiG or a Tomcat? She watched it as she dropped toward a barren and empty plain.

1148 hours
Tomcat 211
Shotgun 2/2

"Hit!" K-Bar yelled. "Splash one MiG!"

"Never mind the damned MiG! Do you see any chutes?"

"Negative, Striker. Negative. No! Wait a sec! At one-five-oh!"

Yes! A parachute! But only one . . .

"Shotgun, Shotgun, this is Shotgun Two-two," Striker called. "I see one chute. That's good chute, good chute at, I make it, eight miles southeast of Sayda Guba. That's map coordinates Victor three-one by Sierra niner-five."

"Striker, this is Coyote. Get back to formation."

"Ah, negative, Shotgun. I can see vehicles on the road below me, heading for that chute. I'm going in to provide cover."

"Shotgun Two-two, this is Shotgun One-one. Return to formation. Execute immediate."

But Striker's full attention was on that lone chute and the vehicles on the ground nearby. Was it Vader or Chris? There'd be no way of knowing until he or she could make contact with an SAR emergency radio.

Keeping his distance, Striker pulled his F-14 into a long, easy circle about the descending chute a mile and a half away.

1150 hours
Over the Kola Peninsula

There was no mistaking the distinctive bulk of that aircraft, huge for a fighter, its wings swept forward for low-speed flight. A Tomcat was circling her, though at this distance Lobo couldn't tell which one it was. The F-14's presence was comforting, however, a sign that her shipmates had not abandoned her.

The ground was coming up faster now. It was close enough for her to make out details—the twin ruts of a dirt road between large patches of mud and snow, a hut or cottage with what looked like a thatched roof, and a nearby barn. There was a town or village a few miles to the northwest. Beyond that was the gunmetal blue-gray of the sea, and a smudge of black smoke where the Marines were storming ashore.

To Hanson, the landscape immediately below her dangling feet looked unutterably bleak, a flat and barren tundra, all bare earth, brown and stunted vegetation, and scattered patches of snow. She twisted back and forth in her harness, still trying to spot McVey's chute. Where the hell was he? Had he managed to punch out? She couldn't see him and that worried her.

And what she could see worried her even more. There, to the

south was a line of vehicles, their shapes indistinct, a convoy of some kind picking its way north along that muddy track of a road.

The ground was really coming up fast now. It looked like she was going to touch down close to that house and barn.

1151 hours
Tomcat 211
Shotgun 2/2

Striker brought the Tomcat almost down to the deck, screaming over flat, empty tundra, patches of snow and earth blurring with the speed of his passage to a rippling brown-white-gray. The enemy convoy was a couple of miles ahead, several trucks and at least one armored vehicle of some kind, possibly a tank. He gentled his F-14 slightly to the left, watching the column of vehicles swell behind his gun reticle, then squeezed the trigger, sending a hail of 20mm shells slashing into dirt, machines, and men.

1151 hours
Air Ops
U.S.S. *Thomas Jefferson*

"Shotgun Two-two, this is Home Plate. Two-two, this is Home Plate. Respond, please."

Tombstone's knuckles tightened around the microphone as he continued to stare at the radar display above the console in front of him. It was cluttered with aircraft, friendlies and hostiles. Russian planes had been coming up from every air base in the Kola Peninsula, and the American aircraft were fighting for their lives.

Striker had broken formation, was circling the area where Shotgun One-four had gone down. Damn it, why wouldn't he respond?

"Shotgun Two-two, Home Plate. Come in, please."

1153 hours
Tomcat 211
Shotgun 2/2

He'd lost sight of the chute. Chris—it *had* to have been Chris!—must be on the ground now.

He felt a small stab at the thought, then dismissed it. He scarcely knew Chris's RIO, McVey. It wasn't that he wanted the guy dead . . . but *please*, God, let Chris be alive and in one piece!

"Shotgun Two-two, Home Plate." That was CAG's voice. "Two-two, come in, please."

"Ah, listen, Striker," K-Bar said from the back seat. "Don't you think we ought to respond?"

"Screw 'em," Striker said. "We got radio difficulty."

"Oh. Right." K-Bar chuckled. "Yeah, I've been having all kinds of problems with this set."

"Just so you don't have any trouble tuning in on the SAR freak."

"Roger that. I'm listening, but there's nothing yet."

"Well, keep on it, damn it!"

Shit. He was angry at himself for his own conflicting emotions, angry for disobeying orders, scared to death that Chris might be dead, and here he was taking it out on K-Bar by snapping the guy's head off. He tightened the F-14's turn, scanning the ground for more Russian troops. Several vehicles were burning on the road below, but others were still closing on the area where the chute had gone down.

There was the chute, blowing free across the ground! And had that been a lone figure he'd glimpsed running through a patch of snow?

Damn it, they needed a SAR flight in here, and right now! "Home Plate, Home Plate," he called. "This is Shotgun Two-two. I've got a man on the ground, repeat, man on the ground. I don't think she's hurt—"

"Striker! I've got her on the SAR!"

"Let me hear!"

". . . on the ground, about eight miles southeast of Sayda Guba. This is Lobo, calling Mayday, Mayday . . ."

"Chris!" he cut in. "Chris! This is Steve!"

"Steve! What are you doing here?"

"Looking after you, babe. Listen. I'll stay with you until a SAR chopper can reach you. Keep your head down. There are some bad guys about two miles south of you, and they looked real mad last time I got a close look."

"Christ, Steve! Get out of here!"

"Not a chance. Now find yourself a ditch and stay down!" He'd just glimpsed several more Russian vehicles to the south. Joy sang in the back of his mind. Chris was alive!

He brought the Tomcat into a long, flat trajectory, lining up for another strafing run.

1154 hours
Air Ops
U.S.S. Thomas Jefferson

"How about it, Jim?" Tombstone asked the Operations Officer. He'd heard Striker talking to someone on the ground and inferred that it must be Hanson, though her SAR radio didn't have the range for him to pick up what she'd said. "Can we get a Search and Rescue helo out that far?"

"Not a chance, CAG. We can call the Marines. Maybe they can send something out from Red Beach. They're close enough."

"Do it, then." He raised the microphone again. "Shotgun Two-two, Two-two, this is Home Plate. RTB. I say again, return to base!" The hostiles were closing in, and one lone Tomcat wouldn't stand a chance by itself.

"Shotgun Two-two, this is Home Plate. Respond!"

1154 hours
Near Sayda Guba

Chris was on her knees on a low rise on the ground, staring toward the south. Even without binoculars, she easily recognized the squat, open-topped turret, the quad-mounted 23mm guns. The vehicle was a ZSU-23-4, a deadly mobile flak battery called a Shilka by the Russians, but popularly known as the "Zoo" among American fliers. She estimated that it was still better than a mile off, sitting in the middle of that dirt road she'd seen from the air.

She grabbed the small survival radio clipped to her flight suit, pressing the transmit key. "Steve!" she shouted. "Steve, back off! There's a Zoo-twenty-three down here!"

The turret had already slewed to the right, and its big, blunt radar antenna, code-named "Gun Dish" by NATO, was tracking something to the west and close to the horizon. She could see that the cannons were firing, raising a haze of smoke above the vehicle. A moment later, the sound reached her, a steady, far-off *thud-thud-thud-thud* as the Zoo tracked and fired . . . and then, God, God, *no*! There was Striker's Tomcat, streaking low across the tundra dead in the Zoo's sights, and then smoke was trailing from it, a white smear unraveling astern of the aircraft as it began to break into pieces, and she heard the roar of the Tomcat's engines rising above the thud of the triple-A guns, and then there was nothing but flame and smoke as Steve's plane slammed into the ground.

Several seconds later, the dull *whump!* of the crash reached her.

Oh, God, please, no!

1158 hours
Air Ops
U.S.S. *Thomas Jefferson*

"I'm sorry, sir. Shotgun Two-two is down."

Tombstone replaced the microphone, his eyes still on the radar screen. That was two down out of Shotgun, plus another damaged and limping back to the boat.

"White Lightning is now over the target," the Operations Officer announced. "Lead plane has just dumped his bombs."

Tombstone dragged his attention away from the blank spot on the map near Sayda Guba to the ragged shores of the Kola Inlet near Polyarnyy. The Intruders were swinging one after the other into their attack vectors, bearing down on the naval bases and depots lining the western shore of the inlet. He could hear the aviators and B/Ns calling to one another as they made their runs.

"*White Lightning One-two-two! Pickle's hot! I'm going in!*"

"*This is One-two-oh! I'm in!*"

"*White Lightning Two, this is Lightning One-one. Watch that flak over the inlet. They've got some ships down there, a couple of corvettes, maybe a light cruiser. We're getting heavy fire from the face of the cliff above the base too.*"

"*Roger that, One-one. I can see the gunfire.*"

"*SAM! SAM! I've got a SAM launch at zero-nine-five!*"

"*Watch for fighters. Echo-Whiskey's got bandits spotted at one-eight-zero. . . .*"

The *hell* with this! Angrily, Tombstone picked up a telephone receiver and punched in a number. "Fred? Tombstone. What's the status on the CAG bird?"

"Uh . . . she's up and ready, CAG. But—"

"Bring her to ready and put her on the line. I'll be on the roof in ten minutes."

"Aye, aye, sir."

He hung up. "Operations Officer!"

"Yes, sir."

"You've got the watch here. I'm going up there."

"Uh, yes, sir. Should I tell—"

But Tombstone had already left the compartment.

1200 hours
Near Sayda Guba

Hanson had started moving in the direction of the crash, her eyes still sweeping the leaden sky, praying for the sight of a parachute. Still, though, there was nothing . . . nothing . . . and then she stumbled into an unseen ditch and fell heavily to the ground.

She grunted with the shock, then rose, slowly, mud-covered and shaken. *Get a grip, woman!* she told herself savagely. *You start blundering around in enemy territory without thinking about what you're doing and you're going to end up dead!*

Voices. She heard voices . . . and the sound of a truck's engine. Turning, Hanson saw a light truck on the dirt road a hundred yards behind her, much closer than the Zoo. Armed men were piling out of the back, calling to one another as they began fanning out across the field.

Coming for her.

Groping at the hip of her flight suit, she drew her pistol, a 9mm Beretta automatic. She counted twelve men now, and clearly they'd already seen her. The line was spreading out, the men on the flanks running now to get around her from either side.

She considered running . . . but where could she run to? They were already close enough to shoot her if they wanted to. She also considered opening fire, going down in some kind of heroic, John Wayne last stand, but that was just plain silly. At a hundred yards, she wouldn't be able to come close to hitting them with a handgun, while they were carrying AKMs, assault rifles accurate to four hundred yards or more. Hanson had never thought much of the old, ultra-macho idea of death rather than surrender.

"*Stoy!*"

The command snapped at her from her right, and she spun, surprised. Damn! How had he gotten so close so quickly? A Russian was standing less than twenty yards away, his AK aimed at her.

"*Stoy!*" he barked again, gesturing with the rifle. "*Zdavay-etees'! Brawste arujyee!*"

She wished that she could speak Russian. Still, it was clear what he wanted. Carefully, making no quick moves, she extended the hand holding the Beretta and dropped the weapon to the ground. The soldier stepped cautiously closer. "*Rukee v'vayrh!*" The rifle snapped up, a savage gesture, and she raised her hands over her head.

He looked Oriental, not Chinese exactly, but with a Mongolian's flat face and puffy, slit eyes. Those eyes widened as he got closer, and Hanson was uncomfortably aware that he had just realized that his prisoner was a woman. He spat something harsh. It didn't sound like Russian. His eyes were twinkling and his face was marred by an unpleasant grin as the rest of the soldiers hurried up.

She stood there uncertainly, arms still raised, as rough hands groped and pawed and patted, spun her about, then groped again. One grabbed her left arm, jerked it down, then pulled off her wristwatch and pocketed it. Another grabbed her SAR radio and jerked it from her flight suit. She tried to concentrate on the uniforms surrounding her, instead of the grinning, too-eager faces. Green camouflage . . . but with a peculiar, high-peaked, visored cap. They wore shoulder boards with the letters BB on them in gold. She knew that the Cyrillic letter that looked like a B was actually a V. What did VV stand for? She was sure that they weren't speaking Russian as they jabbered at one another.

After they had searched her with elaborate thoroughness, someone produced a length of heavy twine and tied her wrists tightly behind her back. She was expecting them to take her back to the truck, but the one who'd first captured her appeared to have a different idea. *"Vpeeryad!"* he ordered, and the muzzle of his AK jammed into the small of her back just below her bound hands.

"I don't understand you!" she told him. "I am American, understand? Amer—"

"Skaray!" He prodded her again, this time in the buttocks, and she stumbled forward, then fell to her knees as the men around her laughed and hooted. Two of them grabbed her then, one taking each of her arms, hauling her to her feet and dragging her forward. They were taking her, she saw with mounting horror, toward that nearby barn she'd noticed during her descent.

Inside, the light falling through the gaps between the boards of the walls was filtered through drifting dust, and the air was thick with the mingled smells of hay and manure. Someone grabbed her arms from behind, holding her tightly while the rest closed in.

"No!" she yelled, desperate, angrier now than she'd ever been in her life. "No, you bastards! *No!*" She tried to kick, but they held her legs while a grinning Mongol stooped to unlace her boots. Another reached up and started tugging at the zipper to her flight suit.

Evidently, that proved to be too slow. Knives gleamed in the half light as three or four of them roughly began cutting every stitch of clothing from her body. It was slow going, for the material of the survival garment beneath her flight suit was thick and tough, like a wet suit. The men chatted back and forth as they worked, sometimes laughing as though at a hilarious joke.

Then she was on her back in the hay and they were all around her, pinning her down, spreading her legs, fondling her, laughing as she cursed and twisted helplessly beneath them.

The hay prickled the bare skin of her back and legs, and the air was so heavy with the stink of barn and animals and unwashed, sweating men that she could scarcely breathe. She'd heard about things like this happening, heard horror stories about Russians raping women in Germany in World War II, about Serbs raping Moslem women in Bosnia . . . but it couldn't, *couldn't* be happening to her.

Somehow, she managed not to start screaming until the first of them dropped his trousers and lowered himself onto her body. . . .

CHAPTER 27
Tuesday, 17 March

1200 hours
The Kola Peninsula

One after another, the Super Stallions descended from the sky like lumbering, green-and-gray-camouflaged insects. On the LZ perimeters, AH-1 Cobra gunships circled and darted, evil-visaged dragonflies that hovered, stooped, and spat deadly flame as hostile positions were identified and targeted. On the ground, Marine spotters called in death from above. Cobras and blunt-nosed Harrier II jumpjets screamed in at low altitude, slamming enemy strong points, vehicles, and troop concentrations with 2.75-inch rockets, TOW missiles, and rapid-fire cannons.

On the high ground above Polyarnyy, elements of the 1st and 3rd Battalions, 8th Marines, spread out from their initial LZs, taking up positions on the windswept, barren heights overlooking the Kola Inlet. A cluster of SAM sites and a radar station, smoking ruins now after repeated air and cruise-missile strikes, dominated the top of the cliffs, overlooking a sprawling naval docking facility on the water.

The Marines had just been flown ashore from the LHA *Nassau*, a floating, flat-topped warren of gray passageways and compartments that experienced Marines referred to, with teeth-gritting sarcasm, as a "Luxury Hotel Afloat." Some of the old hands joked that after sleeping in tiny racks stacked five and six deep with nineteen hundred other Marines for the past six weeks, the 1/8 and 3/8 were more than ready to take on anything the Russians could throw at them.

Russian Naval Infantry were still holding the ruins, but most scattered after a pair of Harriers shrieked in low across the cliff tops, slashing at the sheltering Russian troops with rockets and free-fall iron bombs. As the Marines moved forward, a dozen tired and ragged-looking men in camouflage uniforms emerged from a tumble-down of bricks and I-beams, hands in the air.

Lieutenant Ben Rivera reached the edge of the cliff, an M-16 gripped in trembling hands. He was scared, yes, but more than that he was excited. He'd missed out on the fighting in Norway the year before, and he'd been dreaming of this moment ever since he'd entered the ROTC program in college.

From the beginning, though, he'd wanted to be a Marine aviator, and he'd made it too, learning to fly Marine F/A-18s . . . and burdened by no false modesty, he could freely admit to being one of the best.

But Marine tradition still firmly held that *all* Marines, whether pilots, tank drivers, or cooks, were first and foremost combat riflemen. More to the point, Marine aviators were expected to take their turns as Forward Observers, aviators assigned to the infantry to serve as advance ground controllers.

He'd thought that he'd enter Russia in a Hornet. Instead, he'd come in by Super Stallion, attached to the 1/8. He didn't really mind, for his training had prepared him for just this sort of assignment.

It was just that when the low, rumbling thunder of Marine or Navy jets rolled across the snowcapped peaks of the Kola Inlet, he could grip his rifle and look up from the mud and imagine that the other aviators definitely had the better deal.

Or at the very least, a wider view of the war.

Local resistance appeared to have ceased, and he was searching now for a good spot for an Observation Post. Fifty meters ahead, the ground crested in a low, rounded hummock occupied by concrete block ruins still smoldering from last night's air strikes. Signaling to his radio operator, Gunnery Sergeant Ed Larson, Rivera dashed for the rise, head down, alert for movement ahead of him.

He reached the ruins and picked his way through them, probing the shadows and blind corners. At the east side of the hill, he came to a broken wall, with blast-broken crenellations like gray dragon's teeth rising from a bleached and monstrous lower jawbone. From there he was able to look down into the Kola Inlet itself.

His hilltop actually rose above the head of a smaller inlet opening into the broader waters of the Kola, which measured a good three miles across at this point. Across this smaller inlet to the southeast was the town of Polyarnyy itself, an ugly, dismal-looking clutter of buildings that immediately reminded Rivera of some military or industrial towns he'd known, all smokestacks and crane gantries and warehouses, stained gray to black by decades of pollution and neglect. Several hundred meters below Rivera's position, the slopes overlooking the water flattened out enough to shelter a waterfront town, smaller than Polyarnyy, but identical in its ramshackle-looking collection of warehouses, factory chimneys, and blocks of military apartments with dingy, neo-Stalinist facades. Moles reached out from the hillside to enclose a rectangle of dirty gray water directly below Rivera's OP. Piers and docks extended from the shore into the inlet on both sides of the moles and across the inlet in Polyarnyy itself, and he could see a number of vessels tied to the quays.

Most were submarines. Rivera easily identified the enormous, broad-beamed bulk of an Oscar SSGN; two of the oddly humpbacked Delta IV PLARBs; a half-dozen smaller, sleeker attack subs, Alfas and Victors; and three diesel-electric Kilos, conventional attack subs with antiair missile-defense systems hidden in the long, squared-off sail. A few larger surface ships were tied up there as well, frigates and corvettes and a single Udaloy-class destroyer.

The majority of those ships and submarines showed damage from air attacks, though as he watched, white smoke spouted from the bow of the Udaloy destroyer, then unraveled into a knife-edged contrail arrowing straight up into the sky, then rapidly curving off toward the north. Udaloys, Rivera knew, were equipped with SA-N-9 missiles as their primary surface-to-air armament, advanced missiles similar to the American Sea Sparrow.

There appeared to be some sort of large, concrete structure built onto the hillside Rivera was crouching on, but from his position he couldn't see what it was. Still, this was an ideal Forward Observer's eyrie, with a smorgasbord of targets that gave new meaning to the expression "target-rich environment."

A rippling, fluttering sound shivered through the air. An instant later, part of Rivera's hillside erupted in a geysering column of black smoke, mud, and debris. Clutching helmet and rifle, Rivera dropped for cover, tumbling into a shallow hole behind the wall, knee- and elbow-deep in mingled mud and snow. The first blast was followed by another, a savage thump that jarred Rivera through the ground and sent loose concrete blocks clattering down the hill in front of him. The next explosion was closer still . . . then another passed overhead, exploding behind him.

Raising his head just enough to peer between the dragon's teeth of the shattered wall, Rivera brought his binoculars to his eyes and studied the slopes across the narrow inlet rising just to the west of Polyarnyy. He thought he could see the source of the arty there, several low-slung vehicles that might be 2S3 or 2S5 self-propelled guns. As he watched, he saw a silent flash among the squat shapes; seconds later, he heard the ripping-cloth sound of an incoming round and ducked for cover. The blast shook the ground.

His company radio man was crouched behind the rubble ten meters away. "Larson! Get your ass over here!"

Another explosion showered both men with grit and broken gravel, but Larson crawled up to Rivera, who took the radio handset. "King Three! King Three!" he called. "This is White Knight Five! Over!"

"White Knight Five, this is King Three. Go ahead."

He took another sighting on the far hilltop, comparing it with a small map he'd carried folded up in his breast pocket. "King Three, immediate suppression, grid Charlie Delta Three-five-niner-one-one-two. Tracked vehicles, believe two-Sierra-five mounted artillery, Hill Eight-nine. Authenticate Sierra. Over!"

"White Knight Five, King Three, immediate suppression, grid Charlie Delta Three-five-niner-one-one-two, tracked vehicles . . ."

As the voice at the other end repeated back the message, Rivera marveled at the stupidity of modern politics. Time and time again, the U.S. Marines had come under vicious, slashing attack, not by a foreign enemy but by American politicians eager to cut military budgets, or to eliminate what they saw as Pentagon waste.

There'd been waste in the military, there was no denying

that, though Rivera had always felt that the military all too often became a scapegoat for congressmen trying to divert attention from waste closer to Capitol Hill. In recent years, however, things had gotten out of hand. During some of the sillier periods of the Clinton Administration, attempts had been made to eliminate the Marines entirely, or at least to pare them back; one move still being debated called for eliminating Marine artillery, with the idea that artillery should be strictly the prerogative of the U.S. Army. By that way of thinking, letting the Marines field their own artillery, even for counter-battery fire, was a needless duplication of effort.

In the same spirit of efficiency, they'd blocked letting the Marines buy their own modern M1A1 tanks, forcing them to continue relying on relic M60s. Another target, one not yet successfully hit, had been Marine Air; after all, why should the Marines have their own combat aircraft when America had an Air Force?

Of course, those ideas had been fielded by the same folks who thought that the Navy should lose its strike aircraft. The blind, stupid REMFs who made such suggestions, Rivera decided bitterly, had never been in a foxhole with enemy artillery ranging in on their position.

The bombardment of the Marine position continued, gouts of mud and smoke thundering into the sky with each shrieking rattle of incoming fire. Moments later, though, a Marine sheltering nearby poked his head up and shouted, "Here come the A-6s!"

"Go Marines!" another voice echoed, but Rivera already had his binoculars pressed to his face, studying the gray, blunt-nosed planes howling down over the Kola Inlet from the north. "Those aren't Marines," he yelled, reading the block letters printed on each fuselage. "They're Navy!"

"Go Navy! Go Navy!" Traditional interservice rivalries were forgotten as the Intruders skimmed the hilltops above Polyarnyy in a north-to-south run, coming in impossibly low. Bombs spilled from wing pylons, flashing in the sun as they tumbled end-for-end . . . and then the hill above Polyarnyy vanished in a volcanic eruption of churning orange flame, fireballs boiling hundreds of feet into a smoke-splashed sky.

"Not bad, for squids," Larson said with a casual shrug. "Marines would've come in lower."

But it was better than "not bad," Rivera knew. Those A-6s had been dead on target, and the pounding of the 1/8 and 3/8 positions had instantly ceased. Raising the radio receiver to his ear again, he began to pick out targets among the ships and subs clustered in the water below his position, calling them back to the battle-management people waiting offshore.

In the distance, as the hilltop continued to burn, the first Marine Super Stallions were already touching down outside of Polyarnyy itself.

1230 hours
Kandalaksha Command Center
Kola Peninsula

"I thought you said you would be ready!" Karelin thundered into the mouthpiece of the red telephone he held clenched in one hand. "You should have been at sea by now!"

"We *are* ready, Comrade Admiral," Chelyag's voice replied. "We have been ready for the past eight hours. But the Americans—"

"Audacious Flame cannot wait on the Americans, and it cannot wait on you! If your vessel is ready to put to sea, then go! Immediately!"

"Sir, there are reports of American Marines landing on the heights above Cavern Three. Our forces are scattered or in retreat. A Naval Infantry colonel told me five minutes ago that there is fighting inside Polyarnyy now! The skies above the Kola Inlet are commanded by their planes! It is twenty-five kilometers to the open sea. We would never make it all the way!"

Karelin paused, then took a deep breath, forcing himself to stay calm. Chelyag could have no idea of what was at stake here. "Listen carefully to me, Comrade Captain. Your original orders called for you to reach a strategic bastion before surfacing and carrying out the final part of your orders. But at this point, the launch itself is of more importance than the continued threat of your vessel. You could launch immediately, as soon as you are clear of the cavern."

There was a long silence on the other end of the line. Karelin waited patiently, the phone to his ear. In the distance, outside the walls of his bunker, he could hear the dull thunder of a far-off bombing raid, the crump of antiaircraft guns, the distant wail of a siren. Things were going wrong, very wrong. Hours ago, Leonov's 5th Blue Guard had crossed the Volga at Simbersk. Krasilnikov's senior strategists felt they were making an all-out drive on Novgorod, four hundred kilometers east of Moscow. Leonov's forces had to be stopped *now*, before they managed to isolate Moscow and the far north from loyal troops and supplies east of the Urals.

"You want me to launch as soon as I am clear of the cavern."

"Exactly, Comrade Captain. One missile, targeted on Chelyabinsk. After that, you will make your way up the inlet and into the Barents Sea."

"If possible." Chelyag sounded bitter.

"Yes, Chelyag. If possible."

"American air superiority—"

"*Fuck* American air superiority! I am giving orders now to the 23rd and 47th Frontal Aviation Regiments at Revda and Kirovsk to scramble immediately, to put everything they have into the skies over the Kola Inlet. The American air groups are tired and over-extended. They have already suffered heavy casualties. In one hour, you will see nothing but MiGs above Polyarnyy. You have that long to get *Leninskiy Nesokrushimyy Pravda* under way."

There was another hesitation. "Very well, Admiral. It will be done."

"I am counting on you, Chelyag. Marshal Krasilnikov is counting on you."

"I am very sure my men will appreciate that. Sir."

Had that been sarcasm putting a bite to Chelyag's voice? As he hung up the phone, Karelin could not be sure.

1245 hours
Viper ready room
U.S.S. *Thomas Jefferson*

Tombstone walked into the ready room changing area without knocking. After all, most of the squadron's flyers were either in the air or up in Ops or the CIC. But Lieutenant Commander Joyce Flynn was already there, and Tombstone caught a

glimpse of long legs and small, bare breasts before he hastily
looked away. Carefully avoiding either looking at her or too
obviously looking away, he began pulling off his own uniform.

"I heard you're going up, CAG," Flynn said behind him. He
turned to answer, and blinked. Wearing nothing but a pair of
plain, white panties, she was watching him with a frank lack of
embarrassment or self-consciousness. In one hand she held one
of the bulky, rubberized survival suits. "Whatcha say, sailor?
Can I hitch a ride?"

He gave her a wry smile. Nightmare had been disgusted at
having his aircraft downgrudged, but he'd accepted Tombstone's suggestion that he make himself useful in Ops without
argument. That had left Tomboy, his RIO, with some unexpected downtime. As hard as everyone in the squadron had
been driving, he'd not expected her to squawk about *that*.

"You know, Commander," he told her carefully, "that might
not be a real smart career move."

"Hey, you need an RIO, right?" She ran her free hand
through her red brush-cut hair and dramatically tossed her
head. She had pale skin highlighted by densely scattered
freckles that went clear down to her chest and shoulders, green
eyes, and an impish grin, all of which contributed to her
decidedly less-than-military look at the moment. "I'm your
man!"

Damn, he *did* need a RIO. The F-14 could be flown solo,
barely, but it wasn't a pleasant experience—about like playing
piano with one hand while typing a letter with the other—and
it was suicide in a dogfight. He'd not been thinking ahead.
Hell, maybe he needed someone in the back seat just to watch
over him.

Tombstone sighed, then shook his head. "Get your shit on,
Commander. And move your tail. We don't have much time."

CHAPTER 28
Tuesday, 17 March

1305 hours (Zulu +2)
Flight deck
U.S.S. *Thomas Jefferson*

Twenty minutes later, helmets in hand, Tombstone and Tomboy strode side by side across the flight deck toward Tomcat 200, parked on *Jefferson*'s port side just aft of the island. The "CAG bird," normally reserved for Tombstone when he wanted to log some hours, was being readied by several men in green shirts with black stripes, the air wing men who performed aircraft maintenance.

Before boarding, Tombstone and Tomboy both circled the aircraft, checking for faults, open access panels, and tugging at the weapons to make sure they were secure. Four Sidewinders and four AMRAAMs were slung beneath its belly and wings. Stores of AIM-54Cs had been running low, and in any case, the fighting over the Kola had mostly been close-in combat, a real waste of the high-tech, million-dollar Phoenix missiles. As Flynn settled into the rear seat and pulled her helmet on, Tombstone finished his walk-around, then clambered up the ladder and swung into his seat.

"You're already checked out and on the flight plan, CAG!" the plane chief, a burly man in a brown jersey, called up to him. "They're squeezing you in on Cat One right behind a KA-6."

Tombstone saluted his acknowledgment, then began running through his preflight list. He wasn't entirely sure why he was doing this . . . except for the obvious fact that his people had taken some heavy losses so far, and maybe he could help fill in.

Morale was still bad, and it would be worse when they started realizing their losses. More of them might be tempted into stupid stunts like the one that had killed Striker and K-Bar.

Maybe if the Old Man put in an appearance, it would help pull things together.

Hell, he was guessing and he knew it. Coyote and Batman were doing fine out there without him. But he wanted to *be* there. With them. With his people.

"Now hear this" blared from a 5-MC speaker on the carrier's island. "Now hear this. Rig the barricade. That is, rig the barricade. Crash crew, fire and medical personnel, stand ready on the after deck."

Uh-oh. Tombstone twisted in his seat, studying the hazy sky aft of the *Jefferson*. That would be Shotgun One-three coming in. He'd been following the damaged plane's progress down in Ops, and he'd reluctantly agreed to Arrenberger's request that he try to trap on *Jefferson*'s deck rather than eject over the sea. There was still no response from his RIO. If Blue Grass was still alive, the violence of an ejection—or of plummeting unconscious into ice-cold water—would almost certainly kill him. Slider wanted to bring his crippled F-14 in—a risk, certainly, but the only way to save Blue Grass's life. Tombstone had been in the same position once, years before, trying to get down on the deck with a wounded RIO.

Just aft of where Tombstone and Tomboy were sitting—a fifty-yard-line seat if ever there was one, he thought—two lines of deck personnel were busily erecting the crash barricade, a horizontal ladder of wire and fabric strips designed to stop an aircraft that, for whatever reason, could not make a normal arrested landing. Tomcat 209 had one engine out, and if his tailhook failed to engage an arrestor wire, he wouldn't have the power necessary to complete a touch-and-go and would bolter off the forward end of the flight deck again. For that reason, Slider and Blue Grass would be making a barrier landing.

Nearby, men in red jerseys with black stripes stood ready to go, fire extinguishers in hand, some of them crouched atop deck tractors rigged out as fire-fighting vehicles. Men in white with red crosses were hospital corpsmen, standing by with first-aid kits and wire-frame Stokes stretchers. The ungainly struts and braces of the four-wheeled aircraft-handling crane known as "Tilly" loomed above them in the lee of *Jefferson*'s island. One man standing on the crane was completely anonymous, clad head to toe in brightly reflecting flameproof silver. He had one job only. If Shotgun One-three crashed and burned, he would be the one to brave fire and exploding fuel in an attempt to pull Slider and Blue Grass from the wreckage.

Looking aft again, Tombstone saw the Tomcat, dropping toward *Jefferson*'s roundoff. Across the deck from him, the LSO and his crew were at their station in front of *Jefferson*'s meatball, guiding the crippled aircraft down its long glidepath toward the steel deck. Closer . . . closer . . . nose high, flaps down, gear down . . . With its wings extended, the F-14 was a "floater," generating tremendous lift, and now it appeared to be suspended, hanging almost motionless in the sky astern of the carrier. Tombstone found himself willing the aircraft safely onto the deck . . .

. . . and suddenly it was dropping with alarming speed, plummeting after its own shadow across the roundoff, slamming down with a shriek of rubber on steel, sweeping ahead with a deafening roar into the barricade. Smoke boiled from the starboard engine . . . and then the nose wheel gave way, and the nose smacked onto the deck with a shattering rasp and showering sparks, plunging through the barricade. The fluttering straps of the barrier seemed to gather Slider's Tomcat in, before collapsing across the aircraft's wings and tail.

The crash crew was already rolling, surrounding the plane in seconds, the yellow-painted Tilly lumbering forward with its crane extended, the sailor in the flameproof suit clinging to one of its struts.

Tombstone found he was holding his breath. In seconds, someone had the Tomcat's canopy up, and they were helping Slider out of the cockpit. It took a few moments more to get Blue Grass out. From some two hundred feet away, Tombstone could see the sickening slime of blood covering the RIO as the crash crew pulled him free and strapped him into a Stokes stretcher.

"My God," he heard Tomboy say. "His legs are gone!"

Whatever had hit Tomcat 209 had slammed up through the belly and severed Blue Grass's legs between hips and knees. The man was dead; he must have bled to death moments after he was hit.

"You still want to go?" he asked Tomboy over the ICS.

"Yes." There was none of the usual imp's humor in her voice. "But let's move it, okay?"

Around them, the carrier's deck operations continued their never-ending dance-on-the-deck. Launch ops had slowed their tempo quite a bit to accommodate aircraft coming in for recovery, and the Air Boss was alternating launches from the bow cats with traps astern. After the frantic activity of earlier that morning, and with brief, adrenaline-charged intervals such as Slider's barrier trap, the work load seemed almost light, the men going about their tasks with a casual jauntiness that belied their exhaustion.

The initial checkout complete, with Tomboy reporting all circuit breakers set and systems go, he switched on the engines. As the power built, he felt the aircraft shuddering, as though yearning to free itself from the confines of steel deck and sheltering hangar, to fling itself at the sky.

"Tomcat Two-zero-zero, Air Boss."

Uh-oh. If it was coming, here it was. "Two-double-oh. Copy."

"CAG. I got someone here wants to talk to you."

"Put him on."

"CAG? This is Admiral Tarrant."

"Yes, sir." Tombstone had been gambling that Tarrant would take no notice of his unauthorized launch . . . or better, that he wouldn't find out until after Tombstone was away from the *Jeff*. Tombstone would not refuse a direct order to stand down, but he desperately hoped that that order would not be given.

"Stoney, Air Ops reports real heavy action over the Inlet above Polyarnyy. Watch your ass in there, do you hear?"

"Yes, sir!"

"That's one expensive item of machinery you've got there. Bring it back in one piece."

"Aye, aye, sir!" Tombstone found himself grinning idiotically.

A plane director was backing away ahead of the Tomcat, motioning Tombstone on. Carefully, he let up the brakes and followed, threading the thirty-ton aircraft past Slider's and Blue Grass's fallen, nose-down F-14 and toward the bow catapults.

Captain First Rank Anatoli Chelyag leaned out over the edge of
the cockpit, located high atop the Typhoon's sail. Naval
Infantry troops lined the pier to which *Leninskiy Nesokrushimyy Pravda* had been moored, the younger ones among them
looking scared as the sounds of gunfire continued to echo
distantly through the cavern.

Line-handlers ashore had already cast off the enormous wire
ropes securing the Typhoon to the bollards. Chelyag was
watching now as the distance between pier and the sloping
flanks of the behemoth he commanded gradually widened.

"We're clear to port now," he said, speaking into a telephone
handset. "Ahead slow."

"Ahead slow, Captain" came the reply from the officer at the
helm in *Pravda's* control center.

The huge submarine picked up momentum, gliding through
the filthy water with a sullen *chug-chug-chug* of her enormous
screws. Chelyag remembered again Karelin's voice as he'd
ordered the *Pravda* out of the cavern and into the hellfire
outside. Reach the Barents Sea? They would be lucky if they
cleared Polyarnyy Inlet and made it to the main channel.
Admiral Marchenko had been sending down hourly reports.
That last one had spoken of Marines on the hillside directly
above *Pravda's* hiding place.

But there was no refusing Karelin's orders. Chelyag would
do as he'd been commanded, clear Tretyevo Peschera, then fire
missile number one, already targeted on Chelyabinsk. After
that . . . well, their survival depended entirely on the Frontal
Aviation units now closing on Polyarnyy from the south.

He brought the telephone to his mouth again. "Commander
Mizin. Pass the word ashore to open the cavern doors."

"Yes, Comrade Captain." There was a pause. "Captain? We
have a message from Admiral Marchenko."

"Read it to me."

"He says . . . 'Good luck, *Pravda*. Go with God.' "

Chelyag could almost see the sneer, the curl to Mizin's lip, as he recited the message. His First Officer was a good atheist, a man who'd hoped with an almost religious passion that the return of no-nonsense hard-liners to power in Moscow would mean an end to the religious mania that had exploded throughout the nation during the days of Gorbachev and Yeltsin.

Evidently, he'd been disappointed.

"Tell Admiral Marchenko, 'Thank you. Message received and very much appreciated.'"

And what, he wondered, did Mizin think of *that?*

1317 hours
Tomcat 200
Over the Kola Inlet

"We're coming up on the coast," Tomboy said over the ICS. "Feet dry."

"More or less," Tombstone replied. "We're not over land yet."

He'd swung far out to the east of the carrier battle force, skimming past the Marine amphibious fleet, then cutting south down the Kola Inlet itself. The mouth of the gulf was four miles across here. East were the low, rounded hills of the island of Ostrov Kil'din. Military-looking settlements were scattered along both coastlines, among bare-faced cliffs and gleaming patches of ice and snow. Ice still sheeted over much of the waterway, though the center of the narrow gulf had been kept open by icebreakers.

Smoke coiled away into the sky to the right. The western shore of the inlet at this point was held by American forces, the east by Russians. A large ship—Tombstone thought it might be a destroyer—lay half-submerged in the shallows near the west bank, beneath a greasy pall of smoke and surrounded by ice. Beyond, helicopters darted, insect-like, beneath the writhing tendrils of high-altitude contrails.

"Ninety-nine aircraft, ninety-nine aircraft" sounded over the tactical frequency. "This is Echo-Whiskey Two-one. We're picking up large numbers of bogies coming in from the south, probably from the airfields at Kirovsk and Revda. This could be a general attack."

"What, more bandits?" Tomboy asked. "You'd think they'd be running out of MiGs by now."

"Haven't you heard, Tomboy? They've got an inexhaustible supply. Somewhere they've got factories cranking out MiGs as fast as we can shoot them down. Check weapons."

"Hot and ready. Shame the bird farm was out of AIM-54s."

"That's okay. We'll just have to sucker them in close."

"Wonderful plan, CAG. You have anything else in mind?"

Tombstone was scanning the surface of the water. Sunlight flashed from a silvery something skimming over the inlet. "Yes, actually. Let's ride in with that A-6 flight down there."

"That'll be Red Hammer One," his RIO told him. "Some of our boys off the *Jeff*."

"Good enough. We'll ride shotgun for them for a ways. Call the leader and let him know we're here."

"Rog."

More Russian aircraft, mustering to the south. Obviously, the hammer-blow air and cruise-missile strikes over the past twenty-four hours had not been as successful as originally thought. That was often the pattern in modern warfare; high-tech weapons were wonderfully destructive and accurate . . . but the enemy always seemed to have reserves, an adaptability, a *cleverness*, not accounted for in the original planning. Too, weapons thought to give ninety-percent-plus accuracy were later found to be sixty-percent accurate or less. Men grew tired or careless, Or discouraged.

Of course, the same moral problems would be affecting the other side as well. One of the real challenges of military strategy was knowing when the enemy had reached the end of his reserves, to the point where one more small push might topple his seemingly faultless defenses and bring them crashing down.

Which side, he wondered, would break first in this contest?

1319 hours
Intruder 504
Over the Kola Inlet

"CAG?" Willis Payne twisted in his seat, trying to see behind and above the low-flying A-6. "What the shit is *he* doing out here?"

"Slumming?" Sunshine replied, her face buried in her radarscope. "Or maybe they're really getting hard up back in Ops. They're sending in the REMFs."

"Hey, lady, from what I've heard, Magruder's no rear-echelon mother—"

"Aw, shit, he's a four-striper, ain't he? Sits at a desk, writes up fitness reports, fills out requisitions, wipes noses. Coming up on nine miles to Polyarnyy. Weapons armed. Pickle's hot."

"Rog. Listen, I hear that guy was flying the Hornet that took down the *Kreml* last year. You know, the big Russian carrier? The guy's got more medals than you could push with zone-five burners, and a combat record as long as *Jefferson*'s flight deck. He's not a prick and he's a damned hot aviator. That makes the son of a bitch fuckin' A-okay in *my* book!"

"I copy."

"Why're you so bitter about four-stripers anyway?"

"Oh, I don't know. The morale aboard the *Jefferson*'s gotten pretty grim lately."

"The morale aboard the *Jefferson* sucks."

"Like I said. Maybe I just figured it was *his* fault."

"Shit, guys like him may be all that's holding *Jefferson*'s people together right now. You should've seen him at the Blue Nose initiation last week."

"The what?"

"Uh, never mind. Old news. Whatcha got on the scope?"

"Lots of stuff coming up. Inlets to the right. You should be seeing some smokestacks up ahead. That'll be Polyarnyy."

"Got it. God, there's a lot of smoke."

"That won't stop us. I'm switching to FLIR."

The Intruder shrieked south toward Russia's most vital submarine facilities.

1319 hours
Tretyevo Peschera
Near Polyarnyy, Russia

The huge, massive barrier separating the Third Cavern from the outside world had slid ponderously up and out of the way. Beyond, sunlight danced on the waters of the Polyarnyy Inlet. Holding his binoculars to his eyes, squinting against the dazzling light, Chelyag picked out some of the submarines that had been moored outside the sheltering rock walls of the cavern. That was Kolosov's boat, a humpbacked PLARB of the type known to the West as a Delta IV. The boat was listing thirty degrees against its pier and had settled somewhat by the bow. It looked like a cruise missile had arrowed in just ahead of the sail.

Damn! Over there was Lovchikov's boat, one of the fast-attack subs. Known as the Alfa in the West, those high-technology boats were so expensive the Russians called them *Zolotaya Ryba,* the Golden Fish. God, what had they done to it? The sail crumpled, the periscopes bent like matchsticks. *That* Golden Fish would never swim the ocean depths again.

And *Leninskiy Nesokrushimyy Pravda* would be in no better condition very soon, if Karelin did not honor his promise to send additional Frontal Aviation interceptors.

"Clear the weather bridge," he snapped. "Everyone below."

A spiral staircase, incongruously trimmed with wooden railings, led down from the weather bridge, through massive double hulls and all the way to *Pravda*'s attack center, which rested between and astride the Typhoon's side-by-side inner hulls like a saddle on a swaybacked horse.

"Captain on deck!" a rating cried as Chelyag stepped off the ladder. From consoles around the compartment, pale faces watched him, some expectant, some fearful.

"Missile Officer!" he barked.

"Sir!"

"Missile status."

"Hatch number one is open, Captain. Prelaunch check is complete, and all codes have been verified and authenticated. The missile is targeted and ready to fire."

"Very well. Stand by. We will launch as soon as we are clear of the mooring bay." He at least wanted water enough beneath him that the shock of launching the sixty-ton missile would not slam his keel against the bottom.

On a television screen above the helm officer's station, the entrance to open water was looming larger.

1319 hours
Tomcat 200
Over the Kola Inlet

"Bandits, Tombstone! Multiple bandits!"

"How many and where?"

"Ten . . . twelve . . . A hell of a lot, coming in at low altitude, from one-six-oh to one-eight-oh! Range, five miles!"

"Here's one," Tombstone said, choosing one target out of many displayed on his HUD. He flipped a selector. "Going with AMRAAM." There was a pause, then the satisfying warble of a radar lock in his earphones. "Lock! And that's a fox one!"

Below him, the Intruders had spread out but were still bearing south, arrowing scant yards ahead of their own shadows on the water. Elsewhere, the sky was empty, save for wisps of contrails far overhead.

"This is Tomcat Two-zero-zero," Tombstone called. "Coming in north of Polyarnyy. I've got a flight of Intruders that could use some help about now."

"Two-double-oh, this is Shotgun One-one. Tombstone, what the hell are you doing out here?"

"Getting my ass into trouble, Coyote. Where the hell are you?"

"Retanking at angels base plus ten, Delta Three-five-five, Charlie One-eight-one." Tombstone glanced at his map. That put Shotgun about eighteen miles to the northwest. "We're on our way back to the *Jeff* after covering White Lightning."

"Any of you already tanked up?"

"That's a roger. Three of us are anyway."

"If you're still armed, we could use you at Polyarnyy. Multiple bogies coming out of one-eight-zero."

"I see 'em. Okay, Tombstone. Cavalry's on the way."

"Good to hear that, Coyote." Tombstone locked onto a second target, then squeezed the trigger. "Fox one!"

"Hey, leave a few for the rest of us."

But as the MiGs exploded out of the southern sky, Tombstone knew that Coyote needn't have worried on that score.

In seconds, MiG-29 Fulcrums were everywhere, sleek aircraft with twin stabilizers, clutching deadly pods of weapons beneath their wings.

Then Tombstone and Tomboy were fighting for their lives.

CHAPTER 29
Tuesday, 17 March

Lieutenant Ben Rivera balanced himself against the ragged top of the wall, staring down into the dock facility at the base of the hill. From his vantage point, at the top of a seventy-degree slope perhaps two hundred feet above the waters of Polyarnyy Inlet, it looked as though a monster was sliding out of the rock beneath his feet.

Dark gray, most of its surface covered with a brickwork effect, or tiles like those on a space shuttle, it was Leviathan himself. Even before half of it had moved into the open water, Rivera knew that he must be standing directly above the entrance to one of the secret Russian submarine pens he'd been briefed on before the landing. There were supposed to be a number of caverns piercing the cliffs overlooking the tangled inlets near Polyarnyy, each sheltering some of Russia's most powerful boomers, and by chance he'd been dropped right on top of one.

That monster sliding into the inlet was as long as forever! A Typhoon ballistic-missile sub, it had to be! Nothing else could be so huge. As Rivera watched, that long, long forward deck continued to slide out from beneath the rocks, its upper surface showing the sharply chiseled grooves of two rows of missile hatches down the forward deck.

And . . . most merciful God in heaven . . . one of those hatches was *open*! Rivera nearly lost his hold on the wall as he found himself staring down into the gaping hatch, meeting the gaze of the round, white eye of an SS-N-20 ICBM peering back from its depths.

"Larson!" He scrambled back from the edge of the cliff, the spell of awe and surprise that had pinned him there broken at last. *"Gunny!"*

The Typhoon's sail slid into view, and then the afterdeck, shorter by far than the forward missile deck. The rudder had the span of an A-6, and that broad, flattened, eighty-two-foot beam that made it look as fat as an aircraft carrier. Hell, with an LOA of 557 feet, it was two thirds the length overall of the *Nassau*, well over half the length of the *Jefferson* or the *Eisenhower*.

Larson handed him the radio phone, and he clutched it to his head with a trembling hand.

"King Three! King Three!" he called. "This is White Knight Five! Over!"

There was no immediate answer.

"King Three! This is White Knight. Jesus, Mary, and Joseph, *answer me!"*

1322 hours
Intruder 504
Over the Kola Inlet

"Red Hammer, Red Hammer," the Intruder flight leader called. "This is Red Hammer One-one. Target change. We have a new target request from Marine Air Control."

"Red Hammer One-three, we copy," Willis said. Then, "God, what do they want now?"

"Probably another truck park," Sunshine replied. "Shit, you'd think they'd find something interesting for us to clobber once in a while."

But as Willis listened to the new instructions from One-one, he realized that this target was nothing if not interesting.

It was almost damned dangerous. He brought the aircraft slightly to the right, carefully studying the panorama of mountains and water unfolding ahead.

1322 hours
Tomcat 200
Over the Kola Inlet

"Hit!" Tombstone yelled. "Splash that MiG!"

"Watch it, Tombstone!" Tomboy called from the back seat. "Two are coming around behind us!"

"I see 'em! Hold on!" He jinked right, then rolled to the left, sending the F-14 into a high, floating barrel roll that took him up and out of the two Fulcrums' aim. The sky was filled with aircraft, *all* of them Fulcrums, it seemed. Ahead, there was a flash and an angry puff of orange disgorging a burning meteor plunging toward the waters of the Kola Inlet. Their second AMRAAM had scored.

"That's two . . . *oof!*" his RIO said as Tombstone kicked in his afterburners in a hard, tight turn pulling out of the barrel roll. The two MiGs on their tail had just flashed past on the left, then split apart, one cutting to the left, the other toward the right, almost directly in front of the Tomcat. Tombstone started to follow, then abruptly pulled back and swung left again, letting the F-14 drop a thousand feet toward the water.

"Hey, CAG!" Tomboy called. "What . . . are you feeling generous? You had a great setup there. Why'd you let him go?"

"Take a look up ahead!"

Red Hammer, the A-6 flight, had split up their original tight formation, but each aircraft was maintaining speed and altitude, already into the beginning of their approach run. A Fulcrum coming in from the south had spotted them, wheeled about, and dropped onto the six of one of the Intruders. And Tombstone was bearing down on the six of the Fulcrum.

"I'm going to Sidewinder," he called. "I've got a good shot here, right up his tail."

He let the Sidewinder glimpse the MiG's hot tail pipes, then squeezed the trigger. "Fox two!"

"We've got another one behind us, Stoney. No, make that two!"

"How long till the cavalry gets here?"

"They're coming. Another thirty seconds. Threat warning! They have a lock!"

Tombstone pulled up violently, dumping chaff into his slipstream as he climbed.

He needed to cover Red Hammer's tail while they made their attack, at least until Coyote and the others arrived. Right now, though, the chances of Tomcat 200 surviving those next thirty seconds were not very good at all.

1323 hours
Intruder 504
Over the Kola Inlet

The Intruder rocked violently, and Willis had to pull the nose up slightly to steady it.

"What the hell was that?" Sunshine asked, her face still buried in her scope.

"Fulcrum on our tail," Willis said, glancing back over his shoulder. "Someone just took it out with a heat-seeker up the ass."

"Rog. Thirty seconds!"

Eight hundred feet.

"On manual." The target, according to the Marine air controller who'd fed the data to Red Hammer, was moving . . . and surrounded by numerous other targets. Willis wasn't going to trust the computer on this one. At his side, Sunshine was flipping rapidly back and forth between search radar and FLIR mode; if his own system crashed or if he became disoriented, she would be able to keep him on track.

Seven hundred feet . . .

1323 hours
Tomcat 200
Over the Kola Inlet

The radar homer sliced past to the right, seduced by Tombstone's chaff and Tomboy's vigorous ECM jamming. Now tracer rounds slashed past their canopy, high and leading the Tomcat by a good hundred yards. Tombstone hit the F-14's air brakes and pulled the nose up sharply. Floating at the ragged edge of a stall, the Tomcat slewed to the right just as the Fulcrum, surprised by Tombstone's maneuver, flashed past, so close that Tombstone could read the regimental markings on the other plane's fuselage.

"Guns!" he snapped, and the HUD shifted to gun mode just as the MiG started a hard, climbing turn to port. The maneuver spoiled Tombstone's shot. He was now in what was called a lag pursuit, behind his opponent but with his nose aiming to the rear of the other aircraft instead of leading it. As the MiG continued his left-hand turn, Tombstone decided to counter with a low yo-yo, going briefly to afterburners and diving to the left, picking up speed as he cut beneath the Fulcrum's track, then pulling up hard, coming out of his dive just after the MiG passed overhead. He kept his eyes on the other plane as it passed overhead; a sharp opponent would ease his turn, then plunge on the other plane from above—the preferred counter to a low yo-yo—but it looked like the MiG's pilot had lost sight of the Tomcat. *Yes!* He was holding his turn, angling back toward the Intruders. Tombstone brought the Tomcat up, using gravity to kill his speed, sliding neatly onto the MiG's tail at point-blank range, less than four hundred feet behind him.

Tombstone squeezed the trigger and the Tomcat's M61 cannon thundered, yellow tracers floating across the gap between MiG and F-14. For a moment, the MiG absorbed those globes of light, holding course, lining up with an Intruder just ahead and below . . . and then Tombstone saw bits of metal flaking off and a shimmering haze spilling from the Fulcrum.

Then they were past, the MiG sliding off to the left.

"He's smoking," Tomboy told him as he brought the F-14's nose up. "He's going down. He's ejected!"

"Tomcat Two-oh-oh, this is Shotgun One-one. Nice shooting, Stoney!"

"Coyote! It's about time you got here!"

"Thought you would hog all the fun for yourself, did you?" Batman's voice chimed in.

"Just like these superCAG types," a woman's voice added. "Always grabbing the glory for himself!"

"Roger that, Brewer. Heads up! Bandits at two o'clock high!"

"Tombstone!" Coyote called. "Watch it! You've got two coming around on your six!"

"Never mind us," Tombstone replied. "Just help me keep those MiGs off the Intruders!"

1323 hours
Intruder 504
Over the Kola Inlet

"*There!* Target acquired," Sunshine said. "Come left two degrees. Range one mile."

Another seven seconds. Excitement pounded in his breast, and he could hear the mingled rasps of both his and Sunshine's breathing over the ICS. Damn, they were using the O_2. His own pucker factor was damned high, fifty psi at least; he figured the lip-lock he had on his seat right now would keep him anchored against a minus-five G outside loop. Sunshine sounded as cool and as hard as the ice clinging to the hillsides flashing past either side of the hurtling A-6. On his VDI, his bomb-release marker slid rapidly down his course line.

Five hundred feet . . .

1324 hours
Tretyevo Peschera
Near Polyarnyy, Russia

Leninskiy Nesokrushimyy Pravda was well clear of the submarine docking area outside of the cavern, slipping easily through oily water into the main Polyarnyy channel.

"Helm," Chelyag said. "Come left five degrees. Make revolutions for ten knots."

"Comrade Captain!" the radar officer called from his console. "Enemy aircraft, approaching from the north!"

So much for Karelin's promises. "Maintain course," he said, keeping his voice as calm as ice. "Weapons officer, stand by to fire missile number one."

"Missile one ready, Comrade Captain."

"Fire number one!"

1324 hours
Intruder 504
Over the Kola Inlet

Willis could see the target now, a Typhoon ballistic-missile sub just sliding clear of the moles sheltering a Russian submarine base. It had turned its huge, blunt nose toward the north, toward him, giving him a narrower target than he'd hoped for.

But the thing was still over five hundred feet long, a target almost indecently difficult to miss.

Triple-A filled the sky, rocking the Intruder violently. Something struck the plane's nose, but he held the stick steady. A little bit more . . .

The release pipper hit the bottom of the screen, and Willis squeezed the pickle. Five-hundred-pound bombs *bump-bump-bumped* clear of the Intruder's belly, spilling into the air in a deadly rain.

1324 hours
Near Polyarnyy, Russia

Rivera had a perfect view of the attack, the huge ballistic-missile sub turning ponderously into the Polyarnyy channel, the Intruder sweeping down from the north through a sky suddenly crowded with antiaircraft and missile fire. Bombs cascaded from the A-6's belly. One . . . two . . . three struck the water close alongside of the Typhoon's nose, raising towering gouts of water that cascaded back across the submarine's deck in a white avalanche. Then a five-hundred-pound bomb struck the Typhoon's sail squarely where its rounded foot met the forward deck. The detonation erupted in an orange fireball that preceded the sound of the explosion by several seconds . . . then another bomb struck, and another, opening a gash in the Typhoon's flank next to the sail and peeling back the outer hull like a flat slab of clay. More detonations in the water . . . and another on target, this one far aft, close by the wing-like thrust of the huge fin. Thunder echoed back from the far hills. . . .

A final, cataclysmic blast, this one from the open hatch just in front of the torn-open sail. White flame gouted straight up into the air as though bursting from the throat of an exploding volcano.

Secondaries! Rivera thought. Something had touched off the missile's solid-fuel core. . . . Oh, Blessed Virgin Mary, the missile must have already been fired when the first bomb hit, rupturing the ICBM's hull, or maybe a five-hundred-pounder had dropped right down the open hatch. . . .

The explosion engulfed half of the Typhoon, rupturing its double hull, flinging burning debris hundreds of feet into the air. The shock wave raced out across the water and surged against the base of the cliff. The sound struck Rivera, an impact that staggered him back a step and sucked the wind from his lungs. Another blast, this one farther forward as another missile ruptured and exploded. For a terrified instant, Rivera wondered if a nuke had been set off, but the multiple explosions were nothing more than the violent detonation of SS-N-20 solid-fuel cores.

Flames raced out across the surface of the water.

1324 hours
Intruder 504
Over the Kola Inlet

"Wheeee-oh!" Sunshine called, and her gloved left hand slapped down hard on Willis's thigh. "Way to go! Way to go!"

The Intruder lurched again and Willis barely recovered. Glancing quickly back over his left shoulder, he saw the entire breadth of the Polyarnyy Inlet filled with orange fire.

The RAW light flashed—the Radar Acquisition Warning. "We're being tracked."

"Do you see it?"

"Negative! I can't see a damned thing but explosions!"

"Dump chaff!"

In the last instant, Willis saw the missile, streaking up from the forward deck of an Udaloy destroyer moored across from Polyarnyy. He pulled the stick to the left as hard as it would go . . .

The explosion slammed the Intruder in the right side with a

roar like thunder. The canopy beside Sunshine's head crazed to a frosty white, and a roaring sound filled the cockpit. Sunshine slumped to the left, her helmet thumping against Willis's arm. Blood sprayed across Willis, scarlet droplets splattering his windshield, his instruments, and his flight suit.

"Sunshine!" he yelled, half turning, trying to support her while continuing to fly the Intruder. *"Sunshine!"*

**1325 hours
Tomcat 202
Shotgun 2/1
Over the Kola Inlet**

Batman saw the SAM from the destroyer detonate alongside the Intruder, but there was nothing he could do about it at the moment. He'd plunged into the furball and taken down two MiGs in quick succession, but then a Fulcrum had dropped out of the sky like a hawk with talons extended. Tracers drifted past the left side of his canopy and he jinked right, then jinked left again, unable to break the MiG's lock on his tail.

"Two-one" sounded in his headset. "This is Two-three!"

"Brewer! Where are you? I can't shake this guy!"

"I'm on him! When I tell you, break right!"

Batman winced at the *thud-thud-thud* of a trio of shells slamming into his fuselage. "Do it! Do it!"

"Three . . . two . . . one . . . *break!*"

**1325 hours
Tomcat 218
Shotgun 2/3
Over the Kola Inlet**

Brewer had been angling for a clear shot with her last Sidewinder missile, but the MiG had been riding so hard on Batman's tail she couldn't get a clear shot, one that would nail the Russian without accidentally locking onto Batman's engines. When he broke hard right, however, he slipped clear of her targeting pipper and the AIM-9M system signaled a lock on the MiG.

"Fox two!"

The Fulcrum was already into its starboard turn, still dogging Batman, when the missile slammed into its right engine and detonated. Flame spilled from the MiG's tail . . . and then the Russian's fuel tanks detonated into blossoming orange flame.

"Great shot, Brewer!" Batman called.

"That makes the score six-to-six, dead even, Batman!"

"Listen, babe! After *that* shot, we concede. Right, Malibu?"

"That's affirmative," Malibu agreed. "Beer and dinner're on us!"

She laughed. "Who're you calling 'babe,' fella?"

"Anyone who handles a Tomcat like that is one hot babe. Where's Stoney?"

"I got him," Pogie said. "One-eight-five at angels one. He's got troubles."

"Let's help him! Two-one's in!"

"Two-three," Brewer added. "We're in!"

1325 hours
Tomcat 200
Over the Kola Inlet

A Fulcrum had dropped in behind Tombstone for a high, plunging attack. He'd countered by pulling into a steep climb, rolling left. Inverted now, he looked down through the top of his canopy at the Russian plane passing beneath. Damn! Now it was climbing, rolling into a maneuver identical to his.

Rolling out over the top of his climb, Tombstone tried to line up a hasty shot with his guns, but the MiG pilot had already broken into his own climb, forcing Tombstone to overshoot and pass cockpit-to-cockpit beneath the rolling Fulcrum.

The two aircraft were now locked in a deadly maneuver called a rolling vertical scissors, each plane in turn trying to line up on the other, only to have the target evade its diving approach with an inverted roll. Each repeat of the maneuver cost both fighters airspeed and altitude. The altitude ladder on Tombstone's HUD showed seven hundred feet now, and still the two aircraft were rolling around one another, each trying for the upper—and final—hand, neither able to disengage without giving the other an immediate advantage.

"Stoney!" Tomboy warned. "Watch your altitude!"

"I see it!"

They'd just plain run out of sky. A mountain, black rock patched with ice and snow, loomed ahead and Tombstone cut left and high to clear it. The MiG-29 tried to copy the maneuver, pulling nose high . . .

. . . and slammed into the cliff.

"Way to go, CAG!" Tomboy yelled.

Tombstone rolled out, afterburners thundering, fighting for altitude . . .

. . . and then the Tomcat's left wing disintegrated in a blaze of fire. The shock was so sudden, so unexpected, that it took a moment for Tombstone to realize what had happened. Another MiG had been hanging back throughout those repeated vertical scissors, waiting for a chance to fire, and when Tombstone had broken left, he'd given the guy a perfect shot with a heat-seeking AA-8 Aphid.

The crippled Tomcat, still climbing, went into a gentle roll, streaming flame. "That's it, Tomboy!" he called to his RIO. "We're punching out!"

"Go! Go!"

"Eject!" He yanked on the ring. The canopy blew away, filling his universe with roaring, thundering wind. Then the thunder of his ejection seat rocket drowned even that, and he was hurtling out into chill, empty sky.

The snow-patched Russian tundra spun crazily about Tombstone's head.

CHAPTER 30
Tuesday, 17 March

1325 hours
Tomcat 201
Shotgun 1/1
Over the Kola Inlet

"Tombstone's been hit!" Coyote called.

"I see him," Cat said. "Two chutes! Two good chutes!"

"Thank God. Batman! Brewer! Where are you?"

"We're on the guy that flamed CAG," Brewer replied. "Shit, too close! Goin' for guns!"

"Two-three, Two-one! I've got the shot! Clear!"

"You've got it. Breaking left!"

"I'm on him! Splash one MiG!"

"Look at that sucker burn!"

Coyote circled right, scanning the ground below. The sudden appearance of the three Tomcats seemed to have scattered the Russian MiGs. "Cat! Where are the bad guys?"

"On the run, Coyote. I think they've had enough!"

"Okay. Did you see where Tombstone landed?"

"Negative. Negative. There's too much smoke."

"Okay. We'll circle back. Hang on."

"Don't die on me, Sunshine!" Willis yelled, his voice raw. "Damn it, don't *die* on me!"

A hole the size of his fist had been punched through the starboard side of the aircraft, just below the canopy and just behind Sunshine's ejection seat. Air screamed past the hole, and the Intruder shuddered heavily. Something was wrong with his starboard control surfaces too. He couldn't see through the smashed canopy at Sunshine's side, but he suspected he'd taken some pretty bad damage to his right wing.

Bracing the stick between his knees, he turned in his seat, trying to find out where all the blood was coming from.

There. The front of Sunshine's flight suit and undergarment had been torn open just over her right breast. He could see the thumb-sized, ragged hole in her chest, centered in a patch of blood-smeared skin. The blood was frothing with bubbles.

The Intruder thumped hard and Willis had to turn away, concentrating for the moment on his flying. He was at a thousand feet now, well above the hills, on a roughly north-eastern course, back toward the coast. With the aircraft stable again, he returned to his clumsy examination of his bombardier/navigator.

That hole in her chest was an exit wound. Something must have spit through her ejection seat and up into her right side. Pulling off his left glove, he reached around in front of her, probing her side. There it was, a hole as big around as his finger three inches below her right armpit. He felt broken ribs grate as he pushed against it. She groaned, then choked. He reached up and pulled her mask off. The oxygen would do her no good if she drowned in her own blood, and there was a lot of it on her face, leaking from her nose and mouth.

That bubbling blood in her chest wound meant her lung had been shot through—which was obvious enough from the trajectory of the shrapnel. A sucking chest wound would collapse her lung in seconds, would kill her in minutes if he didn't plug it tight.

With a blood-slicked hand, he unzipped his flight suit's shoulder pocket, then fumbled for the pack of cigarettes inside. Quickly, he stripped off the cellophane wrapper, discarded the cigarettes, and tore the now-slippery cellophane in half. One half he pressed down across Sunshine's chest wound. As she drew her next liquid, rasping breath, the cellophane almost disappeared into the hole, an air-tight seal that would stop her lung from collapsing. Reaching over her again, he stuffed the remaining cellophane in the wound in her side, then pulled her upper arm tightly against her body to keep the makeshift bandage in place.

And there wasn't another damned thing he could do for her now, except get the wounded Intruder down as fast as possible. He could tell from the feel in the stick that they would never make it all the way back to the *Jefferson* . . . and Sunshine sure as hell wouldn't survive ejecting into the sea.

He needed something closer at hand.

**1328 hours
Over the Kola Peninsula**

Tombstone dangled beneath his chute, watching the snow-patched tundra rushing up toward his feet. He bent his knees, keeping his feet together . . .

. . . and then the ground swept up into him. He hit, *oofed!* . . . and rolled, coming up with a double armful of parachute risers, gathering in the chute with swift, pummeling strokes.

He looked up into a contrail-painted sky. He could see Tomboy's parachute. She was coming down half a mile to the west. To the east, vast clouds of smoke piled into the sky from the holocaust in the Polyarnyy Inlet.

With his chute discarded, he gave his survival gear a quick check: first-aid kit, flares, SAR radio, knife, pistol. Many Navy flyers carried revolvers, but Tombstone had always favored the satisfying heft of the M1911A1. The big .45 automatic was virtually a relic now, replaced years before as the Navy's standard-issue sidearm by the 9mm Beretta, but still carried by some personnel who felt that the Colt was more reliable.

Not that a pistol would do them a hell of a lot of good. They

were almost certainly behind enemy lines. Tombstone had two
seven-round magazines, one in the pistol, the other in a flight
suit pocket. Fourteen shots . . . against MVD troops or Naval
Infantry with full-auto assault rifles. Still, it was something.
Drawing and checking the weapon, he dragged the slide back,
chambering a round, then flicked up the safety. "Cocked and
locked" now, he hurried toward Tomboy's chute.

1330 hours
Intruder 504
Over the Kola Inlet

"Okay, Navy. You're clear to land, south-to-north. There's only
one runway so you shouldn't get lost."

"Thanks, Marine," Willis replied. "Have a corpsman standing by. My B/N's pretty badly shot up."

"That's a roger."

It had been sheer luck that he'd found the place, a Russian
airstrip on the coast overrun by the Marines a few hours earlier.
They'd been using it as an advance base for their Harriers and
Hornets, but they'd cleared it now as an emergency runway for
the incoming Navy Intruder.

Sunshine groaned. The blood on her face was bright, bright
red. "Sunshine? Sunshine, you hear me?"

No response. *Oh, God, don't let her die!*

The vibration was getting worse, and he wasn't getting any
response from his right-side flaps. When he flipped the
landing-gear switch, he didn't get any response there either.
Shit! His wheels were stuck up. He'd have to belly in.

The Marines were sending out a radio beacon for him to
home on. He could see the airstrip now, a single runway on the
brown tundra, next to a handful of buildings. Smoke stained the
sky to the east. There was still fighting going on out there.

His altimeter was reading 650 now. The air controller had
already told him that the base he was angling toward was at an
altitude of 275 feet, so the ground was sweeping past his belly just
375 feet below. Easing back on the throttle, he kept the Intruder's
nose high, balanced just ahead of a stall, dropping now at a
thousand feet per minute . . . lower . . . lower . . .

The runway expanded in front of him with breathtaking

speed. He tried the air brakes—no good—and the flaps again—still nothing—and cut the throttles back to nothing, and then he was over the runway and dropping like a stone. His tail struck first with a sound of rasping metal . . . and then the Intruder's keel struck tarmac, tortured steel and aluminum shrieking, and he was battling the controls, trying to keep sliding in a straight line, but his right wing was coming around anyway, and he was out of control, sliding, sliding, sliding down the runway as flames exploded behind him like the wake of a powerboat.

Stopped! With a final lurch, the Intruder halted, its nose tipped into a rubble-filled crater, smoke boiling away from the aircraft's engines.

He hit the canopy release, praying that it would work, and it did. Then he was fumbling with his own harness and with Sunshine's. The aircraft was on fire, and he had to get the two of them out!

"That's okay, Mac," a gravel voice said beside him. Hands grasped his arms, pulling him from his seat. Fire extinguishers *shooshed* and hissed as Marines hosed down the flames. "We'll get your buddy."

"Get her out! Get her out! She's hurt bad!"

"Her? Oh, Christ . . ."

"Quit staring, Mike," another Marine snapped. "Lend a hand!"

"Lady there. Got her into the Stokes."

"For God's sake, take it easy with her," Willis said. "Best fuckin' B/N I ever had . . ."

His legs gave way as he stepped onto the tarmac. He never did remember being helped away from the plane.

1340 hours
Near Sayda Guba
The Kola Peninsula

Tombstone saw both the parachute and the man and broke into a run, the heavy Colt clutched in his hand. The guy wore a camo uniform but had a high-peaked cap, and he carried an AKM slung over his back, muzzle down. His back was to Tombstone, and he was bending over Tomboy, who was lying on her back, still in her parachute harness with the chute billowing and tugging in the breeze.

The soldier appeared to be alone. His back was to Tombstone, his total attention on the woman at his feet. Stoney raised the pistol but kept on running, trying to center the sights on a target that bobbed with each step he took.

From fifty feet away, Tombstone fired . . . a clean miss. The soldier turned, gaping at this apparition charging him with a pistol, then reached for his AKM, fumbling with its strap.

Tombstone fired again. *Damn!* It looked easy on the TV cop shows, but a pistol was a ridiculously inaccurate weapon, especially when fired while running. The Russian raised the AK's muzzle . . .

Again, Tombstone squeezed the trigger . . . *miss!*

Then there was a sharp crack and the Russian staggered forward, still clutching the AKM. Tomboy, still on her back, had her revolver out. She'd shot up into the Russian's back from a range of four feet. The man tried to raise the AK again. . . .

Tombstone stopped, braced his .45 in both hands, and squeezed the trigger three more times in rapid succession. One of the rounds at least hit the Russian in the chest, pitching him backwards, sending the rifle spinning from his hands.

He dropped to his knees at Tomboy's side. "Tomboy! You okay?"

"Hi . . . Stoney." Her face twisted with pain. "Bad landing."

Glancing back, he saw her left leg twisted back under her body at an impossible angle. It looked like she'd snapped both her tibia and her fibula just below her knee. There was blood on her leg too, and a gleam of white bone visible through a tear in her flight suit—a compound fracture, and a nasty one.

Quickly, Tombstone scanned their surroundings. The Russian soldier was dead, and there was no one else in sight. He could just make out the peaked roofs of a small village or settlement some distance to the east. They were sheltered to the north by a low rise, little more than a snow-covered mound on the tundra. Nothing else was visible in any direction but mountains, ground, and sky.

He touched the transmit key on the Search and Rescue radio strapped to his flight suit. "This is Tomcat Two-double-oh,

Tomcat Two-double-oh, broadcasting Mayday, Mayday." He stopped, listening intently, but heard only the hiss of static, and once a garbled burst of something that might have been a partial transmission leaking across from a neighboring frequency.

Nothing. His transmitter might have been damaged in the landing, or else no one was listening on the frequency at the moment. He set the SAR radio to broadcast an emergency beacon, then turned to Tomboy.

"Let me take a look at that leg," he told her. First, he pulled a morphine syrette from his first-aid kit, pulled open the tear in her flight suit, squeezed a handful of skin and muscle, and jammed the needle home. "That ought to make you feel real good," he told her.

"A real . . . high."

With a grease pencil included in the first-aid kit, he marked the letter "M" on her forehead, and the time. The small ritual was comforting, an acknowledgment that they were going to get out of this.

"You don't really think we're gonna get rescued, do you?" she asked. Her eyes were glassy, the words slurred. He thought she must already be in shock.

"Course we are," he told her. "Brace yourself now. This might hurt, morphine or no morphine."

It did hurt; she fought back a yelp as he straightened her leg. Tombstone looked around for a splint, but there wasn't a thing to be found but the soldier's AKM. He'd hoped to use the weapon—an AKM with a thirty-round magazine was better than a pistol any day—but he also needed a splint, and even with an assault rifle, he wouldn't be able to hold the enemy off for long once they showed up in force. He used his knife to cut generous lengths of nylon cord from the parachute, as well as strips from the canopy that he could use as bandages and padding. He removed the AKM's banana magazine, did his best to straighten out Tomboy's leg, then began tying the rifle above and below the break, keeping her leg rigid from thigh to ankle. He tried just once to set the bone, but he stopped when she screamed. Unable to see what he was doing, and unwilling to damage her leg more than it already was, he settled at last for simply immobilizing it, wrapping it in swaths of parachute nylon.

After a while, Tomboy opened her eyes as he worked. "Hey, CAG." Her voice sounded dreamy now, and she smiled. "Is it true what some of the girls are saying?"

"What's that?"

"That some sailor snuck into our shower and took photographs of us in there."

"Where the hell did *that* come from?"

"All the girls are talking about it."

How did news spread so swiftly through a ship's company? Tombstone had hoped the women would never find out about that episode. Obviously, though, he'd not counted on the incredible speed and power of the shipboard dissemination of rumor.

"It's true."

"Any in there of me? Heard there was."

"Yes. One."

"I must've . . . looked awful without my makeup."

"Oh, from what I could see, you looked pretty good."

"I'll bet. Ha! So much for all those women's issues sensitivity sessions. You're not supposed to notice things like that."

"So much for privacy aboard ship. Even one as big as the *Jeff*." He straightened up. "How's that feel?"

"It hurts like hell. CAG?"

"Yeah?"

"We're *not* going to get out of this, are we?"

"Sure we are. We've got our beacon out. They'll hear us."

"Yeah, but *they* can hear it too. You'd better take off without me."

"Nope."

"The Marine lines can't be more than five or six miles north of here. Damn it, Captain, why should both of us get caught? Why should *you* get caught?"

"Why don't you shut up? You women talk too much, you know that?"

"You bastard! Get out of here now, while you can."

"And how effective a CAG would I be after that, knowing I'd run off and left one of my men, half stoned on morphine and lying out here in the mud? What are you trying to do, Tomboy, ruin my career?"

She laughed, an involuntary snicker. Then the pain in her leg hit her and she gasped. Biting her lip, she shook her head. "Tombstone, if you don't—"

"Hush!" Tombstone raised his pistol. He could hear the rumble of an engine, nearby and growing closer. The source was masked by that low mound of earth and snow to the north. Slowly, Tombstone rose to his feet. "Something's coming. . . ."

Troops spilled over the crest of the rise, spreading out to either side. It took Tombstone a shocked half-second to recognize the uniforms, to put up his pistol.

"I'm Sergeant Bradley," the lead Marine said. "You Navy guys pick the God-damnedest places for LZs!"

"What?"

"You got yourself a shit-load of Russians heading this way, sir, but we beat 'em out by about two minutes. Come on. We've got a hummer on the other side of the ridge. We'll take your pal here."

Gathered up by the Marine recon patrol, Tombstone and Tomboy were escorted back to a cluster of camouflaged vehicles waiting a few yards beyond the ridge. Overhead, a trio of Tomcats boomed low across the tundra, the sunlight flashing from their wings.

The reality of his and Tomboy's rescue didn't hit home until that moment.

1443 hours
Kandalaksha Command Center
Kola Peninsula

Admiral Karelin never did find out that *Pravda*'s missile had not made it clear of the launch tube. He'd heard the sub's weapons officer shout the word "fire," but then he'd waited, and waited, listening for some confirmation of launch, and heard nothing but static.

But the missile had to have gotten clear, had to have arrowed into the sky over Polyarnyy on its way to Chelyabinsk. The sub base had been under attack, he knew that, and it was possible that the *Pravda* had been hit within seconds of the launch, but nothing could stop an ICBM once it was clear of its tube, nothing!

But there was no further word from Polyarnyy, and no

confirmation from Moscow that the missile had descended on Chelyabinsk. Perhaps, after all, something had gone wrong. . . .

Damn the American carrier forces! Somehow, they'd managed to take out the pride of the Russian Northern Fleet, spoiling for a second time an attempt to end once and for all the civil war destroying his country.

Always, it seemed, it was the U.S. Navy, the Americans and their far-ranging carrier aircraft. Ironically, it was not the U.S. Navy at all, but an F-117 Stealth aircraft that punched home the final seal of Karelin's destiny.

The Kandalaksha base had been identified the day before by its microwave transmissions. During the night, several cruise-missile attacks and bombing strikes had been made against Karelin's bunker, a low, concrete blockhouse squatting on the plain north of Kandalaksha's military air base. Now, a Stealth Fighter was holding a targeting laser steady on the target, a three-foot-wide ventilation grill on the bunker's roof. The bomb, released moments earlier, was gliding toward the spot of reflected laser light, its control surfaces twitching this way and that to keep its glide path on target.

Smoothly, as though placed there by hand, the one-thousand-pound bomb slipped through the ventilator, bursting through aluminum slats and fittings as though they were cardboard, penetrating yards of concrete and steel before detonating at last in a savage blast.

Admiral Karelin never felt the explosion that killed him.

1530 hours
Flight deck
U.S.S. *Thomas Jefferson*

The SH-3 helicopter settled gently to *Jefferson*'s deck. Tombstone unsnapped his harness and, clutching at his cranial with one hand, jumped through the open door to the deck. Ducking to avoid the still-spinning rotor blades, he trotted across the flight deck toward the carrier's island.

Admiral Tarrant, Captain Brandt, Coyote, and several aides stood there, waiting for him.

The fighting ashore was winding down, though God alone knew how much longer it would continue. The last word he'd heard was that the Marines now held a twenty-five-mile perimeter from Polyarnyy to Port Vladimir, but that they would be pulled out soon. The Marines who'd picked him and Tomboy up off the tundra had regaled him with stories of the fighting, including a hand-to-hand gunfight inside one of the huge, underground Russian sub pens.

For the most part, it seemed, the Russian defenses were collapsing. Dozens of their ICBM subs had already been seized, dozens more crippled or destroyed by the constant bombing raids. Everywhere, Russian troops were surrendering. The civil war had had a terribly demoralizing effect on them, and the situation had been complicated by continuing problems with logistics and poor communications. Morale throughout the Red Army was virtually nil, and some POWs brought with them tales of food shortages, of corruption or cowardice among the officers, even of mutiny and defection among the enlisted men. The crew of the *Jefferson* might have been facing morale problems, but nothing as serious as *that*.

He'd learned something else while he'd been with the Marines ashore. Late during the previous afternoon, a Marine patrol had entered the town of Sayda Guba after a sharp, short firefight with some rather raggedly undisciplined MVD troops. There, they'd found a wire cage with Lieutenant Hanson locked inside. Gang-raped and badly beaten, she was still alive. The Marines had flown her out to the LPH *Iwo Jima*, which had an excellent and well-equipped three-hundred-bed sick bay. Tomboy had been heloed out to the *Iwo* as well, as had a badly wounded female RIO from VA-89 called Sunshine.

At last report, all three women were going to be fine . . . although some wounds might take longer to heal than others. Chris Hanson, he'd been told, might never recover fully, though Tombstone wasn't willing to take odds on that. Naval aviators were tough—they *had* to be—and if anyone could find the strength and resiliency and sheer willpower to bounce back from an experience like that, Tombstone thought Lobo could do it.

But . . . had the Great Experiment been worth it? He wondered. Women in combat. They'd proven they could take stress as well as men, or better in some cases. And in the acid test of combat, they'd shown that they were just as capable as any man they flew with. God knew they'd earned the right to fight for their country. Tombstone had never disputed that.

Balancing all of that, though, were the undeniable problems sexual integration had raised. The morale problems alone had put his entire air wing at risk, and possibly the entire battle group. If he'd learned nothing else from this episode, it was that the U.S. military was not the place for social experimentation by politicians or by liberal activist groups like DACOW-ITS or NOW. The Navy, for all the scandals uncovered during the past decade, for all the problems it had endured, was still America's first line of defense, the projection of America's military might that kept the ambitions of nuclear-armed madmen like Krasilnikov at arm's length.

Any nation that tampered with the efficiency and combat readiness of its military services in *this* day and age did so at its peril.

Tombstone reached the silently waiting commanding officer of Carrier Battle Group 14 and the men waiting with him. He saluted, then addressed Brandt. "Permission to come aboard, sir."

"Granted," Brandt said. "Damn you, Stoney, I ought to give you permission to visit the brig."

"I get him first," Tarrant said, "Tombstone. What did I tell you about bringing back your airplane?"

"I guess I misplaced it. Sir."

Tarrant shook his head, then laughed. "I ought to make you walk back and get it. Well, welcome aboard anyhow. And welcome back!"

"Good to be back, Admiral."

"How'd you like playing with the grunts?" Coyote asked.

"Oh, not bad. Marines are almost human, once you get to know them."

"I see you also lost your RIO," Tarrant added. The twinkle in his eye told Tombstone the admiral knew that Tomboy was safe aboard the *Iwo*. "What happened, Stoney, you decide you have enough of women in your air wing and leave her in the Kola?"

"Terrible thing, sir," Coyote said, grinning. "But you know what they say. Women and salt water just don't mix."

"I don't know about women or salt water," Tombstone said. "But Tomboy, Lobo, and Brewer and the rest are *aviators*!" He grinned widely. "They can fly with me *any*time!"